Losing Lila

Also by Sarah Alderson

HUNTING LILA

FATED

SARAH ALDERSON

Losing Lila

SIMON AND SCHUSTER

First published in Great Britain in 2012 by Simon & Schuster UK Ltd
A CBS COMPANY

1 3 5 7 9 10 8 6 4 2

Simon & Schuster UK Ltd
1st Floor
222 Gray's Inn Road
London
WC1X 8HB

www.simonandschuster.co.uk

Simon & Schuster Australia, Sydney

Simon & Schuster India, New Delhi

A CIP catalogue copy for this book is available
from the British Library.

ISBN: 978-0-85707-197-2
E-BOOK ISBN: 978-0-85707-198-9

This book is a work of fiction. Names, characters, places and incidents are either a
product of the author's imagination or are used fictitiously. Any resemblance to actual
people, living or dead, events or locales, is entirely coincidental.

Printed and bound in Great Britain
by CPI Group (UK) Ltd, Croydon, CR0 4YY

For Nichola and Vic, for always being there for me, even though we're thousands of miles apart.
With love,
S x

1

I stared back at my reflection in the bathroom mirror. My hair was loose, my eyes dark-circled. I looked pale and a little gaunt. Alex was standing behind me, bare-chested and in jeans, his hands resting lightly on my shoulders. The bruise on his cheek had faded and there was only the faintest trace of a scar running at an angle across his cheekbone up to his eye. He looked tired too. The strain of the last week was starting to show.

'Just do it,' I told him.

He looped my hair, twisting it up like a rope, then pressed the scissors against the nape of my neck and cut. Blonde strands fell to the floor, but I kept my eyes on Alex, so focused on the job in hand. The only thing that was keeping me sane, keeping me from running straight back to California to find my mum and Jack, was him. Eight days zigzagging south over the border, trying to shake the Unit off our tail, had brought us here, to the sweltering heat of Mexico City, and this tiny hotel room.

After Alex was done, he put the scissors down and bent to kiss my bare neck. I drew in a breath, goosebumps rippling down my spine, and gripped the edge of the basin tighter. Alex looked up, caught my eye in the mirror and gave me one of his half-smiles.

'You look beautiful,' he said.

I stared at myself in the mirror. My head felt lighter all of a sudden. My eyes were massive in the pale oval of my face. I had expected to look more like a child, but I looked older somehow. The angles of my face were sharper, my neck longer. It was as if I'd lost the last vestiges of childhood along with my hair. Alex dipped his head once more, tracing kisses slowly up my neck towards my jaw, his fingers running through my cropped hair. He turned me round and, holding my face, kissed me full on the lips.

Despite everything I was feeling – a lurid, unwieldy mixture of fear and desperate hope – I couldn't help but respond. I wrapped my arms round his neck and pulled myself close against him.

Ever since the night in Joshua Tree when we'd faced the Unit and Jack had been shot, I had felt like I had lost my balance – that the world was rolling under my feet. Alex was the ballast, the anchor that was stopping me from floating away. Just like he'd been when my mother died. But she wasn't dead, I reminded myself. She was alive. And so was Jack. I had convinced myself of that, if only to avoid the crushing feelings of loss and guilt that threatened to sink me whenever I thought of what might have happened.

No, I told myself for the millionth time. They were *both* alive and we were going to find a way to rescue them.

Alex suddenly broke off from kissing me, the muscles across his shoulders and arms tensing. I glanced up at him, confused. He was looking over towards the bathroom door, as if he'd heard something.

'Stay here,' he said, pushing past me and reaching for the door handle. I heard it too then – a screech of tyres, the slamming of car doors.

My heart started to pound, my stomach constricted. Alex left me standing there and edged out into the bedroom, his hand automatically moving to his gun which was stuck down the back

2

of his jeans. I looked round the bathroom – at the lack of places to hide or things to throw – and then followed him.

Alex was standing by the open window, pulling on a T-shirt as he scanned the street below. He turned to look at me over his shoulder.

'They've found us,' he said.

The ballast shifted inside me. From the expression on his face it was clear who had found us.

'Come on, let's go!' Alex grabbed my hand and pulled me towards the door. The words were still sinking in and my feet were unresponsive. 'Lila, come on!' he shouted. 'There's no time, move!'

The Unit had found us. How on earth had they found us?

I let Alex pull me through the door of our hotel room. He threw our bag over his shoulder and we started sprinting down the hallway towards the fire exit at the far end. Just before it there was a cleaning closet. Alex opened it, unshouldered the bag, threw it up onto the highest shelf, then closed the door behind him. The bag contained most of our money, a couple of guns and our clothes. Before I could ask him what he was doing, he had taken my hand once more and was tugging me towards the fire exit.

He cracked the door open a centimetre. The boom of footsteps thundering up the fire-escape stairs hit us. The Unit men were about two floors below us, and moving fast in our direction.

Alex swore under his breath and turned to look at me, frowning. I hated that frown. Then he took a deep breath, pushed the door wide open and pulled me through after him. With our backs flush to the wall, we sidestepped up the stairs as silently as possible. The men below were gaining on us; the noise of their steel-toe-capped boots pounding the concrete steps was echoing off the walls, ringing in our ears.

My breath was ragged in my throat. I hugged the wall, expecting, with every step, to feel my head explode with pain and my legs fall out from under me. It would come soon. I knew it would. And I knew, when it did, I would fall to my knees. Alex's grip on me tightened as if he was expecting it too and was getting ready to catch me.

We made it to the sixth floor at the same time as the men below us hit the fourth, barrelling through the exit we'd just come from. The door flew back against the wall with an almighty crash and Alex opened the door onto the roof at the same time, the noise muffled by the shouts and footsteps below us.

I stepped ahead of him onto the flat roof of the hotel. In the distance I could see the dome of the cathedral, but no way down to the street below. We were trapped on an open expanse of concrete about the size of a basketball court.

'Which way now?' I asked.

Alex ran to the edge of the building, dropped to his knees and scanned the alley below. He ducked immediately, leaning back against the wall out of sight of whoever or whatever was below. The rest of the Unit were probably down there covering the exits. We were fish in a barrel. I looked at Alex and saw a panic so real cross his face that my insides liquefied.

I spun round. There was no way off the roof. I ran back to the door. The footsteps were heading our way now. Voices were calling out, barking orders. They knew we were here. *Damn it. Damn it.*

I glared at the door, focusing my mind, and it slammed shut with a crash. There was a discarded plank of wood lying twenty or so metres away. I spun it across the roof and into my outstretched hands, then rammed it beneath the door handle, hoping it would buy us a few more seconds.

'Lila!'

Alex was on the other side of the roof. I sprinted across to him and peered over the edge. There was an empty, garbage-strewn alley running down the side of the building. The Unit didn't appear to be guarding it, but there was no way of getting down there. We were six floors up. I looked at Alex, wondering what he was thinking. He wasn't looking down, though. He was looking across at the opposite roof.

'We've got to jump,' he said.

'Are you kidding?'

He wasn't kidding. The thump of metal slamming against metal made us both look round. The plank of wood I'd placed against the door was buckling. There was a whole army of men on the other side of the fire exit. We had maybe ten seconds to get off the roof before we were staring my mother's torturers in the face.

I paced back a few metres then took off, hitting the ledge and throwing myself forward, feet pedalling emptiness until I felt them make contact with brick. I stumbled and rolled until I was lying flat on my back, the wind knocked out of me. I glanced up and saw the top of Alex's head. He was staring at me in disbelief. Then he took off. It was an easy jump for him. He landed by my side in a crouch.

He shook his head at me, pulling me to my feet, and we raced to a doorway on the far side, ducking behind it just as we heard the sound of metal shearing. The Unit had broken through the fire exit. We could hear their footsteps running to the sides of the building to look down, searching for our escape route.

'Why aren't they firing?' I whispered. I wasn't talking about bullets. I meant why weren't they firing the weapon that made my head explode like a swarm of wasps stuck inside my skull.

'They've only got one shot,' Alex whispered back. 'They'll want to save it until they have you in sight.'

One shot. That would be all it would take to bring me to my knees anyway. And then I had one minute before they could fire another round. Not that they'd need to. I'd be writhing on the concrete in agony after the first one.

'This way,' Alex said.

We moved to the edge, still well out of sight. The roof of this building ran straight into the next, with just a low ledge separating it. We dropped over the side and skirted a pile of garbage until we were on the adjacent roof. There was a fire exit on this one, but it was locked from the inside. Alex thumped it with his fist and swore again.

'Over here!' a man's voice shouted behind us.

I peered round the wall. Four men on the roof of the first building were taking running leaps to clear the distance onto the next roof.

'Lila, can you open the door?'

Oh God. I looked at it. It was a metal fire door. Plain, with no handle on this side. I normally needed to see something in order to move it. I tried visualising the handle on the other side.

Nothing happened.

'You might want to hurry.'

'I'm trying,' I hissed.

'Try harder,' Alex said through gritted teeth. He had his back flat to the wall, his gun cradled in both hands. I squeezed my eyes shut and tried to visualise the handle again. Imagined how it would feel to push it down.

The door popped with a clang and swung open. I grinned at Alex. He grinned back and we darted through into a dark, musty stairwell. I slammed the door shut behind us. We hit the ground floor at a run and paused, breathless, before the final door onto the street. I nodded at Alex. He pushed the door a fraction with his foot and glanced out.

'OK, it's clear. I'll go first. Keep against the wall, we're going left. Move fast, keep down.'

The alley we came onto was a rat run, just a few metres wide. I glanced up. We were in partial shadow. A ledge jutted out above our heads, giving us about fifteen centimetres of cover. A stone or something fell from the roof, throwing up some trash by my foot.

'Watch out!' Alex yelled, as I realised it wasn't a stone but a bullet. The Unit were on the roof, firing down on us. Alex's arm was pinning me back against the wall, just in case I felt like playing dare with a semi-automatic.

'They're not real bullets. They're rubber,' he said. 'They don't want to kill us. They want to take us alive.'

I glanced at him. Was he trying to make me feel better?

Just then we heard shouts coming from around the corner. They were closing in on us from every direction. I peered over Alex's shoulder and fixed my gaze on the metal dumpster at the end of the alley. I imagined pushing it across the uneven ground, and suddenly I felt the shunt of it as it rolled slowly across the alley. When I felt it meet the wall opposite, I pushed harder, wedging it firmly between both sides of the alley, creating a metal barrier between us and the Unit. I smiled widely at Alex as the dull thud of bullets began to ricochet off the metal.

'Run!' I shouted, grabbing Alex by the hand. And we did, trying to stick as close to the wall as possible, bullets dancing around our heels, spitting up dirt and gravel.

We rounded a corner into another alleyway, this one wider than the last. After thirty metres Alex shouted at me to stop, and threw his weight against a wooden door which splintered open with a loud crash. I stumbled through the doorway, my mouth falling open. Two half-naked men, with towels slung round their waists, were standing in front of a row of battered metal lockers. A wooden bench ran down the centre of what was obviously some kind of changing room. Clouds of steam billowed overhead, but I barely noticed. Alex had stopped in the middle of the room to look back at me and was now yelling at me to move. I dodged past the two men, muttering an apology as I went, skipped round a pile of dirty towels and grabbed Alex's hand.

We burst through a door into a long service hallway, sprinted past several people wearing what looked like maids' uniforms, and then finally crashed through another door, spilling out into the luxurious hush of a grand hotel lobby. Several guests sitting in the adjacent bar area glanced at us, and the concierge yelled out a warning for us to stop. Out of nowhere a security man appeared, blocking our way. I glanced over my shoulder, close to tears, panic taking root, but Alex gripped my hand tighter, nodded at the gun he was holding, and the security man jumped aside.

We shoved our way through the revolving door, exiting onto a street that was flooded with tourists, all heading towards the Zócolo – the giant square in front of the cathedral.

'Walk ahead of me,' Alex murmured, dropping his pace instantly to a stroll and ducking his head. 'Keep next to those people.' He nodded at a group of tourists just ahead of us who were following a guide with a yellow umbrella. I slipped into their midst, keeping my head down, my ears pricked for any shouting or gunfire.

Once we broke into the wide cathedral square, Alex caught up with me. I felt him just behind me, his breath scorching the back of my neck. 'Keep walking, keep walking,' he said quietly. 'Follow the group inside the cathedral.'

It took all my willpower not to run. The square was too bright, too exposed; we stood out too conspicuously amongst this band of camera-wielding, guidebook-clutching tourists. I wanted to slip down one of the darkened streets and disappear into the chaos of the city, but I listened to Alex, keeping my pace steady as we moved in a pack towards the cathedral.

The light was murky inside, and it was cold enough to make me shiver. It felt like being trapped in an underwater cave. My eyes were still adjusting to the dimness when Alex slipped his hand under my elbow and started steering me down a side aisle towards a chapel at the far end. Without a word, he pushed me into a curtained confessional.

We stood facing each other in the latticed gloom. I pressed myself against his chest and felt his arm come round my back, his hand flatten against my spine.

'You OK?' he whispered.

'Yes,' I nodded.

'I can't believe you made that jump.'

'I can't believe they found us. What are we going to do?'

He didn't answer, he just held me tighter. We stood there for a few seconds in silence. My heart was pounding so loudly I almost didn't hear him at first.

'It must be one of us,' he murmured.

'What?' I looked up at him, not understanding.

'They tracked us all the way here. They knew exactly where we were. Exactly. Down to the room we were in. They stopped at the fourth floor.'

I shook my head, pulling out of his arms. I wasn't sure what he meant.

'It's got to be one of us.' He was thinking, his eyes scanning me from top to toe. 'It can't be you. They didn't have a chance to plant anything on you.' He stopped talking then and we stared at each other. I caught up with his thinking. He meant a tracking device.

'It's not on my clothes.' His clothes and watch were new, bought two days ago at a border town. 'It's not in the bag. The bag was in Jack's car. It was unauthorised. The Unit didn't know he had it in there. It was just for emergencies. I checked everything.'

Alex stopped for a second, thinking, then he handed me his gun, and in one quick move, pulled his T-shirt off over his head. We both turned our heads to stare at his upper arm. In the darkness we could just about make out the tattoo of crossed swords, the words *Semper Fi* inked indelibly above. He ran his fingers over it. I followed suit.

'Are you serious? You think they planted a tracking device on you? I mean, *in* you?'

'Here, here, feel this.' He grabbed my fingers and pressed them into the muscle. There was a tiny bump under the skin, almost imperceptible, like a raised scar. My eyes went wide.

'I've seen this done,' Alex whispered, tracing the tiny bump again with his fingertips. 'Not on us, but when someone goes undercover. They plant a device just under the skin so they can track them. It's almost undetectable. I just didn't think for a second—' He shook his head, pulling his T-shirt back on.

'But if they've been able to track you this whole time, why didn't they come after us from the start?' I asked. 'When they thought Demos had caught us, when we both disappeared, why

10

didn't they just follow the tracker then? Why wait until we were in a different country?'

It didn't make sense.

'I don't know.' Alex shook his head, frowning at his arm.

'What are you going to do?' I asked, running my hand under his sleeve and over the minuscule bump.

He didn't answer. Instead he pulled a switchblade from his back pocket. I took a step backwards, my shoulders bumping the grille behind me. Alex rolled the sleeve of his T-shirt up and lifted the blade to his arm. And then the door flew open.

A priest in black robes was standing there, his mouth gaping as he took in the scene before him – Alex holding a knife and me clutching a gun. He grabbed the rosary hanging around his neck and started squawking loudly in Spanish, his eyes rolling heavenwards. I glanced at the chapel behind him. Several people had turned to stare.

'Sorry,' I muttered to the priest as we barged past him out of the booth. The priest shouted something to our backs as we slipped out of the chapel and made our way towards the central aisle of the cathedral, which was now heaving with people. I clutched the gun against my thigh and tried to look inconspicuous, but I could feel the ripple of eyes and the swivel of heads as we passed.

Alex skidded to a sudden stop in front of me, almost yanking my arm out of its socket. He spun us a hundred and eighty degrees and started heading back the way we'd just come, towards the angry priest. I glanced over my shoulder at the entrance. Six men in black combats had burst through the crowd gathered there. They stopped to let their eyes adjust to the gloom and we took the opportunity to hustle our way down a length of pew and disappear into a pack of tourists standing and admiring the altar. I

11

risked another backwards glance over my shoulder. Two of the men from the Unit had headed off to the chapels on either side of the entrance, two more were heading to the other side of the church away from us, and the last two were moving down the central aisle straight towards us. One of them was holding a small palm-sized device which he kept glancing down at.

With a final push, we shouldered our way through the crowd towards a little side door behind the altar. Alex reached for the handle and I took a final glance round the cathedral. I spied what I was looking for in a chapel on the far side, away from where the crowds were gathered. A statue of a saint stood in a little alcove high above the entrance. There was no one below it so I said a little prayer then tipped the statue off its plinth. It fell with a splintering crash that rocked through the muttering quiet of the church like a tidal wave. Instantly people started screaming, and running towards the exits and, in the blur of noise and chaos, Alex and I slipped silently through the little door.

The room we came into was some kind of dressing room. A giant crucifix dominated one wall and choir robes hung from hooks on two other walls. Several candles were burning beneath the crucifix.

'I'm so going to hell,' I said, looking around.

'Well, I'm going with you,' Alex replied.

He pulled the sleeve of his T-shirt up once more and I watched in horror as he ran the blade quickly through a candle flame before pressing the tip of it into the skin of his arm.

'Oh God.' I leaned against the door, feeling suddenly woozy, but unable to take my eyes off the knife.

Blood started to trickle down Alex's arm. He grimaced, and I grabbed a long scarf thing hanging on a hook behind me and handed it to him. Alex held the knife out towards me. On its bloody tip was a tiny metal ball.

'That's it?' I asked.

'Yep,' he said, flipping the knife and letting the ball fall to the flagstones at his feet. He crushed it underfoot before grabbing the cloth out of my hands and wrapping it round his arm, tying it in a knot.

'Right, let's go,' he said when he was done.

We ran again, through doorways, beneath arches and through empty rooms, until we reached a heavy wooden door that came out at the side of the cathedral. The sun was starting to go down and the shadows were lengthening, spiking the square with oblongs and pyramids of dark.

We hung there, in the shadows, waiting. Alex pressed against me, sheltering me against the wall. After a minute he shifted position. 'Here they come,' he said under his breath.

I peered out from under his arm, spotting the men from the Unit as they came running out of the cathedral, like spiders disgorged from a nest. They scanned the square, searching for us, people scattering in panic out of their path. The one holding the black device in his hand was frowning and shaking his head.

We watched as they headed over to a black van that had pulled up on the far side of the square, and climbed inside. After another minute it drove off and disappeared into the flow of traffic.

'Where to now?' I asked Alex, feeling suddenly like I needed to lie down.

'Back to the hotel. We need that bag. It's got all our money in it.'

Technically it wasn't really *our* money. It was the money we'd got from selling Jack's car back in California. But it was all we had and we were going to need every cent of what was left to get ourselves out of here to somewhere the Unit couldn't find us.

'Are you sure it's a good idea to go back to the hotel? Won't they look for us there?'

He shook his head. 'They'd assume we wouldn't be that stupid. It's probably the safest place to go right now.'

I sighed. 'OK. So we go back and get the bag and then what? Find somewhere else to sleep?'

'No. No sleeping. We have one more thing to do tonight.'

I studied his face. He looked grim. I was guessing the *one more thing* wasn't a candlelit dinner and a movie.

2

We'd retrieved the bag from the cleaning closet and broken into an empty room on the top floor of the hotel, with a view of the street below. Alex was now busy sorting through the bag, laying everything out on the bed next to me. I was watching him. There was about fifty thousand dollars, give or take a few thousand; three guns; several clips of bullets; our passports; and a change of clothes for both of us. Alex repacked everything, emptying a pile of dollars into his wallet. We'd fixed up his arm with some surgical tape and a bandage. I reached out a hand and stroked up his arm. He stopped what he was doing and looked down at me. Then he pushed the bag aside and lay down on the bed, putting his uninjured arm round me. I curled into him.

'How are you doing?'

I didn't answer. How was I doing? I wasn't sure. I tried prodding my brain like it was flesh and I could feel where the bruises were, but it didn't work like that. It just shut down like a clam wherever I poked it. I was trying not to think about anything else other than Alex right here, next to me, holding me.

'He'll be OK, Lila.'

Jack. He meant Jack.

'Hey, don't cry.'

I hadn't realised I was, but tears were trickling down my

cheeks and onto his chest. I tried to stop them, but they just kept coming.

'We left him. We just left him, Alex.'

Alex's grip on me tightened. His fingers went under my chin and he forced it up so I was looking him in the eye.

'We had to, Lila.'

I stared at him. *Did we?*

'It was the only thing we could do,' he said. 'If either of us had gone to help him, we'd have been shot too. We've talked about this. Jack would have done the same thing. He would have wanted you to be safe.'

A part of me knew what Alex was saying was true, but it wasn't enough to make the guilt untwist the knots it had made in my gut.

'But Alex, what if he's—'

I thought about Ryder lying dead in the dirt and of Jack at his side with a bullet wound in his chest and scrunched my eyes shut. He wasn't in a good way. That's what Key had said. He was in a coma. He could be paralysed. He could be *dead*. And I didn't know because I was here. And Jack was there. And so was my mum. And there was no way of getting to either of them because between us and them was the Unit.

Alex put his hands on either side of my face. I opened my eyes. He was looking straight at me. 'Jack's fine,' he said, 'I know it. He's too tough not to be. And anyway, Jack has a very good reason to stay alive.'

'My mum?' It was a good reason. We had thought she was dead, but she wasn't.

'That,' Alex said, a smile pulling at the corner of his mouth, 'but I was thinking more that he'll want the opportunity to kick my ass.'

16

I laughed through my tears. 'Yeah, he wasn't too happy, was he?'

'No more than I deserve.'

'No, don't say that.' I scrambled to sit up. 'You can't do that to me again. You can't leave me again because of Jack. Because you're scared of what he thinks. I can't – I won't go through that again—'

I thought back to the days just before all this kicked off. To Alex's promise not to hurt me, and the way he'd left me so easily, thinking he was doing the right thing. When I thought about it, it made me feel as if the Unit had fired that weapon of theirs right at my heart.

Alex sat up too and took my hands in his. 'Lila, I promise you I'll never leave you again, ever. I promise you that I'll keep you safe and that we'll find Jack and your mum, and I promise that even if Jack does kick my ass, which one day I hope he will, I will still never leave you.'

I weighed his words, analysing their content. Alex had been known to twist the meaning of things. He'd tricked me that way before. I considered him: the arctic-blue eyes, the bruised shadows beneath them, the dark blond crew cut growing out, the soft curve of his lips, the familiar frown line running between his eyes that always made me want to reach out and smudge it away.

'I promise, Lila,' he said. 'No hidden meanings. I'm not going to leave you.'

He leaned forward and kissed me, still smiling. My whole body melted away, the muscles becoming as soft as sponges dipped in a hot bath, all the guilt and worry disappearing back into the corners of my consciousness, where I preferred them to stay.

After a few minutes Alex pried me off him. I sat up grudgingly as he swung his legs off the bed and watched as he bent to plug the light back into the socket. We had taken to unplugging electrical equipment as a precaution every time we moved to a new hotel room. When it came to proximity to Alex, I couldn't control my ability and we didn't need to be advertising our presence to the Unit with a Vegas-style sound and light show.

'Seriously, we have to focus,' he said, rearranging his T-shirt and running a hand through his hair.

'What do we have to focus *on*?' I had thought the bed was a pretty good thing to concentrate on.

'Get up,' Alex said.

I narrowed my eyes in suspicion, but slowly got up off the bed and stood in front of him.

'OK, we need to practise.'

I groaned. 'I'm so tired.'

'I know,' he said, 'but you really need to be able to defend yourself if you have to. So, don't argue, OK? We just have one more thing to do then we'll get out of the city and find somewhere safe to wait for Demos and the others.'

I froze, looking up at him. 'We have to wait here. They're coming *here*.' I couldn't hide the note of panic in my voice.

Alex shook his head at me. 'We can't stay in Mexico City. The Unit will be looking for us here.' He softened his voice. 'Don't worry, Nate and Key will find us wherever we go.'

I hoped he was right. I hoped they hadn't been caught. When we'd left them back in California, they'd been trying to draw the Unit north, away from us. A pretty futile exercise it now turned out because the Unit had been tracking us this whole time anyway. But it had been over eight days since we'd last had contact with Demos. When I'd suggested it would have been a good idea to swap cellphone numbers, Alex had rolled his eyes and given me a rudimentary introduction to evade-and-resist tactics, which apparently called for the ditching of all electronic, traceable objects. I hadn't yet pointed out that he should also have ditched his arm. I must have been looking worried still, because Alex took my hand.

'They'll find us,' he repeated. 'They found us before, didn't they?' He tugged me to my feet. 'Now come on, practise.'

How could I resist a face like that? Anything, he could ask me anything, and I'd do it.

He turned in a flash and picked up the gun from the bed. His finger was on the trigger before I had flung it out of his grip and back onto the pillow.

'Good,' he said, reaching to pick it up. 'But you need to be quicker.'

Quicker, huh? I spun the gun out of his reach to the foot of the bed.

He looked at me with a wry smile and I smiled back. 'Quick enough?'

He considered me for a long moment and I felt my pulse start to speed up. Finally he strolled around and stood directly behind me. I stayed where I was, feeling his breath tickling the back of my neck and trying not to let it distract me.

'So, if someone comes up behind you like this, what do you do?' Alex asked, stepping even closer, his lips brushing the edge of my ear.

'Smack him over the head with something?' I suggested, trying to focus on the question and not the feel of his lips.

'No,' he said. 'You can't let people know about your ability. Try this instead.' He put his hand on my shoulder and then, reaching over with his other hand, took my left hand and put it on top of his. 'Now twist, like this.' He showed me and I practised until I was able to extricate myself from a headlock. And then we kept practising, purely because I liked the feel of his arms wrapping round me, although I told Alex it was because I was trying to commit the move to memory.

Alex finally called a halt to the lesson and came to stand in front of me. 'Do you want to try moving me?' he asked.

I rolled my eyes. 'You know I can't. We tried already.'

'You can. I know you can do it. Look what you did today, moving that dumpster. You just need to try.'

I sighed at him. 'I'm not Demos, Alex. I can't stop people in their tracks just by looking at them.'

'Maybe not, but I've seen you move objects, big objects.'

He was talking about Humvees – cars as big as tanks that the Unit used. I wasn't sure how I'd done that, though, except that they had been bearing down on us and there had been no other option other than a future as roadkill.

'You can move a man,' he said. 'You just need to practise.'

He held his arm out in front of me. I stared at it. But all I saw was his arm – tanned and smoothly muscled – and all I could think about was how it felt when that arm held me in the night. Alex cleared his throat.

'It's too distracting,' I said, flushing and shrugging at the same time. 'It's *your* arm. I can't concentrate.'

He tried not to smile. 'OK, try this.' He stood behind me and put his arm round my neck in a stranglehold.

'It's still your arm.'

He squeezed a little until it was uncomfortable. I concentrated on trying to break his hold. Nothing happened.

'Imagine I'm Rachel,' Alex whispered in my ear.

20

His arm almost tore out of its socket as I flung it off me. He staggered back away from me.

I spun round. 'God, I'm sorry, are you OK? Damn – I didn't mean to – you just – you really shouldn't mention her name . . .'

Alex was nursing his shoulder, his eyes wide with surprise or possibly shock. Then his face split into a wide grin.

'Again,' he said, wrapping both arms round my waist.

I closed my eyes and visualised Rachel's beautiful, sneering face and the smirk when she told me that my mother was still alive. It took a few seconds but Alex's grip broke apart as easily as if I was peeling a banana.

I opened my eyes and turned round. Alex was appraising me now with something approaching awe. At least I hoped it was awe. He stepped towards me with his arms outstretched. *Rachel*. I punched his arm away with my mind and it jolted backwards. This could be fun. Now I had it, it was easy. And all along Rachel was the key. I wasn't sure why I was surprised, or why I hadn't figured it out sooner. Every time I got angry or otherwise emotional, I lost control of my ability, so it made sense that Rachel would be my biggest trigger.

Alex was keeping his distance now and his smile had faded. He seemed almost too nervous to make another move towards me. And there – was that a slight wince of irritation I caught in his eyes? It vanished as soon as I noticed it and he gave me a brief smile.

I wondered suddenly if I could make him step towards me. Put his arms round me? Take off his T-shirt? Lie down on the bed again? Kiss me? I couldn't stop the grin from taking hold of my face. A whole world of opportunity suddenly opened up, involving a lot fewer clothes between him and me and a clear way past Alex's resolve.

21

No, bad Lila, I told myself. *Bad, bad Lila. Control.*

'You don't need to make me do that,' Alex said softly, moving towards me and stopping just a few centimetres from me. The pull was too great. I leaned into him, running my hands up the ridges of his stomach and chest until they looped behind his neck.

'Damn, you can read my mind,' I murmured.

'No. I just know you,' he smiled and kissed my ear, then the hollow at the base of my throat and I felt the tremor in my body as my pulse quickened. I pushed my forehead against his shoulder and breathed in deeply. In all this mess, with this nightmare going on around us, at least I had this.

3

The taxi driver asked if we were sure.

'*Sí*,' Alex replied.

I could only follow a bit of the conversation, my Spanish being remedial at best. I could order a burrito and ask for a double room and that was about it.

'Why does he keep asking if we're sure?' I whispered to Alex.

'Because tourists don't usually ask to go to this part of town.'

'I can't think why,' I muttered to myself, looking out of the window. There were a lot of red lights and dark alleys and flashing signs for Negra Modelo and Corona. It was nearly two in the morning and the streets were eerily empty. Even the locals obviously had more sense than to come out after dark.

I turned to face Alex across the back seat. 'So, remind me once more what we're doing here?'

'We both need new passports. And we need them fast. We can't use our old passports to cross back into the States. The Unit will have an APB out on us by now.'

'And illegal passports aren't something they sell in the super-market. I get it, but why are we *here*?' I wasn't seeing a flashing sign for a passport shop.

'I asked the driver to take us to the worst part of the city.'

'OK,' I said as if I understood.

Alex turned to the driver and spoke to him in fluent Spanish and I stared at him in surprise, wondering how many more skills he had that I didn't know about.

'*Aquí?*' the driver said, gesticulating at the area around us like it was a plague zone. I was on the driver's side. This didn't look like too safe a place to be getting out for a stroll, even with Alex and his gun for company.

They spoke for a few more minutes before the driver, shaking his head, took the money Alex was holding out to him and killed the engine. We were sitting on the side of a narrow road, parked between two other cars. About fifty metres down the road was a building with boarded-up windows. A dark reddish light was escaping through the slats.

We sat in the dark for another ten minutes until I noticed that Alex was watching a man half-hidden in the shadows. He was hovering in a doorway, and every so often a car would pull up and the man would bend down and speak to the driver. An exchange would happen and then the car would drive off.

'I thought we came for passports, not crack,' I whispered to Alex.

'Follow the street crime, which leads to the local dealer, which leads to the boss.'

'What kind of boss? Who do they work for?'

'The Mafia,' Alex said, not taking his eyes off the man in the shadows. 'In Central America there are various cartels. They control it all – the drugs, money laundering, arms, passports.'

I stared at him, wide-eyed, processing only the word *Mafia*. He didn't look like he was joking. I nodded slowly. 'So, we walk up to the nice man on the corner,' I said, 'convince him in Spanish to take us to his Mafia boss, and ask him nicely to give us new passports. Good plan.'

'Thanks,' Alex said, ignoring my sarcasm.

'OK,' I said, taking a deep breath, 'are we going to stay here all night, or are we going to go introduce ourselves to the man on the corner with the drugs?'

We reached for the door handles, but then Alex turned suddenly back towards me, putting a hand on my thigh. OK, we could stay here all night. I sank back into my seat.

'Lila—' Alex started then stopped.

'What?'

He shook his head and removed his hand. 'Nothing. I was going to say stay close to me, but I don't think I need to tell you how to look after yourself.'

The same look of irritation I'd seen earlier flashed through his eyes, making the blue momentarily darken. I had an instinct about what was causing it. I leaned over, putting my hand over his. 'I still need you, Alex,' I whispered.

He gave me a smile in return, but it didn't reach his eyes, and then he turned away and opened his door. I sat there for a few seconds before I followed him out. The taxi sped off with a screech of burning rubber as soon as I shut the door.

I looked around at the dark street and steeled myself, then followed Alex over to the man standing on the corner. He saw us coming, and his eyes darted up and down the street as if he was expecting the police to leap out at any moment from behind parked cars. We stopped in front of him.

He smiled a nervous kind of smile, revealing a black hole where his front teeth should have been. His feet were jittery on the sidewalk. I checked him up and down for any sign of a gun or a knife, realising that at some point in the last month surreptitious weapons checking had become my immediate reaction on meeting someone for the first time. I saw a familiar bulge under his shirt and his right trouser leg was rucked up as if he had something holstered to his ankle. I decided I'd go for the gun on his waist if I needed to.

Alex and the man had a brief conversation. The man didn't seem to be playing ball. He kept shaking his head. I caught sight of Alex slipping the man a folded wedge of dollars. The man looked at it and then finally he shrugged, muttered something under his breath and started walking down the street. We followed him.

'What did he say?' I whispered to Alex.

'He said, "*It's your funeral,*" but he's taking us to see the boss.'

'Great,' I said.

'I shouldn't have brought you,' Alex muttered, frowning as he looked over his shoulder.

'You had no choice, Alex,' I reminded him, nudging him with my elbow. 'You're not allowed to leave me, remember?'

He put his arm round me in answer, pulling me tight against his side, but I could see the way his jaw was clenched.

We headed down a back alley and stopped in front of a heavy, reinforced door. The dealer knocked loudly three times. A bolt slid back on the other side and then the door cracked open a fraction. There were raised voices inside – the dealer was talking to someone behind the door. Whoever it was didn't sound too happy. I clutched Alex's hand tighter and prayed he knew enough Spanish to get us through this. And that if he didn't, he had enough bullets in his gun.

The door finally cracked open another few centimetres and the dealer stepped out of the way, letting the light from inside fall in a strip on Alex and me. I threw back my shoulders and tried to look as relaxed as Alex did. He was veering on the nonchalant, acting as if fronting up to drug dealers was something he did every single day of his life. There was a moment's silence and then the door swung wide on its hinges. We stepped inside and the door slammed shut behind us with a solid *clang*.

Before I could get a glance at the room or who was in it, a hand shoved me roughly against the wall. Other hands started patting up my legs, working their way up to my hips and waist – where the patting became more like groping. I let out a yelp as a hand squeezed my butt, then drew in a deep breath, trying to remember what Alex had said about not revealing my ability unless I absolutely had to. The hand slid round my ribcage and I gritted my teeth, wondering at what point we reached absolutely.

'*La chica no tiene armas!*' Alex shouted. 'She's unarmed! We're both unarmed.'

Alex was unarmed? I twisted my head to look at him, forgetting all about the hands groping me. Alex was spreadeagled against the wall next to me, as the biggest man I'd ever seen held a gun to the small of his back and patted him down for a weapon. I gaped at Alex. For an entire week, he'd been surgically attached to his gun and then, when we pay a visit to a Mafia boss, he decides it's time to detach himself from weaponry? He shook his head at me ever so slightly, a warning look in his eyes.

The man holding me against the wall let me go finally and I jerked round. I was ready to lash out, could feel the anger coiling inside me, as I tried to shrug off the lingering sensation of fat fingers pressing into my thighs, but it drained away instantly, ice-cold fear flooding my system instead as I registered the four men in front of us.

The one who'd been groping me had a scar running the length

of his cheek. It was puckered like a silk scarf that had snagged on a thorn. He was staring at me, glassy-eyed, his tongue poking out between his teeth. The one beside him had a tattoo flowering from his chest and winding up round his neck of a snake twined round a naked, large-breasted woman. The third man – the one who'd been patting down Alex – was a solid mountain of muscle. It would take a battering ram just to get through him, never mind the door. I edged closer to Alex instinctively as my eyes finally lit on the fourth man.

He was sitting behind a table at the back of the room. He was older than the others, his hair shaved to the skull, and he had razor-sharp cheekbones below eyes as sunken and dark as pits. His shirt was open to the navel and a large crucifix hung against his tattooed chest. He didn't exactly look like Tony Soprano, but he was, without doubt, what my dad would have called *of the criminal persuasion*. He could definitely pass for a Mafia boss. Or a psycho killer. Whichever. Alex took a small step forward, as if he could somehow block me from the man's snake-like, unblinking gaze.

'American?' the man asked, staring straight at me.

'Yes,' Alex answered.

'You're looking for something I hear.' His eyes slowly travelled to Alex, narrowing to pinpoints.

'Yes,' Alex said again, keeping his voice even. 'I've been told you might be the man to ask.'

'I might be,' the man said, rubbing a hand over his stubbly chin. 'Depends who's asking. And how much they're paying. Drink?' he said, nodding at the unlabelled bottle sitting in front of him on the table.

'Sure,' Alex answered.

I saw his head turn as he studied the room – was he assessing our exits? Or the odds of us getting out alive? I couldn't tell, but I was starting to question his judgement in bringing us here and, more particularly, the wisdom of drinking whatever the hell was in that bottle – it looked like a shrivelled-up worm was floating at the bottom of it.

Alex finally walked to the table and I followed, sitting down in the chair beside him, acutely aware of the three men right behind us. They were all armed – two with guns, one with a knife the size of a sword. Our exit was blocked. There was only one other door directly behind the desk, but it was shut and possibly even locked. The room we were in was clearly where the deals went down. I wasn't sure what kind of deals, but from the bits of foil and the weighing scales sitting on the table in front of us it wasn't too hard to guess. My foot started tapping and I rested my hand on my thigh to try to still it.

The man sloshed whatever was in the bottle into three smeared shot glasses. He pushed one across the table towards me. I looked over at Alex. His eyes were locked on the man and, though his face was as impassive as ever, I could sense the tension in his body. I could see it too – in the straight line of his jaw, the set of his mouth and the bulge of tendons in his forearm, resting casually on the table.

'*Salud*,' the man said, downing the liquid and slamming his glass down on the table. His eyes never left my face and I could feel my skin starting to prickle as though fire ants were grazing on my neck. Alex picked up his shot glass and drank it back in one gulp without taking his eyes off the man.

'And you?' the man asked, nodding at my untouched glass. 'What's your name, *Señorita*?'

'Lila,' I said, casting a nervous glance at Alex, wondering if I should have given my real name.

'You not drinking your drink, Lila?' the man asked, nodding his head at my almost overflowing shot glass.

What was the etiquette here? 'Um, I'm not thirsty,' I hazarded.

'I think you should drink,' the man said.

It was an order. I thought for one second about disobeying it, but then I remembered the three men behind me so I picked up the shot glass and tipped whatever was in it down my throat. *Burning, burning!* I spluttered and coughed. Alex started smacking me hard between my shoulder blades.

The man laughed as I tried to breathe through the fumes filling my mouth and nose. 'My name is Carlos,' he said.

Great. I was on first-name terms and drinking Tequila with a Mafia boss. My dad would be ecstatic.

'So, you want papers? Passports?'

'Yes,' Alex said.

Carlos grunted. Then he turned to me. 'You running from something, Lila?'

I held his gaze. 'Not anymore,' I answered. His expression showed an instant of puzzlement before the dead-eyed stare returned.

'Ten thousand American dollars,' Carlos said to Alex. 'You pay now.'

'Half now, half on receipt,' Alex countered.

Carlos appraised him slowly as I sat there, gripping the seat, willing Alex to just get out his wallet and pay up in full so we could leave with all our body parts still attached.

Carlos finally laughed under his breath. 'For a *gringo* you got balls. OK, *sí*, half now, half later.' He lit a cigarette, his eyes falling back on me as he drew in a lungful of smoke.

'How long?' Alex asked.

'I assume you want express delivery – so let's say twenty-four hours. You got photos? Names – you don't get to choose. You get what we give you, what we got in stock, but they'll be American passports. Real nice. You'll have no trouble.'

Alex reached into his back pocket and pulled out an envelope. It had passport photos of both of us in it, taken just a few hours ago down in a metro station. He counted out five thousand dollars in hundred dollar bills and placed them on the table. Carlos checked it was all there. Then he said something to one of his men, the one with the naked woman writhing with a snake tattooed on his chest, and he came and took the money and photographs and disappeared through the internal door.

'Tomorrow, we deliver to you.'

'Midnight, at the McDonalds near the cathedral,' Alex said, standing and pushing back his chair. I followed suit, glancing nervously at the internal door – how did we know they'd actually do it and not just take the money? I really didn't want to have to come back and ask them to return our five thousand dollars.

'You not going to stay?' Carlos asked me. 'Have another drink.'

'No, we're good, thanks,' I answered, taking Alex's hand and edging back towards the door. 'We should be going.'

'OK, OK, I see that you two have a thing going on. You're a lucky man, Mr American.'

Alex didn't say anything. I turned to the door. The man who looked like a giant pork joint was unbolting it – slowly. The other man said something to Carlos in Spanish and Alex's grip on my hand tightened as he pulled me closer towards him, his eyes planted firmly on the door, which still hadn't been opened.

A harsh laugh burst in my ear and stinking breath lapped my

face. I screamed as a strong hand grabbed hold of me from behind, fingers digging into my waist, trying to pry me free from Alex's grip. Alex shouted something and distantly I heard the scrape of metal, but before anyone could make a move I'd spun the guy with the snake tattoo off me and launched him halfway across the room. He went crashing into the far wall head first, before slumping to the ground. He moaned and rolled onto his side, clutching his head in his hands, blood trickling between the gaps in his fingers. *Uh-oh*. I couldn't meet Alex's eye. I wasn't sure if he'd agree that what had just happened had constituted absolutely necessary.

Instead I turned to Carlos. He was staring at me, unblinking, his shot glass dangling precariously in his hand.

'Please tell your friend to get out of the way,' I said, indicating the enormous man behind us who was barring the door. 'I don't want to hurt him.'

Carlos studied me for a moment and the room fell ominously silent. Even the guy on the floor stopped moaning. Then Carlos threw back his head and started laughing like a madman, his fists hammering the table.

'You want a job?' he asked me when he had finally pulled himself together and wiped the tears from his eyes.

I weighed my response carefully. 'No thanks.'

He shifted his gaze to Alex. 'I see why you brought her,' he said, nodding approval. 'She's a good bodyguard.'

'Yeah,' Alex said, smiling tightly, 'she's pretty ninja. You don't want to get on her bad side.'

4

It took twelve hours, driving just under the speed limit, to make it to the coast – to a place so beautiful it looked like the setting for every suncream advert ever filmed. The white sand, topaz sea and blazing sun were such a contrast to Carlos's drug den and to Mexico City that it took a while for me to absorb it. I stood with my toes buried in the sand, staring back at the three thatched cottages nestled under a grove of palms, waiting for Alex who'd gone to book us a room. Even through the fog of exhaustion I couldn't help but look over my shoulder and stare down the deserted beach, convinced that at any moment the Unit would appear, black-uniformed men sprinting towards me.

I turned back, squinting against the sun, and saw that Alex was walking towards me across the burning sand, one arm flung up to shield his eyes. I was wearing his Ray-Bans. He hadn't asked for them back.

'I got us a room,' he called out.

He pointed over his shoulder to one of the cottages with a palm thatch roof and a hammock stretched out across the balcony. It had a clear view over the Caribbean Sea and fronted the beach. The other cottages seemed unoccupied.

If someone had told me a few weeks ago that I'd be in Mexico with Alex and that he'd be walking across the beach with a smile on his face, having just booked us a room, I'd have dropped dead from excitement. I would have needed defibrillators to bring me round. But here he was, walking across the sand towards me, and he was mine. And I hadn't dropped down dead. On the contrary, I felt very, very alive.

'They only had a double,' he said, when he reached me.

I met his eyes; the amber in the aquamarine was sparkling.

'That's too bad,' I said, trying to look annoyed.

'Uh-huh,' he nodded, one eyebrow raised in amusement. He wasn't falling for it. Ah, the trials of not having a poker face.

'How did you know about this place?' I asked as we wandered back towards the room.

'My parents have been coming here every year since their honeymoon. We needed somewhere to rest and wait.' He shrugged. 'This place sprang to mind.'

'So, how long are we staying?' I asked. Beautiful as it was, as much as this had been a fantasy a few short weeks ago, now it wasn't where I wanted to be. I needed to be in California. I wanted to be doing something to get my mum and Jack back. Waiting was torture.

'We stay until we have a plan. And until Demos finds us.'

I glanced at Alex. He was so confident that they'd find us, but they'd be looking for us in Mexico City, not here on a beach in the middle of nowhere. Sure, they had ways of finding us, but Nate and Key couldn't fly around the globe like satellites trying to spot us, and Suki and Alicia couldn't read every mind in the world until they happened across us hanging out here building sandcastles.

Alex avoided my look and led me up the stairs instead. 'Come and check out the hammock,' was all he said.

We lay together, rocking peacefully and talking quietly, until the sun dissolved into the sea and the stars lit up the sky. It was so beautiful and such a contrast from the last few weeks that I kept having to squeeze my eyes shut and pinch myself to make sure that it wasn't all a dream, that my brain hadn't been fried by one of the Unit's weapons back in Mexico City, and left me hallucinating.

'Why didn't they fire that thing at me?' I asked, twisting in the hammock so I could see Alex's face. 'When we were running away . . . they had the chance, but they didn't do it. Why not?'

'I've been wondering the same thing,' Alex said, 'and the only reason I can come up with is that they still don't know about you. We didn't know for sure, not after what happened at Joshua Tree, but if they didn't fire on you when they had the chance, it means they don't know you're a psy.'

I raised an eyebrow and propped myself on one elbow to look at him. 'But if they don't know about me – about what I am, what I can do – then why were they firing at us at all? Why are they even bothering to chase us?'

A pained expression crossed his face. He looked away, up at the sky. 'I broke my oath, Lila. I broke into the base and kidnapped two prisoners.'

'They weren't prisoners, they were hostages,' I retorted angrily.

'That's not how they see it,' he sighed. 'And I fired at my own men.'

I sank back into the hammock. It wasn't fair. What choice had he had?

I felt his lips press against my forehead and I knew he was trying to tell me in his own way that it didn't matter – but it did. He'd been forced to do all those things because of me. If the Unit

35

caught me, they would discover what I was most probably, and then they'd experiment on me, but if they caught Alex – what would they do to him? I didn't dare ask. Instead I changed the subject.

'So, now you're John Bartlett and I'm Emily Roberts,' I said, referring to our new passport names, 'are you sure they won't be able to find us?'

'Yes,' Alex answered, 'but we'll still need to be careful when we cross back into the States. They'll be watching the borders closely now they know we're in Mexico.'

We rocked silently for another minute, then Alex turned his face to mine. 'So, tell me again what happened when you were with Demos.'

I paused, running over the conversation in my head. I'd thought about it so much while we were on the run. I'd already told Alex about Demos and my mum. How he was trying to get revenge on the Unit for killing her, that he had loved her and that she had gone to him when she needed help, just days before the Unit killed her . . . or pretended to kill her. I still couldn't understand how they had faked the murder. That was the least of the things to get my head around, though. Ten days ago I hadn't even known that people like me existed and then, within the space of a few hours, everything I'd ever understood had been exposed as lies. I guessed it was still a shock to Alex too, which was why he was asking to hear it again.

'Demos loved her. I couldn't believe it until he showed me the photo of them together. Then it all just made sense. I could see it in his eyes, Alex. The way he looked at me, like I reminded him of her. Like all this love was just there under the surface still.'

'You do look like her. I told you.'

I sat up suddenly, throwing my legs over the side of the hammock, making it rock wildly. 'What are they doing to my mum, Alex?'

It was a question I'd been too scared to ask up until now. I waited, my stomach clenched hard as a stone. Alex leaned up and put his arm round my shoulders. 'I don't know,' he said quietly. 'Honestly, we never knew they were experimenting. We thought they were just containing people like—' He stopped.

'Like me?' I finished for him.

'Yes,' he sighed. 'Yes, like you, but people who had committed crimes, Lila, as we believed, and who couldn't be imprisoned in a normal facility—'

'I saw him,' I said, cutting him off.

Alex fell silent, but I knew he was thinking of Thomas as well – of the bundle of rags that Jack had pulled from the car, the zombie-like shape, shuffling and stooped over. Thomas had spent five years contained – imprisoned – by the Unit. God knows what they had done to him in their efforts to understand how he could project out of his body. I had tried to imagine what those experiments might look like, but every time it felt like I was pressing my face to the window of a car crash. I didn't want to see what horrors were inside.

I heard Alex sigh again. He dropped back into the hammock behind me and I turned so I could see him. His face was haunted and silver in the moonlight.

'Whatever they did to Thomas they're doing to her too, aren't they?' I asked.

He hesitated before he answered. I could see his eyes were shut. 'Yes, probably,' he said after a while.

I got up and walked shakily to the edge of the balcony, listening to the surf crashing onto the beach as if it was trying to reach us all the way up here. Alex came and joined me, his arms snaking round my waist.

'She's alive, Lila. That's what you have to focus on. A week ago you thought she was dead.' He bent to whisper in my ear. 'You'll see her again.'

'How?' I shouted, twisting out of his arms.

It was impossible. How would we ever get back on the base? How would we ever get anywhere near her? The Unit were a small army. We were just us. And even if Demos and the others found us, we still weren't enough to take on the Unit, that much had been proven in Joshua Tree. Ryder had *died*; how many more people were going to risk their lives for a fight that wasn't their own? Demos had a reason – he loved my mum. But Suki? Nate? Key? Amber? Why would Amber want anything to do with us now the man she loved had been killed?

Tears started to slide down my face. Ryder had been so good to me. And now he was dead. Killed by the Unit right in front of me.

'How will we get onto the base, Alex? It's impossible.'

Alex was looking out at the dark expanse of sea. 'There's always a way in,' he said, turning slowly back to face me. 'That's what they taught us. There's always a chink in the armour. We just need to find it.'

5

'I love you,' I whispered.

I had said the words only once before, the first night we'd run from Joshua Tree, leaving Jack lying bleeding out in the dirt and Ryder dead beside him. Alex had skidded the car into a truck stop an hour down the road. I was shaking, my arms wrapped round me, trying to contain the spasms, the sobs trapped in my chest making me gasp for air. Alex had unbuckled my seat belt, reached across and pulled me into his lap, rocking me, holding me, trying to get me to calm down. I had gripped him back fiercely, my fingers claws, and he'd taken my face in his hands and, with his lips against mine, whispered to me in the dark, over and over, that it was all going to be OK.

It had taken a while for the shaking to stop, for my hands to loosen their grip on his shoulders and for my breathing to calm. He held me the whole time, his voice low and steady in my ear, his hands warm against my skin, and when I had found my voice, with my lips against his neck and my body slumped against him, I whispered the same words I whispered now: *I love you.*

Even though for the last seventeen years I had whispered them in my head – hell, I'd shouted them, yelled them, sung them, screamed them in my head for most of that time – the words were so new between us they practically had a price tag still attached.

39

Heat flooded my face and my legs turned to jelly, even though I was lying down. 'I love you,' I said again, this time holding his gaze.

'I know,' Alex answered, unplugging the light with his free hand and pulling me close. 'Since you were five.'

I poked him in the ribs.

'I can't believe I never saw it.'

Yeah, neither could I. I couldn't have been more obvious if I'd tattooed his name and a love heart across my forehead.

'I never in a million years expected you to like me back,' I murmured, running my hand over his chest. It was an action I'd never, ever get tired of doing.

'Why?'

'Because.' I shrugged. As though it needed explaining.

He laughed then traced a finger up my cheek and across my lips, leaving a low, burning throb in its wake. 'You have no idea how hard you were to resist. Not when you were five,' he added quickly. 'Cute as you may have been back then, I have to say I never thought of you like that until you came back a few weeks ago.'

'Yeah, well, you could have fooled me. You didn't act like you thought *anything* of me.'

'What can I say?' Alex shrugged. 'I'm trained in subterfuge. You remember that night you stayed at mine? After the alarm went off at the base? I was awake all night.'

'Are you serious?' I laughed and rolled onto my back. I had been torturing myself that night with the belief that Alex liked Rachel and had spent eight sleepless hours wishing that Rachel would strut her perfect body in front of a bus. 'But the next day at dinner, at the bar even, you were so cold with me,' I said, sitting

40

up so I could look at him better. 'You acted like I didn't even exist.'

'Yeah, sorry.' He pulled a guilty face. 'Trying to distance myself. I never expected—' He broke off suddenly.

'Expected what?' I asked.

He took a deep breath before letting it out with a sigh. 'This,' he said. Then, after another pause, 'You've always been in my life, Lila. I knew you before you could even talk.' His head flopped back on the pillow. 'God, I miss those days.'

I elbowed him in the ribs again.

'What I mean is,' he said, turning towards me, catching my hand in his and holding it tightly, 'I was used to thinking about you one way – as Jack's little sister – and then,' he laughed softly, 'there you were. No longer little. No longer Jack's kid sister. You were all grown up.' His eyes swept up the length of my body before settling on my lips. 'And far too sexy for your own good,' he added. '*That* I wasn't expecting.' He ran the flat of his hand up my arm. 'I guess this proves you can't fight the inevitable,' he said, with the faintest of shrugs.

I narrowed my eyes at him. 'The inevitable, huh?'

He paused and gave me one of his looks, the kind that melted me like I was butter in a hot pan.

'Yes, the inevitable. Maybe you're right. Maybe it was that moment when you were five, when you broke your leg. You saw it before me, that's all.'

I tried to suppress the smile, lying down again and nestling my head under his chin. 'When did you know?' I asked. 'Was it my grand entrance? When I fell down the stairs? Is that what you meant?'

The last thing Alex had told me before leaving me with Demos was, *When you fell down the stairs, that was the moment.*

41

'Because, you know,' I continued, 'that was an orchestrated move on my part. It had nothing whatsoever to do with clumsiness or nerves. I fully intended to land at your feet.'

Alex laughed under his breath. 'Yes, that's what I meant. The stairs. I didn't want to let you go when you fell on me.' His fingers were lightly stroking up my arm.

'But you did,' I murmured, closing my eyes.

I heard him sigh into my hair. 'I had to. Jack was right there.'

'Inevitable.' I toyed with the word in my mouth. It felt good. I tipped my head back so I could look at him and smiled what I hoped was a seductive smile, though it had hitherto not had the desired effect. 'So, if this is inevitable like you say, unavoidable, completely and utterly meant to be,' I tiptoed my fingers up the taut lines of his stomach muscles as I said each word, 'why are you fighting it now?'

'What?'

Oh, this was embarrassing. 'You know what I mean,' I mumbled, wishing for the first time I still had long hair and could hide behind it.

He looked at me, confused. I stared at the bed sheet. It was tastefully embroidered.

He finally figured it out. 'Because, Lila,' he said, stroking my cheek, 'you're tired, there's a lot going on in here,' he tapped the side of my head, '. . . too much . . . and there's a right time. It isn't now. Besides,' he added, 'it's still illegal in the state of California. You're not eighteen for another four months.'

I leaned up on one elbow. 'We're not *in* California,' I said, scowling at him. And besides, why was he caring about the illegalities of that when we'd broken at least fifty other laws and were on the run from a team of special ops Marines who wanted to kill

42

us? It wasn't like I was going to file a police report in the event. But Alex just laughed at me.

'You'll thank me later,' he said.

I wouldn't thank him later, but there was no point arguing.

6

'Are we interrupting something?'

'Suki! It's Suki!'

Alex was already halfway across the room. I scrabbled like a crab over the surface of the bed, pulling the sheet round me, then leapt after him.

She was banging on the door. Alex opened it and she burst through. I stumbled crazily towards her, pushing Alex out of the way and throwing my arms round the tiny Japanese girl with sunglasses the size of dinner plates and a dress so mini it would barely cover a Bratz doll.

'Suki! You found us! You found us!'

She hugged me back. 'Of course we found you. What did you expect?' She pulled her sunglasses down and peered at me over the top of them. 'What did you do to your hair?' she shrieked.

'Hi, Lila.' Demos was standing behind her, in the doorway.

I extricated myself from Suki's arms and turned to Demos. 'Hi,' I said.

He smiled at me. There was little joy in it, though. He glanced down at my sheet toga and then at Alex in his boxer shorts. A wry smile formed on his lips. Then he took hold of Suki's elbow. 'Come on, Suki.' He pulled her towards the door. 'We'll see you downstairs,' he said over his shoulder.

'Bye,' Suki called out, her eyes so glued to Alex's bare chest that she failed to watch where she was going and walked straight into the doorpost. We heard her giggling all the way down the stairs.

'Where's Nate? Where's Key?' I asked, looking around and feeling all my elation drain instantly away.

Demos, Suki, Alicia and Harvey were sitting on sunbeds beneath the shade of a palm tree, quietly conferring. There was no sign of Nate or Key. I frowned and did another headcount. Amber and Bill were missing too.

Demos stood up and walked towards us. 'Nate's in his room, resting,' he said. 'Key's gone back to see if he can find out what's happening to Jack.'

At the sound of Jack's name I felt a familiar lurch in my stomach. Demos must have realised how I was feeling because I felt his hand on my shoulder. I looked up into his flat blue eyes and something passed between us – some kind of reassurance that he understood how I was feeling and that everything would be OK. Or maybe he was doing some kind of Jedi mind-trick on me – I wasn't sure, but I did feel calmer.

'Where are the others?' I finally asked.

'They're in Mexico City,' Demos said.

'What are they doing there?'

'Thomas needed medical help.' He glanced darkly in Alex's direction and I stepped slightly in front of him as though I could block Demos's anger. Alex hadn't known what the Unit was doing to Thomas; it was hardly fair to blame him.

'And Amber? Bill?' I asked.

Demos's expression turned darker still. He looked at me.

45

'Amber's not in a good way. Bill's doing his best to look after both of them.'

Of course Amber wasn't in a good way – she'd seen the man she loved killed right in front of her. I didn't know what to say to that.

'Demos.'

I looked up. Alex had stepped forward and was holding out his hand. 'I'm Alex Wakeman. We never got to meet properly.'

There was a moment when no one breathed. We all stared at Alex, wondering what Demos would do. Whichever way you looked at it, Alex and Demos had been fighting on different sides of the war until just over a week ago. No one was sure whether the truce had been temporary or if it would hold.

I looked at Demos. His eyes were a match for Alex's in both the blueness and the as-inscrutable-as-a-rock stakes. He considered Alex for a few seconds before taking his hand and shaking it. We all breathed out in unison.

'Thank you for fighting with us back there,' Demos said.

Alex nodded. 'It was the least I could do. I'm sorry.'

'You weren't to know. I'm sorry I kidnapped Lila from you.'

A scowl crossed Alex's face. Then he took a deep breath and walked over to where Alicia was sitting. She looked up at him. The bruise on her face was still there. It had mellowed to a yellowish colour, but it was still a clear reminder of her recent imprisonment.

Alex knelt in the sand in front of her. 'I'm sorry,' he said.

Alicia grinned at him. 'Apology accepted. And thank you for springing me out of that place. We're cool.'

Alex grinned back at her and stood up. Demos introduced him to Harvey and I watched the three of them fall into a small huddle and start talking as if a fortnight ago they hadn't all been trying to kill each other.

46

'Did you find us OK?' I asked, turning to Suki.

She raised a perfect eyebrow. 'We're here, aren't we?'

'I mean, was it difficult? We had to leave Mexico City. The Unit found us. There was a tracker in Alex's arm.'

'We know. Nate was there in the cathedral; he won't stop going on about it – particularly the part where Alex took his T-shirt off.'

My mouth fell open. Nate had been in the confessional *with* us?

'He followed you here too,' Suki went on, without pausing for breath, 'but by the time he got back to us, we were way behind you. It took us a while to drive down here – nice place by the way – and we had to stop in Mexico City, of course.' Her face puckered.

'How is Amber?' I asked.

'Not good,' Suki said with a sigh. 'She's angry. Very angry. With Demos. With the Unit. With everyone. She didn't want to come with us.'

'How did you get the Unit off your tail?' I said, changing the subject as I saw Suki's lip tremble.

'They were never on it,' she said. 'We drove north, but they went south almost immediately. They were following you from the get-go. Once we realised, we turned straight round and tried to get to you before they did, but it wasn't so easy. We got pulled over three times by the police and they tried to stop us at the border too.'

'What happened?' I asked. 'How'd you get through?'

'Demos.' Suki shrugged. 'He just froze them and we drove on by.'

Not for the first time I felt a stab of jealousy at Demos's ability. It made things so much easier. He would never have to befriend a psychotic Mafia drug lord or be manhandled by his minions.

'A who?' Suki burst out. 'What did you just say about a Mafia drug lord manhandling your minions?'

'Nothing.' I frowned at her. 'I didn't say anything.'

It was making me wonder now why we'd bothered with the fake passports. We could have just waited for Demos and crossed the border with him.

'What are you talking about?' Suki asked, her smooth forehead creasing.

'It doesn't matter,' I said quickly. 'Come on, show me where Nate is. I want to say hi.'

She bounced up, grinning, her black hair flapping like a crow's wing. 'He's going to be so mad he didn't get to see Alex in his underwear.'

'Wait, hang on a second,' I said, grabbing her by the wrist, 'what about Rachel?'

I noticed everyone had fallen silent. Alex's own head had pricked up at the sound of Rachel's name. Last time we'd seen Rachel she'd been fighting tooth and nail as she was hauled onto the bus.

'Urgh, her,' Suki groaned. 'Yeah, she's still with us. And she's still a pain in the *culo*. I'm learning Spanish,' she said brightly. '*Culo* means ass.'

'Yeah, I'm aware of that. Did you get any information out of her?' I asked, unable to keep the hope out of my voice. I looked anxiously over at Demos and the others.

'Nothing helpful,' Suki said. 'She just keeps singing nursery rhymes in her head every time Alicia and I try to read her mind. Over and over. If I hear her singing *she'll be coming round the mountain* one more time, I think I'm going to have to shoot her.'

Get to the back of the line, I thought to myself.

'We know where they're holding your mum, though,' said Demos. 'We got that out of her. She's still on the base at Pendleton

– down in prisoner holding.' He glanced at Alex. 'We were hoping you could help with the plans of the building and the entry codes.'

Alex shook his head, his expression grim. 'They'll have changed the codes and barred my access,' he said. 'And we'll need more than just a layout of the building. We need a plan of how we're going to get in there. I won't be able to go anywhere near the base. And the whole place is rigged with alarms so none of you can either.' He paused. 'Let me speak to Rachel, see if I can get something out of her.'

And if that doesn't work, I thought to myself, *just let me at her*. It would make what I did to that Humvee back in Joshua Tree look like tossing a pancake.

7

'Oh, Nate, if only you could see what I've just seen!' Suki sighed, dropping down onto the bed Nate was stretched out on. We were in the room next to mine and Alex's. The others were all outside, sitting under some palm trees, talking. We could see them through the open door, but couldn't hear them over the roar of the surf outside and the whir of the fan overhead.

Nate rolled over sleepily and smiled widely as he saw me.

'Hey,' I said.

'Hey,' he answered, rubbing his eyes. 'What's going on?'

'Oh, just Alex half naked, that's all,' Suki smirked.

Nate sat bolt upright. 'I missed it?' He sighed and lay back down. 'Oh well, I've seen him completely naked already.'

I leapt off the bed. 'Please don't tell me you were following us the entire time, Nate?' I begged. Oh God, what had he seen? I squeezed my eyes shut, recalling some of the more graphic moments Nate might have been witness to, and let the blush swallow me whole. A loud gasp from Suki made me cover my ears and scrunch my eyes even tighter shut, as if that might somehow stop her from getting a visual on the images running wantonly through my mind.

'La la la la la la la la la la,' I started singing, trying to picture a blank white wall instead of Alex in all his naked perfection.

'Nate has been following you all the time,' Suki said, cutting through my la-ing, 'and yes, he has seen everything. And reported back to me. So I'm all up to speed.'

I opened my eyes and started scanning the room for something to launch at her head.

'Nice work, Lila,' Suki continued, lowering her voice. 'Shame you can't get him to – you know . . .'

'I can't believe you guys!' I yelled.

'All in the name of duty,' Nate beamed. 'Someone had to make sure we didn't lose you. If it wasn't for me following you guys, we wouldn't have known where you'd run off to and we might never have found you – and then what? Seriously? Who chooses a romantic beach getaway at a time like this?'

I glared at him. And at Suki. A serious talk about the concepts of privacy and invasion was going to be occurring when I had calmed down.

'We're sorry, please forgive us,' Suki said, nudging Nate, who nodded, the corners of his mouth turning down as he attempted a contrite look.

'Well, don't do it again, OK?' I hissed. 'You've found us now. There's no more need to spy. Agreed?'

Neither of them said a word. They just shot each other a look out of the corner of their eyes.

'Agreed?' I growled. Nate opened his mouth to argue, but Suki elbowed him in the ribs and he shut his mouth quickly and nodded.

'And you,' I said, turning to Suki, 'stay out of my head, OK? It's really starting to get annoying.'

'Easier said than done, but I'll try.'

I held her gaze, imagining in graphic, bloody detail what I

would do to her if she or Nate spied on me again, or on Alex. Or on the two of us together.

'OK, I get it!' Suki yelled, throwing her hands up. She patted the bed and, after a few seconds, I relented and went and sat back down.

'What happened to the bus?' I asked, referring to the giant RV tour bus that they'd been travelling in up until now.

'We had to get rid of it – it was kind of obvious as Batmobiles go. Harvey was very sad, but Demos bought him a BMW instead – actually, he stole it, he didn't buy it. And he also stole a van, because we needed somewhere to put Rachel. You know, it's not such a good idea driving around with a gagged girl in the front seat of a car. We didn't want people thinking that we were trying to kidnap her.'

'We did kidnap her,' I reminded Suki. 'So, where is she?' I tried to sound like I didn't care. I was itching to go and see Rachel right that second, but I also knew that if I did, I might not be able to control myself.

'I think she's still in the van,' Suki said, her eyes narrowing at me as she read my mind. 'She's not very compliant with our wishes. Every time we take the gag off she starts screaming about how her father's going to kill us when he finds us.'

'But not before he rips open our brains and finds out what makes us so freaking special,' Nate butted in.

'Nate!' Suki shouted, glaring at him. 'Lila doesn't need to hear this.'

'Whoops, sorry,' he said, biting his lip.

I shrugged it off as best I could and glanced through the open door to where I could see Alex. He was sitting on a sunbed, locked in conversation with Demos, but he sensed me looking and

52

glanced over. He said something quickly to Demos then stood up and strolled towards us, hesitating at the door until Suki waved him in. He crossed to where I was sitting on the bed and dropped to a crouch by my side. Suki and Nate fell silent. I could have sworn I heard one of them sigh.

'Nate, hi, nice to meet you properly,' Alex said, extending his hand. Nate blushed to the roots of his hair and I tried to suppress a laugh.

'Hi,' Suki answered for him, in her tinkling sing-song voice, 'it's nice to meet you too – properly, I mean. Nate's already met you, so to speak. He follows you a lot.'

Nate blushed even harder, glaring at Suki. Alex laughed it off, shooting me a puzzled look. I shrugged. It was better all round not to go there.

'Are you sure you want to do this?' Alex asked me, his face suddenly turning serious.

'Are you kidding?' I answered, standing up.

'Only the last time you saw Rachel you wanted to kill her,' he said, looking at me doubtfully.

'Yep, I still want to kill her,' I said, 'but not before she tells us everything we need to know.'

He looked even more worried. I shrugged. What did he expect? That suddenly I'd feel like sharing milk and cookies with the woman? This was the person who was behind the Unit, behind my mother's imprisonment and probable torture. Yes, I wanted to kill her.

Alex considered me for a minute, probably trying to work out whether or not he could trust me to control myself. I was still trying to work the same thing out, but I wasn't about to tell him that and I hoped Suki wouldn't either.

'OK, let's do this,' he finally said, clearly having decided that he could trust me. 'She's next door, in Demos's room.'

Rachel sat on the edge of the bed, her ankles and hands bound together and a gag in her mouth. She was wearing a pair of ugly grey sweatpants, cheap white sneakers and a T-shirt three sizes too large, with the slogan 'Tijuana makes me HAPPY' stamped on the front in big red letters. The whole picture combined to make *me* very happy.

Rachel's eyes were vacant, her face blank. She looked like a recently salvaged thrift store mannequin, one where the sheen had worn off the plastic limbs and the wig had taken on a life of its own.

'OK, go ahead and unfreeze her, Demos,' Alex said, and it was only then that I noticed Demos looming over her, giving her one of his *you will do exactly as I say* stares.

Demos stepped aside and Rachel suddenly blinked into consciousness. A sneer instantly replaced the vacuous, glazed expression. Her eyes widened immediately at the sight of me and Alex standing in front of her.

My gut tightened, my jaw tensing so hard that my teeth ground against each other audibly. Both Demos and Alex turned and shot me warning looks. *OK, OK,* I whispered silently to myself. *Control. I've got it under control. I can do this. I will not kill her. I will not kill her. At least not quite yet.*

Suki was focusing hard on Rachel, her brow furrowed with concentration. I wondered if Rachel was busy singing nursery rhymes in her head, but she seemed too distracted by the sight of me and Alex in the room and her eyes were darting all over the place as she struggled to get her bearings. I noticed her gaze fly to

Alex's arm, where the bottom of a bandage could be seen poking out from under his sleeve, and a frown gratifyingly puckered her forehead.

Alex walked over to her and pulled the gag down. 'Rachel,' he said, by way of greeting.

'Alex,' she replied coolly, 'how lovely to see you.' Her eyes flicked towards me like a serpent's tongue. 'Still babysitting the mutant, I see.'

'You not going to play nice, Rachel?' Alex asked in a pleasant tone.

She blew her hair out of her face, unable to use her hands. 'I just don't get it, Alex,' she said.

'You don't get what?' he asked.

'What you see in her.'

I felt her gaze travelling up my body like a rash. I hadn't ever realised what hackles were, but now I was feeling them rise. The urge to take something heavy and smack Rachel over the head with it was growing. There was a wide-screen television fixed to the wall. I wondered how hard it would be to tear it from its hinges and spin it at her, Frisbee-style. Then the thought vanished, along with any desire to do violence. I felt floaty good. I glanced at Demos out of the corner of my eye. He raised his eyebrows at me in warning. He was right, I knew. In this situation I was the one who could afford a little magnanimity. I was, after all, the one with Alex. Not the one bound and gagged and wearing questionable clothing. But still . . .

'You know what *I* don't get?' Alex said after a beat. 'I don't get why you're doing this.'

'Doing what?' Rachel answered.

'You know what. Why is the Unit doing this?'

'Oh, come on, Alex, don't be naive. Money makes the world go around.'

He stepped backwards, shaking his head. 'That's what this is all about?'

Why was he asking her this? We *knew* that's what this was all about. Demos had already told me the Unit was trying to find a way of tweaking the genetic code that made us this way so they could create new weapons, which they would then sell to the highest bidder. Ergo – all about money.

'What else would it be about?' Rachel laughed, a high, braying noise that could have shattered glass.

'Have you even considered the consequences?'

'Oh please, don't get all righteous on me. Wars will happen regardless. Man has always found a way to inflict harm. This way we get to at least choose the winning side. We get to make the world safer, Alex.' Her eyes were burning brightly, lit by some kind of scary evangelical fervour.

'Safer according to who?' Alex snapped back. 'According to whichever madman pays you the most?'

Rachel considered him for a moment. 'Hmmmm. You know your problem, Alex?' she said after a while. 'You always get bogged down by morality. You could do with losing a few scruples. You'd sleep easier.'

'I'm sleeping pretty easy, thanks,' Alex said. 'Be sleeping even easier if I knew the Unit was no longer in existence.'

'Keep dreaming,' she sneered at him. 'You think you and your band of sub-mediocre *Heroes* rejects here have any chance of putting us out of action?'

Alex looked at Demos and then me before turning back to her. 'I think we made a pretty good start, don't you?' he said. 'We're here, after all. And you're the one trussed up like a Thanksgiving turkey.'

'So, you managed to put a few teams out of action.' Rachel shrugged. 'There are plenty more where they came from. You're just foot soldiers. Useful, but expendable.' She took pleasure in the last word, spitting it at him and watching greedily for his reaction.

Alex stared at her for a few seconds. His face remained inscrutable. But I could see that his eyes had turned to ice.

'You can't take one step on that base, Alex,' Rachel continued, the southern twang of her voice adding a warmth that the words belied. 'You'll be history. The military police will come down on you so hard you won't know what hit you. You fired on your own men. You think what *we* do is bad? Just wait till you're locked in a six by eight cell with a psychotic Marine for the rest of your life, you'll be wishing you had less scruples then.' She laughed and for a second she looked like a deranged Barbie doll. Then her face blanked out, the fire dying in her eyes and the sneer dropping off her face.

I looked over at Demos who was now giving her one of his *just be quiet* stares. Once again I envied the man.

'What are you getting?' Alex asked, turning to Suki.

Suki pulled a face. 'Just the same old craziness. She has some interesting ideas about what she wants to do to you – and let's just say they're not the same ideas that Lila and Nate have.'

'OK, unfreeze her again,' Alex said to Demos.

Once more Rachel blinked then scowled up at Demos, baring her perfect white teeth as if she wanted to tear out his jugular with them.

'What's the Unit working on?' Alex asked, his voice gentle, almost kind.

I shook my head. Was this how they taught them to interrogate in the Marines? Maybe it was time we skipped the non-violent Gandhi approach and started on the Jack Bauer method. I would be happy to take the lead.

'Whoa.' Suki suddenly reeled backwards.

'What?' I asked, thinking that maybe she'd heard my thoughts.

'What is it?' Alex asked simultaneously.

'They're doing some kind of weird experiments – I'm not sure – it's not clear.' Suki had turned as white as a sheet, her eyes locked on Rachel.

Rachel smiled smugly up at her. 'Well done, you read correctly. Give the girl a gold star – I was wondering whether you actually were a mind-reader or not. We are experimenting – and we're this close to a breakthrough. You know,' she said, looking at me now, 'your mum's been really helpful, Lila.'

I felt my heart come to a shuddering halt and Demos's hand squeeze my shoulder, another warning.

'Soon we won't be needing her anymore,' Rachel went on. 'We'll be looking for other freaks to experiment on. Maybe we could start with you.'

Demos cut her off before she could say anything more, freezing her with her mouth wide open and twisted into a snarl. Alex stepped quickly forward and pushed the gag back in.

I spun round and headed for the door before I lost it completely. The television was wobbling on its bracket, and I wasn't sure if I could get through the door without using it to decapitate her.

Outside the room I turned to Alex. 'So, what do we do now?' I asked, crossing my arms over my chest. 'Can we use Rachel as collateral? Offer her in exchange for my mum?'

Alex shook his head. 'I've thought about that already, but I can't see how it'll work. I know him. Richard Stirling wouldn't put Rachel ahead of his business interests.'

'Who's Richard Stirling?' I asked.

'Rachel's father,' Demos answered, appearing behind Alex. 'Richard Stirling is the man who set up the Unit. He's the man who bribed the senator your mother was working for, who ordered your mother's kidnap and who then faked her murder.' I watched the way Demos's jaw tensed as he spoke and realised how shocked and angry he still was. He seemed to be the only person other than me who felt it in the same way. I'd had a week to absorb the news that my mum was actually alive, and I was still reeling with disbelief. It looked like Demos was struggling to come to terms with it too. He carried on talking.

'Stirling has a business empire so wide and so pervasive that not even the taxman can follow its loops and trails. He has business interests in every country America is at war with, officially and unofficially. He's on first-name terms with half the military dictators on the planet.'

'I met him once,' Alex spoke up. 'Two years ago. He came to the base. He didn't come all that often – he left Rachel in charge of business there. He lives in Washington.'

'We can't use Rachel as an exchange,' Suki piped up, 'because, let's face it, who'd want her back? So, what do we do? How do we rescue Lila's mum?'

'And Jack,' Demos added, before I could.

I looked round at everyone then took a deep breath. 'I have an idea,' I said.

8

'No way.' Alex stood up from where he was kneeling in front of me and walked away.

I felt the painful stretch of the invisible ties – electrons or protons or whatever they were – that connected me to Alex. They snapped and fizzed with every step he took further from me. I got up and went after him. He had his back turned to me and was standing in the doorway of our room, looking out over the ocean. I'd brought him back here to talk to him in private about my idea. Now I was glad that I had.

'Alex,' I said, putting my arms round his waist and resting my cheek against his shoulder blade, 'just hear me out.'

He ran his thumb along the length of my arm and then turned to face me, his expression hard. But after a few seconds it softened and he nodded. We went and sat on the edge of the bed, side by side.

I took a deep breath. 'They don't know about me. Only Rachel knows what I am.' I stopped abruptly, thinking back to Joshua Tree, wishing that I'd never given myself away. It was a big mistake. I could tell from Alex's pursed lips that he wished the same. 'You said it yourself,' I continued, taking his hand, 'otherwise the Unit would have fired that thing at me. They don't know anything other than that Demos kidnapped me and that you and Jack busted Alicia and Thomas out in order to rescue me. They have no clue that I'm one of them – that I'm a . . . psy.' I hated using the word; it made me sound like I should be locked up in a padded cell wearing only a straitjacket, but for want of another term, I used it anyway.

'It's too dangerous,' Alex said, standing up and marching across the room once more. 'If they find out about you . . .' His words trailed off as he spun round to face me.

'They won't.'

'They will. You take one step inside their headquarters and you'll trigger the alarm.'

I frowned. 'You said the alarm only triggers if someone uses their power – well, what if I don't?'

I could see him pausing to think about it. 'Is that right?' I pressed. 'Could I get inside?'

'Yes,' he finally agreed, 'but it's too dangerous, Lila. I can't let you do this.'

I sighed. 'I have to go, Alex – I have to try. It's the only way. You said we needed a way in. Maybe I'm the way in. If I'm on the base, if I'm in the headquarters, then maybe I can find that chink – maybe. I know it's a long shot, but it's the only idea we've got right now.'

Alex held my gaze, his eyes the blue of the sea just outside. 'What will you do if I say no?' he asked.

I hesitated. He saw the answer in my eyes and the flare of anger that crossed his face sent a stab of pain right through me. 'Please. I need to go back,' I said, walking across the room and taking his hand. 'I can tell them you let me go. That I was slowing you down – that you were scared of them catching up with you. I'll say that you knew you were in trouble for breaking the rules, for turning on your own men, so you're running. They'll have to let me see Jack. I'm his sister.'

'They know you were with Demos. They'll assume he told you about what the Unit is really doing, and about your mum.'

'I'll act like he didn't say anything. I'll tell them that he tried to kill me like he killed my mother.'

'You're the world's worst liar,' Alex countered, pulling his hand from mine.

I'd already considered that. I'd been working on this plan for a few days. 'Well,' I said, 'I'll tell the truth, just not the whole truth. That way I won't have to lie.'

He cocked an eyebrow at me. 'Sara will see through you. She's trained to interrogate people who are far more skilled than you at lying.'

I shook this thought off. 'We don't know what Sara knows,' I argued, 'or how involved she is. She could have been fooled like you and Jack.' I could hear the desperation in my voice and tried to rein it in. I needed to sound confident not desperate. 'We might be able to get Sara on our side. She loves Jack. I can't believe she's one of them.'

Alex sighed. 'I can't either. But if you'd told me two weeks ago what the Unit was really doing, I wouldn't have believed that either. It's too dangerous, Lila. There has to be another way.'

I took a step closer towards him. 'Alex, you know there isn't. If there was another way, believe me I'd take it. But I have to do this. This is my mother and brother we're talking about.'

Alex stared at me fiercely. 'This is *you* we're talking about.' I felt my resolve falter.

'I'm coming with you,' he said. 'You're not doing this alone.'

I smiled up at him. 'I was hoping you'd say that.'

9

Key was waiting when we joined the others back in Nate and Suki's room. He jumped up as soon as he saw me.

'Your dad's with him,' were the first words out of his mouth.

I stared at him, wondering what he was talking about. I looked around the room to see who he might be talking to. Whose dad was with Jack?

But when I looked back at Key, he was still staring straight at me. 'Your dad,' he said, 'he's in the hospital with Jack.'

'What?' Alex interrupted.

'I just got back from another recce of the base. Your dad is at the hospital. I didn't hang around long – figured you'd want to know.'

'My dad?' A bubble of realisation burst through the meniscus of my brain. Oh God.

'Didn't you speak to him?' Alex asked, rounding on me.

I swallowed, my throat suddenly as dry as ash. 'Not exactly. I couldn't get hold of him so I left a message with Maria, our house-keeper. I told her we'd all gone on a camping trip to Death Valley and that we'd be back in a week. And then, maybe, I sort of forgot to call him.' I gave him a big, fake, apologetic grin.

Alex didn't say anything, he just continued to stare at me, his lips pressed together, turning slowly white.

'He really believed that one,' Key muttered under his breath. 'He's in California. At the base. And he's wondering why Jack's been shot and is under arrest and why you're missing.'

'Jack's under arrest?' I burst out.

'Well, what did you think was going to happen when he got into a gunfight with the Unit?' Key asked, looking at me like I was stupid. 'He shot his own men. They're not going to be giving him the Medal of Honor any time soon.'

'Hey, hey, don't worry her,' Alex cut in.

'Don't worry me? My brother's lying in a coma, possibly paralysed and under arrest, and my dad's just walked right into all this. And you're saying *don't worry me*?' The full awfulness of the situation settled on me. 'What's he even doing here?' I asked, panic making me breathless. 'He always said he'd never come back to the States. That he'd never set foot on US soil again. Not after what happened to my mum.'

I felt Alex's arm come round my shoulders and I turned to him. 'God, he doesn't know about her, Alex. He has no idea she's still alive. Why did he have to come back? He can't be involved in all this.' I pressed my head into Alex's shoulder. 'That's my whole family, Alex, right there. The Unit has them all.'

There was a deathly silence.

'What does your dad know about the Unit?' Harvey finally said. He was puffing on a cigarette by the open door.

'Nothing,' I said, still reeling from shock, my legs feeling wobbly and my voice wavering. 'He doesn't know anything about them or us. He knows nothing.'

'Actually, that's not quite true.'

I looked at Demos. 'What?'

His gaze flashed to Alex and then to me. He cleared his throat.

'Your father knew about your mother – about her being a telepath.'

'He what?'

'He knows. And he knows about the Unit too, but he believes that the Unit's mission is to contain people like us – contain psys – because we're dangerous. He thinks I killed your mother, because that's what the Unit told him.'

My jaw fell open. The silence thickened as I tried to get my head round the fact that my father had known about my mother's powers all this time. It suddenly made sense – why he'd dragged me straight on a plane to London after my mother's funeral. Why he'd been so mad at Jack for staying behind. Why he'd freaked out about me coming back. Oh God. I put a hand to my head to try to contain all the thoughts banging against my skull. How much more freaking out would he be doing now? With me missing?

This was so bad. So, so bad.

'There's more,' Demos said, because clearly he could tell I wasn't panicked enough already. I looked up warily, bracing myself.

'Your father's been working on something all this time.'

I waited.

'He's been carrying out research to find out what makes us this way.'

'No, he hasn't,' I laughed, but my laugh sounded empty and false. 'He's a paediatric specialist. He researches childhood diseases. He writes papers. He's always at conferences and stuff. I've been to the hospital where he works.'

Demos just shrugged. 'For the last five years your father's been trying to find a medical *cure* for what we are.'

'But we're not sick,' Suki spoke up from the corner of the room.

'No,' Demos said. 'But to Lila's dad, we're suffering from a kind

65

of cancer and he's been trying to invent what you might describe as a type of chemotherapy, some way of *curing* us.'

No one spoke. It seemed like this was news to everyone – not just to me.

I drew in a breath. All this time. The whole time we were in London. The trips abroad, the hours spent in his study, in his lab, working, working, working. And never enough time for me. And there I was thinking my dad was just working to put my mother out of his mind when all the time he'd been working with her right at the forefront of his mind. *For* her. Because he thought if he could find the answers to curing us, he could what? Stop Demos? Undo what had happened? Fix something? Is that what my mother had wanted too? To be cured? Because I wasn't sure it was what *I* wanted.

'How do you know this?' Alex asked.

'Because I've been keeping a close eye on him,' Demos answered, his eyes darting to me. 'And Lila. And Jack. I promised Melissa that I would look out for them and protect them if anything ever happened to her.'

'You've been spying on us? Since when?' I shouted.

'Lila,' Demos said, his voice shot through with weariness, 'I was only interested in making sure you were safe. When your dad took you to London I breathed easier, but I still needed to make sure the Unit weren't going to try something. Luckily they didn't see the need to.'

'Why not?' I demanded.

Demos chewed his lip. I guessed he was trying to evaluate how many more surprises I could take, which I had to admit wasn't many.

'We think the Unit knows about your father's research. It makes sense. It explains why they've left you both in peace.'

Why we're still alive, he meant.

Suki stamped her foot. 'Can someone please start explaining everything to me in simple English. I'm just not getting it. Any of it. And it's very annoying.'

'They want Lila's father's research,' Alex said, almost as if he was speaking to himself, 'because it might help them unlock the secrets about what you are. He's helping them – without meaning to.'

'Alex is right,' Demos said. 'The Unit is waiting until Michael unlocks the answers to the genetic code that makes us this way. There's almost no better person to do the job. He's an expert in childhood diseases – hereditary ones.' He paused and I thought about what he was saying.

Whatever we all had that made us this way, it was genetic. Everyone seemed to agree on that. But no one knew how many people had the gene, or how many people it was active in. I had it but Jack didn't – why that was, was a total mystery. But perhaps not to my dad.

'And more than any person on the planet,' Demos continued, 'Michael's got the incentive to find the answers. They don't even have to pay him.'

'So, what? They're waiting until he cracks the cure or whatever the hell he's doing and then they'll steal it? I don't get it. They don't want a cure. They don't want to destroy the gene or whatever the hell it is that makes us this way, they want to generate it. They want to create more people like us.'

'The science is the same,' Alex said, glancing at me, but his thoughts were miles away, already evaluating what new mess we were in. 'To fix something you've got to understand first how it works. Your dad thinks he's making things better. But really he's making it worse.'

'Why didn't you stop him if you knew that the Unit were wanting to steal his work?' I yelled at Demos.

'Stop him *how* exactly?' he asked.

'Er,' I looked at him like he was lobotomised, 'you know that little ability you have? Could have been useful, don't you think?'

Demos rolled his eyes at me. 'I couldn't spend my life following your father around freezing him. I do have other things to do. And besides, he thinks I killed your mother so he's not likely to listen to anything I have to say, is he?'

I scowled at him. I didn't want to listen either. I got up and walked unsteadily to the door.

10

Alex dropped onto the sand next to me a metre or so away. I glanced over at him. He was sitting like me with his knees drawn up, his arms wrapped round them, staring out at the sun as it melted into the sea. The beach was completely deserted. I stopped toying with the leather bracelet wrapped round my wrist and shifted in the sand towards him until I could rest my head against his arm. He reached out and curled his fingers through mine.

'I just can't believe my dad has been working on this all this time,' I murmured. Alex didn't say anything.

'And I don't know how to feel about it. Or the fact he's trying to cure me. I don't want to be cured, Alex. There's nothing wrong with me.'

He glanced at me out of the corner of his eye, a smile twitching at the side of his mouth. 'Debatable,' he said. I kicked sand at him and he pulled me down so we were lying flat on our backs, looking up at the purple sky.

'Why'd my dad have to come back?'

'Same reason you're going back. Same reason I gave you. When you love someone, you don't have a choice.'

I turned my head to look at him and he held my gaze. I felt tears pricking the back of my eyes and turned to stare up at the sky so Alex wouldn't see.

'I should go back and apologise to Demos for storming out like that,' I said, making no move to get up.

'Tomorrow,' Alex answered. 'I talked to the others. I told them your plan. They thought it might work. But we'll discuss it tomorrow and everything about your dad, because first I need to do something.' He pulled me closer towards him until our lips were almost touching.

'What might that be?' I managed to stutter, closing my eyes, anticipating the warmth of his lips against mine. But the kiss didn't come. I opened my eyes. Alex had jumped to his feet.

'Swim,' he said, grinning at me. 'Come on.'

'Swim?' I pouted, unable to hide my disappointment that he wanted to swim rather than make out with me.

Alex pulled his T-shirt off in one swift move. My eyes fell straightaway to his chest – which was tanned, smooth and ripped with muscle, and which, when you studied it as I had done, in fine detail, you discovered wasn't a six-pack but actually a twelve-pack. My eyes flitted to the shadowed hollows where his hips disappeared into his shorts, causing a flutter in parts of my body that up until three weeks ago had been flutter-dormant. Alex's hands dropped to his shorts and he started undoing his belt.

I reassessed the swimming option. I could definitely do swimming.

He shrugged off his shorts, but before I could catch an eyeful of anything, he was off, jogging towards the water. I paused for a nanosecond, weighing up my embarrassment at stripping naked over my desire to follow him. With a deep breath, I tore off my dress then kicked off my underwear and started running towards the sea, praying Nate wasn't doing a fly-by.

The water was warm and flat as a bath. I could see Alex in the distance, his skin gleaming in the now inky moonlight. When I got close to him, his hand snaked under the water, wrapped round my waist and pulled me towards him. I didn't resist because I'd forgotten in that instant how to swim. And then he kissed me and I prayed silently and fervently that he took my shudder to be the effect of the cold water.

I tried sticking myself onto him like a barnacle, but eventually Alex managed to pull himself free, holding my wrists in his hand so I couldn't reattach. His resolve was as solid as a nuclear bunker's walls. Alex had said there were always chinks. But I couldn't seem to find the one in his armour. He swam two long strokes away from me. I trod water and stayed where I was, feeling confused, glad that the night was dark enough to hide my expression.

'I'm just trying to protect your honour,' he said, guessing it anyway.

I groaned and rolled my eyes. When was he going to understand that I was happy for him to protect every other part of me, just not my honour?

He swam silently back to my side.

'I know we have to leave,' I sighed, 'but it feels like this is the only place in the world right now where we're safe. Where nothing bad can happen.'

'We'll come back,' Alex said, his hand reaching under the water to stroke down my back.

'You think?' I looked at him hopefully.

'I know so,' Alex said, pulling me close once more. 'I'll bring you back here. It's inevitable.'

I couldn't work out if it was the salt water that was making me float like a jellyfish on the water or him.

11

'I like it. Lila, it's a genius idea.'

I hadn't said anything. I'd just been thinking idly, following random ideas this way and that in my head while the others talked about Stirling Enterprises and how we were going to destroy them – as if bringing down global corporations was as easy as knocking down a house of cards.

'What? What idea?' I glanced over at Suki. She was bouncing on her heels and clapping her hands.

'Carlos. The Mafia man.'

Carlos? What? 'I didn't have an idea. I was just thinking,' I blurted, suddenly fearing where this might be heading.

'What were you thinking?' Demos asked, swivelling to me.

'You were talking about how we needed to bring down Stirling Enterprises,' I said, squirming in my seat. 'Not just destroy the Unit, but the whole company, and I was thinking about how to do that.'

'And she thought about this man.' Suki bounced forward. 'This Carlos. With the bald skeleton head and the mean eyes and the baddie tattooed bodyguards. I like this plan.'

'It's not a plan,' I almost shouted.

'No, there's something there. Wait,' Alex said. He took a few seconds to think. Everyone waited.

'It was stupid,' I interrupted before he could think any further. 'I just thought that the only way to really hurt Richard Stirling and destroy his company would be if we could set him up somehow.'

'And she thought drugs,' Suki said, still bouncing on the balls of her feet.

'I thought about drugs and money,' I corrected her. 'Which made me think of Carlos. But not seriously. It was just a random thought. It wasn't meant for public consumption.'

'This Carlos guy – he's the guy you got the passports from?' Demos asked.

'Yes,' Alex answered.

'She's onto something,' Alicia spoke up, her face brightening.

'No, I'm not onto anything.' Everyone needed to calm the hell down.

'DEA. That could do it,' Harvey said, nodding.

'DEA?' Suki asked. 'What is this DEA?'

'Drug Enforcement Agency,' said Alex. 'They'd have to investigate. If we could tie some drugs to Stirling, a *lot* of drugs to him—'

'What? Make it look like Stirling Enterprises was a massive drug-laundering cartel?' Key asked.

'Yes,' Alex nodded. 'Exactly. Stirling would lose all its government contracts, the Unit would be shut down. And Richard Stirling would face a trial and prison.'

'I like the sound of this DEA. See, it's a good idea.' Suki was beaming. 'I told you.'

Demos was scratching his chin. 'You know, it might just work.'

'Are you serious?' I announced, standing up. 'What's the plan? We break into Carlos's drugs den, take out his henchmen and steal all his drugs?'

'And his money. We need dirty money too,' Harvey said, lighting a cigarette. 'Lots of it. Money that can be traced back to Carlos.'

'OK, and then what?' I asked sarcastically. 'We're not X-Men in case you hadn't noticed.'

'No, we're way better than them,' Demos answered. 'What next?' he asked, smiling. 'We plant it.'

'Where?' I assumed he wasn't meaning in the ground.

'All over Stirling's office and house. We link the money and drugs to him so clearly he can't deny it. A watertight case neither he nor his lawyer can buy their way out of.'

'And how the hell are you going to do that?' I spluttered.

Alex looked over at Demos and they grinned at each other like two college kids planning the prank of the century.

'We can't. We just can't,' I said in growing panic, looking round the room for someone to back me up, but everyone was grinning like they were on something.

'You got a better idea?' Key asked me.

'No, she doesn't,' Suki answered.

12

'We need a sifter,' Demos said, from his position at the head of the table.

We were still in Suki's room, which had become the unofficial headquarters of the stupid and ridiculous plot to bring down Stirling Enterprises. It was already past 3 a.m. I could feel my eyes starting to close, my head tilting dangerously near to the table we were sitting round.

'Go and lie down,' Alex whispered to me.

'No, no way,' I said, getting up and moving to the minibar for a Coke.

'Getting in and getting out are easy. It's the part where we don't want them coming after us that's the problem.'

We were discussing the plan for Carlos. So far all we had was a strategy for getting into the place and for getting our hands on the drugs. The plan involved Alex giving directions, Demos doing his mind-control thing, Harvey and I stealing all the money and drugs and carrying them out to the getaway car, which Nate had decided he was driving and the rest of us had decided that Harvey was driving.

That was the extent of our plan. Even though I'd spent three hours arguing with everyone about the insanity of said plan and shooting graphic death thoughts at Suki for having read my mind yet again, no one had listened. Not even Alex. And Suki was ignoring me. Which meant I had no choice but to eventually sit down and join in. And I also had to concede, though not out loud, that the plan wasn't actually all that bad.

But there was one major issue – in amongst all the millions of minor ones – and Demos had hit on it. How to avoid having the Central American Mafia on our tail afterwards. We had the police and the Unit on it already. Adding an angry Mexican drug lord to the equation seemed like asking for trouble.

Ryder's name hung in the air like a ghost we were all trying to avoid. He had been a sifter: able to rearrange memories, even remove them entirely. Without him, we were stuck.

'I know a sifter.'

It took a few seconds for everyone round the table to register and take note of Key, sitting on the floor by the door. We'd thought he was sleeping. He wasn't. He was watching us with his yellowing, dusty eyes.

'I know a sifter,' he said again.

'Who?' Harvey asked.

'My mama.'

'Grandma's a sifter?' Nate yelled from across the room where he and Suki were huddled together doing something on a laptop.

'Yes, she is,' Key sighed.

I didn't remember falling asleep, but when I woke, it was to find Alex's arms wrapped round me. We were back in our room – he must have carried me there. I stretched and rolled over. Alex was still sleeping, his face bathed in the slatted golden light coming through the window. I watched him, listening to the soft sound of his breathing and studying his face, trying to etch it onto the surface

76

of my mind. As if it wasn't already imprinted there in indelible pen. A memory flashed into my head all of a sudden – of lying just like this in a motel room only a few weeks previously, watching Alex as he slept. I smiled to myself, remembering how his eyes had flashed open as though he'd sensed me watching him. And how he'd leaned towards me and kissed me for the first time and I'd known right then that nothing would ever be the same again.

Alex stirred and, finally, his eyelids flickered. He gave me a long, sleepy smile. 'Morning, beautiful,' he said, his hand reaching out to brush a strand of hair out of my eyes.

My stomach contracted and I felt the stinging burn at the back of my throat and behind my eyes. This was our last morning waking up together – hopefully not forever, but for a while at least. These moments ahead of us were it. Tomorrow I wouldn't be waking up in these arms. I might be waking up in a cell about to have my head hacked open by the Unit as they experimented on me.

I sat up in bed, fumbling at the leather bracelet on my wrist with an urgency that surprised me. I needed to get it off. I tugged and pulled until Alex grabbed hold of my wrist.

'What are you doing?'

'I want to get it off.'

'Why?'

I could see he was confused. The bracelet had been yo-yoing between us for years as a goodbye present. First he'd given it to me five years ago when I left for London, then I'd given it back to him on his birthday just a few weeks ago, then he'd given it to me just before he'd left me with Jack. And now here I was needing to give it back to him for yet another goodbye. I had this crazy feeling that it would protect him. Keep him safe when I couldn't be near him.

'I want you to have it again,' I said.

'Hold on, wait,' he said, sitting up. He rolled out of bed and crossed to the chair where he'd thrown his clothes. He fumbled in a pocket and came back with his switchblade by which time I'd managed to untie the knot.

'Here,' he said, 'give it to me.'

I realised what he was thinking and handed the bracelet to him. He cut through the leather strand, stiff with salt water and faded beyond a light brown, and then tied one half round my wrist. When he was done, he picked up the other half and tied it round his own wrist. I helped him out with the knot. It felt suddenly solemn. Like we were making each other a promise that nothing would divide us ever again, and I held on to that thought as though I could force it to come true.

The others were waiting for us, sitting under a palm tree on the veranda outside Demos's room. There was no sign of Rachel and I noticed that Alicia sat apart from the others, her knees drawn up to her chest, looking out towards the sea. Key too was nowhere to be seen. Then I spotted him in the distance, striding back and forth down the beach, his trousers rolled up to the knee.

'Harvey, Alicia, Nate and Suki are coming with me to Washington once we're done with Carlos,' Demos was saying.

I looked over at Suki and Nate. Suki had a heavy gold chain hanging around her neck and was wearing a pair of ripped jeans with white sneakers. I hadn't known that Suki owned any jewellery quite so bling or any shoes less than three inches tall. She looked incredibly short and weighed down. Nate had attempted to tie a bandana round his afro, but his hair was springing out from underneath as though attempting a prison break. He was wearing reflective sunglasses and a white tank top, which only served to emphasise his skinny shoulders and arms. It crossed my mind that he and Suki had probably been up all night researching the fashion preferences of the Mexican criminal underworld and that this was their quite serious attempt at going undercover.

'Alex is going with you back to Oceanside, Lila,' Demos said, 'but he has to keep a distance from the base. Key's the only one of us who isn't known to the Unit so he's going back with you as well – at least he'll project back there. He won't be there in person.'

I smiled at Key. It made me feel a whole lot better knowing that Key would literally be my shadow – like having an invisible lifeline to the others.

'We'll keep his body with us,' Demos continued. 'It's safer all round for him and that way he can get back to us instantly and let us know if you're in any danger.'

'But remember,' Alex said, pulling up a chair, 'Key can't go into the Unit's HQ or within five metres of the perimeter wall or he'll trigger the alarm. You'll be OK, though; you can walk straight through the front door like everyone else. Just be very careful not to use your power when you're inside or anywhere nearby. The alarm works by picking up any changes to the electromagnetic field, so as long as you keep it under control, you'll be fine.'

I noted the extra emphasis he put on the word *control* and the look he was giving me, his eyes fairly bulging in his head.

'Under control,' I repeated, 'got it.' Though to myself I was thinking *CRAP*.

'Second point,' he said, moving swiftly on. 'If the alarm sounds when you're inside, you won't be able to get out. Not just because it will floor you, but because the whole building goes into lockdown.'

79

I nodded at him. 'Control. I heard you.'

'The cells are buried deep underground in an area called prisoner holding. They're off grid. Before, when we rescued Alicia and Thomas, we needed Rachel to get us in there. We used her access codes. Only she and a few others have that kind of clearance.'

'So, how am I going to get down into this prisoner holding place?' I asked, trying to focus again.

'You're not getting down there, Lila,' Alex said, shooting me a black look. 'When the time comes, we'll all go together. At the moment our only option for getting in is Sara.' He frowned as he said her name. 'But we don't know if we can trust her. We need you to try and figure that out.'

'Lila,' Demos interrupted, his voice a red-flag warning, 'Alex is right. You're not to try anything stupid. It could mess up everything. You wait. Understand?'

It was like he had read my mind. I felt my jaw clenching and unclenching with the effort it took to nod.

'Your priority is to gauge whether we can trust Sara and to find out what's happening with Jack,' he said, holding my gaze firmly. 'They're treating Jack in the military hospital on the base which is outside the Unit's jurisdiction. But don't do anything suspicious, don't try to break him out, don't try to rescue your mother – don't do anything except keep your ears and eyes open. Gather intel and wait for us.'

'OK, I got it the first time,' I muttered. They all continued staring at me in silence – even Alex. 'What?' I burst out. 'I promise!'

Demos nodded, a smile brushing his lips. 'The timing needs to coincide exactly with what we've got planned in Washington. There's no room for error in this.' He looked at me as he said it.

Jeez, I thought, *enough already with the lectures.*

Suki snickered behind me.

'Alex will follow after you, Lila,' Demos said.

'What about Rachel?' I asked. 'What are we doing with her?' I had a few ideas about what to do with Rachel, but I didn't think Demos would want to hear them.

'We'll leave Rachel in Mexico City with Bill,' he said. 'He's staying to look after Thomas anyway. They have an apartment there. She'll be hidden and out of the way.'

'And Amber? What about Amber? Is she staying with Bill and Thomas? Or is she coming with us?' Nate asked. The rest of us fell silent.

'We'll see,' Demos replied, his mouth set in a grim line.

Key suddenly appeared in the doorway behind him. 'Well, we got ourselves a sifter,' he announced.

13

I kept getting flashbacks as we drove through the streets of Mexico City at dusk, my eyes darting between the traffic, trying to spot anyone in black combat uniform or an SUV with blacked-out windows on our tail. Alex was on edge too, barely saying a word as we wound our way through the city in the BMW with Harvey, Suki and Nate. Demos was in the van ahead of us with Alicia and Rachel.

The apartment Bill and Amber were staying in with Thomas was on the tenth floor of a grey, nondescript apartment building in the centre of the city. Harvey pulled into the underground car park and killed the engine.

Demos suddenly appeared and yanked open the door so fast I almost fell out.

'Coming?' he asked me.

I glanced at Alex. He gave me a small smile of encouragement. I wasn't sure I wanted to go inside and see Amber. What on earth would I say to her? And then there was Thomas. I really wasn't sure I was ready to see him – to see what the Unit had done to him, or worse, hear about it in detail. But Demos was waiting and the others were staring at me so I undid my seat belt and followed him, dragging my heels all the way to the elevator as if I could somehow delay the moment.

Alicia came too, so it was the three of us who strolled through the lobby and took the elevator to the tenth floor. We walked silently along the carpeted hallway until we came to the last door. We knocked and, after a few seconds, Bill opened the door. He ushered us inside, motioning with a finger to his lips for us to be quiet.

'How's Thomas?' Alicia whispered.

'Come and see for yourself,' Bill replied, leading us through a small living room and down a short hallway. He opened the door to one of the bedrooms and I glanced in, struggling to make out the shape of a bed and a person lying in it amidst the gloom.

Alicia crossed straight to the bed. I knew I should follow her. Half of me did want to see him, but I couldn't take a single step. I was rooted to the spot.

'He's getting better,' Bill said softly, going to stand next to Alicia. 'He just sleeps – he hasn't really woken up – but there are no more nightmares. He seems calmer.'

I noticed Demos scowling at Bill, obviously warning him to watch what he said in front of me.

Bill cleared his throat. 'He's going to be fine,' he said. 'Give it another week or so and he'll be back to normal.'

I took a small step forward towards them and the insubstantial shape in the bed. Alicia was blocking my view. She stepped aside and I gasped and clapped a hand over my mouth. Thomas was as white as the sheet, whiter in fact, and his face was sheened with sweat. His breathing was so shallow that at first sight he appeared to be dead and I had a sudden thought that this was some kind of trick they were playing on me – bringing me to see a corpse. Then I noticed the slight rise and fall of his chest. But whatever Bill had just said was clearly just meant to placate me, because it sure as hell didn't look like Thomas would be awake and back to normal this time next week, or any time this decade for that matter.

'What did they do to him?' I asked under my breath.

Bill exhaled loudly. 'He hasn't been coherent enough to tell us anything. We're not even sure if he can hear us. Amber only sees whiteness when she looks at him.'

'The point is, he's fine now. He's going to be fine,' Demos said as if the conviction in his voice could make us all believe it. But no one said anything in reply and so his lie fell flat.

He should be in the hospital, being looked after, I thought angrily to myself. How else was he going to get better?

'It's not safe for him to be in hospital. The Unit would find him,' Alicia answered my silent question. 'And Bill here used to work as a nurse.'

'Paramedic actually,' Bill murmured.

Oh. I hadn't known that. To look at, you would have thought Bill made his living from cage-fighting. He had a bald, well-dented head and a neck almost as wide as my torso. But once you got to know him, you realised this softly-spoken, gentle man was a perfect example of not judging a book by its cover. I seemed to remember that Bill had been accused of several crimes by the Unit, including murder, but I couldn't imagine him hurting so much as a fly. Then I remembered how he'd flipped one of the Humvees with the Unit soldiers inside. I studied him once more. He was a man of contradictions.

'Alicia, can you hear anything? What's going on inside his head?' Bill suddenly asked.

'Nothing,' Alicia answered, almost too quickly. 'I can't hear anything.'

She turned her back on me so I could no longer see her face, putting me instantly on alert. Was she lying? Why? I glanced at Thomas. What was she seeing in his head? God – this was far worse than I had imagined. I had expected Thomas to at least be sitting up in bed, conscious and talking. Was this what my mum would look like?

The rage came out of nowhere – a tornado bursting out of me without warning. I tried to rein it in, but it was too late. Before I realised what I was doing the water glasses on the bedside table had gone spinning to the floor, smashing into the bedpost and shattering into millions of tiny shards.

I felt my breath coming in great heaving waves. Alicia's arm reached round my shoulder. 'We shouldn't have brought you,' she said.

I shrugged her off. No, they shouldn't have brought me. Why had they? Did they think that seeing and hearing this would make me feel better? I just wanted to get out of here; the room was so small. I couldn't breathe. I wanted to find Alex. I needed to see him.

I turned on my heel, unsteady, aware that I was swaying, and headed to the door, ready to march out of there, when all of a sudden Amber appeared, blocking my way. She looked terrible. Her normally wild red hair was scraped back into a knotted pony-tail, her face pale and completely bare of make-up. She looked like she hadn't slept in a month.

She stared straight at me, then her face twisted into a grimace and she looked away. I drew in a breath. What colour had she seen? Was it my rage that had hit her? Rage was the colour red. I probably looked like a giant ball of flame to her.

'Amber,' Demos said quietly.

Her grey eyes flashed angrily at him then she walked abruptly past him to the window, pulling back the curtain.

'You know, Demos,' she said, scanning the street below, 'I'm not sure what's better, looking at the people out there or looking at you. Out there there's so much colour.' She laughed, but it was a noise as bitter as bile. 'The world carries on,' she said quietly.

I let out a long breath, feeling my anger dissipate with it. I knew what she was talking about – knew it well – a feeling that the world should somehow stop, cease to be, because someone you loved was no longer in it. That's how I'd felt after my mother died. Or after I had *thought* she'd died.

'You know, I never knew that pity had its own colour.' She glanced at me as she said it and I looked away, embarrassed, realising that that was what I was now feeling instead of rage. 'But you, Demos,' she carried on, 'you have your own colour. Did you know that? It's not pity you're feeling, is it? It's something else. Guilt. And that has a colour all of its own.'

Demos shuffled uneasily next to me. Amber got up slowly from the chair and strode towards him. 'Why are you here?'

'We're worried about you, Amber,' Demos answered.

'Oh really? I don't think so, Demos – that would actually require you to care about someone other than Melissa and to actually be thinking of something other than revenge.'

I felt Alicia stiffen beside me.

'Amber,' Demos said, 'this is about more than just Melissa. You know that. It's about stopping the Unit from capturing any more of us and doing to them what they've done to Thomas. But if you want to talk about revenge – what about Ryder? Don't you want revenge for what they did to him?'

Amber's face contorted for a second, but then she spun away from Demos and headed over to the window once more, planting herself there with her back to us.

'Don't you want to put a stop to all this?' Demos asked more quietly.

I could sense the fury rising off Amber in waves – I didn't need to see auras to be able to feel it. I glanced over at Alicia to see what she was thinking, but she was just staring at Demos with an expression which seemed to be part sadness and part confusion. And Bill was just staring between all of us like an umpire at a tennis match, shifting from foot to foot, obviously uncomfortable with the whole situation.

Amber finally turned round. She'd composed herself a little. 'You know, Demos, you're just as bad as Richard Stirling,' she said. 'Trying to make people do what you want. Using people like they don't matter. You made Ryder believe that we had to fight them. And you made him think we actually had a chance of winning.'

I felt my heart lurch into my mouth.

'We can't fight the Unit,' Amber said, her voice getting louder, until I was sure even Thomas would be able to hear her. 'We can't win. And everyone will die following you, or end up like Thomas: being experimented on like a rat in a cage. This is your fight,' she said, 'yours and hers.' She nodded at me. 'It's not mine. And it's not theirs,' she said, tilting her chin at Bill and Alicia.

I felt as if something was constricting my chest. Demos said nothing back. He just stood there, staring at the floor, his head lowered.

Bill cleared his throat. 'I think maybe you should, um, leave.'

Demos opened his mouth to say something to him, but Alicia's hand on his arm stopped him short. She shook her head at him silently. With one last glance at Amber, Demos walked to the door, beckoning for me to follow. I stood there for a moment, unsure of what to do.

'Amber,' I said finally and saw her back stiffen. 'I'm so sorry,' I whispered.

She didn't even look round.

14

A taxi screeched to the kerb as we walked out of the lobby, its chassis scraping the tarmac in protest. We stepped back out of the way as the driver threw open his door in our path. Demos halted, throwing his arm across me, and I instantly froze. But the driver just cursed in Spanish, ignored all four of us, and marched to the trunk where he started fighting with the rope securing the contents that were threatening to spew all over the sidewalk.

Key got out of the passenger side and tried to help him. We stared bemused as five suitcases were disgorged and Key threw some notes into the driver's hands. The man was still yelling and pointing at the car, which was leaning oddly to one side like a see-saw.

The back door opened at this point, causing a passing bus to swerve and honk. Then a woman emerged from within. She was as round as a dough ball and dressed in what was clearly her Sunday best – a pale green Jackie O-style hat with a small veil, a matching two-piece suit and, clasped in her gloved hands, a white patent leather handbag. The woman was like a mini planet with its own gravitational pull – the car was bending towards her as she heaved herself out. Key rushed round to her side and took her arm, dragging her out of the way of oncoming traffic, to the safety barricade that her suitcases, piled on the sidewalk, provided.

'This sho ain't the Hilton, Joe Junior,' the woman remarked, looking up at the grey cement face of the building. 'You said you got me the finest suite at the Hilton.' She looked around her, up and down the street. 'I don't see no Caribbean Sea or palm trees swaying over white sand either.'

Key rolled his eyes heavenwards. 'Mama, I told you that we needed you to do one little thing for us first and then you'd get your vacation. I explained all this on the phone and in the taxi.'

Half an hour in a taxi with his mama had clearly taken its toll on Key – he looked frazzled. I was speechless, unsure how such a woman shared the same genetic code as Key and Nate who were both so skinny they were like exclamation marks when you looked at them from the side. This woman was a full stop. Round, complete and, from this first impression, someone who obviously liked to have the last word.

'Mrs Johnson, it's a pleasure to meet you,' Demos said, stepping forward and giving her his most charming smile, the one that occasionally made me realise what my mother had seen in him.

Mrs Johnson melted. Her gravitational pull threatened for a moment to suck Demos in like he was a dying star falling into a black hole. I wondered whether his power would work on her or whether it would have no impact. Maybe it would be like trying to scream in space. She blushed, smoothed her hat and took his proffered hand, all the while batting her eyelashes as if she had something stuck in her eye. 'So, you're one of Joe Junior's friends?' she purred.

'I hope so,' Demos replied.

'I'm Lila,' I said, reaching out my hand, trying to take the pressure off Key.

Mrs Johnson took me in with an expression which seemed to

suggest I needed to get some meat on my bones before I would be worth talking to.

'I'm Alicia, thank you so much for coming, Mrs Johnson,' Alicia cut in across me. I was glad. Alicia's tone and her smile had a much greater effect.

Mrs Johnson beamed widely at her. 'I was just telling Joe Junior how happy I am to be here,' she said.

'Mama, come on, this way,' Key said, putting a hand under her elbow. 'Nate's waiting to see you.'

'Awwwwww, that sweet grandson of mine, where's my baby? I've been so crazy worried – you didn't even think to call your old mama. Boy, what, you think I'm telepathic or something? You couldn't even find time to call me and let me know where you were?'

They walked off, leaving us all standing there gaping after them.

'Nathaniel, what have they been feeding you?' Mrs Johnson screeched when she saw Nate. She rounded on Key. 'What you been feeding that boy? A diet of water and laxative pills?'

She clutched Nate to her bosom and I wondered if he'd suffocate. 'You so skinny, my boy, you gonna break in two if you not careful. And what you wearing that bandana for? You better no' be messing up in no gangs, you hear me?'

Suki was hopping up and down behind them, her feet tapping as Nate backpedalled his arms, trying to break out of the embrace. She danced forward. 'Nate's grandma, I'm pleased to meet you. I'm Suki.'

Mrs Johnson released Nate and clutched Suki to her bosom instead. Suki disappeared almost completely; just her white sneakers and a slash of her black bob could be seen.

'You the girl that's been taking such good care of my Nate? Well, bless you, you angel, you're so kind. Nate been telling me all about this lovely girl Suki.' She winked at us over Suki's buried head. Clearly the woman was no telepath.

She pushed Suki back, holding her by the shoulders, and looked at her sideways. 'You best not be no gang member either.'

I heard Nate and Suki start to protest, but then I got distracted. Alex had threaded his fingers through my hand. He bent his head to whisper, 'How'd it go with Amber?'

I shook my head. 'Amber's not coming with us.'

I saw a trace of a frown pass across his face. He pulled me out of the way of the others, behind the van. 'What happened?'

'She said that it was Demos's fight. Demos's and mine. And she said we'd all die or end up like Thomas if we carried on.' I hesitated. 'Do you think that's true?'

Alex shook his head. 'No, Lila, I don't. And it isn't just your fight, it's *our* fight. It's not just about revenge – I told you that before – it's something bigger. It's about stopping them. I would fight this battle even if it wasn't about your mum. Or about you.' He touched my chin lightly so I'd look up at him again. But I couldn't smile. I kept seeing Thomas in my mind, lying there, trapped in his own head.

'Did you see him? Thomas, I mean,' Alex asked, just at the very moment I was trying to erase the memory of him.

I nodded. Alex seemed to understand that that was all I could do – that I couldn't talk about it – because he didn't ask me anything else. He just pulled me close and kissed the top of my head.

15

'You sure know how to treat your mama.' Mrs Johnson was still ranting at Key. 'Mrs Williams, she got a plasma television from her boy Marlon Junior. But what do I get? I get a trip to the parts of Mexico City not even the missionaries go to. And it's after three a.m. Who we going to see at three a.m, I ask you? Ain't no right-minded, God-fearing folks gonna be awake at this o'clock of the morning.'

'Mama, I told you, once we're done here, you're heading straight to the Hilton in Acapulco. We booked you the nicest room you can imagine, sweet sounds of the ocean just outside, palm trees swaying, beach so white it makes your eyes hurt. You're gonna love it.'

'I'm just saying I'm not seeing no palm trees swaying, Joe Junior. Plasma television,' she muttered under her breath.

Key's head was thrown back. He was contemplating the roof of the rental car as though he wanted to do it extreme violence. I was wedged next to him, Mrs Johnson on his other side. Alex was driving and Suki was in the passenger seat. The others were in the van in front of us, which had been emptied of its Rachel load. Demos had deposited her in the same apartment as Thomas. I worried about the wisdom of leaving her in Amber's vicinity, but then I remembered that Amber was blaming Demos and not the

Unit for Ryder's death. And then I remembered that I didn't care what happened to Rachel and hoped that Amber had a change of heart about who she blamed.

We parked about two blocks down from Carlos's little hideout. The streets were just as empty as they had been when Alex and I had come here a few nights previously.

'How did Joe Junior get the nickname Key?' I asked, making conversation before Mrs Johnson could launch into another tirade or ask about when she was going to be getting to Acapulco.

She turned to me, righting her hat which had slid slightly to the left, before placing both hands on top of her handbag. 'Well, you see, when he was a boy, Joe Junior knew all these secrets. Things he shouldn't have been knowing if he had any sense in that head of his. And every time we'd be saying, *That boy he knows all the secrets, it's like he has the key, like he can unlock the things everyone be hiding away*. So we nicknamed him Key.' She patted her hair, making sure it was all in place. 'Course that's before we knew what Joe Junior could do.'

'Demos wants to know if we're ready,' Suki announced, leaning round to face us.

I glanced towards Alex. He was looking at me in the rear-view mirror. I couldn't see his mouth, but I knew he was giving his reassuring smile.

'Has Nate been in?' I asked.

'Yes,' Suki said, having a silent conversation with Alicia in the van in front of us. 'Alicia says that Nate counted four of them in there. One big fat one on the door, two others with guns and the Carlos man. I cannot wait to meet him.'

'Sounds like the same men as before,' said Alex. 'Did he check all the rooms?'

Suki paused, running the question in her head and waiting for a reply. 'Yes, he's been through the whole building,' she nodded.

'Oh, my poor Nate,' Mrs Johnson exclaimed. 'I don't like the way you're putting him in danger. Why you letting my poor boy go in there all on his own?'

'He's fine, Mama.'

'He is fine, Mrs Johnson,' Suki said. 'And look, he's back from his recce.' She pointed at Nate who was in the van in front waving out of the back window. 'He says hello.'

Mrs Johnson started waving back. The car rocked and I ducked as her handbag swung in my direction.

'I'd rather he was saying hello from the balcony at the Hilton – you understand what I'm saying?'

Alex got out of the car and opened the back door, releasing me from its crush. I clambered out and Alex leaned in past me. 'You guys stay here until we call you. Lock the doors,' he said to Suki who looked like she was about to argue with him. 'Here,' Alex said, handing a gun to Key, 'just in case.'

Mrs Johnson's eyes grew round. 'Mary mother of Jesus, what you doing with guns? Joe Junior, what kind of trouble you getting yourself mixed up in? And why you dragging your poor old mama into it? Mrs Williams' boy never goes getting himself into trouble. And if he did, he sho wouldn't bring his mama into it.'

Alex slammed the door on them and we walked to the corner of the road, hoping Key didn't turn the gun on his mother before she'd done her sifting business. Demos, Harvey and Alicia fell in behind us.

'Lock your door,' I mouthed to Nate as we walked past his van. He looked like a little puppy, waiting for his owners to return.

'Are they going to be OK out here?' I asked, looking around at the eerily dark streets.

'They'll be fine,' Alicia said. 'I can hear if anything goes wrong.'

Two telepaths, I thought. *Handy*. Like having our very own silent walkie-talkies.

The others fell back as we approached the door.

'Good luck,' Alex whispered, before disappearing into the shadows at my side. I heard my footsteps getting louder, my heartbeat pounding like a drum in my ears.

Demos took up a position on the left of the door and nodded at me. I took a breath and knocked. A part of me, the inner voice which had been quiet over the last few days, started screaming at me to run – to run very fast in the opposite direction. But the door opened before I could unglue my feet and obey my survival instinct.

The man who answered was the tank-shaped one. The one I'd thought we'd need a battering ram to get through. Hopefully Demos was just as good. The man squinted at me, then he recognised me and his face contorted in disbelief. He cast his eyes up the street behind me.

'About that job . . .' I said before he could notice the car and the van parked there.

He looked back at me, uncertain whether I was insane or if he'd misunderstood my English, but then he grinned a leering kind of grin and called out over his shoulder, something in Spanish I couldn't understand. He let the door fall open. And Demos stepped right in front of me.

We all strolled in, past the tank one, frozen now mid-leer, and stood in front of the other two who had been caught by Demos mid-step, confused expressions slapped on their faces. Carlos was sitting behind the desk, one hand resting on his gun which was lying flat on the table and the other setting down a shot glass.

Harvey and I went straight for the guns, easing them with glances out of their hands and floating them towards us. Alex walked over and patted the frozen men down, removing three knives and one machete in the process. He threw them into the corner of the room and took the gun I hovered in front of him.

On the table in front of Carlos were stacks and stacks of white bricks wrapped in cellophane. One brick lay slashed open like an upended bag of icing sugar, spilling its powdery contents all around. There was a razor blade and several hundred-dollar bills rolled up next to it. I had seen scenes like this before on *CSI*.

'We hit the mother lode,' Demos said with a smile, surveying the room.

Alex grinned back. 'Easy as stealing candy from a baby. Lila, can you help?'

'Sure,' I said, lifting the stacks with just a glance in their direction and depositing them into the bags that Alex was holding open.

'We need the money too,' Alex said to Demos.

There was no money in sight, except for the rolled-up dollar bills on the table. 'Wake him up or whatever it is you do,' Alex said, nodding at Carlos.

'Alicia, you ready?' Demos asked.

'Yep,' she nodded.

Carlos blinked at us, his eyes focusing immediately on the gun Alex was pointing at him. He grabbed for his own gun, realised it wasn't where it should be and frowned. Then he noticed his men were all frozen solid and I watched the panic flare across his face.

'You,' he growled at me.

'Yeah, me,' I shrugged at him. 'Hi, we've come for all your money and all your drugs. So, tell us where the money is or else this man over here is going to do really bad things to you.' I pointed at Demos who was busy focusing on the henchmen. This negotiating with a Mafia boss was more fun than I'd expected it to be.

'Where's the money?' Carlos repeated, laughing, banging his hand on the table. 'You think I'm going to tell you where my money is? Jesus!' he yelled.

I thought he was swearing. 'Jesus!' he yelled again, which was when I realised he wasn't swearing, he was calling to one of the men behind us whose name must have been Jesus.

'Your friends can't hear us,' Alex answered. Carlos scowled again, confusion in his eyes.

'It's in a safe,' Alicia interrupted. Carlos's mouth fell open and I caught a glint of gold. He switched his gaze to Alicia.

'Where's the safe, Carlos?' Alex demanded.

'You think I'm going to tell you?' Carlos shouted, tipping the contents of his shot glass down his throat. He reached for the bottle and I noticed his hand was shaking.

'It's next door. Under the floor,' Alicia said.

'Hey, how are you doing that?' Carlos shouted, leaping from his seat.

'Uh-uh,' Demos tutted, freezing him instantly. Carlos blinked, struggling against Demos's invisible hold. I wanted to stay and watch, but Alex dragged me into the adjoining room.

There was a table in the centre of the room. I shoved it to one side with a flick of my eyes and it slammed into the far wall. The rug beneath lifted up and Alex took hold of an iron ring set into the floor and started to pull. I leaned over his shoulder and helped.

The door in the floor flew back revealing a hole, about two metres square. Face-up in the hole sat an old-fashioned bank safe with a combination lock.

'We need numbers. The code!' Alex yelled through the open door to Alicia.

'I'm not telling you anything. *Nada*,' Carlos spat.

'You don't need to tell me anything, I can read your mind,' I heard Alicia say. '5 – 12 – 63 – 18 – 71,' she called out and Alex spun the dial.

The safe clicked. Alex reached in and pulled it open. It was spectacular. The bricks of money were just there, waiting for us, like gift-wrapped presents in a stocking.

'Lila?' I looked up. Alex was nudging me with his eyes.

'Oh sorry,' I mumbled, taking off my backpack. We started transferring the contents of the safe into it. The money floated upwards and I stacked it in fat towers inside my bag and, when that was full, I started loading up a duffel bag that Alex had brought with him. He hefted the bags onto his shoulder.

'Allow me,' I said, grabbing them out of his hands before he could do anything and whisking them through to the other room. I let them hover in front of Carlos.

'How are you doing this? Who are you people?' Carlos asked, his stare turning bug-eyed and a vein starting to pop purple on the side of his temple. 'You think you're going to get away with this?'

Alicia looked at Demos, and then at me and Alex, before turning back to Carlos. 'Yeah, I think so,' she grinned at him.

'I know your faces. I know your name, *Lila*. I'm going to hunt you down,' Carlos hissed. 'You're never going to sleep sound again because you know I'm going to be there in your nightmares. And then one day,' his voice dropped to a whisper, '*boof*, I'm going to be there for real. And that day you're going to wish you'd never been born.'

A hooting laugh interrupted his monologue. It was Demos. 'You've been watching too many *Godfather* movies, my friend,' he said. Then he leaned in close to Carlos and winked. 'And besides, you've not yet met Mrs Johnson.'

16

We could hear her long before we could see her.

'There'd best be twenty-four-hour room service in this hotel, Joe Junior,' she was saying. 'And a robe. I want one of those white fluffy bath robes and a jacuzzi too. I bet Oprah got herself one of those—' She stopped short when she walked into the room.

'How in the name of Jesus my saviour are you doing that?' She stared wide-eyed at the scene in front of her.

'That's Demos. Like I told you, Mama, he's got a very special power. He can stop people doing what they want to be doing. Make people do stuff they got more sense not to be doing.'

'Well, that's a quite remarkable thing,' Mrs Johnson said breathily, her hands fluttering.

'Mrs Johnson,' Alicia said, 'I know this is an unusual scene and a strange request, but we'd like you to, um . . . use your power on the people in this room . . . remove every memory they have of us from tonight.'

'And from before, any memory they might have of Alex or me,' I butted in.

'Yes, all the memories they have of Alex and Lila too,' Alicia agreed.

Mrs Johnson spun on her axis towards me. 'What's a little bitty girl like you doing getting yourself mixed up with people like this?' she said, pointing her handbag in Carlos's direction and tutting loudly.

'It's complicated,' I offered weakly.

'Remember I told you a little of what was going on, Mrs Johnson?' Alicia said sweetly. 'About how these men were going to help us, in a roundabout way, rescue Lila's mother and brother from some bad people?'

Mrs Johnson looked a little uncertainly back at Alicia. 'What? Bad men like this? I know you asked for my help, but these men don't look like the kind of men I want my Nate getting involved with. What was in those bags I saw floating on out of here?'

'Nothing to trouble yourself with, Mrs Johnson. Just some stuff we needed to borrow,' Demos spoke up, his gaze still on the middle distance, as he focused on holding Carlos and his men.

Mrs Johnson wiggled her shoulders, settling her bosom like a ship in a dock, and offered Demos a look that could have given him a run for his money when it came to freezing people. 'You think I'm stupid, young man?'

'No, Mrs Johnson,' Alicia said, shooting a warning glance at Demos. 'It's just that we know how much you love Nate and Joe Junior and they speak so highly of you and your ability, and poor Lila over here,' she pointed at me and I obliged by looking as sweet and innocent as I could, which wasn't as sweet and innocent as I might have looked a month ago, 'Lila needs our help.'

Mrs Johnson observed me for a moment. 'You poor child,' she said at last. 'What they did to your mama.' She shook her head and reached into her handbag for a handkerchief. 'It's a crime. That's what it is. You need my help, Nate's asked me to come down here, so my help's what you gonna get.'

She rounded quickly on Key. 'But I'm expecting to see one of those big drinks with the little bitty umbrellas and the cherries on sticks waiting for me on the balcony when I get to the Hilton. I want a vacation that's going to make even Mrs Williams stop talking about that badass boy Marlon Junior and that vacation he took her on to Florida last Christmas.'

With a monumental effort, Key kept his mouth shut and nodded. Mrs Johnson turned her round body towards Demos. 'Now you tell me who I've got to work on first.'

Demos nodded his head in Carlos's direction. 'I'm going to let him go. Be ready.'

'Lord have mercy,' she muttered as she shuffled over to the table. She put her handbag down and I hoped she hadn't noticed the white powder it was now resting in. She reached across the table, muttering to herself in distaste, and put her hand on Carlos's temple, like she was being forced to touch a dead rattlesnake.

I saw Alex move quickly to stand behind Carlos and wondered what he was doing. 'OK,' he said.

Carlos snapped into consciousness, immediately trying to pull back from the ginormous woman in her Sunday best who had appeared from nowhere and who was now holding his head like it was a bowling ball she was about to slam for a strike. Alex rammed him down into his seat, holding his shoulders so he couldn't move. Mrs Johnson didn't let go either. I saw Carlos's eyes go wide then start to turn dreamy.

After five seconds Mrs Johnson said, 'OK, you can freeze him up again or whatever in the name of Jesus it is you're doing. No point in me doing this if you're just going to let him see you all again, is there?'

She shuffled over to the other men and with each one the

episode was repeated until the three of them had their memories wiped as clean as a disinfected surface.

When they reached tank man, Alex paused. 'Lila, I'm going to need some help on this one. Can you hold his arms?'

I looked at the arms, like uprooted tree trunks. 'I'll give it a go.'

I focused on the arms, imagining they were just sticks, twigs even. When Demos unfroze him, he made an instant lunge and Mrs Johnson went skittering backwards. It was like wrestling against the tide, but then I got him under control, pinning his arms to his side. I noticed Harvey and Alicia glancing at me. They hadn't known quite the extent of my power – that I could move people now as well as objects. I wondered whether I was a whole new category of subhuman. I wasn't quite like Demos, but I knew Harvey and Bill couldn't move people.

'Right, let's go,' Alicia said once Mrs Johnson had finished wiping memories.

Key moved to escort his mother out of the building. She was still talking about Acapulco as he pushed her into the van.

We followed after them, leaving Demos inside to hold them all until we got clear. Suki pulled up in the car and Alex and I jumped in. I turned round and checked the trunk. We were in possession of several hundred kilos of cocaine and what was probably well over a million dollars. Demos climbed into the back next to me.

'I love it when a plan comes together,' he said, winking at me.

17

'I am very annoyed that I didn't get to meet this Mr Carlos,' Suki huffed, sticking out her bottom lip.

'Don't be,' I said as I dropped the last bag of drugs on the floor of the hotel room we'd rented using some of the money we'd stolen. We'd gone up in the world, taking over the entire penthouse floor of the Four Seasons hotel.

'Why did Alicia get to see inside his head? I wanted to do that.'

'Because, Suki, Alicia can speak Spanish and you can't.'

She grunted. 'I know how to say *culo*.' She pouted some more. 'I always miss out on the fun bits,' and then she started rifling through the white and green bundles stacked on the table.

Harvey and Demos were making neat towers of the money and the drugs, counting it out and weighing it. It was more than we'd ever hoped to get. More than we would need.

Suki read my mind instantly. 'Does this mean there's going to be money left over for some shopping?' she asked Demos. 'Because I need new shoes.'

Demos chuckled, which was a sound I'd never heard him make before. It almost made me smile to hear it. 'Suki, you've almost as many shoes as Imelda Marcos.'

'Who?' she demanded jealously.

'We didn't tell you,' Harvey said, 'but the reason we got rid of the RV was because you'd turned it into a giant dressing-up box.'

Everyone burst out laughing as Suki stood glaring in the centre of the room. Maybe it was the tension evaporating, maybe it felt good to laugh, but I couldn't join in. I got up instead and went to find the bathroom.

I stood in front of the mirror, staring at my reflection, at my elfin cropped hair and the dark smudges of shadow under my eyes. Would I ever look like a happy, normal, well-rested seventeen-year-old girl again or was that girl gone forever? I was about to turn the tap on when I heard Demos's voice on the other side of the door. I tiptoed over and pressed my ear to the wood panel.

'You heard something, didn't you?' he was saying. 'When you read Thomas's mind – what did you hear?'

I heard someone take a breath. 'It wasn't what I heard – it was what I saw.'

It was Alicia talking. I strained harder to hear her, hoping she wouldn't pick up on my proximity.

'Demos – it was awful,' she said. 'Like he's trapped in some nightmare – there were just fragmented pictures, images of things that they did to him. I can't even explain it – I'm not sure what they mean. I just saw white rooms and flashes of faces. The things they're doing in there – I could just hear screaming. It brings it all back.' Her voice became muffled as if Demos had taken her in his arms. 'That could have been me,' she murmured.

'Did you see Melissa?' Demos asked.

'Yes,' I heard Alicia say, more clearly now. 'I saw her.'

My whole body went rigid, my heart hammering so wildly I was sure that Alicia would hear it.

'Is she OK?' Demos asked.

Alicia paused again. I heard her sigh. 'No, Demos, she's not OK. We need to get her out of there.'

I closed my eyes and was aware that they'd both fallen silent on the other side of the door. I held my breath and waited a full minute trying to compose myself. When I left the bathroom, Demos was standing just outside, leaning against the wall, waiting for me.

'Hi,' I said, jumping half out of my skin. I hadn't expected him to still be there.

'You heard,' he said by way of reply. His face was heavily shadowed in the gloomy hallway.

'Maybe,' I shrugged.

'I'm sorry.'

'You know,' I said, swallowing what felt like a golf ball that was lodged in my throat, 'it's not your fault. What Amber said earlier – it isn't true. She just wants someone to blame and you're the nearest person. But none of us think it's true.'

Demos studied me for a few seconds. 'I don't know, Lila, maybe she's right. This did all start because I wanted revenge for what they had done to your mother. What am I doing asking the others to help me now – after what's happened to Ryder and to Thomas?'

'I don't believe you ever asked us, Demos. We don't need asking. This is not your personal battle – it belongs to all of us. It's our fight. All of ours.' I remembered Alex's words earlier.

Demos still didn't say anything. 'We're going to win,' I said quietly, the conviction in my voice surprising me.

I realised I was saying it, forcing myself to believe it, because losing wasn't an option.

* * *

Alex was staring at the clock on the mantelpiece, his chin resting on his hands, when Demos and I walked back into the living room, but as soon as he saw me he stood up.

I guessed time was up. I slowed my pace, trying to stretch out these last seconds. My legs started to shake. How was I supposed to say goodbye this time? And with an audience? I could sense everyone staring at me.

I kept my eyes locked on Alex. He was wearing a V-necked black T-shirt and dark jeans, his blue eyes studying me, a thousand different emotions passing behind them which I could read as easily as if I was Suki. With a shock, I realised that either Alex was losing his ability to look inscrutable or I was just getting better at reading him. Either way I preferred it.

He was going to travel by car with the others back over the border. They would be able to bypass border control while Demos froze the guards. The Unit would be watching the airports. They had to see me arrive on my own. My story had to hold water.

Alex walked over to me, took me by the hand and led me away from the others. 'Please don't do anything impulsive,' he said, once we were alone in the hallway.

'Impulsive? Me?' I tried my innocent face.

He smiled ruefully. 'You know what I'm saying.'

'OK, I promise you. Nothing remotely reckless,' I said, stroking up his arm. The bandage was off, but the cut he'd made to remove the tracking device hadn't yet healed. There was a thin red scab across his tattoo.

'Remember your first day at elementary school?' Alex suddenly asked.

My hand stilled on his arm. 'Yeah,' I said, frowning up at him. Why was he bringing that up?

107

'You were really scared,' he said, seeing my confused expression. 'Do you remember? You didn't want to go. But you didn't want your mum or dad or anyone else to walk you in either. You insisted on going all by yourself.'

I frowned some more. I did remember. I remembered how determined I'd been not to look like a little kid. I also remembered I was wearing a Harry Potter backpack. The memory made me cringe. There I was, standing knock-kneed on the steps, looking up at the school building, trying to will myself to walk through the doors as hundreds of older kids barged past me. It had been terrifying.

'We were there,' Alex said, interrupting the horror show in my head. I frowned at him some more. 'Jack and I,' he continued. 'We were watching you the whole time, hiding behind some cars in the teachers' lot. We were watching you from the minute you got off the bus. You had a Harry Potter backpack on, and some kid said something about it – teased you.'

They were there? Alex saw that?

'Jack wanted to leap out from behind the car and beat the kid up, but I held him back. And you said something to that kid anyway and he walked off looking like you'd just told him zombies had eaten his pet dog.'

I laughed under my breath. He was right. That *had* happened. Though not the zombie put-down part.

'And then you walked up those steps and in through the door without once looking back. And as far as I recall, you made it through the rest of the year in one piece.'

I shook my head at Alex in silent wonder, still not quite believing he had either been there or that he remembered it. He smiled at me. 'And when you were eleven, on Halloween you went out trick or treating with some friends.'

I felt a twist in my gut at the memory of having had friends, of having once lived a normal life, doing normal kid things. I had unwrapped presents under a tree once upon a time with my family, had eaten turkey at Thanksgiving and even had sleepovers involving ice cream and Hannah Montana. The memories were so vague and foggy they didn't feel real. It was more like remembering a show I'd once watched on the Disney Channel.

'You were dressed as a pirate,' Alex said. I blinked at him, speechless.

'Jack and I tailed you all the way down the block and around the neighbourhood. He was dressed as Nacho Libre.'

I burst out laughing. 'What were you?'

'The Joker. From *Batman*.'

'Why were you following me?' I asked, though I already knew.

'To steal your candy,' Alex answered, smiling before his expression turned serious once more. He raised his eyebrows. 'Why do you think?'

I shrugged. 'Because you're both overprotective to the point of needing treatment for OCD?'

He contemplated me for a moment, then took a step closer so I could make out the day's stubble on his jaw and feel the warmth radiating from him. 'What I'm trying to tell you, Lila,' he said, his voice husky in his throat, 'is that I've always been there, looking out for you, even when you didn't know it – even when you couldn't see me.'

My stomach flipped. Alex took hold of my hands and squeezed. 'Nothing's changed. I'll be right there, I promise. You might not be able to see me, but I'll be there.'

18

I made it through immigration and saw that Alex had been right. The tail wasn't even subtle. A man in black combats followed me out of the terminal, practically stepping on my heels. The Unit seriously needed to work on its camouflage uniform and under-cover routines, but then again, I supposed they didn't care about blending in or being subtle. This man wanted me to see him and for me to know that I was being followed. But I did what I'd been told and pretended to be oblivious, hailing a taxi to take me straight to the base.

At the gate to Camp Pendleton an armed Marine leaned in the window and asked what I was there for.

'I'm Lila Loveday. I'm Lieutenant Jack Loveday's sister,' I said, giving Jack his full title. 'I think he's here. I need to get onto the base to see him.'

He walked away and conferred over a radio with someone and a few seconds later I got waved through in my yellow taxi. The building was a way onto the base. It rose up like a square, mirrored fortress and I took a couple of deep breaths when I got out of the cab, my legs feeling suddenly elastic, incapable of propelling me forward towards it. But my mum was somewhere inside that building so I got a grip and forced myself to walk.

The pod doors at the front of the building were swishing open.

I half expected to see Rachel sashaying through them just like she had the last time I'd been here. How I'd hated her instantly. And not just because of the infinite supermodel legs, symmetrically perfect face and the way she'd practically poured herself over Alex like she was the hot sauce and he was a nice juicy steak. I hadn't liked her because I had good instincts. From now on I was going to start trusting them.

I edged up to the building, expecting the alarm to sound at any second and the searing pain that went with it to scrape the bone from the inside of my skull. What if Alex had it wrong? What if I triggered the alarm just by being near it? I hadn't understood a word he'd spoken about electromagnetic fields. But I had no choice but to trust him.

I kept walking towards the building. Ten metres, eight metres. I took a deep breath. Five metres. And then I was right outside, in touching distance of the doors, and no alarm was ringing. I was still standing. I was OK. *I was OK.* I looked up at the sky – was Key up there? Hopefully, if he was, he was keeping a safe distance.

I approached the pods and looked for a buzzer or a bell, but as I stood there dumbly, one swished open. With a final glance upwards at the sky, I stepped inside.

The doors locked behind me, sealing me for an instant inside a vacuum. There was no way back anymore. The glass in front of me swished opened and I stepped out into a wide, marble-floored lobby. Footsteps were clicking across the tiles towards me.

'Lila!'

I looked up sharply. Sara was striding towards me, her face a picture of relief and distress and worry and hope all blended into an expression that I wasn't sure how to read. So much for trusting my instincts. My instincts were bats in a cave right now.

She threw her arms round me, pulling me into a hug. 'Lila! Lila! What are you doing here? God, where have you been?'

My hands were hanging limply at my sides. With a huge effort, I forced myself to lift them and hug her back, telling myself that there was no evidence that she knew what the Unit were doing. Sara might be our only hope so right now I needed to act convincing. I needed to act like I didn't suspect her of a single thing.

'I just . . . Alex . . . he made me come back,' I stuttered.

Sara pulled back instantly. 'Is he here? Is he with you?' she asked breathlessly. She was still clutching me by the tops of my arms, her wide brown eyes searching my face.

'No. He's not here. He let me go. After you traced him to Mexico City he didn't want me around anymore.' I said this last part to the floor, hoping she wouldn't notice my cheeks burning. 'He said I was slowing him down.'

It was only then that I noticed the two men standing a few metres behind her – or rather I noticed their boots. I glanced up. They were staring blank-faced at me, as expressionless as tombstones. I frowned. They were both familiar – maybe I'd met them before when Alex brought me here to the base for a run and introduced me to his team. Maybe they were the same people who had been chasing us over the rooftops of Mexico City just a few days ago. Possibly they were the same people who'd shot Jack and killed Ryder. I had no idea. I tore my eyes away from them.

'Come on, this way,' Sara announced, spinning round and heading off across the lobby.

I started and grabbed for her hand, pulling her back. 'Jack? Jack – where is he? Is he OK?' I demanded. 'Are you taking me to see him?'

112

She paused, looking at me oddly. 'You don't know?'

Why did she think I would know? Was this some kind of test? 'No,' I stammered. 'How is he?'

She linked her arm through mine and began walking towards the elevators. 'He's not good. He was shot. You were there, right? You saw what happened?'

'Yes. I saw.' And I wouldn't forget it in a hurry. Jack running to Ryder's side and the expression of disbelief on his face when the bullet smacked home. He'd been looking straight at me.

'He's unconscious, Lila. The doctors are doing everything they can.'

'Is he going to be OK?'

Sara hesitated, glancing over her shoulder at the men behind us. 'They say so, but Lila, it's not quite so cut and dried. When he wakes up, there are going to be questions. Lots of questions.'

I dug my heels in. I didn't want to get in the elevator. Where was she going to take me? 'Where is he?' I asked, stalling for time. 'Can I see him now?'

'Not just yet. We need to debrief you first.'

'Can't that wait?' I asked, my voice rising in pitch. 'I need to see Jack.' I didn't want to be debriefed. I couldn't lie well enough and I wasn't sure whether debriefing would involve any testing – of the lie-detecting or genetic-code variety.

'No, sorry, orders,' Sara said. Her eyes were glistening with tears. They looked genuine enough. 'Your father's here too. He flew straight over. He said that you'd called and left a message that you were all going away on a camping trip?'

'Yeah, Alex made me.' Sara threw me a look. As if Alex would ever have to make me do anything. She knew that. Damn it.

She led me into an elevator. I glanced at the illuminated panel

113

of numbers. Alex had said prisoner holding was level -4. Four whole storeys beneath the lobby and as impenetrable as a nuclear bunker. For a split second, as we all crammed into the narrow space, I imagined myself taking out the two soldiers behind us and knocking Sara unconscious with one of the moves that Alex had taught me. But without using my power, I had no hope. I was a seventeen-year-old girl up against two elite commandos and Sara – and who knew what moves she had? And if by some billion to one odds I actually made it down to prisoner holding – what next? Was I going to ask about visiting hours or something?

So I didn't do anything. I just stood there in the elevator feeling the hysteria rise within me and trying to focus on what Alex had told me, but his words were just fuzziness in my head. He could have spoken in Spanish for all I remembered his instructions. I let Sara lead me out of the elevator and into a small, square, white-panelled room. There was a recording device on the table and a two-way mirror on the far wall. Was this an interrogation room? I felt suddenly chilled and crossed my arms over my chest. My eyes kept pulling back to the smoky mirror. Was someone on the other side watching me? Studying and judging my every lie-ridden move? Sara pulled out a chair and indicated I sit opposite her, facing the mirror. The door opened just as I was about to sit and another person walked in.

'This is Dr Pendegast,' Sara said, introducing him.

'Ethan,' he said, holding out a pale, manicured hand.

I took it like it was some creature dredged from a pond, still covered in slime, wondering why a doctor needed to be involved in my debrief.

Dr Pendegast sat down, indicating I do likewise. I dropped into

114

my seat as though it was an electric chair, my hands gripping the edges to force myself to stay sitting.

'Lila,' Dr Pendegast said, 'we just need to ask you a few questions. To help us get a better understanding of what went on prior to the shoot-out at Joshua Tree and to understand why Alex and you ran rather than coming back here where you would have been safer. We would have heard him out. We still would.'

I nodded slowly and glanced at Sara, but she had her head down, her hair falling like a veil in front of her face. She was scribbling notes on a pad in front of her. Then she reached over and hit a button on the recorder before looking directly at me, wearing the face of a professional now, clinical and detached. I studied her. Her eyes were dark-ringed. Had she been sitting by Jack's bedside every night, holding his hand, willing him to wake up? To live? Or had she just been working round the clock trying to catch us? Could I trust her?

'Tell us what happened the night of Alex's birthday,' she said, giving me a brief smile. 'You left the bar.'

Wow, she was straight in there with the questions. I took a moment to steady myself and to remember what I'd rehearsed. 'Er, yeah,' I said, 'I took a taxi. I went back to Jack's.'

'Why?'

'Because I . . .' I looked at the man, Dr Pendegast. He wasn't writing anything. He was sitting with one leg crossed over the other and leaning back in his chair. He was in his thirties I guessed, with thinning brown hair and round, invisibly-rimmed glasses which made his eyes look double-glazed. He was chewing a pen and looking at me with undisguised interest. 'I saw Alex with Rachel,' I said, sitting up straight. 'I didn't want to stay after that.'

Sara looked up and gave a slight nod. She understood. She

115

knew how I felt about Alex. She'd been the first person I'd ever admitted it to. Hell, she'd even encouraged me to tell him, back when the thought of uttering the I love you words out loud made me break out in cold sweats and dream of burying myself in a deep hole.

'So, you got back to the house,' Sara said, not following up on the Rachel line of questioning which surprised me. 'And then what happened?'

I took a deep breath. My heart was drilling a hole resolutely through my ribcage. 'I got back to the house and I was just hanging out.' I wasn't going to tell her that I'd gone back to the house, hacked into Jack's computer, found out what the Unit were really up to, and that I'd been about to pack my bags and leave before they found out that what they were searching for was in fact *me*, when Key burst in to warn me that Demos was on his way.

'What happened, Lila?' Sara asked again.

'Then Alex came by,' I answered.

Alex had followed me home from his birthday party at the bar and had dragged Key and me out of the house just seconds before Demos had arrived. Of course that had been before we knew the truth about Demos and the real remit of the Unit – before we discovered that the bad guys weren't Demos and his people at all, but rather the Unit.

'Why? Why did Alex leave his own birthday party and follow you?' Sara asked.

I shrugged. 'I don't know. Because he felt bad? Because he saw I'd gone and he wanted to check up on me?' I tried to hold her gaze even though I could feel my skin starting to prickle as though I had heat rash. 'You know what Alex and Jack are like. He was

116

probably worried that Jack would be furious if he found out I'd left and gone home by myself.'

'So, what happened next?'

'I don't remember anything. Demos arrived. He did something to my head.'

Sara stared at me. Dr Pendegast stared at me. Their eyes narrowed and I felt my pulse rise. I thought I might vomit all my nerves up onto the table.

'We won't beat around the bush, Lila,' Dr Pendegast spoke up. 'You know now as much as we do, possibly more, about these people. We call them psygens – psys for short.' I didn't say anything.

'We've been studying them for some time. Your brother and Alex have been helping us contain them so that we can find a way of curing them.' The way he said *cure* with a little curl of his lip made my stomach revolt. 'We were hoping you could give us more information about the group of people that was holding you. With your help, we could stop them. Wouldn't you like to help?'

I wondered whether Dr Pendegast's doctorate was in patronising people. 'Yes. I want to help.' I nodded and smiled in what I hoped was an eager-looking way. 'But first I want to know what's happening to Jack.'

'We'll talk about Jack in a moment,' he said brusquely. 'Do you know who Demos is, Lila?' he asked, pen poised over paper.

It was a trick question. I hesitated a fraction. 'I know he killed my mother.'

'How do you know this? Did he tell you?'

'No. Alex told me. He said that the Unit had been chasing Demos for years.'

Sara frowned. 'Let's get back to the story, then,' she said, looking down at her notes. 'You said Demos arrived at the house and from that point you don't remember what happened.'

I made a non-committal sort of sound, a gurgle in my throat.

'So, at what point *do* you start remembering?' She looked up expectantly.

'Um, I'm not sure how long after, but the next thing I knew we were in their bus and driving somewhere. Then the bus stopped and Demos told Alex he had to go back to the base to break a prisoner out and he said that if Alex did it, he would let us both go.'

'Right. And Alex said yes?'

'He had to,' I blurted. 'They were going to kill me if he didn't.'

Sara bit her lip and studied me for a few seconds. 'What happened to the car? Jack's car? It disappeared – turned up in a second-hand car dealership outside of Palm Springs. The owner said a young couple on their way to Vegas to get married had traded it in.' She raised an eyebrow. 'Know anything about that?'

'Yes, it was us.' I had my lie ready. 'Demos made us do it. He wanted the money.'

Sara was chewing her lip. This was the weakest part of the story. She knew as well as I did that Demos didn't need money. He robbed banks for a living. 'And I think he wanted to leave a trail so you'd think we were on our own.'

Sara nodded and wrote something down. 'So, in the two days you were with Demos,' she said, continuing on, 'did you have a chance to talk with him? Did he say anything to you?'

'Not really, no.' I looked down at the table. 'He didn't speak to me. He only spoke to Alex.' More scribbles. I sat in silence, swallowing, breathing, trying to stop my feet from jigging up and down.

'And Jack? How did Jack get into this? Why did Alex call Jack and arrange for him to meet you?'

'Demos told him to.'

'Why?'

'Because Alex said he couldn't break into the base by himself. That he needed help. They let him call Jack.'

'And when Jack met you, what did he say?'

'He wanted to kill Demos. He tried to, but you can't fight Demos. He's impossible to fight. He makes you do stuff. Stuff you don't want to do.' I petered out at the sight of their blank faces.

'So, Demos made Jack and Alex come back to the base to break out two prisoners,' Dr Pendegast said. 'And when they brought the two prisoners back and Rachel, what happened then?'

'They did the exchange. Demos demanded they give him Rachel too. They didn't want to, but he just took her. Then the Unit arrived and we were caught up in a huge gunfight. It was really scary.' To my own ears I sounded like the world's worst liar, like the kid in the school play who only gets given one sympathy line and even that is delivered so poorly the entire audience cringes.

Sara didn't cringe, though; she just nodded. I swallowed again. She leaned across the table and took hold of my hand. 'Lila, Jack and Alex fired on their own men. Did Demos make them?'

I didn't like blaming Demos, but it wasn't as if it was going to hurt him any. The Unit had already sentenced him to death. What were a few more guilty verdicts going to do? Increase the wattage? And this way, I reasoned, I was protecting Jack and Alex.

'Yes,' I answered.

Sara leaned back heavily in her seat.

'But you have to understand,' I carried on, 'they had no choice.

They were being controlled. Demos, he has this amazing power. I'm telling you he can make you do things. *Anything!*'

'In which case, how did you manage to get away?' Dr Pendegast asked.

'After Ryder got shot and Jack . . .' I closed my eyes, trying to push the image away. 'After that, it was chaos. I think Demos must have lost control or something because Alex pushed me into the car and we managed to drive off.'

Again there was silence. The two of them were just nodding at me thoughtfully.

'And Rachel? What happened to her? Did you see?'

I looked between them both then shook my head. 'I saw her being put in the RV – the bus – by Demos. But I have no idea what happened after that.'

'Here's the thing, Lila,' Dr Pendegast said, uncrossing his legs and leaning forward across the table. 'What we can't understand is why you would leave Jack and why both of you wouldn't just come straight back. Instead you've been on the run for over a week and when the Unit got close to finding you – to bring you in for your own safety – you ran from us. Can you explain why?'

The labyrinth of lies was just getting so deep I wasn't sure I'd be able to find my way out. I took a deep breath. 'Alex knew he couldn't come back here. Not after what happened. He knew you'd be angry with him for breaking those prisoners out. I tried to convince him – I told him we had to come back – that you'd understand. I told him we had to find out about Jack, but he wouldn't listen. And then, when you found us in Mexico City and almost caught us, he told me that it was getting too dangerous and that he didn't want me around anymore. I don't think he ever really wanted me around, he just didn't know how to tell me.' I looked at my hands twisting in my lap then forced myself to look up straight into Sara's eyes. 'So, I came back,' I said.

'Why'd it take you so long to make that decision?' Sara whispered, hurt in her eyes.

I felt a sob in my chest heave its way into my mouth and suddenly I was crying. Actually crying. Real tears were rolling down my cheeks. 'Because I wanted to stay with Alex. I love him.' It was about the only true thing I'd said so far.

Sara handed me a tissue and came and sat next to me, putting her arm round my shoulders. 'You poor thing. I'm sorry for all the questions. We're just trying to understand what happened.' I nodded through my sobs.

'Lila, just one more thing,' she said. 'Do you know where Alex is right now? I know you probably don't want to tell us, that you want to protect him, but we really do need to talk to him. If you can tell us where he is, it would be really helpful.' She squeezed my arm.

As if, I thought. *You can shoot me with a thousand of your brain-frying guns before I'll tell you anything.*

'We just need to speak to him,' Sara said with a tired smile, 'to verify your version of events.'

'You're doubting them? You think I'm lying? Why would I lie?'

She looked uncomfortable for an instant. 'No, Lila, that's not what I meant. Look, honestly, we just want to talk to him, and to Jack when he wakes up. We understand they can't have been acting of their own accord. We realise that they were under the influence of Demos. Do you know where Alex is now?' she asked again.

'No, I don't know where he is,' I said. 'The last time I saw him he was putting me on a plane in Mexico City.' I managed to produce more tears at that point.

After a few minutes I wiped my eyes and looked up. The machine was still recording. Dr Pendegast was still writing notes, his pen scratching the paper furiously. Sara was just watching me and across the smoky grey glass of the mirror, I was sure I saw a shadow flicker.

'Can I see Jack now?' I asked, pushing my chair back and standing up. 'Can I see my dad?'

19

'Lila.'

He walked towards me, his face grim with anger. But then he grabbed me hard in his arms and I didn't feel any anger, just waves of relief and love.

'Sorry, Dad,' I mumbled.

He didn't let me go. 'God, you had me so worried,' he whispered in my ear. Then he took stock of me. I'd not seen him in almost a month, but I was aware I'd changed in a lot of ways, not least my hacked-short hair. He shook his head and then pulled me back against his chest. It felt good. It went some way to soothing the ache I was feeling between my ribs.

We were in a hospital room reserved for family in the intensive care unit. The hospital was a military one, bang in the centre of the base. It already felt like Jack was under arrest. The whole place was swarming with uniforms. Even the doctors were Marines, wearing uniforms under their white coats. There was an armed guard outside Jack's room, just in case he woke up from a coma, discovered he wasn't paralysed and decided to escape, I assumed.

'Where they hell have you been?' my dad said, dropping into a chair. I noticed now how wretchedly awful he looked. Like he hadn't slept in days. As if he was living on coffee and vending-machine food. 'And what happened to your hair? Why did you cut it?'

'I'll explain later,' I said, casting my eyes about the place. Alex had warned me that the Unit would most likely have bugged Jack's room and that they'd definitely put a bug on me too. Something in my clothing because they couldn't get me drunk and tattoo me as they'd done with him and Jack. I wasn't sure if they'd bugged me already, but I wasn't about to risk opening up to my dad and telling him everything.

'Have you seen him? How is he?' I asked to put a brake on his asking any further questions about where I'd been.

'He's OK. They've done everything they can. We just have to wait. He's lucky. It only hit his spleen, but another few centimetres and the bullet would have hit his spine. As it is, it lodged very close to one of the vertebrae. They had to operate to remove it.'

I closed my eyes and heaved in a breath or two. When I opened them, my dad was looking at me, waiting, expectation hanging like smog in the air.

'Are you going to tell me what happened?' he said. 'They won't tell me. Sara's been great, but she can't say anything. Damn security nonsense.'

I thought the effort of not speaking was going to kill me. The voice in my head was screaming, *Mum's alive. Mum's alive. She's here. She's right here.* But I couldn't open my mouth. The screaming just carried on in the vault that was my head.

'Can I see him? Can I see Jack?' I mumbled, unable to meet my dad's eye. He led me through into Jack's room with a sigh.

The first thing I noticed was the insistent beeping of a machine. Then the *hush-hush* of a ventilator. I walked slowly over to the bed and there was Jack, looking like he was sleeping and dreaming of kittens. His face was so peaceful, without a trace of his habitually raised eyebrows and ironic half-smile. I took his hand in my own. It was warm but lifeless. The bruising on his knuckles from where he'd punched the tree after finding out that I was a psy was now barely visible. I steeled myself and glanced down at his body. There was a large gauze bandage covering his lower abdomen which, other than for the suckers covering his upper chest, was otherwise bare.

I bent down. 'Hey, It's me, Jack. It's Lila. I'm here,' I whispered quietly in his ear.

Nothing. The machine kept up its rhythmic beeping and the ventilator told me to hush. After what felt like just a few minutes my dad tapped me on the shoulder. 'Come on, let's get you out of here. It's late.'

I glanced up. The clock on the side said 21.23. I had been awake for something like thirty-six hours and it suddenly felt like it. It had been over twelve hours since I'd said goodbye to Alex. I wondered where he and the others were now. He'd said it would take them just over a day to make it across the border.

'You need something to eat and we need to talk,' my dad said, hovering by the door. I kissed Jack goodbye, gave his hand one last squeeze and we left.

'Has Sara been to see him at all?' I asked my dad as we made our way out of the hospital.

'She's been here every day. I take it she and Jack are,' he paused, cleared his throat, 'dating?' I nodded.

'She seems like a lovely girl.'

I nodded again. I had thought so. Now I had no clue whether she was lovely or a two-faced bitch. And I had no clue how I was going to find out either.

'Where are we going?' I asked my dad.

'I thought we could go back to Jack's. I've been staying here in the visitors' room,' he indicated a door off to the right, 'but I could use a decent bed tonight and I think all your things are still at Jack's.'

I let out a sigh of relief. That's exactly where I wanted to go. Where I knew Alex would look for me, but would the Unit just let us drive straight off the base? 'How are we getting there?' I asked my dad.

'Sara's arranged for a car. I told her the plan and she said it was fine. They'll have security at the house, though.'

'Why?' I asked, feigning innocence.

My dad stopped in his tracks and looked at me. 'Lila, you were almost kidnapped just the other day from that house. Until they catch the . . . until they catch him we're having round-the-clock security.'

Him. He was referring to Demos. I looked away, my teeth grinding so hard my jaw hurt.

I stood to one side in the hallway, watching my dad carefully. His eyes lit first on the coat rack. He stood there startled, blinking at it in confusion. Then his gaze fell on a painting hanging on the wall and he winced. I kicked myself. I should have warned him that half the furniture here was from our old house in Washington, but I hadn't been able to open my mouth in the car. I'd been so scared that if I did, I'd let something slip.

My dad wandered through into the living room. I followed him and found him standing in front of the bookcase, staring at the photograph of my mother.

She's not dead! I wanted to scream it out loud again. Instead I bit

126

down on my lip and went into the kitchen to put the water on to boil. After a few minutes my dad joined me.

'So, are you going to tell me where you've been?' he said when I put a cup of tea in front of him. 'I was worried sick, Lila. I thought I'd lost you. What the hell happened? I get a message saying that you'd all gone camping. I phoned the Unit and they told me that Jack and Alex were on a mission. I come over and find my son in a coma and my daughter's disappeared. Then suddenly you're back and acting like nothing has happened.'

I didn't say anything. I just kept stirring my tea.

'Lila, you can't do that to me,' he said, and beneath the anger gravelling his voice was a note of utter desperation, a choking sadness that made tears spring burning to my eyes. 'This is why I didn't want you back here,' he said.

'I know,' I said, looking up at him.

'It's not safe.' Well, he was right about that.

There was a pause. My dad looked down and studied the tabletop. 'But I guess you've figured that out by now.' Another pause. 'They told me he'd kidnapped you,' he said in a strained voice. 'Did he hurt you at all?'

I was startled. 'Huh?'

'Did he hurt you?' he repeated, this time through clenched teeth.

'No, Dad.' I shook my head. *He wouldn't hurt me; he didn't hurt Mum. Demos is a good man.*

'What did they tell you?' I asked, swallowing. 'What did the Unit tell you happened?'

'When I got to the base, they said you'd run off somewhere with Alex. They didn't know where. They told me you'd been kidnapped by . . .' He couldn't say Demos's name. I reached across the table and took his hand. He looked up at me and gave me a quick smile. 'Sara told me that the Unit had gone after you and that Alex and Jack had rescued you. What they won't tell me is how Jack got shot. And they wouldn't tell me where you and Alex were.'

I nodded, trying to buy time. My dad was pretty much in the dark, then.

'Where were you?' he asked again, pleading this time. 'Why didn't you come back?'

I needed to tell the same story I told Sara I realised, just in case the Unit was listening in on this conversation. 'Alex was scared to come back,' I said. 'After . . . after what Demos made him do.'

At the mention of Demos my father stood up from the table, his chair scraping the floor. He stood with his back to me, his hands resting on the edge of the sink.

'I tried to get him to come back,' I said.

'I don't understand this. I'm going to talk to whoever's in charge. This is ridiculous. Alex and Jack saved your life and now they're in trouble. It's outrageous.' He turned back to me. 'Don't worry, Lila, I'll sort it out. They won't be in any trouble.' He came and knelt down by my chair. 'Do you know where Alex is?'

I pressed my lips together and shook my head. 'No.'

'I didn't want you to know about any of this, Lila.'

I looked at him, confused.

'I hoped you'd never know about the people who killed your mother. I was trying to protect you.' He pushed his hands through his hair.

'I know,' I said.

He sat down again at the table. 'So, you know about Demos. I guess you know everything.' I knew more than he could ever guess.

'You know what he can do?'

I nodded. *I know about Mum too. I'm one of them.*

My father got up once more and went and stood by the window, looking out. 'The Unit has got to stop him,' he murmured to his reflection.

20

The beeping of the machine was driving me insane.

Goddamn you, wake up. I need you.

The door opened and I glanced over my shoulder. It was Sara. Her face was drawn, stress marking clear lines round her mouth. She crossed straight to Jack's side and took his hand in hers, leaned over and kissed him on the forehead. I watched her out of the corner of my eye.

'How's he doing?' she asked.

My dad was standing at the end of the bed, studying Jack's chart. 'No change. Vitals are good, though.'

'How long will he be in a coma for?' she asked.

'Who knows? The doctors won't tell me much even though I am one.'

A little frown puckered Sara's brow. She sank into a chair. 'This bureaucracy is crazy.'

'What will they do when he wakes up?' my dad asked Sara.

She took hold of Jack's hand again and started to stroke his hair. 'They'll move him to the Unit's HQ.'

'Why?'

'Because they need to question him, Dr Loveday.'

'Michael, please, call me Michael.'

'OK, Michael. Jack's in trouble. He opened fire on his own men.

Several men were wounded, three were killed. Even if he was acting under duress, they still need to follow protocol and investigate.'

My dad hung Jack's chart back up. 'That's ridiculous,' he said, using his doctor voice. 'Of course he was acting under duress. Lila's already told you that. What else would he have been doing? For God's sake, this is absurd. He should be commended for bravery – not treated like a common criminal.'

'Dr Loveday – Michael – I know. It's not my decision.' She looked genuinely upset. 'We operate under military rules. There has to be an investigation.'

'Well,' my dad said, moving to the door, 'I want to talk to whoever's in charge.'

Sara glanced at me quickly before looking back at my dad. 'Actually, that's why I came,' she said. 'There's someone who wants to speak to you. He's waiting back at HQ.'

I was left alone with a silent Jack and my anything but silent mind. I crossed to the door and opened it a crack. The view was barred by a black statue standing to attention in front of the doorway. No escape there, then. How on earth were we going to be able to break Jack out of here? I crossed to the window. We were on the second floor. And even if Jack was conscious, I doubted he'd be able to abseil down. He might never be able to walk again. When I'd asked my dad about that, he'd told me not to worry, that until Jack woke up no one knew anything for certain, but I had seen the way he kept staring at Jack's legs. He was just as worried as I was.

I sat back down and stared at the beeping machine, and the tubes tangled like intestines poking out of Jack, and tried to think of a way out of this.

* * *

'What was that all about? Who wanted to talk to you?' I asked, springing to my feet as soon as my dad walked through the door.

'Richard Stirling.'

'Who?'

'Richard Stirling. He owns Stirling Enterprises. The Unit is a division of that.'

I turned away, trying to mask my horror. After a few seconds struggling to compose my expression I turned back round. My dad was studying Jack's chart as if in the last half-hour his condition might have changed.

'What did he want?' I asked.

'He offered me a job.'

For several seconds I stood there, unable to speak. 'He did *what?*' I asked eventually, my voice strangled.

'He asked me to come and work for him.'

I continued to stare at him. 'What did you say?'

'I told him I'd think about it. My priority right now is your safety.' He came over and put his arm round me. 'I don't want you in California where Demos can find you. He's out for revenge, Lila. And I'm not giving him a second chance.' He paused before adding, 'Richard said that they could arrange security for us.'

I cringed at the first-name usage. I bet they could arrange security for us. It would probably entail having one of the Unit's soldiers supergluing himself to me for the rest of my life.

'Why do they want you to work for them?' I asked. I knew they wanted his research, but they didn't need him to work for them for that. They were already stealing it. What did this mean?

'They need my help, Lila,' my dad answered.

'With what?'

He sat down in a chair by the window and patted the chair next

132

to him. I walked over to him, feeling the ground swaying slightly beneath me. 'Well, for the last few years, Lila, I've been trying to find a cure for whatever it is that Demos has.'

And that Mum had. And what I have, I thought, sinking down into the chair. 'A cure?'

'Yes. I've been researching the genes, trying to find a way of unlocking the DNA so we can stop people like him. Make them better.'

'Better? So it's an illness, then?'

My dad frowned at me. My tone was a little aggressive. I had to curb it. 'Not exactly,' he said, 'it's like cystic fibrosis or sickle-cell anaemia. There's a gene that lies dormant in a tiny percentage of the population. And then sometimes that gene gets woken up and you get someone like Demos.'

And people like my mother. Had he forgotten that?

'Right. So, you're trying to fix it, like it's a kind of cancer?' I asked.

'Yes,' he nodded, pleased that I'd understood.

I stood up and went to stand by Jack, resting my hands on the bed. 'So, you're going to work for the Unit?'

'Well, it seems that we're both trying to achieve the same thing. Seems silly not to work together on it.'

'But you said you'd never come back here,' I said, rounding on him.

'And maybe I was wrong. Jack stayed. He stayed because he wanted to find who killed your mother. I left. I wanted to protect you. I had to.'

'Yeah, I know,' I said, watching Jack's chest rise and fall in time with the respirator. 'But you were so angry with Jack for joining them.'

My dad sighed and came over to stand by my side, looking down at Jack. 'Because I was scared something like this would happen. He was just a kid, still at college, of course I was mad. And besides,' he said, his voice dropping, 'it wasn't his job to stop Demos. It was mine.'

I clamped my lips shut.

'There's something else, Lila . . .' I turned, my stomach already churning and my body tense with foreboding.

'They'll drop the charges against Jack,' my dad said. 'Hold a closed inquiry, not a criminal one. He'll be free to go.' He shrugged. I noticed his suit was creased. 'All I need to do is agree to work for them.'

I stared at him and didn't say a word. I couldn't.

'I'll do anything I need to do to protect you both,' he said finally.

21

I stared at my dad's watch and then did the calculation. It had been over twenty-four hours since I'd been back, which meant Alex had to be somewhere nearby already. I remembered what he said about being there, even when I couldn't see him, and the butterflies started tumbling in my stomach. And I felt braver because of it, like suddenly the impossible had become possible.

I closed my eyes and pictured his face, remembering the way it felt when his arms wrapped round me, closing out the world. How in the water his hands had stroked fire up my back and set my spine alight. To any passing shoals of fish I must have looked like an electric eel. I breathed in the memory of his lips, the softness of them, and how they felt tracing across my skin, leaving ripples of goosebumps in their wake.

'What's up?' my dad asked. 'You just made a groaning sound. Do you have a headache?'

'No, no,' I said, feeling the heat radiate from my face like a mushroom cloud. 'I'm fine.' I squirmed towards the back door. 'I'm going upstairs,' I said, letting the screen door slam behind me. I walked through the kitchen, leaving my dad on the outside veranda going through his research notes.

I flopped onto the bed in my room and buried my head under a pillow. How on earth was Alex going to get near me with the

Unit stationed outside the front door and with surveillance all over the place? I sat back up and looked around, wondering whether there were any cameras hidden anywhere that maybe I'd missed. That's when I noticed Alex's T-shirt – the one that I'd been wearing the first night in Oceanside when I came downstairs for a glass of water and he startled me in the kitchen. The one I'd subsequently almost died of humiliation while wearing. It was lying beside me on the bed, folded neatly. I hadn't left it there. I most certainly hadn't folded it neatly either.

It was a sign. Alex had been here. I got up and ran to the closet, throwing open the door, not exactly sure what I was looking for, but feeling the nudge of disappointment when I didn't find Alex hiding there amidst Jack's dress uniform and old shoeboxes. I threw back the covers of the bed. Nothing. Then I tossed the pillows aside. There it was. A piece of paper. I smiled widely and picked it up.

It just had one sentence written on it in Alex's neat handwriting.

1 a.m. Previous escape route. x

I frowned. Previous escape route? What did that mean? Then I smiled, figuring it out. When I'd run out on him before, I'd jumped the back fence into the neighbours' garden. I lay back down on the bed, grinning at the ceiling. I was going to see Alex soon.

My dad stayed up late working. I offered to make him hot milk, but he just looked up from his papers and eyed me suspiciously. I even thought about ransacking the bathroom cabinet for some Valium to lace his dinner, but Jack didn't do drugs – of the medicated or non-medicated kind – so I scratched that idea. Just after midnight, when I thought I was going to have to hit him over the

136

head with a frying pan to knock him out, he finally went up to bed. I waited, fully dressed, under the covers for another fifty minutes, before slipping out of bed and sneaking back downstairs.

Two cars were still stationed at the front of the house. I hoped to God the Unit security detail wasn't going to be prowling round the neighbourhood in the dark. The garden backed onto other gardens so they couldn't park there, which meant it was probably the safest route out of the house. I had to hope Alex had thought about this – he was trained in reconnaissance so I assumed it was likely.

I tiptoed across the squeaky linoleum in the kitchen and eased the deadbolt at the bottom of the door. It was a dark night, the moon shrouded heavily by cloud. I waited for my eyes to adjust to the gloom, focusing on the fence at the back of the garden, which I had to get over. A hand suddenly grabbed me from out of the shadows, catching me round the waist. Before I could scream another hand covered my mouth.

Then lips replaced the hand, and I was in Alex's arms, kissing him back so hard that I couldn't breathe, my hands fumbling to hold on to him and pull him closer.

He drew back and I was about to speak when he put a finger against my lips. Then his hands dropped to my waist, and his fingers were suddenly tugging at my jeans, undoing the buttons. I looked at him in surprise. What, here on the veranda? With the Unit out the front and my dad just upstairs and the laws of California still in force? He'd chosen a funny time to abandon his resolve. Then I realised what he was doing and with a twinge of disappointment started helping him out, pulling my T-shirt off over my head and shaking off my jeans until I was standing in the shallow moonlight on the decking, completely naked.

137

Alex handed me a pile of clothing and then held my gaze with a smile, his eyes not dropping for a single moment as I fumbled my arms through a tank top and hopped into a pair of jogging bottoms. *Going commando with a commando*, I thought, as I watched Alex kneel and start rifling through my discarded clothing. He held something up near my face. I could see it was a little metal thing, similar to the one we'd pulled out of his arm. When had they planted that on me? I watched as he dropped it back into the front pocket of my jeans. Then he folded my jeans up and put them in a pile with the rest of my clothes under the table.

We crossed the garden and ducked behind a tree. Alex cupped his hands together and I stepped one foot into them and hauled myself up and over the fence. He dropped down next to me half a second later, took my hand and in silence started pulling me towards the next fence. We hopped over three more fences, dropping quietly into bushes either side, before dashing across lawns and skipping over garden furniture and toys until the final fence gave onto an alley filled with trash cans.

I glanced around. 'You sure choose the most romantic places for dates,' I said.

Alex pushed me up against the fence, one arm round my waist and the other holding the back of my head, and kissed me.

'OK, I take it back,' I murmured against his lips. 'God, I'm so glad you're here.'

'Me too. Come on, let's get out of here,' he said, snatching my hand and pulling me down the alley.

'Where are we going?' I asked.

'Away from here so we can talk.' We stopped by a huge dumpster and I burst out laughing.

'Excellent,' I said, grinning in delight at the sight of a sleek black motorbike.

Alex handed me a helmet. I put it on and then climbed on behind him, wrapping my arms tight round his stomach. 'You know, you promised Jack you'd never let me ride on a bike again.'

'I never promised,' Alex said, grinning at me over his shoulder.

A sudden scream of sirens shattered the night-time quiet. Alex revved the engine and we flew out of the alley.

22

'Are you sure they haven't followed us?' I asked, looking over my shoulder once more. We'd only driven about half a mile. Alex had parked up by the pier and we had jumped the barricade closing it off and were now walking out along its length.

'Yes, I set up a little distraction.'

I looked sideways at him. 'What kind of distraction?'

'I made a phone call to the local police department, pretending to be a concerned citizen who'd spotted two suspicious vehicles parked on your street.'

'Clever,' I said, my eyes drinking in his face, feeling the magnetic pull of his lips.

We walked in silence to the end of the pier, our bodies synching, Alex's hand round my shoulder, my head resting against his body. Everything felt lighter all of a sudden, easier. The doubts and fears that had started to plague me were soothed away just by the sight of him.

'So, what happened when you got back to the base?' Alex asked as we dropped to the edge and dangled our legs over the side of the pier. There was no one else out here at this time of night and we were hidden from view of anyone on the beach.

'Did Key not tell you? I thought he was here?' I asked. My eyes were drawn up to the dark sky above us. Was he here right now following us? Was he listening to this conversation?

'He saw you go into the headquarters and then come out. I had a call from Demos – Key had reported back,' Alex said. 'What happened – did they question you? Did you see Sara?'

I turned my attention back to Alex. 'Yeah, she was there – she met me as soon as I walked in the door. She was the one who questioned me. And there was a man with her, a Dr Pendegast. He just took a lot of notes. I think I did OK. It's hard to tell what they believed. But they let me go, though; that's got to be a good sign, right?'

Alex nodded. He was staring out at the ocean, the line running between his eyes giving away his anxiety.

'Did you hear about my dad's job offer?'

He looked back at me. 'Yes. Key heard you and your dad talking about it.' He nodded to himself. 'So, Richard Stirling's here. Did you meet him?'

'No,' I said, shaking my head.

If I ever met Richard Stirling, I would probably inadvertently kill him. Or maybe not so inadvertently. I gazed down at the black waves slapping the pier beneath us. Then my eyes lit on an orange buoy out in the ocean about fifty metres away and just like that it started to move, as if it was a jet ski, tearing through the dark mass of water until it became a pinprick in the distance before vanishing over the horizon.

'Hey, hey, Lila . . .' I tore my gaze from the waves and looked back at Alex. He seemed troubled. I reached a hand over, unthinking, and stroked the line between his eyes until it disappeared. He took hold of my fingers. 'You can't lose it, Lila. You have to control your power. Especially, and I mean *especially*, around the Unit. If you do meet Richard Stirling, you can't let him know how you feel. You can't give yourself away. Promise me.'

'OK,' I whispered.

He held my gaze for a few more seconds, his lips pursed in an anxious way. He was right to worry. My record for self-control with regards to both him and my power was pretty terrible.

'Have you heard anything from Demos and the others?' I asked, hoping to steer him away from any more lectures about control.

'They're good,' Alex said. 'They should be in Washington soon.'

'How long will they need to get everything in place?'

'A day or so.'

I chewed my bottom lip, thinking about how long that gave me to figure out an escape plan. 'I don't know how we're going to get Jack off the base, Alex,' I finally admitted. 'There are soldiers all over the place. And the headquarters is like some kind of Fort Knox – there are all these security checks to get through to even use the elevator.'

'I know,' Alex said quietly.

'So, how will we get in? Let alone out?'

'Maybe having your dad working for them isn't such a bad idea,' Alex said quietly.

I looked up, startled, snatching my hand out of his. 'What?'

Alex said nothing for a while then he turned to me and I saw the moonlight had turned his eyes a pale blue topaz colour. 'It could help having someone on the inside,' he said.

'No way!' I shouted. 'He needs to know, Alex. Imagine if it was me and you thought I was dead? It's killing me not being able to tell him. It's like this voice in my head is screaming all day long at me to tell him. We have to! We can't let him work for them. It's just too horrible.'

Alex shook his head at me. 'If we tell him, he might not react so well. I know I'd struggle to act rationally in the same situation. And we can't risk having him blow our cover. Right now we need to be able to control as much of the situation as we can. He's an asset, but we have to keep him in the dark until the time comes when we can make use of him.'

I thumped the pier with my closed fist. It sure didn't feel like the right thing to do. It made me feel sick just to contemplate my father working for the Unit. But Alex was the Recon Marine – and, though I didn't like to admit it, maybe he was right. If my dad found out now, he'd probably try to do something crazy or stupid – like call the police – or, I drew in a breath, he might not even believe me.

Alex laid his hand on my arm. 'We'll just keep him in the dark for a few more days. And anyway, if he takes the job, then it also helps remove any suspicion off you,' he said. 'They'll assume that if you did know about the Unit, or the fact they're holding your mother, that you'd have told him.'

I sighed. I could see he was right. 'I suppose.'

We sat thinking in silence for a minute, the waves slamming into the struts of the pier below us as if they could sense my own feelings of frustration and anger.

'What about Jack?' I finally asked. 'They're going to transfer him to prisoner holding even if my dad takes the job. They said they'd still need to process him even if they're going to drop the charges.' I looked at Alex. 'Do you really think they'll let him go like my dad says? Do you think they're telling the truth?'

'No.' Alex shook his head. 'There's no way, not if they think he might know the truth about what they're really doing. It's too dangerous for them to risk it.'

'So, shouldn't we try to spring him now while we still can?'

Alex shook his head again, grimacing. 'I think we might have to let them transfer him to prisoner holding. It's easier having just

143

one target. If we're trying to break Jack out of the hospital and your mum out of headquarters, our focus is split, as are our resources. And there just aren't enough of us. It would be easier to mount just one offensive against the headquarters.'

He saw the look on my face. 'Lila, this was my job. This is what I'm trained for, remember?'

'But what if we can't get inside the headquarters?'

'We will,' Alex answered calmly. 'When the time's right. You need to trust me.'

I leaned into his shoulder. 'I do trust you,' I whispered. It was all just so frustrating. I didn't know how he could stay so calm.

'Do you trust Sara?' Alex asked.

I turned to him. 'I don't know. For the most part I think she's genuine. I really want to trust her, but . . .'

'But what?'

'I don't know. I just don't know.'

'Always listen to your instincts, Lila. If you aren't sure, she stays out of this. Don't tell her anything, OK?'

I nodded and buried my head once more in his shoulder.

23

'I think you should take the job, Dad.'

My dad looked up from his papers and put his mug of tea down on the table. 'You do?' he said.

'Yes.' I took a piece of toast and started spreading butter on it. 'Like you say, Demos needs to be stopped. If you can help, you should.'

Lying, lying, lying. I was actually getting better with all the practice. My face was no longer turning as red as a stoplight and my voice no longer went up a pitch in tone.

'Well, I still don't know,' my dad said. 'It would mean moving over here and I've not given any notice back in London and—'

'You could ask for compassionate leave. For Jack. I'm sure the hospital would understand.'

He paused. I knew he would already have done the maths on this. I was just giving him my endorsement.

'Well, if you're sure. I don't want you here, but on the other hand, I actually think we might be better off near the Unit, with the security they can offer us. And I'm not going anywhere until Jack's on his feet again—' He broke off abruptly, realising what he'd just said.

I kept spreading butter. 'You should tell them today. You know, get the ball rolling. Keep busy,' I added, taking a bite of toast which instantly got lodged like a burr in my throat.

My dad nodded to himself then swept his papers up into a loose pile and walked through into the living room to make the call.

I watched him go then put my toast down and sat with my head in my hands.

'Will you be OK if I leave you here for a moment?' my dad asked. 'I need to speak to someone about starting work. I need to get into a lab. There's some things I need to set up.'

'I'll be fine,' I answered weakly. 'I've got an armed guard on the door, remember.' I glanced at the opaque glass of the hospital door, through which the wavy black shape of a Unit soldier could be seen.

My dad came and ruffled my hair. 'I like your hair by the way. Suits you,' he said before he turned to open the door. 'Back soon.'

I swivelled to face Jack. Same old, same old. The damn beep of machines and wheezing *hush* of the ventilator.

'Wake up, goddamn you,' I hissed. 'I need you to hear me.'

Nothing.

'You need a shave.'

Nothing.

'Dad's working for the Unit.'

Nothing.

'He's looking for a cure for people like Demos.'

Nothing.

I sighed then bent forward until I was right by his ear.

'I'm madly in love with Alex and while you've been sleeping he kidnapped me and took me to Mexico and we went skinny-dipping. And let me tell you – it was A. Lot. Of. Fun. I'm sure you want to kick his ass, but oh, what a shame, you're in a coma.'

146

Nothing. Then the machine, the beeping machine, started going faster. It was momentary, but the read-out showed a spike in his heart rate.

'You can hear me,' I said, blinking at Jack's inert body in astonishment. Was I imagining it or had the peaceful expression on his face changed? Was that a muscle twitching by his eye? I bent down again so my lips were pressed against his ear. 'Did I tell you about the double room?'

The machine definitely hiked for a second.

Beep. Beep. BEEP.

I laughed under my breath, wondering if I should keep going to see if I could get him to wake up. Then I sat firmly back in my seat. I didn't want to give him a stroke. I leaned forward one more time. 'Please don't kick his butt by the way.'

'You must be Jack's sister.'

I very nearly fell out of my chair. I spun round. A man was standing in the doorway. He was wearing military uniform underneath a white doctor's coat. I caught the flash of medals slung across his chest. He was early thirties I guessed, with short dark hair and quick brown eyes. He crossed to the bed and picked up Jack's chart.

'I'm Dr Roberts. Your brother's doctor,' he said.

I studied him as he read the chart. He was about five foot ten, average build. He didn't have the square musculature of the soldiers from the Unit, nor was he wearing black, but you never knew. I wasn't going to trust anyone, especially not in this place.

He unwrapped his stethoscope from where he had it looped round his neck and pressed it against Jack's chest, waited a few beats then noted something down on the chart. Then he crossed to the machines and started checking the read-outs. After a few seconds he looked over at Jack then back at the chart.

147

'Something the matter?' I asked.

'No,' he answered, still studying the read-out. 'It looks like he had a spike in his heart rate a minute or two ago. I'm not sure what caused it.' He frowned at the read-out and then he frowned directly at me.

I flashed him a wide-eyed, innocent smile and looked back at Jack. 'How's he doing?'

'He's healing well. Very well. We'll take a look at how the wound is doing tomorrow. His vitals are fine, though. You should keep talking to him. There's a chance he can hear your voice – it'll help him come round.'

Or induce a heart attack.

'Will he be able to walk?' I asked, clearing my throat.

The doctor stared at me with what I imagined was the expression he wore when passing on bad news to relatives. 'It's impossible to tell at this stage how serious the damage is,' he said. 'The bullet went in here,' he pointed to Jack's stomach. 'It nicked the rib here at the front and then lodged against his spinal cord here at the back. Until he wakes up and we can do further tests we won't know whether or not he's lost the use of his legs.'

I closed my eyes for a moment. 'When will he wake up?' I asked.

'Who knows? He was heavily sedated at first, but we've eased up on that. These guys,' he said, nodding at the bulky shadow of the Unit soldier standing on the other side of the door, 'they want him up and about last week already. They're putting pressure on me to bring him round, but there's little I can do – he'll wake up when he wakes up – his body needs time to recover from all the trauma. But now they're talking about moving him soon to their headquarters. They don't care if he's conscious or not. I don't know who these people think they are but . . .' He muttered something under his breath.

My heart was hammering. The Unit were going to move Jack? I knew that Alex had said it might be for the best – all that stuff about split assets and resources – but now it was actually happening it suddenly didn't seem like the best idea. I realised the doctor was still talking to me and in a daze turned back to face him.

'I'm just still a little concerned about the way his stats are spiking,' he was saying. 'If it keeps happening, I'm going to have to keep him here under observation.'

He was staring at me intently, then just like that, he turned and walked out. I stared after him, blinking, wondering if I might have misheard or misinterpreted what he'd said or the laser-beam stare. But no, he'd clearly been offering a suggestion – a way to help keep Jack here in the hospital under observation. I smiled to myself. Maybe, with a bit more luck and a few more innuendoes whispered in Jack's ear, I could find a way of getting my brother out of here before they transferred him. But was that the best plan? Or was I just panicking?

I got up and walked to the door, feeling frustrated. I threw it open and the man guarding it turned to face me, barring my exit with a gun the size of my arm held against his chest. I looked up, glaring, ready to demand he moved when I stopped short, drawing in a sharp breath.

'Jonas?' I stuttered.

The man in front of me was actually a boy. He was only a year or two older than I was. He had chestnut eyes and skin like burnished copper. In another lifetime, in a world without Alex, I might have found him hot.

'Lila,' he said, smiling. He gave a quick look up and down the corridor which was empty for the moment. 'I didn't want to disturb you.'

'So, you're what? On duty?' I asked.

He flashed me a smile that showed off the white of his teeth and made him look about six, playing dress-up in commando clothes.

'Yeah.' He looked embarrassed, which was something I supposed. 'This whole thing with your brother and Lieutenant Wakeman, it's kind of big. They're just wanting to make sure he's secure.'

Right. Until they could transfer him to prisoner holding and keep him there indefinitely. That kind of secure.

He saw me wince because he started to mumble. 'I mean, I don't think Jack did anything wrong. It wasn't like he had any choice . . . what with you being taken and then Demos and . . . what else could he do . . . ?' He started scuffing the floor with the toe of his boot.

I didn't want to hear it. Making small talk with a boy holding a gun, who would shoot me without a second thought if he knew what I was, wasn't exactly high on my list of priorities.

I squeezed past him. 'I'm going to get a coffee,' I said as politely as I could before starting to walk fast down the corridor.

'Lila,' he called out after me. I turned round, plastering a smile on my face. 'I was just thinking, wondering really, would you like to get a coffee with me later?'

I stood there, in the middle of the corridor, trying to process his request. It seemed such a bizarre question given the circumstances. We were in the hushing lull of an intensive care unit. He was effectively guarding my brother, who was lying prisoner in a coma on the other side of the door. And I could, if I so wanted to, snatch the gun from his hands before he had time to react and turn it on him. Was he seriously asking me on a date?

I started to open my mouth, my brain formulating a weak excuse about Jack and my dad not letting me date anyone in uniform, when I realised I was staring a gift horse in the mouth. A gold-plated, diamond-encrusted gift horse. I was meant to be gathering information after all. Jonas was maybe the chink we were looking for.

'Sure,' I said to Jonas, smiling widely, 'that would be nice.'

24

At lunchtime Sara arrived. She looked stressed. She was wearing a pale grey silk blouse and a pencil skirt with black high heels. She went straight to Jack and followed her usual routine, stroking his brow and taking his hand before kissing him. I was being so sceptical and unfair. Maybe she genuinely was the tragic girlfriend. I really hoped so because I didn't want Jack to wake up from his coma and discover his girlfriend was an evil, two-faced psycho. It might affect his rehab.

'Sara?' I said, taking the chair opposite her.

She looked up at me and I saw again with a pang of guilt how tired she looked. The circles under her eyes were darkening, making her face look grey, while her eyes themselves were pink-rimmed. She looked like she'd been up crying all night. I felt my words catch in my throat. It would be so good to tell her everything. I pressed my lips together to stop myself. I was being impulsive. I'd promised Alex no reckless behaviour.

Aside from the fact Sara could be one of Richard Stirling's evil minions, we were bugged. I had found the little metal splinter inside my jeans again. God only knew who was breaking into the house every day and rooting through my clothes – hopefully not Jonas – because despite my daily laundry missions, they kept on reappearing.

I needed to weigh my words carefully. 'Do you think Jack will be OK?' I asked.

'Yes,' she said, 'yes, he'll be fine. He has to be.' There were tears glistening in her eyes. She suddenly let out a sob which startled me. 'You have no idea how scared I was, Lila, when they brought him back to the base. When he disappeared, I was terrified. He didn't tell me where he was going. I guess he didn't trust me.' She wiped her eyes with a tissue and I shifted uncomfortably in my seat.

'And then, when we found out they'd broken out the prisoners and taken Rachel . . . I came under so much scrutiny. They thought I must have known. That I was a part of it. I told them I didn't know anything. I'm not even sure they believe me now.' She rested her head in her hands.

'But you didn't have anything to do with it,' I said.

'I know. But I wish,' she paused, looking up and holding my gaze, 'I wish that Jack had trusted me. I'd do anything for Jack,' she said, her bottom lip trembling. 'Anything.'

I felt my heart ratchet up a notch. 'Do you know about my mum?' I asked, taking a deep breath. It was innocuous enough as questions go – I wasn't asking her straight up whether she knew my mum was being held and experimented on. I wanted to see if there'd be some kind of spark, something registering on Sara's face that she knew about Mum being alive, but her face stayed blankly innocent and she simply asked, 'What about her?'

'About what happened to her?' I said.

'I know why she was killed,' Sara answered guardedly, frowning at me as if she wasn't sure she understood the question. 'I know that Jack and Alex joined the Unit to find her killers. And that Jack would do anything to stop them. As would I.' Again with the long stare.

I sat back in my chair and looked at Jack. If Sara did know about my mum being held by the Unit, she deserved an Oscar for this performance. It was flawless. But why, then, was my instinct fighting against my desire to tell her everything? Was it just because there was too much at stake? Or because we were bugged? Or was it simply that I didn't believe her?

25

My dad was staring at me as if I'd just waltzed into the room speaking fluent Japanese and wearing a clown costume.

'He asked you for coffee?' he spluttered.

'Don't have an aneurysm, Dad, it's just a coffee.'

'Er, well . . .'

My dad had never had to deal with the issue of me and boys before because I'd never had a boyfriend – until now. But he didn't know about Alex. True, we'd skipped the whole movie, popcorn, first base, prom thing, but Alex still qualified as my boyfriend. Maybe. It wasn't as if we'd had time to discuss it. Perhaps one day we'd get to do something normal like go on a real date. And act like we were a normal couple as opposed to a mutant teenager with mind-control issues and a special forces operative trained to kill me.

'It's not serious,' I whispered to my dad, aware that Jonas was stationed on the other side of the door.

'Yes, right, well . . .' I could see my dad was struggling to cope with the idea of me and boys in the same sentence let alone in the same room, drinking coffee. 'I guess that's fine. I mean, at least you'll be safe. You're not going off the base, are you?'

'No, Dad, we'll stay right here. Just the cafeteria.'

'OK, then.' He nodded at me and I squirmed like a worm in a Petri dish. I wondered what kind of a reaction I'd get from him if

155

I told him where I'd been and what I'd been doing with Alex just a few days ago.

I bent to say goodbye to Jack. Still beeping. Still unresponsive. Then I opened the door. Jonas was there waiting, gun slung across his chest.

'Hi, Lila,' he said, beaming at me. Again I was struck by the contrast between his boyish smile and the huge black machine gun he was holding against his chest. He looked like a five-year-old wearing a GI Joe costume. Why did they need to recruit someone so young? Then it struck me that Jack and Alex had barely been older when the Unit had recruited them.

'Hey,' I said back.

'I just have to wait to be relieved,' he said, pointing at the door.

'OK, I'll go and order coffee. See you down there,' I smiled. I hoped the smile was warm and flirty, but I had a feeling I looked more like I'd swallowed my own vomit.

The cafeteria was on the ground floor. Ten or so plastic tables and a coffee concession stand to one side. I saw Dr Roberts at a far table. He smiled over at me before carrying on a conversation with a couple of nurses.

I bought some coffee and then on a whim some cookies. I didn't think I could actually find the words to flirt with Jonas so I'd just give him the cookies – like a third-grader. I didn't know how to flirt. That much had been proved with regards to my failed attempts to seduce Alex over the last few years, not just the last few weeks. And besides, it felt wrong. So wrong. Even with the mitigating circumstances it felt like a betrayal.

A gun appeared on the table – on top of the cookies. It seemed symbolic, but I couldn't work out how. I automatically scanned the gun for the safety catch, thinking how strange it was that a couple of weeks ago Alex had had to show me how to hold a gun

156

and aim straight and already I felt like a pro.

'Um, do you always bring your gun on dates?' I said, looking up at Jonas.

'Is that what this is? A date?' he asked, flashing a huge white smile at me.

For a moment I felt really sorry for him. I was being so unfair using him like this. Then I remembered who he was working for and the guilt evaporated.

Jonas dropped into the seat, moving his gun off the table and resting it upright against the table leg. I pushed his coffee across the table towards him. 'So, how's your brother?' he asked.

'He's OK, I think.'

'I hear your dad's starting work for the Unit. Cool.'

Yeah, it was really, really cool. 'Yeah,' I said.

'What's he working on?' Jonas asked.

I paused for a second. I had to assume that as Jonas was a lower rank than Alex or Jack, he probably didn't know that much, if anything, about the real work the Unit were doing.

'He doesn't really tell me much. I'm not sure,' I shrugged.

'You know,' Jonas said, leaning across the table, and letting his voice drop, 'I heard the other day that they're doing tests on them.'

I swallowed some coffee and it burnt my tongue.

'Demos and his people – when the Unit catches them. They're testing them to find a way of fixing them.'

'Really?' I asked, anger flooding through my body. I looked at the cookie and it moved a fraction of a centimetre across the table. My heart dived after it. *Damn it.* I looked up, terrified. But Jonas hadn't noticed, his eyes were fixed on my face.

'So, what was he like?'

'What was who like?' I stammered.

157

'You were with him, right? Demos?' He said his name in a hushed tone as though Demos was a celebrity he couldn't believe I'd met. 'What's he like? I can't believe you actually got to, like, meet him. The Unit's been trying to catch him for years. He's like the big boss. Did you get to talk to him?'

'Well, he kidnapped me so I guess that counts as meeting him.'

'What did he do to you? Did he use his power on you?'

'Yes.'

His eyes widened. 'Wow, what did it feel like?'

'It wasn't very nice,' I said, remembering the feeling I'd had of being lassoed round the ankles and slammed against an invisible concrete block.

'How did you get away?'

'He was busy fighting off the Unit. He couldn't hold everyone so we managed to escape.'

Jonas was listening, bug-eyed, his mouth hanging open.

'Were you there?' I asked. 'At Joshua Tree?'

'I was in the third vehicle,' he said. 'They turned it over. We were all inside. It was nasty.'

I flushed. 'But you were OK?' It had been weighing on me. Just a little. Not as much as my mum or Jack or the thought of getting caught were weighing on me, but the knowledge that I'd hurt people, that Alex had maybe killed people, was there – a monster lurking in the recess of my mind, prodding me with angry fingers, trying to make me face it. So far I'd kept my back turned on it. There was just too much else to deal with.

'I was fine,' he smiled at me, throwing back his shoulders. 'A couple of the others in my team came off a bit worse. A broken leg and a broken collarbone, that sort of thing. But Alpha team got hit hard. They lost three men.'

158

His eyes were shining bright with tears and I looked away and started fiddling with the cookies, breaking them apart and crumbling them onto the table. Alex had tried to tell me there were always casualties in war. That this was a war. That he'd have shot every single one of them if it meant protecting me. His words had registered on some level but a remote one. All I cared about at that point were Jack and my mum. The men from the Unit didn't figure at all in my reckoning. They hadn't figured at all until now.

But here was the reality. People were dead. They were dead because of me and because of Alex. People who didn't know the truth – who were just cannon fodder for Stirling Enterprises.

No, I reminded myself sternly, they weren't dead because of me or because of Alex. They were dead because of one man and one man only – Richard Stirling.

I focused back in. Jonas appeared to have blinked away the film of tears and was now describing the carnage I'd caused.

'. . . totally destroyed the Humvees. No idea they could do that. It's amazing. Just imagine being able to do that. Just by looking at something.'

Yeah. Just imagine. I sipped my coffee.

'We only got one of theirs.' Jonas was still talking.

A scalding splash of coffee spilled over my hand. That was Ryder he was talking about. *Ryder.* I wanted to shake him by the arms and yell Ryder's name in his face, but I didn't. I sat there and ground my teeth and tried not to let go of my precarious control.

'We took a giant hit. We're down to just fourteen men. They're training some more at the moment, lots more, I hear another four teams, but they won't be operational for another week or so.'

I looked down at my coffee and gave it a stir. The odds were not moving in our favour.

'Where do they recruit them from?'

'They take the best of the recruits from out of special ops training.' His chest puffed out. 'We're the best of the best.'

I thought of Suki and Nate and Amber and the others. They might have mind powers but it wasn't going to be enough. They weren't soldiers.

I gave Jonas a once-over. He looked like a high school quarterback not like a soldier who'd completed special ops training and come out top of the class.

'How old are you?' I asked.

'Nineteen,' he answered, jutting out his chin, 'nearly twenty. And like I told you, we're the finest trained Marine force in the world. You've got the best protection you could want.'

Huh. Great. That was great. I tried to look relieved and not utterly destroyed by the news.

'And the guys in the lab are making a breakthrough,' he added because he obviously thought I still looked panic-stricken.

I looked up. 'They are?'

'Yeah, so I hear.'

'What kind of a breakthrough?'

'I'm not sure, some way of being able to trace them better – so we can find them easier. That's the biggest problem. They just stay one step ahead all the time; we can't get close.'

'Oh yeah?'

'Yeah, not sure what it is, but it's gonna be big. The guys are all talking about it.'

My stomach lurched. 'You don't have any idea what it could be?' I said, trying not to sound like I gave a damn when really I was this close to snatching up his gun with my mind and holding it against his head until he told me or went away and found out.

160

'No, but exciting, huh?'

I made some kind of noise, a strangled gurgle, which he took for agreement.

'So, soon enough you won't have to worry about a thing. This is going to be over before you know it.' He reached across the table and took my hand.

It took a moment to register and another moment to fight the urge to shake it off – mentally. *Control, control*, I repeated over and over in my head. His hand felt hot and heavy on top of mine.

'So, you want to go see a movie sometime or go for pizza one night? I mean . . . only if you want to . . .'

'Um, I need to check with my dad. He's kind of overprotective. Like Jack.'

I saw the disappointment on his face as he stood. 'OK, well, let me know.' He smiled, embarrassed, his cheeks flushing. 'Because I'd really like to hang out some more.'

I nodded and tried to smile.

'I've got to get back to HQ,' he said. 'Sorry. I'll see you tonight, though.'

I nodded absently, then did a double take. 'Tonight?'

'Yeah, I'm on duty for the first part of the evening. I'm stationed outside your house – your very own security detail, just like the President has.'

'Well, in that case, I'll see you later,' I said, forcing myself to keep smiling when all I really wanted to do was rest my head on the table and cry.

After he'd gone I sat for a few minutes staring mutely at the tabletop until the remaining cookie lifted a few centimetres off the table and hurtled to the floor.

26

The problem was that I was bugged. And I had no phone. And I couldn't go anywhere without an armed guard. So technically, it was more than one problem I had to deal with. It was several.

I reminded myself of what Demos had said about what the Unit would have the potential to do when they made a breakthrough. It didn't exactly spell world peace. Stirling Enterprises made its money through weapons dealing, legitimate and otherwise. They'd sell their weapons to the highest bidder and farewell world as we knew it. Hello crazy new world order. I could hear Jack in my head calling me melodramatic, but from where I was sitting it seemed a pretty good assessment. He was in a coma. What did he know?

'Miss Loveday?'

I looked up, startled. A man in black combats was towering over me. I felt a kamikaze nosedive of fear. Was this it? Was this the moment I'd been waiting for? Then I came to my senses and started to assess his size and weapons. I could take him. For sure I could. If he touched me, I'd take his arm off. Then go for his gun. Then make a run for it.

'Miss Loveday?' he said again.

'Yes,' I said as defiantly as I could muster.

'Would you mind coming with me, miss?'

I studied him. He was about six feet four tall, solid, oblong shaped – even his head was a rectangle with buzz-cut fuzz decorating the top. His face was expressionless. He reminded me of Robocop. I glanced round the cafeteria. It was empty except for a humming orderly clearing cups off the tables.

I looked back at the man. 'Where to?' I asked. I already knew, of course. He wasn't here to take me on a guided tour of San Diego zoo.

'There's someone who wants to see you.'

I waited a beat, but he wasn't any more forthcoming. 'Who?' I asked.

'If you'd just like to come with me, please,' he said, pulling the back of my chair out.

I stood up, gripping the edge of the table for support. 'Um, I think I need to tell my dad where I'm going so he doesn't worry.'

'That's been taken care of.'

Taken care of? That did not sound good. Had they taken him too?

My mind bounced around, pinging back and forth, trying to figure out whether to make a break for it now or to wait. If he took me into the Unit's headquarters, it would be too late. But I couldn't act now. What if it was completely innocent? I would blow everything if I let them find out about me.

Before I could figure out what to do, we were outside and the man was steering me by the elbow towards a jeep. Act? Not act? I thought again about dislodging his arm, throwing him backwards and then hopping in the jeep and driving off. But I knew I wouldn't get far on a military base in a stolen jeep. He pushed me into the passenger seat before I could decide what to do. Maybe he was taking me back to see Dr Pendegast. Did they want to interrogate me again? I clutched the seat and tried to think straight.

Less than a minute later we pulled up outside the Unit's mono-lithic headquarters. I clambered down and followed the man like he was my executioner. I had to go inside. It was too risky to make a move. We stepped into one of the pods, brushing arms as we walked, and I felt myself start to sweat, my skin prickling even in the air-conditioned cool. The door swished open and we walked into the lobby. It was too late to act. I froze, stock-still, in the middle of the lobby, my heart fluttering in my throat, making me feel like I was going to throw up. I should have tried to escape. And now it was too late. My guard looked back scowling over his shoulder and then beckoned me to keep following. I unglued my feet and walked on.

We stepped into an elevator and the guard swiped our entry onto the top floor – the fifth. At least he wasn't taking me down to prisoner holding. Though – my stomach lurched – that was where my mum was. But now there were nine floors between her and me. That might as well be nine solar systems for how far away it felt and how impossible to cross.

The man led me down a hallway and through a door into a room that had windows on two sides and an enormous oval-shaped board table in the centre. A man in a dark grey suit was standing at the far end of the room with his back to me, staring out of the window.

The door shut with a whispering click and I spun round. My guard had left. I turned slowly back to the room. The man had turned too and was now looking straight at me, appraising me. He was late fifties perhaps, well over six feet tall, with steel-coloured hair and the tan of someone who spent his weekends sailing in the

Bahamas. He seemed vaguely familiar. I looked him up and down carefully, trying to place him. There was something about the piercing blue of his eyes and the straight-backed arrogance of his bearing which reminded me of someone. He didn't look like a doctor. Or a soldier.

The breath rushed out of me as I figured it out. He looked exactly like I'd imagine the boss of a multi-billion-dollar company to look.

'Miss Loveday, thank you very much for coming,' he said, striding towards me.

Richard Stirling. Rachel's father. The man behind all of this. The man responsible for my mother's pretend murder. The man sanctioning the experiments. That was the man walking towards me and holding out his hand. And I was expected to shake it without hurling him through the window. My whole body tensed with the effort to control the urge.

'I didn't have much choice,' I said through gritted teeth.

He stopped short, frowning a little. Then he recovered, giving me an apologetic nod of the head. 'Ah yes, the boys from the Unit, not the most subtle, I'm afraid. I'm very sorry if my request to see you has put you out in any way.'

I knew I had to behave. That I needed to play the game as Alex would call it, and use him to get information, but my brain didn't feel too strategic. All I could think about was how much I wanted to kill him. I took a deep breath, forced myself to smile, though it hurt to do so, and then I spoke. 'No, it was no problem. I just wanted to get back to Jack, that's all.'

'Yes, of course, I understand. Well, thank you for your time. I'll keep it brief. Here,' he pulled out a heavy chair, 'have a seat.' I considered it and then sat down, perching on the edge.

He stayed standing. 'It's about my daughter. I understand you were one of the last people to see her?'

'Yes,' I answered. I held his gaze and wondered if he could see the hatred burning in my eyes.

'Can you tell me what happened?'

'Um, I already told Sara and that doctor what happened,' I said, grasping at my lies, trying to remember what I'd told them.

'I know, I read the report.' He smiled though his eyes stayed cold. 'Thank you for all the information, it was most helpful. I was just wondering whether you'd thought of anything else in the mean time?'

Er, like the fact your daughter is bound, trussed and stashed in a hotel room in Mexico City? And that one day I'm going to kill you?

'No. Nothing,' I said, shaking my head. 'Sorry.'

His eyes narrowed slightly. 'So, you've no idea where they might have taken her or what they want from her?'

'Sorry, no idea.'

He stared at me, slightly puzzled, obviously unused to people not giving him the answers he wanted. He stepped closer, leaning against the table by my chair. 'So, how was your time with Demos and his little friends? Enjoyable?'

My heart wasn't so much beating as gasping. Did he know?

'Obviously, I'm sure it must have been very traumatic for you.' I nodded slowly, unable to pull my eyes from his face. 'So,' he continued, 'you must see the absolute necessity of containing Demos and all the people like him before things get any more out of hand.'

He waited again for me to show some sign of agreement. I nodded once more. He smiled and then came to perch on the table right by me, his leg brushing mine. I stared at his neatly manicured hands, resting on his knee. 'Because,' he said, 'we wouldn't want anyone else in your family to get hurt now, would we?'

My eyes flew back to his face. Was that a threat? He merely raised his eyebrows and gave the tiniest of shrugs, almost imperceptible through the cut of his suit. I sat on the edge of my seat, toying with the idea of shoving him hard through the plate-glass window behind him. It would only take a flicker of a glance. But then he turned around and his question almost shoved me off my seat.

'Your father's told you all about the Unit's mission, I'm sure. Actually, you probably knew all about our mission before he did – didn't you?'

I sat speechless. What mission was he referring to? The pretend one my dad thought they were working on, to find a 'cure', or the real one, to create new weapons of mass destruction?

He smiled as if he understood my confusion. 'It's still early days,' he continued. 'We're not quite as far advanced as I'd like to be, but we're making progress. Good progress. With your father's help, we're going to crack it soon.'

It.

'We're starting to unlock the secrets behind the telepath gene.'

Oh my God. This had to be the breakthrough Jonas had mentioned. My eyes flitted round the room like a butterfly trying to settle on a piece of solid ground.

'If we can hear their thoughts then we're so much stronger. We're still trying to crack that one, but the exciting news is that, thanks to all our research, and your father's research, of course, we've had a breakthrough.'

My gaze travelled from the floor back to Richard Stirling's face.

He waited until he had my undivided attention. 'We've found a way of blocking telepaths. Isn't that something?' I stared at him blankly.

'You know,' he said. 'It's their telepaths who hear us coming. Now it'll be like pressing the mute button on a phone. They can't hear us – so they won't see us coming. It's a very handy tool for the arsenal. Soon we'll be able to read their minds too.'

It felt like my seat was tipping, as if the floor was tilting under me.

'It's amazing the research we've been doing.' He paused. 'Obviously, it helps having two telepaths to research on. Well, only one now . . . since your brother and Jack broke Alicia out.'

. . . *Mum . . . my mum* . . . I looked into his eyes. And my heart stilled in that instant. He knew. He knew that I knew about my mum. It was obvious in the smile contorting his face.

'Though for obvious reasons your father is going to have to be kept in the dark as to our guinea-pig situation. But once we get him working in our labs, it'll be no time before we've cracked the telekinetic gene code.' He stared at me unblinking. 'We just need to get our hands on one.'

I flinched back in my chair, before I could stop myself. He paused again, smiling at my reaction. 'But of course this is all for one end. As you know. To catch Demos,' another pause, 'and his people.'

And his people. Meaning me.

The table slanted to a forty-five-degree angle. No, it didn't. That was my head, sliding down my arm. It felt like I was running off a cliff face. Pure panic and a wall of terror rushing up to meet me. They knew about me. My breathing was coming in fits and starts. My lungs were screaming. I couldn't get any air into them. I flattened my hand on the tabletop, trying to steady myself as the room spun around me.

'You should get back to your father, Lila. He'll be worried.'

I looked up. Richard Stirling looked hazy, as if he was painted in watercolour. I knew it was the tears filming my eyes and tried desperately to blink them away. I gripped the table edge and stood up, suddenly unsure of how to walk. He was letting me go? Why was he letting me go?

'Oh, Lila,' he called as I reached unsteadily for the door handle. 'I'm sure you know how much we value your family's contribution to our little project.'

I gripped the handle for support.

'Your cooperation is something I personally am very grateful for. I understand it must be hard for you. But I know you want Jack to get the best care imaginable and I know it must be a relief having your father nearby.' Another pause while he waited for me to give some sign that I had understood his true meaning. 'And the protection we can offer you and your father is second to none. We wouldn't want what happened to your mother to happen to any of you, now would we?'

I stood there as still as if Demos was in the room freezing me and watched as Richard Stirling strolled towards me.

'No one can reach you now,' he said softly. 'You're entirely safe. So you shouldn't worry. This will all soon be over.'

So that was why he was letting me go. It was with a warning. If I did anything stupid, he'd hurt Jack and my dad as well as me.

Something was going to break. The door, his neck, my grip on sanity and my even slenderer grip on my ability. If I stayed one more second, I wouldn't be able to stop myself. I could feel my control slipping. I had to get out of here.

169

'Lila, it's been a pleasure,' he said, putting his hand over mine, sending shudders up my arm. He opened the door. 'Let's do this again sometime. I'd like to get to know you better.'

And with that he shut the door on me.

27

My dad was sitting by Jack's bed. He looked up when I stumbled through the door.

'God, what's happened? Are you OK?' he said, jumping up from his chair and crossing the room towards me at a half-run. I fell into his arms.

'Lila, Lila, what's the matter?' he asked, trying to pull me away from him so he could look at me. I wouldn't be budged. He gave up and just held me. I scrunched my face into his shirt and breathed until my chest stopped heaving. What was the matter?

Richard Stirling knows everything. He knows what I am. He knows. My lungs felt like they were filling up with acid. It hurt so much to breathe.

After a minute or so my dad pried me slightly off him. 'What's going on?'

I stared at him – at his eyes a muddy green colour, his high forehead scourged deep with frown lines. His hands were still resting on my shoulders. I contemplated them. He still wore his wedding ring, a bruised gold reminder to the both of us.

'Nothing,' I said, pulling away from him harshly. *Nothing I can tell you.*

I moved to Jack's side and studied his blank face. Why couldn't I be the one drifting on the edge of consciousness, happily oblivious, while everyone else had to find a way of dealing with the situation?

'Won't you talk to me, Lila?'

I glanced up at my dad, his face fraught.

I took a deep breath. 'Can you make someone telepathic? Are you helping them do that?'

My dad took a step backwards like I'd slapped him. 'What on earth? No – that's absurd. Why would you think that?'

'Er – because Richard Stirling just told me about your little breakthrough.'

'What breakthrough?'

'That you can block telepaths.'

'Oh, that.'

'Yes, that.'

'That's so we can stop them, Lila,' my dad said, shaking his head in bewilderment. 'So we can catch them. We can't stop them unless we catch them. But we haven't made anyone telepathic. That's not what Stirling Enterprises is doing.' He laughed. 'It's not even possible.'

My head had been bowed, but I looked up now, stunned, hope bursting inside me. 'It's not?'

'Well, I suppose theoretically it is possible.'

My heart sank back to where it had been, somewhere at the bottom of my chest. My dad kept talking, oblivious to my expression. 'You'd just have to reverse the logic of what I've been working on. But why would they want to do that anyway? We're trying to find a cure, Lila. So that we can stop them before anyone else gets hurt.'

All my dad was doing was speeding the process to our elimination – and his own. Because once he'd given them everything they needed, it would be goodbye, Dr Loveday. And goodbye to Jack and me – but not before they'd done whatever testing on me they'd done to Thomas and were currently doing to my mum. The only reason Richard Stirling hadn't taken me already and started experimenting on me was because he needed my dad. I looked over at him now, staring at me in confusion, and sighed. Why couldn't he have found a cure for cancer, for God's sake?

Richard Stirling was as good as his word. When we left the hospital, there were two cars waiting for us at the kerb. Our protection had been doubled. He was doing his best to hammer home the message that there was no point running and no point fighting, just in case his barefaced warnings hadn't done the job. That's what the eight men in their mirrored sunglasses were supposed to be spelling out to me. But the only miscalculation he'd made was that I never, ever reacted well to being told what to do.

My dad seemed slightly puzzled by the increase in the security detail numbers as they ushered us into a third car which drove off sandwiched between two others. Jonas was in the passenger seat of our car and I caught him glancing over his shoulder at me. I turned away and stared out of the window, refusing to meet his eye.

'Why the extra car today?' my dad asked the guy driving.

'Nothing to worry about, Dr Loveday,' he answered. 'We just wanted you to know how seriously we take your security. And your daughter's.' My head jerked in his direction. He was staring at me in the rear-view mirror, his eyes shielded by the alien gleam of his mirrored shades. I gripped the door handle tighter. Did he know about me being a psy? Did they all know? Surely if Richard

Stirling did then all the people working for the Unit would know? My breathing escalated at the thought.

'I see,' my dad muttered. He peered nervously over his shoulder as though expecting to see Demos leaping out of the bushes at the side of the road. I clenched my teeth together and pressed my forehead against the cool glass, watching the white stripes of the road slip by.

When we pulled up outside Jack's house, Jonas was immediately out of the car, opening my door for me. 'Don't forget to set the alarm,' he said to me as I got out. 'Oh, and by the way, we've got men out the back too. Covering the lanes either side and the road behind.'

I glared at him – was this another thinly veiled threat? But he seemed genuinely confused by the death stare I was giving him. I hurried up the path to the house, pausing only once to glance back at Jonas sitting in the car. He was still looking at me, chewing his lip. His face lit up as soon as he saw me looking his way. I stumbled. He couldn't know, I realised. If Jonas knew who I was – what I was – there was no way he'd be acting this way – asking me on dates, opening car doors. He was far too transparent. And if he didn't know, that meant the others probably didn't either. At least I hoped not.

Once inside the house, I deliberately ignored setting the alarm and walked into the living room instead. I peered out of the window. The Unit's cars had parked one behind the other forming a metal barricade in front of the house. I drew the curtains on them and crossed to the bookshelf. My eyes were drawn immediately to the picture of my mum. Always, when I saw her picture, I felt like a plunger had been placed over my chest and was trying to suck my heart out through the gaps between my ribs.

I glanced at the photograph next to it, of Jack, Alex and me as children, taken one summer at the lake – smiling, oblivious to anything like this future. I traced Jack's face with my fingertips. The picture had been taken the summer I'd tried to swim across the lake after them and had nearly drowned. Between them Jack and Alex had managed to get me to shore. I felt the surge of frustration that I always got when Jack beat me at something or did something better than me, but this time it transmuted into another type of emotion – defiance.

You think I'm just a girl and that I can't keep up with you and Alex? I thought as I stared at Jack's face. *I am so going to show you.* Then my fingers moved to hover over a thirteen-year-old Alex, hair slicked wet and eyes shining blue. He was grinning widely at the camera, and squinting against the sun. He had one arm thrown round my skinny eight-year-old shoulders, the other round Jack's neck. I wasn't looking at the camera – I was looking up at Alex with what could only be described as a look of awe on my face. The kind of expression normally reserved for saints in medieval paintings as they stared up at the face of God. Embarrassing.

I crossed back to the window and looked out. The men in the car nearest caught the movement of the curtain and turned robotically to stare at me. I stared back for a few seconds before letting the curtain fall.

Richard Stirling's threats still echoed in my head. That man had torn my family apart and now he was threatening to do worse. Except – I took a deep breath – this time I wasn't going to let him. I'd had enough of being on the run – of being hunted. And I'd really had enough of hiding who I was. I was done with being the victim, the little kid, the one who always needed rescuing. There

175

was an anger burning in me which Richard Stirling had just fanned to inferno-sized proportions. But it wasn't the hot anger I was used to, the kind of anger that blinded and was hard to control, the kind that made cookies spin across a table, T-shirts ruck up and buoys zip out to sea. No. This was nitrogen-cold. It was as focused and intent as a gun trained on a target.

Richard Stirling might see just a seventeen-year-old girl standing in front of him, too scared to fight back, too panicked and afraid to do anything but submit. But that was where he was wrong. Richard Stirling was going to need the whole damn United States army guarding him if he was planning on stopping me from kicking his butt. Well and truly. And I wasn't even going to extend him the courtesy of a threat first. I was just going to do it.

I ran upstairs and stood in front of the mirror in my room. The eyes that stared back at me were sea-green; my face was lightly tanned from the sun in Mexico, a flash of colour across the bridge of my nose and forehead. I looked like me still, only not quite. There was something different that I couldn't at first put my finger on. Not older exactly. Not tired, nor wired. Not the shorter hair. Just *different*. Maybe it was the tilt of my chin reminding me of the way Jack looked when he wasn't ready to give up an argument. I stepped closer to the glass, holding my own gaze steady. That was it. There. My eyes. The expression in them. Before they'd been feverish, manic as wind-chopped waves. Now they were still. Completely clear and still like the ocean just before the tide changes.

Half an hour ago I'd been in pieces, but now I was together, completely together. And it felt good. The fear had gone. The yo-yoing of my insides had gone. The thoughts that had been backpedalling like ants in jam were running free. It was about time I started being who I was. I rolled back my shoulders and took a deep breath. It was time I started practising.

I sat down on the bed and visualised the radio sitting on the windowsill in the kitchen, then I twisted the volume button. Pounding drum and bass music started shaking the house. I heard my dad's feet stamping into the kitchen and then the radio fell silent. I smiled to myself, feeling the buzz of excitement start to bubble in my gut. I cast a glance round the bedroom, wondering what else I could practise on. I thought of the shower. Instantly the sound of water splashing into the bath echoed down the hallway.

'Lila?' my dad called up the stairs.

'Yeah, I'm just going to have a shower,' I called back, my heart pounding.

I walked into the bathroom and shut the door with my eyes closed. It felt good to start using my power again – to practise – sort of a release. And I realised with a start that I was getting good. Really good. And controlling it was getting easier too. The meeting with Richard Stirling had been the litmus test. If I could get through that without impaling him under a table leg then I felt pretty confident of my ability to keep control in any situation. No more near eyeball-kebabing unless the situation absolutely demanded it.

I sat on the side of the bath, a fine drizzle from the shower settling on my hair. I felt like I could imagine the ocean, a quarter of a mile away, thumping into the struts of the pier and I could force it to punch through the wooden planks. I didn't need to see things anymore. I just had to think an abstract thought with enough intent and it would be done.

I shook my head. I was being stupid. That was ridiculous. I

knew I could move objects – tanks even. And I had kind of mastered moving people – though I hadn't had much chance to practise other than with Alex and a fat Mexican Mafioso – but now I was suddenly thinking I could manipulate nature. *As if.*

But then again, maybe, just maybe, I could.

I turned away from the shower and walked to the end of the bathroom. I thought about the shower spray hitting the ceiling. The hiss of the water on enamel stopped, became a slap and slosh instead. I turned slowly. The shower head was pointing at the plughole and the water was coming out of it, but instead of falling down towards the plughole, the way water normally does, it was erupting upwards like a geyser towards the ceiling and then water-falling back down towards the bath.

I closed my eyes and opened them once more. The water was defying gravity. The laws of physics . . . I was bending them. Take that, Newton.

With another trace of a thought, the spray of water changed direction, firing towards the window like a car-wash jet. I dodged out of its path and it parted round me, curving round my arms and bouncing back into the bath. I glanced at the tap and it turned off, then I sank to the floor, my knees soaking in the puddles left behind.

Holy crap.

In a good way. Holy. Crap.

28

Dr Roberts was standing by the nurses' station when I walked onto the intensive care ward. He was chatting away with the same nurse that I'd seen in the canteen and from the way she kept touching his shoulder and giggling I could tell she wanted to touch a whole lot more of the good doctor. She frowned at me in irritation when I appeared at his side.

'Hi,' I said.

'Hi,' Dr Roberts replied. 'You're here late. It's outside visiting hours.'

I knew that. It was past midnight. I'd had one of the cars parked outside the house drive me back to the base. I had needed to see Jack.

'Can I just pop in and see him?' I pleaded with a smile.

The doctor nodded, smiling back. 'Sure, just not for long. Fifteen minutes, OK?'

'OK,' I said, already hurrying down the corridor.

I glared at the guard standing like a pillar in front of Jack's room until he moved out of my way. I opened the door, stepped inside, shut the door behind me and then froze.

The bed was empty. I stared at the rumpled sheet and the loosely dangling IV, dripping its viscous saline solution onto the floor. I registered that the hum and hiss of the respirator had stopped. The machine to the left of the bed was flatlining in silence. I turned round slowly, breathing haltingly, my knees shaking. The room was empty. They'd taken him. *They had taken him.* I felt my knees give way. But then something else registered. Why were they still guarding the door if they'd taken him?

I heard the handle to the bathroom being turned and spun round, hurling the vase from the table towards the door just as it flew open. I started, only just managing to catch the vase before it smashed down onto Jack's head. He ducked anyway, and looked up at the floating crystal shape filled with blooms and then over to me. He raised an eyebrow as if to say *are you trying to kill me?*

I stared at him. He was standing upright, unaided, in his boxer shorts, looking like he'd just spent ten days in a spa, not in a coma. How was that possible? The doctor had mentioned paralysis, wheelchairs, physio, and here he was walking around as if he was warming up for a marathon. My gaze fell to his chest, to the place where he'd been shot.

There was no gauze. No wound. Nothing. Just clean, bare, unblemished skin.

I lost my grip. The vase shot towards the floor. Jack reacted before I could blink, diving to catch it before it crashed into a million shards. He straightened up, throwing me a glare, and nodding his head at the door and the hulking shadow looming behind it.

I didn't follow his gaze. I couldn't tear my eyes away from his chest. From the place where there should have been a great big hole, or at the very least the bloody, puckered remains of a scar, and instead all there was to see was perfect eggshell skin.

I found my voice. 'What the—'

Before I could say *hell*, Jack lifted a finger to his lips, returning me to my stunned silence. 'Bugs,' he mouthed. 'Guard.' He put the vase back on the windowsill.

'You were shot!' I mouthed back, enunciating each word into a silent vacuum. 'Jack. You were shot. Where's the hole?' I pointed to his stomach for further emphasis, drawing a circle in the air to indicate a giant hole. I had seen the bullet hit him, had heard it smack into him. I had seen with my own eyes the blood gushing out and Jack falling to his knees in the dirt. I had not imagined it. So, where in hell's name was the bullet hole?

Jack bent his head to look and placed his hands over his stomach at the point the bullet had gone in. Then he looked back up at me and shook his head. He looked as confused as I was. He reached out and took hold of my hand and pulled me into the bathroom, closing the door behind us. He turned both taps on full. I had already disposed of the bug that had reappeared in my jeans – wedging it down the back of the seat in one of the Unit's cars. Hopefully, they would think it had just fallen out. I sat down on the edge of the toilet seat. Jack knelt in front of me.

'What the hell is going on?' he said.

'I was going to ask you that same question. You were shot. How are you walking around?' I couldn't take my eyes off his stomach.

'What are you doing here? Where's Alex?' Jack asked. 'I thought you guys made it out of there?'

'We did. We came back. Alex is nearby. He couldn't come back onto the base. The Unit are after him. You guys are in trouble.'

Jack scowled at the ground then his eyes flew back to me. 'How long have I been unconscious?'

'About two weeks.'

He frowned once more, his hands moving to his stomach. 'Just two weeks?' he asked in amazement. Then he seemed to register

181

something. 'Why'd you come back?' he demanded. His tone was accusatory and I felt my temper flare in response.

'For you, you idiot. And for Mum.'

Jack's eyes darkened. 'Alex should have got you away from here. What was he doing bringing you back?'

'Excuse me for having free will! It's not up to Alex. Or you. It was my decision to come back. The others are coming too.'

'The others?'

'Yes, the others – Demos and the others. We all came back to rescue you and Mum.'

I noted the familiar grinding of his jaw, though I couldn't tell whether it was the memory of Mum or Demos's name causing it. He hadn't exactly had long to process the news about Mum or about Demos before he was lying in the dirt with a bullet in his gut.

'The others are in Washington,' I said. 'We have a plan. It's complicated and I don't have time to explain. The doctor's coming to check on you in ten minutes . . .' My gaze dropped to his chest again. I reached a finger and prodded him where the bullet had gone in. 'This is weird.'

'Coming from you . . .' He looked at me, arching his eyebrows.

Oh my God. My jaw unhinged itself. What was he saying? My mind had automatically been looking for a medical reason for the lack of scar or paralysis – a wonder cure or miracle drug, stitches that were invisible, some skin grown in a Petri dish that they'd grafted over the hole. But what if it was, in fact, none of the above? What if Jack had an ability too? What if he could heal himself?

My eyes flew to his hand, the hand he'd used to punch a tree. It too showed no signs of bruising. His knuckles had been as swollen as balloons just two weeks ago and now they looked totally normal, not a scratch on them.

No. No way. As if. Jack – one of us? A psy? It wasn't possible. It would be the most ironic joke the universe had ever played.

Why no way, though? I'd seen stranger things. I'd witnessed people astrally projecting to the other side of the world while their bodies flopped in front of me. I'd seen church-going, Oprah-worshipping ladies removing memories from drug lords, and I'd suffered a tiny Japanese girl spying on my most intimate, graphic thoughts. For crying out loud, I had personally made water fly against the laws of gravity. Why was I, of all people, having an issue over the reality of my brother being able to heal himself?

Maybe it was because this was the same person who had spent five years trying to hunt people like us down, the guy who had been so mad when he found out what I could do that Alex had had to form a human barricade between us so he didn't kill me. The person who'd used a pine tree as a punchbag to take out his frustration. I didn't see him punching any trees now, though. On the contrary, he looked as though he'd won the lottery and the size of the cheque was just starting to sink in.

Jack stood up, leaving me staring at him like a sea bass from the toilet seat. 'OK, let's get out of here.' He reached out a hand to grab me.

'No!' I yelled, throwing his arm backwards with a glance. I basked in the surprise that lit his face. 'You can't go!' I blurted. 'We have to wait. The Unit's guarding you. And they know all about me. Richard Stirling threatened me. And Dad. We can't go without Dad.'

'Dad?'

'Yes, Dad.'

'What are you talking about?

'Dad. He's here. He's working for them. I told you all this.'

'Unless it escaped your attention, I've been in a coma, Lila.'

I flushed the loo again with a blink of my eyes so the water gurgle would cover Jack's shouting. 'Dad's been here the whole time. He came as soon as he heard something had happened to you.'

Jack hung his head. 'I heard him talking to me. I just thought . . . I thought I was dreaming.'

'No, not dreaming. It was real. He's working for them . . .' I paused, trying to look innocent. 'Did you have any other dreams?'

Jack was staring at the floor, but now he glared up at me through his lashes. That was a scowl. Definitely a scowl.

'Oh yeah,' he said. That was anger. Definitely anger.

'When I'm done sorting out the Unit, Alex and I are going to have a little chat.'

'Over my dead body.'

'I'm thinking more over his dead body.' He glowered at me some more then held up a hand to stop me in my tracks. I thought about making him slap himself. It wasn't like it would cause any damage. Tempting.

'Look, hold up,' Jack whispered. 'Did you just say Dad's working for the Unit? What are you talking about?' He took hold of my shoulders.

'It's not what you think, Jack. Dad's been trying to find a way of stopping Demos this whole time. He doesn't know about Mum being alive. He has no idea what the Unit are really doing.'

His eyes popped. 'Well, why the hell didn't you tell him? How could you let him work for them?'

'Because Alex said he could be an asset. He thought it would give us a way into the headquarters.'

Jack ran a hand through his hair and started pacing the tiny bathroom. 'OK, we can discuss this later,' he finally said, turning to me. 'Let's just get out of here first.'

I jumped in front of the door, barring it with my body. 'We can't just waltz out of here,' I said, frustration mounting on top of my irritation. 'We'll never get off the base – half the Unit are waiting for me outside. With guns. We'll get caught and then what?' Jack looked like he was about to open his mouth and argue back. 'It's OK,' I hurried on, 'I'm meeting Alex in a few hours and he'll have figured something out. A plan. He said he was working on a plan. We need to trust him.'

Jack narrowed his eyes at me while simultaneously cocking an eyebrow. He shook his head finally. 'I don't like this. I don't want to wait till the morning for Alex to come up with a plan. I say we leave now, you get off the base and I'll head straight to the Unit and break Mum out.'

I rolled my eyes at him. 'For one – you're not doing anything without me. And for two – are you insane? You and whose army? You think you can just walk right in there and they'll hand her over? You – we – can't go now. Besides, you'll set off the alarm. If we wait for Demos and the others then we're more evenly matched. And those guys are in Washington right now. Demos is setting something up there with Stirling Enterprises. It all needs to coincide or it won't work.'

'What won't work? What's Demos setting up in Washington? What are you talking about?'

A Mexican drug lord, I thought, *millions of dollars of stolen cocaine and drug money. A big-time set-up operation. You know, that sort of thing.*

'I don't have time to go into it,' I gabbled. 'You need to get back into bed and fake like you're still asleep or something.'

185

'I don't like this plan,' Jack muttered, squaring his shoulders.

'Well, tough,' I said. 'You've been sleeping. I've been having to work things out. I'll come back first thing in the morning. I promise.'

'What about Sara?' Jack interrupted. 'Where is she?'

I got ready to restrain Jack, dropping my gaze to his hands. 'I don't know if we can trust her.'

'What are you talking about?' Jack's eyes flared wildly. 'Of course we can trust her. Why haven't you told her already? She'll help us.'

'No, Jack! You can't go telling her anything. We don't know if she's part of this or not. She might be . . . she interrogated me when I got back. She acts like she doesn't know, but how can she not?'

'Are you crazy? I worked for the Unit and I had no clue. This is Sara we're talking about.' He tried to grab the door handle. 'I've got to see her.'

'No, Jack.' I dodged sideways, blocking him, locking the door with a silent click. 'It's just too dangerous.'

'What?'

'Don't say anything to Sara. Promise me.'

He scowled some more at me, his mouth twisting into a grimace. But he didn't argue, which was the closest Jack ever came to acquiescing.

'Look, I'll tell you everything tomorrow,' I said. 'Just right now get back into bed. Please. Before the doctor comes around. You have to fake it. If he sees you, he'll freak.'

'You think it is me, then? That I did this?' Jack asked, his eyes huge, his hand stroking his stomach like it was a newborn baby. He looked up at me suddenly. 'Do you think I really am like you?'

I raised an eyebrow. What other explanation was there?

'I mean,' Jack went on, shaking his head, 'it's weird. I can sort of feel it happening . . . inside . . . but it's just crazy. I mean . . . how? I wasn't like this before.'

I shot him a death stare. Not two weeks ago he'd thought that people like me were sociopathic nutjobs who needed to be contained, but now *he* could do something cool it was a totally different story. It made me want to scream.

'It's genetic,' I said. 'You knew that. It can be triggered by traumatic events, I think. Look, I'll explain later.' I unlocked the door. Yeah, I'd explain all about that, and about Mum too. Happy mutant families.

'Listen,' I said, 'whatever you do, don't let them take you to prisoner holding. The doctor said the Unit wanted to transfer you, but if they take you there then they'll find out about you and they'll probably start cutting you open to find out what exactly you can heal from.'

Jack started to frown as the reality of the situation dawned.

'You need to pretend like you're dying – make your stats keep bouncing. The doctor said if they kept spiking, he'd have to keep you here. Can you manage that? Do some sit-ups or something when no one's looking. And whatever you do, don't talk to Sara. I mean it. Not until we know for sure we can trust her.'

He opened the door and took a step towards the bed, then he turned and darted back towards me. In silence he grabbed me into a bear hug, then he dropped me just as suddenly and dived onto the bed.

The door to the corridor started to open. I glanced back at the bed and the sheet pulled itself over Jack's inert body and the IV reattached itself to the plaster on his arm. The pads and wires suckered back onto his chest in a polka-dot formation that didn't alter the flatline read-out one bit.

187

'How's things going in here? All quiet?' Dr Roberts asked, closing the door behind him.

'Mmmm, all quiet. Nothing to report,' I said. 'I don't think he's waking up any time soon.'

The doctor smiled at me and walked over to the bed. He paused a second, staring at the horizontal line on the monitor and then at the randomly suckered wires.

'Why are his wires all over the place?' he asked, looking at me. 'Have you moved them?'

I chewed the inside of my cheek. 'Um, I was just trying to figure out how they worked.'

'Want to be a doctor one day, huh?' he said, unsuckering them one by one and placing them in the right positions. The machine started up its rhythmic beat.

'Er, yeah, maybe. I'm not very good at science, though. And besides,' I said, looking at Jack's faking-it coma face, 'I think Jack's the healer in the family.'

Dr Roberts looked up at me and smiled, but then the smile faded away. 'Lila, someone from the Unit just called.' He paused. 'They're moving Jack tomorrow.'

My own smile died on my lips. 'But you said if his stats kept bouncing, he'd be kept here – and they have – his stats have been bouncing – they've been bouncing a lot. See!' I pointed at the read-out jumping all over the place. 'They're bouncing like crazy.'

Dr Roberts shook his head. 'I know. I'm sorry. I managed to keep him here as long as I could. They were going to transfer him tonight and I stopped them, but they're moving him first thing tomorrow. There's nothing more I can do.'

I glanced at Jack. He wasn't faking it so well anymore. His

forehead was creasing, his lips pursing, the heart-rate monitor was spiking like a mountain range.

'He's not awake, though,' I cried.

The doctor pursed his lips and took a deep breath. 'They don't care. They say they have the medical equipment to be able to take care of him now. I really don't understand why they want him so badly – but they do.'

Sure they did. And they were going to want him a whole lot more when they found out what he could do.

'Are you coming? Visiting time's over.'

I stared at the doctor who was holding the door open. Then I looked frantically back at Jack. I bent down, took his hand and whispered in his ear.

'I'll be back in the morning. I promise.'

29

Unsurprisingly I didn't sleep. Instead I sat on the edge of my bed in the dark trying to put my thoughts in some sort of order. It wasn't like they could be catalogued and filed, though. My mind was cartwheeling from one thing to the next like it was performing an Olympic floor routine. I kept thinking back to Jack. How was it possible? How could he heal himself? And why had it suddenly appeared out of nowhere? Maybe the shooting had triggered it. It was a possibility. Wasn't it trauma that triggered whatever the hell kind of gene we both had?

I really wanted to start experimenting – see if I could find out what kinds of injury Jack could sustain and still heal from. A bullet was pretty hardcore. What about an axe? Did he feel pain too? My head jerked up . . . could he die? Another unsettling thought followed swiftly behind – was his power better than mine? No way. It was so unfair. For the first time in my life I had been better than him at something.

I pulled myself together. He might be able to heal himself, but I could control nature. Or at least water . . . Or at least I thought I could. I hadn't had any further chances to experiment since flooding the bathroom.

I sat up and pulled my knees to my chest, wondering what Key would have told Alex by now. Key wouldn't have seen my meeting with Richard Stirling as it was inside the headquarters, but he would have been at the hospital and seen Jack was up and about so he would also know about Jack's new-found ability and about the Unit moving him in the morning.

And Alex would definitely agree that we couldn't let the Unit take him now. So, we'd have to change the plan and rescue him from the hospital instead, and then go back for my mum and to kick Richard Stirling's ass later. Whatever Alex had been planning, whatever he'd said before about split resources, the circumstances had changed, so the plan needed to change too. And Alex would figure something out. I didn't need to worry. I'd meet him in a few hours and we'd make our move then. The Unit wouldn't know what hit them. Hopefully Demos and the others would also be back by then.

But where did that leave my dad? I mulled it over. I couldn't leave my dad behind. But then, I pulled at the cover on the bed, bunching it between my fists, what about my mum? How was it possible to rescue her and Jack and my dad simultaneously from three different places – when they were all under guard?

Oh God, I needed Alex's help. I wasn't known for my tactical planning. I was more of a rash, impulsive, just do it and worry about it later kind of girl. That's why I was here in the first place, wasn't it? Almost stabbing someone in the eye? Impulsive. Stealing my dad's credit card and jumping on a flight to California. Also impulsive.

I'd promised Alex I wouldn't do anything else reckless – but what was the alternative: stand aside and let them take Jack and cut him into little pieces to see if he'd grow back?

I looked up at the ceiling, hoping to God that Key was up there and not taking a pee or rest break. 'If you're there,' I mouthed, 'please tell Alex to figure something out. And fast.'

I lay on the bed staring at the alarm clock on the bedside table. When it flashed 5.51 a.m., I got out of bed. There was a pile of clothes hidden under the bed. A pair of Jack's old shorts and a T-shirt, pilfered from the closet in his room and washed twice. I pulled them on and then sat on the edge of the bed to put on my running shoes. I looked again at the clock on the bedside table.

5.57 a.m.

I got up from the bed and crept to the door, easing it open and then tiptoeing across the landing in the semi-darkness. I bent and slipped a piece of paper under my dad's door. His alarm was set for 6.15 a.m. The note told him to meet me at the hospital by 7 a.m. I'd underlined URGENT three times.

Down the stairs, jumping the creaking one, landing in the hallway by the front door. I paused. Timing was crucial. At 6 a.m. the Unit did a changeover. I needed to head out just before the new cars arrived, when the men who'd overnighted at the house were tired and waiting for relief, and at the moment that would cause the most confusion. Alex had run over the plan with me at least a dozen times when we'd met on the pier.

I opened the door, glancing back up the stairs to where my dad was still sound asleep. I stepped onto the veranda, pulling the door closed behind me, and then bounced down the steps and started stretching, waving to the men in the cars guarding the house. It couldn't look like I was about to give them the slip. As far as they were to know, I was just going for an early-morning run. I noticed the two men in the back of the first car were asleep, faces pressed like lumps of Play-Doh splatted against the windows.

The guy at the wheel swore when he saw me. He poked the guy next to him in the ribs and I watched him rub the blur from his eyes and then confer, looking over his shoulder, obviously trying to evaluate whether to pass it onto the relief cars which hadn't yet appeared or to the car behind them whose occupants were clearly doing exactly the same calculations. Before they could make up their minds I bounded into a sprint, making it to the street corner before I heard the sound of an engine turning over and the black shape of the SUV pulled alongside me. I didn't pay it any mind. This was what we'd anticipated. Alex had been quite right. The timing was perfect.

Once I hit Main Street, my heart was slamming into my ribcage as my feet pounded the sidewalk. Did the Unit soldiers know about me? Had Richard Stirling told them? This could all go horribly wrong if they did. But just then Jonas's face flashed into my mind. He had no idea what I was – I was certain of that. I had to take the risk that the others didn't either. There was no other choice.

I scanned the road ahead. There was more traffic, but it was still early and I needed there to be a few more cars on the road, bigger cars, or it wouldn't work. I slowed my pace a fraction, sighting the red light a hundred metres ahead. I pulled up by a lamp post and started to stretch my calf muscles, peering over my shoulder. The Unit pulled up beside me and the driver wound down his window to glare at me. He'd been on shift for twelve hours and looked like he needed to be heading to bed and not kerb-crawling a dawn jogger. I smiled sweetly at him and started running just as he opened his mouth to say something.

The light turned green up ahead. A truck appeared on the horizon. I cast a quick glance over my shoulder again, checking the SUV was still right on my tail, and then, with my eyes on the oncoming traffic, I stepped right out in front of the Unit's car. The driver slammed on his brakes and I darted to the other side of the road where the lights of the Seven-Eleven beckoned.

Once my foot hit the sidewalk, I swung my eyes to the truck heading towards us and forced it to fishtail across the road. It was heavier than the Humvee, but to me it was easier than pushing a piece of paper across a table with my fingertip.

The back end of the truck swung across both lanes of traffic, right into the path of the Unit's car. I saw the driver from the Unit frantically trying to ram the car into reverse to avoid the oncoming smash and I let him reverse a few metres, scared that the smash would be too big when it came and that someone might get hurt, but once it had cleared a few metres, I held it in a lock. The wheels spun, grinding up the asphalt. I didn't wait for the impact. I turned on my heel and sprinted towards the Seven-Eleven, making it inside just as the sound of metal slicing into metal tore through the air.

I ran down the row of canned goods and noodles, past the place Key had first accosted me – which felt like a year ago already – past the fridges blowing condensed cool air, towards the fire exit looming large at the back and that's when I fell.

The pain was so intense I curled immediately onto my side and tried to wrap my arms round my skull to stop the bone from shattering into a million pieces. I wondered where the axe had come from and who was swinging it at my head. Except it wasn't an axe. I knew what it was. I'd felt it before, only never like this – never this badly. All I could compute was that they knew.

They knew. They knew. How stupid had I been to think that Richard Stirling wouldn't have warned them? Of course they knew!

I tried to roll onto my haunches, dimly aware that there was a man shouting somewhere in the distance or maybe he was yelling right by my ear. But I couldn't understand whatever he was screaming. Was he one of the Unit? I had to stand but I couldn't find the floor. Or my feet. The room was a shrieking, spinning cage. I sobbed and choked, realising I was on my knees, with my head resting on the ground. I needed to get out of here. I needed to get to Alex. With an unsteady arm, I reached out and found something solid to lean on, a shelf maybe. But then the shelf tipped or the room tipped and I tipped with it and I lay there amongst the fallen packets of noodles, feeling the tears slide down my cheeks.

Then I was lifted up. My arms flopped over somebody's back, my head banged against something hard and I groaned. *Put me down. Let me go.* But the words didn't make it past my lips. *Please.* Something bashed my leg and then I was held upside down. No, I was upright. No. I couldn't tell any longer which way up I was.

'Lila, Lila . . .' I tried to raise my head.

'Lila, can you sit? You need to hold on. Can you hold on?'

I opened one eye. It was Alex. He was yelling at me. I frowned, wincing at the pain that shot through my head.

'. . . hold on . . .'

What was he saying? He grabbed both my arms then and hauled me like a sack of potatoes onto something, something unsteady, and I wobbled and wanted to fall to the floor. But he wasn't letting me. He was tugging me upright and he wouldn't let go of my wrists. He had his back to me and I rested my head between his shoulder blades. Then the drilling in my skull was joined by a throbbing sensation that made my whole body vibrate violently.

My head lolled to one side and it was just too much effort to lift it back up so I let it hang there, feeling the lure of the horizontal and the screaming pull of the muscles in my arms and shoulders. Alex was shouting still and I tasted salt and I didn't know why, and then the drilling stopped and the pain receded slowly.

I raised my head from its painful back bend position and felt wind pummel me. The sob that had been crushed in my windpipe burst free and I pushed my face forward into Alex's back to stifle it. I shifted my balance on the bike, squeezing Alex even tighter than he was gripping me.

'Are you OK?' The words whipped away in the wind as he said them. I nodded against his back, hoping he could feel it. Speaking was out of the question.

At some point he slowed the bike to a stop and the noise of the air juddering in my ears faded. My head felt hangover heavy as though I was trying to balance a cannonball on top of a blade of grass.

I let Alex put one hand round my back and one underneath me and lift me, and I curled into him, pulling my head under his chin. But the blunt stick of a memory was starting to poke at my bruised brain. I tried to ignore it. It felt good here folded against Alex, hearing his pulse under my ear, loud and steady.

We were walking on wood. And I could hear the slap of water beneath us. The pier again? I twisted my head to see and cracked open an eye. We were on a jetty, not the pier. There were rows and rows of boats – sailing boats, speedboats, dinghies and one or two super yachts towering over the rest, making them seem like plastic bath toys.

What were we doing here? I needed to be somewhere.

'Key!' Alex's voice vibrated against my cheek. 'Start the engine. We need to go. Now!'

Key? Did he just say Key? I squinted into the shatteringly bright sun and saw a silhouette above us standing on the deck of an enormous boat.

'What? Why is she here? What happened?'

That was Key's voice. But what was Key doing here? Why wasn't he in Washington? Why wasn't he up in the sky floating around?

'We've got to go,' Alex said. 'The Unit know about Lila. They'll be on our tail. We've got to go now.'

What was Alex saying? We couldn't go. I needed to get somewhere. I just couldn't think where.

'What happened?' Key repeated.

'I don't know. But we need to haul ass out of here.'

No. No, no, no hauling. No ass. This wasn't right. The hospital. That was right. I needed to get to the hospital and rescue Jack. I pushed myself away from Alex's chest and threw my legs out in a jerking puppet dance in an effort to get down.

'No, no. Go back. Go back! Down!'

The roar of an engine severed all lines of communication. Alex held me tight, reining my legs in. 'Whoa, calm down. We're going, Lila. We have to go.'

He started shifting my weight so he could throw me over his shoulder and hoist me onto the boat, but I fought him, pried his arms off me with an enormous effort, forcing them apart with my mind. I slid to the jetty, banging my knees as he dropped me. Alex staggered back, rubbing his shoulder, a crease of irritation running between his eyes.

'What time is it?' I asked, looking up at him from my kneeling position, shouting to be heard over the kicking of the engine.

'It's about six twenty. Why?' he shouted. 'Come on, we have to go.' His hand was there, under my arm, pulling me up. I let him, leaning against him for support.

Six twenty? Just six twenty? What had happened to time? It seemed to be compressing and lengthening like the universe was playing yo-yo with the world. It had felt like eighty lifetimes that I'd been writhing on the ground before Alex came and hauled me out of the Seven-Eleven, and then another eighty lifetimes on the bike, but it had been less than ten minutes ago.

'I need to get back. I can't be late.' Why didn't he understand?

'What are you talking about? Late for what?' Alex was looking at me like I'd sustained a head injury. 'You can't go back. They know about you, Lila. The weapon, that thing they used to floor you – it means they must know about you – about what you are. We need to get out of here while we still can.' He reached a hand out towards me. 'Everything's changed now.'

That's when I realised Alex didn't know. He didn't know about Jack being awake or about him being a psy. He didn't know about Richard Stirling threatening me either. How could he know? Key was here, *in person*, not floating around in the ether. The realisation hit me, sent me reeling, clutching a hand to my throat as I felt it constrict – if Alex didn't know about Jack then there was no plan to rescue him. All of this had been pointless. I should have tried to break Jack out last night.

'I know they know about me, Alex,' I shouted. 'But they have Jack. They're moving him this morning to prisoner holding.'

He dropped his hand. 'What are you talking about? How do they know about you?'

I shook my head. 'I don't have time to explain. But they're moving Jack this morning and I promised I'd go back for him – that I wouldn't let them take him.'

198

Alex was trying to stay calm, but his voice was giving him away – he was losing it. 'Lila, if they know about you, there's no way you're going back there. And we talked about this. We agreed that we'd let the Unit move him. I don't see what the problem is.' He placed both my hands on the rungs and his hands on my waist and tried to get me to climb the ladder. 'We'll come back for him and your mum. When Demos gets here. We'll figure something out, I promise you.'

'No!' I twisted out from under his arms. 'There is no later. You don't understand. We can't let them take him. We have to go back now.'

'He'll be OK,' Alex said, frustration marking his words.

'No. He won't be OK,' I said, shaking my head. 'He'll be dissected.'

Alex stopped short, frowning at me. He didn't understand and I didn't have time to explain.

'I'm not waiting for Demos and the others. I'm not waiting until you come up with another plan,' I said, breathless. 'I'm going now. And I'll go by myself if I have to.'

Alex's eyes flashed with fury, his expression hardening. His look flattened me as easily as the weapon the Unit had just fired.

'I'll go with you.'

It wasn't Alex offering. I looked up. Key was leaning over the deck of the boat.

'No. No one's going anywhere,' Alex growled in answer.

'Jack's one of us now,' I blurted. 'He's like me. We can't let them take him.' It was OK me wondering about what injuries Jack could sustain, but the Unit wouldn't just wonder.

Alex was staring at me now open-mouthed. The anger had given way to confusion. 'Jack's one of you? What do you mean? He's awake? Is he OK?'

I nodded, poised on the balls of my feet ready to run, my heart jittering wildly as the adrenaline flooded my system. I noticed Key had climbed down the ladder and was standing just behind Alex. Then Alex strode towards me, grabbed my elbow and yanked me towards the boat. 'You're not going back, Lila. It's too dangerous. I won't let you.'

I didn't think. I just reacted. To an outsider it must have looked like an invisible hand had snatched Alex into the air and thrown him against the side of the boat. His shoulder smacked into the metal railing and he fell to his knees. He cried out and I took a faltering step towards him, but he threw his head up, glaring at me, and it stopped me in my tracks. Then all emotion dropped away and his face turned to stone – to blank indifference. He stood calmly and backed a few steps away, still gripping his shoulder. I felt my ribcage compressing as if someone had dropped a brick on me from a great height.

'Lila, come on, let's go,' Key mumbled. He glanced at Alex and gave a small apologetic shrug.

I paused, caught in a single moment which I knew could lead to two very different outcomes, torn between wanting to run to Alex and needing to save my brother. Knowing that if I stayed, I might lose Jack but if I went, I'd almost certainly lose Alex.

For a long moment we stared at each other, Alex's eyes burning me with their fury, and I saw myself reflected, an insubstantial shape – who turned and ran.

30

Key unlocked the back door to a black, windowless van parked at the top of the jetty.

'When did we get this?' I asked.

'Alex bought it yesterday – we were going to use it as our getaway car when the time came. Guess that time's now.'

I took a deep breath. I was really messing things up. I was ruining whatever plan Alex had set up – and what if it was the wrong thing to do? Should I wait? What if going now meant we couldn't rescue my mum? What if Alex was right and I got caught? But at least I had a chance now of rescuing Jack and that chance was something I couldn't let go of. I had promised him. If the situation was reversed, I knew that Jack would do the same for me.

Key opened the door to the van. Inside there was a wooden bench running along one side. In the centre was a steel table set onto metal tracks inlaid into the floor. On top of the table was a coffin. Two metres of varnished oak with silver handlework.

'What was the plan?' I asked, turning to Key confused.

'Private ambulance. Alex reckoned it was the only way of getting onto the base. He forged the paperwork, says I'm transporting a body.'

I stared at the coffin. How many of us could have squeezed into that?

'We've got to get you hidden,' Key said, climbing in.

'Hidden?' I asked. 'Where am I going to hide?'

Key nodded at the inside of the van. There it was. The solid oak coffin. Grinning at me.

'I'm not hiding in that thing!' I caught the yell in my throat and dropped my voice to a hiss.

'Well, our options are kinda limited right now.'

But *this* limited? There had to be another way. I scanned every bit of the van. It was bare. Other than the coffin.

'This sucks.'

'There are air holes drilled in the sides, you won't suffocate.' He hefted the lid off the coffin. Inside it was lined with crimson silk.

'No way.'

'Lila, come on, we're late. It's just a coffin. I've slept in worse places.'

I stared at him in the gloom of the van. 'Fine,' I snapped. I turned to look at the coffin. *Oh God.*

'Do you need a hand?'

'No, I'm fine,' I snapped, swinging one leg over the side. He steadied my elbow. I climbed in and lay down. The silk was synthetic. It felt cool and scratchy against the back of my legs and arms.

Oh God. Oh God. Oh God. Jack owed me big time for this.

Key's face hovered over me. 'OK, stay cool. We'll be there in ten minutes. Less,' he added when he saw the look of horror on my face.

'I'll come round and let you out then.' Key gave me one last semi-reassuring smile then slid the lid on.

I wasn't prepared for the darkness. It was solid, like I'd been embalmed in tar. Immediately I started scrabbling at the lid and the squashy sides, gasping for air. Were my eyes open or shut? It was so dark I couldn't tell. Then I felt the shudder of an engine underneath me as Key revved the engine and pulled us out of the parking lot. My breathing was so loud it was echoing off the wood ten centimetres above my lips as though it was trying to lift the lid off the coffin. I was starting to sweat. Beads of it prickled the back of my neck, soaking into the synthetic silk lining which in turn stuck to the backs of my legs. I hummed to myself and tried to imagine I was lying in bed with Alex.

It didn't work. All it did was make me wonder if I'd ever get that close to him again – whether he'd ever even talk to me again. That anger – I'd never seen him like that before about anything. I wouldn't cry. Not now. Not yet. But inside, I already knew that there was no way of coming back from this. I'd betrayed him. I'd hurt him. And worse, I'd run out on him yet again.

We slowed. I felt the swerve of the van. Was this the entrance to the base? We stopped. I could hear the muffled sound of voices. I prayed that they wouldn't open the van and look in the coffin. The back of the van opened with a clang. I heard Key's voice, louder now, but I couldn't make out what he was saying. Sweat started to trickle down my forehead. Dead people weren't supposed to sweat. I prayed even harder that they wouldn't open the coffin.

Key's voice came nearer – clearer – still. Footsteps made the coffin shake. A bang above my face as a hand slapped the lid. *Solid oak*, Key was saying.

I took a huge gulp of warm air, crossed my hands over my chest and tried to look dead, though I was sure if they opened the coffin, my heart would literally bound out my chest and smack them in the face.

Footsteps. Slamming door. Blurry voices. Indistinct cries. Engine whine. Tyres on gravel. Picking up speed. I let out a breath.

A minute or two later we slowed, then sped up again and finally stopped. I heard the engine cut out. The doors at the back opened after another second and the van rocked. A dazzling glare of light hit me, a mountain of colours making my eyes water. Air. Fresh, sweet air. I sucked it into my lungs. It tasted rich and cool and succulent. I gulped it down and heaved myself out of the coffin. Key caught me under my arms and helped me stand.

'I want to be . . . cremated . . .' I panted. 'Remember that. If anything goes wrong . . .'

'Right, you ready?' Key asked.

I nodded, took a few more deep breaths, and wiped the sweat off my face with the back of my arm.

We were parked in a bay, down a ramp, behind the hospital. Wide double doors faced us – closed and impenetrable.

'Good luck,' Key said. 'I'll be here waiting. Don't be long.' He shuffled and glanced over his shoulder.

I smiled at him. 'Thanks for this, Key. I owe you.'

'No worries,' he said, winking at me.

31

I took one glance at the double doors and they clicked open. I peeked through into the neon glare of a green tiled corridor. It was, at this early hour, empty. I slipped through and let the door fall shut behind me then started walking, my limbs feeling springy and coltish as the adrenaline and fear began to invade my body. About halfway down the corridor was a locker room. I stepped quickly inside. Rows of lockers covered two walls. I swept my eyes along them, fifty or so doors flying open in my wake with an almighty crash. I glanced over my shoulder, cringing, but the corridor remained empty. I ran to the nearest locker, ransacking it, looking for something I could use.

A nurse's uniform. Perfect. I ducked behind the door and stripped to my underwear in record time, shoving my running gear into the locker I'd stolen the nurse's outfit from. The shoes I took were white clogs, a size too big, but they'd have to do. I stood in front of the mirror and fixed the little hat to my hair with fumbling hands. I didn't look like a nurse, I looked like a stripper. How did nurses work these uniforms with dignity? I shrugged. It would have to do. I took one last thing from another locker – a doctor's white coat. Jack was going to need a disguise too.

The corridor was still empty when I poked my head back round the door. I stepped out brazenly, arms swinging, rubber-soled shoes squeaking on the lino floor. I tried to tell myself to walk like a nurse. Purposefully, like I knew where I was going. Like I was on my way to resuscitate someone. I started running then slowed myself. That was too obvious. Maybe I should pretend I was on the way to empty a bedpan. I slowed my pace to a stroll, but that felt too slow.

I did know where I was going at least. That was a bonus. I'd mapped this whole place out on my search for a vending machine. About three strides before I got to the emergency stairwell I planned to use, a man stepped out of nowhere. He was dragging a mop and bucket behind him and almost collided with me. I stepped round him and caught the question on his face as I kept on past him and rounded the corner. Damn. I couldn't use the stairs now. It was too risky. He was mopping the corridor right by them. I could hear the squelch and slop of water.

I kept walking, trying to remind myself that I could move water – I could flip a man on his backside with a glance. I was invincible. Kind of. And invisible would be better in this situation. But I'd work with what I had.

I passed the sign for the mortuary. Yellowing plastic sheeting hung in place of doors and I picked my pace up to a fast trot. It was quiet down here. Just me and the dead. And the janitor around the corner.

Once at the never-ending corridor's end, I found the elevator. It was risky taking it. The doors opened right by the nurses' station on the intensive care unit, as opposed to the stairwell which was at the far end. What if I walked into one of the nurses or Dr Roberts? That would be a difficult one to explain. There was no other way from here, though. It was either the elevator or back the way I'd come past the suspicious janitor. I pressed the button and waited for the elevator to lumber down. It was empty thankfully. I stepped inside and pressed the button for the second floor and prayed that it wouldn't stop at any of the floors in between.

No one heard my prayers. The elevator slowed and juddered to a halt on the first floor. I looked around for somewhere to hide. The doors started to open and I caught them in a moment of panic, holding them together like the pages of a book. Some fingers appeared in the gap, trying to force them open. I could feel them in my head, like they were pressing into dough, and I squeezed the doors tighter together until whoever it was pulled their hand back, cursing.

'Damn elevator,' I heard them say.

I kept my finger on the button, holding it down, and after a few seconds it obeyed and I felt the hydraulic shunt as we moved up. At the second floor I played the same trick, keeping the doors shut while I pressed my ear to them, listening for footsteps or voices on the other side. There were none, so I opened the doors a fraction and peered with one eye through the slit. I could see the back of someone's legs a few metres away to the left, by the nurses' station. Jack's room was to the right.

What was at the end of the hallway? I tried to think. There were private rooms coming off on either side and then at the far end there was a coffee vending machine. I pictured it in my head. There was a slight tug, like a fish catching on a line – and then I felt it fall. The crash rumbled through the elevator doors then the sound of footsteps followed, taking off in that direction.

I let the doors slide open and stepped out, turning right, expecting to see the guard stationed outside Jack's room, and hoping I could sweep my way past him if I kept my head down. But he wasn't standing to attention there. He was right in front of me, heading towards the commotion at the end of the hallway. I almost walked into him. He was holding his gun in both hands. It was too late to turn back towards the elevator so the only thing I could do was to keep walking and hope he didn't recognise me.

'Lila?'

I froze and glanced up. Jonas was blinking at me in open-mouthed astonishment.

'Hi!' I screeched.

'Why are you dressed as a nurse?' he asked. I noticed the gun hadn't shifted back into its normal at-ease position.

'Er . . .' That was his only question? Why wasn't he levelling his gun at my head? I waited. But he made no move to stop me – he was just staring at my hat. I could see the cogs turning.

'Well . . .' I said, trying to think. His brow was darkening now, his skin folding into stiff creases, suspicion starting to cloud his eyes. 'I thought . . . maybe . . . you'd appreciate . . . the nurse's outfit . . .' I stuttered, unable to believe the words coming out of my mouth.

Neither, it seemed, could Jonas. His eyes widened like dinner plates. 'For me?' he smiled.

'Yeah, I saw the way you were checking out the nurses and I thought maybe you'd like a visit from Nurse Lila.'

Nurse Lila? Oh God. I wanted to grab the gun and shoot myself.

Jonas's eyes lit up like a Christmas tree. He looked up and down the hallway. Then to the zip on my dress.

'Are you serious?' he asked.

Of course I'm not serious, you whacko, I thought, staring at him in disbelief. But another thought was registering simultaneously. He didn't know. I had been right all along. Jonas, for whatever reason – rank or age or just plain luck – didn't know about me.

'But how did you know I was even here?' he asked suddenly.

'Um, the men at the house told me?' I answered, feeling my gut tighten into a string of knots that I couldn't see ever coming undone. Jonas pondered this for a second and then shouldered his gun in a hurry, grabbed me by the arm and started whisking me down the hallway. We thundered past the door to Jack's room. Where was he taking me? Was he arresting me? Then he pulled me into the adjacent visitors' room.

'What are we doing in . . .' My words trailed off as I saw he had shut the door, thrown his gun onto the sofa and was walking towards me, his expression intent.

'Man, this is like the coolest thing ever,' he said, putting an arm round my waist.

I was too shocked to protest; my brain was still trying to process the fact he'd believed my line about having dressed up like a stripper for him and that he wasn't radioing for back-up. Maybe he hadn't heard about my big escape half an hour ago. That was a stroke of luck, otherwise I'd probably be on the floor by now. But actually, it looked like that's where Jonas wanted me anyway.

'What's this thing for?' He grabbed the doctor's coat out of my hand and shook it out with his free hand. My heart thudded to a stop in my chest. He surely had to work it out now. It was like a game of Cluedo – the nurse, in the hospital room, with the doctor's coat. Yet for whatever reason he couldn't seem to join up the dots.

'Doctors and nurses . . . wow,' he said, looking me up and down again, so obviously mentally undressing me that I squirmed. 'This is, like, totally . . . cool . . .'

'Er,' I said, ducking back from the hand that had come to rest on my shoulder and was stroking a damp strand of hair back from my neck. 'Won't you get in trouble? You're on duty.' I indicated the door.

'It's early. No one will notice.' His eyes were running over my dress.

I looked over his shoulder. There was a waste-paper basket in the corner. I lifted it up and brought it in a silent glide towards him until it was hovering about a metre over his head. It would need to be a huge whack to knock him out and I wasn't sure it was heavy enough. His skull was obviously pretty thick.

Before I could try it, though, Jonas's arms came out of nowhere, wrapping round my waist like an octopus, pulling me into him. He was strong. Way stronger than I was expecting. And the shock of his touch in comparison to Alex's gave me a jolt. He took the jolt as acquiescence because before I could think another thought his lips were on mine, warm, pepperminty, alien, his tongue trying to force itself into my mouth.

The basket made a thunking sound when it made contact. Jonas reeled and staggered, his arms loosened and I stepped backwards ready to slam him into the wall. But I didn't have to. Jack had appeared out of nowhere and was standing right in front of me. He took Jonas by the scruff of his neck and hauled him upright. He waited until Jonas was steady and then pulled his fist back. I winced in anticipation.

'That's my sister you're mauling there,' Jack shouted. 'Don't – Ever – Touch – My – Sister!' Then his fist made contact with Jonas's temple. The blizzard of confusion on Jonas's face turned to wonder and then his eyes rolled back in his head and he crumpled to the floor at Jack's feet.

'I thought you were coming to rescue *me*?' Jack said, flexing his fingers and rounding on me.

'I am,' I snapped. 'I had it totally under control.'

'Yeah, looked like it.'

I glared at him. 'Come on, let's get out of here. Put this on.' I threw the doctor's coat at him.

'What about clothes? Did you not bring any clothes?' he asked. He was wearing some green scrub trousers he must have stolen from somewhere, but otherwise he was bare-chested and barefoot.

'Things didn't exactly go to plan,' I shrugged.

'What happened?' he asked, pulling the coat on over his bare chest and bending to pick up the gun that Jonas had discarded on the sofa.

'I'll explain later. We have to go,' I said, yanking open the door. 'Oh, wait!' I closed the door again and turned round, bending to Jonas's side and rummaging in his pockets. 'We need a knife.' I tugged an army switchblade from his uniform pocket and stood up, blade at the ready.

Jack stared at me. 'What are you doing?' He dodged out of my way as I stepped towards him with the knife held high.

'We need to get rid of the tracker.'

'*What?*' He sidestepped me again. 'What tracker?'

'In your arm, your tattoo . . . there's a tracker. We need to get it out.'

Jack paused for a second then peeled back his doctor's coat and ran his hands over the top of his arm, over the image of two crossed swords. 'Where?' he asked.

'Here,' I said, pressing my fingers hard into the muscle of his arm, trying to feel for the tiny bump.

'Damn,' Jack whispered under his breath. 'Give me the knife.'

That was fine by me. I handed it over and turned my back.

There was a second of silence and then a sharp intake of air. I peeked over my shoulder.

'Does it hurt?' I asked, watching the trickles of blood start to slide down his arm.

'Of course it goddamn hurts. Give me something to stop the blood, will you?'

I cast around the room trying to find something. Jonas was sprawled across the floor, his foot resting by a little table with a lace doily on the top.

'Wait . . .' I turned back to Jack.

'I don't think I need it.' He was staring at his arm. The blood had stopped flowing. The cut had sealed itself up, leaving just a faint pink line over the word *Semper*. 'Just something to wipe this up.' He nodded at his arm, where the blood had trickled to his elbow. 'Sometime today,' he added when I made no move for the doily.

I shook my head, trying to dislodge the amazement. My mind had already jumped ahead to the next logical question. If he hacked off his arm, would it grow back? I threw the doily in his direction. He caught it and, frowning, started to wipe the smear of blood off his arm.

'Give me the tracker,' I said, hopping from foot to foot. We were wasting time – the Unit would be here any second. We *had* to go.

'Why?' Jack asked, pulling the doctor's coat back on and picking up the gun again.

'Because I'm going to get rid of it,' I said. I was going to send it to the elevator and let it ride between floors. That should keep them confused for a while when they came looking for us.

Jack handed it over and I took it between my thumb and

forefinger before rolling it under the door, feeling the friction between it and the linoleum floor. I closed my eyes, trying to visualise the hallway and the elevator. With a thought, I pushed the call button and we heard the distant *ping* as the elevator doors opened. I floated the tracker into the elevator, let it roll into a corner and then pressed the buttons for every floor.

'Let's go, then,' Jack said, stepping over Jonas's inert body.

I grabbed Jack's arm just before he turned the door handle. 'What now?' he whispered furiously.

'I forgot something else. We need to wait for Dad.'

Jack's jaw looked like it was about to dislocate. He closed his eyes then opened them again. 'You do all this,' he waved a hand at my nurse's outfit and then at the prone form of Jonas at our feet, 'and then you want to sit around and wait for Dad?' He rolled his eyes. 'Shall I go make us a cup of coffee while we wait? I could call the Unit and ask how many sugars they all take too and tell them to pick up some donuts on their way.'

I pulled a face. 'I told Dad seven. He should be here any minute.'

'Oh, that was a great idea, Lila. No, really, the army should recruit you as a strategist. Why the hell did you tell him to meet us here?'

I shrugged and pulled a face. 'It seemed the easiest way.'

Jack shook his head at me as though he couldn't figure out how we were related. Then he inched open the door and peered round it. I knew Jack and my dad had issues, but leaving him at the mercy of the Unit – he couldn't be serious. I pushed the door shut with a glance, but Jack was already shutting it himself. Without a word, he grabbed my arm, hauled me over the unconscious Jonas and through the door into his room.

'What? What is it? Is it the Unit?' I asked as he shoved me into the corner of the room. He ignored me. He was too busy levelling the gun at the door.

'No, it's a doctor,' he answered.

I jumped in front of him. 'That'll be Dr Roberts. He's a good guy. Not a bad one.'

'Lila, get out the way.'

I stood my ground, clogs spaced a hip width apart. 'No.' With a quick glance, I tugged the gun up so its barrel was pointing towards the ceiling. I heard the door open behind me and twisted round to look. Dr Roberts was standing in the doorway. He did a triple take, confusion performing a Mexican wave over his face, followed by astonishment, before confusion came round for a second tour.

The doctor's eyes tracked from the gun in Jack's hands to me. He opened his mouth and closed it once more as he took in the nurse's uniform. I squirmed. But his attention was already back on Jack. He looked like he'd seen his life flash before his eyes, but it wasn't the gun he was staring at. He couldn't take his eyes off Jack's bare, unblemished torso. I watched him try to figure out where the gaping scar should be and how his coma patient was now up and about, dressed in a doctor's coat and brandishing a gun.

I felt Jack tugging at the gun and turned back to him. 'Jack, he's OK. He's not one of the Unit. You don't need to use the gun.'

The doctor raised his arms slowly and stepped into the room. I glanced at the door and silently pulled it to.

'Lieutenant Loveday,' Dr Roberts said in a low, even voice, 'I think you should listen to your sister, you don't need to use the gun. I'm not going to hurt you.' He took a step nearer Jack, his eyes falling to his abdomen again. 'I would like to examine you, though.'

'No time for that, doctor,' Jack said, letting go of the gun. I only just caught it before it hit the ground. It hovered at knee-height by Dr Roberts. His eyes flew to the gun dangling in mid-air, as though it was attached by invisible puppet strings to the ceiling, then his eyes tracked to me and his mouth fell wider open. Jack didn't give him a chance to say anything. He grabbed hold of the doctor's white coat and dragged him towards the door to the visitors' room. I snatched up the gun and then ran round them both and blocked their way.

'We don't need to lock him up,' I said to Jack, hoping my instinct was right. I turned to face the doctor. 'Dr Roberts, I know this looks really . . . weird . . . and you have no reason to believe me . . . but please, just listen . . .'

He said nothing. His eyes kept flitting between Jack and me. I hurried on, 'The Unit aren't trying to arrest Jack. They want to experiment on him. And on me. And I'm not talking about a simple blood test and an eye exam. Do you understand? They're not what you think they are.'

The doctor's eyes flew to Jack's stomach once again and I saw the questions start to ignite and flare in them.

'My dad is going to be here any minute. And the Unit too. Please,' I asked, 'can you help us?'

Dr Roberts's eyes flashed to the gun I was holding as though doing a rapid calculation of odds times risk times likelihood of family insanity. I realised the nurse's outfit and the gun weren't helping us any. His brows drew together, knotting in the middle, and my heart sank. I was going to have to knock him out and just when I'd thought we could count on him.

'What do you want me to do?' he asked.

I breathed for the first time in about sixty seconds. 'Um, when they get here, stall them so we can get away with my dad?'

Jack shook his head and stepped forward. 'We need to get clear. They have a weapon that can take us out. We need to put as much distance between us and them as quickly as possible.' He turned to me. 'Where's the getaway car?' he asked. 'Tell me there is one. Please tell me that.'

I nodded, grateful finally for having done something right. 'Yes, there's a van. It's out the back.'

Jack turned back to the doctor. 'OK, we'll take the stairs, then. When they get here, can you send them up to another floor and—' He was interrupted by the sound of stamping feet thundering down the hallway.

Speak of the devil, I thought, *and he appears.*

32

Jack hauled me backwards into the visitors' room. I tripped over Jonas's head and he groaned in response. I ignored him, scrabbling into a crouch at Jack's side, edging the knife that Jack had dropped across the floor and into my outstretched hand.

'Where is he?' a muffled voice demanded. It sounded like the Robocop one who'd taken me to see Richard Stirling. There was a moment's pause. I felt a tiny movement as Jack shifted his weight to better balance the gun.

Then Dr Roberts's voice came – quiet, calm, convincing. 'I sent him up for an MRI. His blood pressure was spiking. I needed to make sure we hadn't missed something before you moved him.'

'Is he OK?'

That was my dad. He was just on the other side of the door. Beside me, Jack tensed.

'What floor?' the same guy from the Unit demanded.

'The third,' Dr Roberts replied.

Angry footsteps beat a path out of the door and down the hallway, shouts accompanying them.

'Dr Loveday?' we heard Dr Roberts call out. There was a pause. 'Do you mind staying for a moment. I need you to sign some release papers.'

Footsteps headed towards us and Jack stood up just as Dr Roberts pulled open the door.

My dad took a few seconds to take everything in. He blinked at us both in confusion as though trying to place us, then the expression on his face transformed into a frown as he took in my nurse's outfit. The smile that had started to split his face at the sight of Jack standing faded into a slack-jawed horror mask as we watched his gaze slowly track to Jack's stomach.

'Hey, Dad,' Jack smiled. 'We've got to go. Coming?'

My dad faltered, his mouth opening and shutting. 'But – you—' he stammered, glancing at the doctor. 'I thought – you said he was having an MRI – what the hell is going on?'

'Dad, there's no time to explain,' I interrupted. 'You have to come with us now.' My dad stared at me blank-faced and unmoving.

'Now!' I yelled, taking him by the arm and pulling him towards the door.

Down the fire-exit steps, my dad asking at every turn where we were going. Jack's white coat flapping, bare feet slapping; my heart combusting, breath coming in shallow waves. Expecting any minute for my head to be skewered and barbecued when the Unit discovered our escape and fired one of their weapons.

'Where are we going?' my dad asked.

'This way, come on,' I said, taking him by the hand and breaking into a sprint.

At the end of the hallway I pushed the door back with my mind and it flew open ahead of us, crashing against the concrete walls. I almost sobbed with relief when I saw Key standing by the open doors of the van. He looked hyped on speed, his eyes round balls of worry in his head, his feet dancing on the sidewalk. His face dissolved with relief when he saw us.

Then out the corner of my eye I caught sight of a dark shape.

I twisted round just in time to see Jack raising the gun high above his head. What the hell was he doing? He looked like he was about to smack it down over Key's head. I caught hold of the barrel in mid-air just before it cracked Key's skull open and twisted it out of Jack's hand. He made a grab for it, catching it before it hit the ground.

'What are you doing?' I screamed. 'That's Key! He's our getaway driver. You idiot.'

'How was I supposed to know?' Jack hissed back.

'In! In! Get in . . .' Key, ducking his head, was waving us into the back of the van.

My dad clambered in first then took a reeling step back. 'Why is there a—'

'We've got to get off the base,' I cut him off as I climbed in next to him. Jack jumped up beside me and Key slammed the doors on us, entombing us in the gloom.

'That for me?' Jack asked, nodding towards the coffin.

'Yep,' I answered.

'Nice idea,' Jack said, striding towards it. 'Alex, right?'

I nodded. It had been Alex's idea. But I was kind of insulted that he assumed all the good ideas had to be someone else's.

'Buckle up!' Key yelled from the driver's seat. The engine revved to life. Jack threw one leg into the coffin and climbed in, taking the gun with him for company.

'All set?' I asked him.

He flashed a smile at me. 'See you in the afterlife.'

'What are you doing?' My dad swayed towards us as the van started to move.

Jack looked at me and winked. 'OK, do it.'

I was aware, so aware, that my dad was standing right beside me

219

and that what I was about to do was going to rocket him through the Richter scale of shock from the four he was on to maybe a twenty. But what choice did I have?

'We're coming up to the main gates. Get ready,' Key called to us. I took a breath and flipped the lid onto the coffin, locking Jack inside.

There was a graveyard silence. I edged round slowly. My dad was staring at the coffin. Then his eyes rose slowly to meet mine and a long look of recognition passed between us. It wasn't as bad as with Jack. Jack had been brainwashed to hate us and Jack had a temper. And there had been trees present. My dad, well, I wasn't sure what my dad thought exactly, but I knew he thought people like me were sick and could be cured. And my dad didn't really do anger. He did do shock, though. He did it really well. His face drained of colour, becoming so pale that I thought he was going to faint.

The car swung round a bend and he fell hard onto the bench. I sat and put my arm round him. This would work. This could pass for a grieving father being comforted by a nurse. We slowed. I held my hand tight round my dad's shoulder, keeping my head angled towards him and my ears tuned to the conversation between Key and the guard at the exit gate.

'We're on alert, sir. If we could just look inside.'

'Well, Lieutenant . . .' Key started to remonstrate.

'I'm a private, sir,' the Marine interrupted.

'Well, private, I have a grieving father in the back with his son's coffin. I think it would be more appropriate if you just let us drive on.'

'Orders, sir. I can't disobey orders. We're on high alert. Is the back open?'

Oh God. My heart was so loud it was audible. It surely sounded like someone hammering on the coffin trying to be let out.

Key hesitated. *Think of something*, I yelled silently. *Don't let them open the back.*

'Yes,' Key said.

Oh great.

'Don't move,' I murmured to my dad. He didn't appear to hear me. His head stayed bent, his elbows on his knees. I switched to his other side, so I was further back in the shadows, and straightened my nurse's cap. We might be able to pull this off. So long as they didn't open the coffin.

The back doors suddenly flew open, letting in a swathe of light. I blinked at the silhouettes of two Marines, in full combat gear, guns in hand.

'Excuse us, sir,' one said to my dad. 'We're sorry for your loss, but we're under orders to check every vehicle leaving the base. Apologies once again . . .'

He made to shut the doors on us. I realised I was squeezing my dad's knee so hard it was as though I was trying to crack open a walnut.

'Hold up!' a voice called from somewhere outside.

There was a commotion. I heard Key swear under his breath. My dad looked up. I peered round him. The Marine turned back to us, his stance changing as I watched. His hand dropped from the van door and moved to the butt of his rifle. I didn't wait to see where it was going next. I slammed the door in his face, yelling simultaneously to Key, 'Go, go, go!'

He didn't hesitate; the engine whined as he stepped on the gas and my dad and I went flying down the bench, grabbing onto the coffin to steady ourselves. There was a loud retort followed by a crack that I

221

recognised as gunfire. A dent the size of my fist hammered into the side of the van less than two centimetres above my head.

I stood up and threw myself forward so I could see out of the front window. There was a wooden barrier about five metres ahead of us on the road. Key was aiming straight for it. I hurled it to one side with a quick glance before switching my attention to the two Marines manning the other barrier, ripping the guns straight out of their outstretched arms and into the bushes behind them. Key was praying. His hands were rigid on the wheel, his head bent forward almost on top of them, his foot flat to the floor, the van protesting noisily.

I put my hand on his shoulder. 'It's fine. Keep driving. Just keep driving.' He just kept praying.

We had maybe half a minute's head start and it was a ten-minute drive to the jetty, I estimated. I needed to create a roadblock. I stumbled my way to the back of the van, tripping on the metal runners, and threw one door open. The wind took hold of it like a sail, trying to slam it back into my face. I blew it outwards, directing the wind to back the hell off. It worked. The door hung limply, and the wind tunnelling through the van died down. For a single second I stood there, feeling a current of energy surging through my body.

'Lila! They're on our tail. Do something . . .' Key's voice was loud and clear, echoing through the van.

I stopped marvelling at what I'd just done and looked up. Three jeeps were spinning after us out of the road from the base. I sighed. I was getting tired of destruction. There was a stream of trucks in the far lane. We were drawing parallel to one now. I saw the driver, cap pulled low against the morning sunshine. He was staring out of his side window at me, gesticulating wildly with his hand.

'Sorry!' I mouthed to him before shifting my focus to the wheels underneath his cab. I watched as the back of the truck jackknifed beautifully across four lanes of traffic. The cab turned a hundred and eighty degrees, the tyres leaving black slashes across the road. There was a single beat of silence followed by the squeal of dozens of brakes being slammed on, followed by the violent shriek of metal creasing and ironing out. Then finally came the crunch and tinkle of glass hitting the asphalt. The crash seemed to lift us into orbit before slamming us back to the ground.

'What the hell is going on?' I heard Jack yelling and banging from inside the coffin and turned my head to lift the lid off. He sat bolt upright, the gun clasped in both hands and pointed at me.

'Just a little distraction,' I called over my shoulder, my attention already back on the carnage I'd left in our wake. 'They were right behind us.'

I looked at my dad. He was staring at me like he'd just witnessed a poltergeist in action. The wind had started up again; it was trying to get my attention, snapping at the van door. I let it take hold of it and bang it shut, ignoring the look on my dad's face. Instead I wobbled my way to the front and spoke to Key who was veering the van across three lanes like he was drunk.

'Whoa, Key, hold it steady,' I said, putting my hand on his shoulder. 'That should stop them. For a while . . .' I glanced in the wing mirror. The road behind us was empty thanks to the metal roadblock I'd created behind us.

'You're getting good at that,' Key muttered with a nervous laugh, nodding his head at the destruction in the mirror.

'Hmmm,' I replied. Yeah, good at destruction. That was me. Something to be proud of.

I glanced at my dad. It appeared he didn't agree.

33

Footsteps made me turn my head. Alex was sprinting towards us up the jetty.

The relief that flooded through me made me instantly weak-kneed – though that could also have been down to the litres of adrenaline leaching out of my body. I stumbled down the wooden steps onto the jetty, leaving my dad standing by the van with Jack and Key. I managed about three woolly-legged paces before Alex reached me. I waited to feel his arms wrap round me, for him to murmur something about forgiveness while scooping me up. I wanted him to kiss me and carry me back to the boat and . . . all he did was march straight past me and over to Jack.

'Did they follow you?' he demanded.

'No,' Jack growled back, glaring at him.

Alex tensed and looked like he was about to say something else to Key, but then he turned to my dad. 'Dr Loveday,' he said, his voice measured and calm, 'please, this way.'

My dad just stared at Alex as if he was a ghost. I watched him contemplate the man in front of him. The last time he'd seen Alex had been three years ago. They'd been boys then, he and Jack, and now Alex towered over my dad. My dad took him in, having to tip his head back to meet his eye. Then he glanced round at his surroundings, obviously wondering what we were doing on a jetty. Finally he looked back at Alex and followed him wearily down the steps. They both walked past me without so much as a word or a glance in my direction.

Key just shrugged and jogged after them with Jack bringing up the rear, still scowling. 'Come on, Lila,' he called over his shoulder.

But I couldn't move. Alex hadn't even looked at me. There was a sob building in my chest threatening to crush me. I swallowed it down and forced myself to put one foot in front of the other until I was standing by the rungs up to the boat. I glanced up and saw Alex hanging over the side, offering me his hand.

The panic melted away as I took it. I smiled up at him. It was all a big misunderstanding. He wasn't mad at me. He'd just been blanking me because Jack and my dad were there. That made sense. An instant surge of electricity shot up my arm as I took his hand and he pulled me up. I fell against him as he hauled me onto the deck, feeling the hardness of his chest and his warmth, and feeling suddenly like crying with relief. But in the next instant Alex pulled his hand out of mine. His lip curled in anger and his eyes, unlike his body, were devoid of warmth. It was as if he couldn't stand touching me.

My smile died. Alex didn't even notice – he'd turned away and was already climbing another ladder to the wheelhouse above. A few seconds later the engines burst into life and we started to move, the boat edging out of the harbour, picking up speed as we made it round the harbour wall and out into open water. I glanced up and saw Alex giving Key directions on how to steer the boat.

'Lila.'

I turned stiffly round. Jack was standing next to me. 'Dad's downstairs. We need to tell him what's going on.'

Oh crap. I wanted to drop to the floor and curl up in a ball. I

225

couldn't handle this right now. My whole body felt like it had gone into shock – I could feel myself trembling and my head was all fuzzy. Every time I looked at Alex I felt a sharp blade of panic piercing my heart. Was that it? Were we over? Were we over before we'd even properly begun? I was back and I was safe. Why was he so angry still? I'd rescued Jack. We hadn't been caught. Why wasn't he glad?

A shadow fell over me. I looked up. Alex had appeared. I watched his eyes dip to Jack's stomach and saw him pull up short. I wished Jack would just put on a shirt and stop showing off. Jack squared his shoulders and narrowed his eyes in response to Alex's stare. Alex lifted his head and met Jack's gaze head-on, refusing to look away. I frowned, puzzled. What was going on? Was this about *me*? If it was, it was so ridiculous. I wanted to yell at them both. We had way more important things to deal with than Jack's issues with Alex and me. Besides, it didn't even look like there was an Alex and me. Not any more.

'Come on, we need to explain to Dad,' I said, tugging at Jack's sleeve. 'And we need to figure out how we're getting Mum back.'

Alex walked on past us both, his jaw set, still refusing to meet my eye. I might as well have been captured, I thought, for all the difference it would have made. I caught Jack's arm as he was about to follow Alex.

'Please, just let it go,' I hissed.

'Let what go?' Jack asked innocently.

'You know what! This thing about Alex and me. It's nothing to do with you.'

'You're my sister,' Jack growled. 'He's my best friend. And he brought you back here. I'm going to kill him. He should have been looking out for you, not . . .' he struggled to find an appropriate word, 'doing whatever the hell he was doing with you.'

226

I should never have opened my mouth when he was comatose. I dropped my voice so no one could hear. 'Jack, for God's sake, don't you think we have more important things to deal with right now?'

Jack glared at me, his mouth twisting with the effort he was making to keep it closed. 'OK,' he finally said, 'let's go talk to Dad.' He stood back to let me walk ahead of him down the stairs. 'I'm still going to have it out with him, Lila. You're my sister,' he muttered to my back.

Was he ever going to stop this? I paused and walked back up a step so I was in his face. 'Jack, I know you think you have to look out for me and take care of me, but you really don't. I can take care of myself. I think I've proved that. And don't get me wrong,' I continued, 'I love you for wanting to look after me, but I love Alex as well.' I heard my voice catch and tear as though love was a serrated word.

Jack faltered on the step above me. 'Love?' he asked incredulously.

'Yes,' I glared at him. 'Four-letter word, Jack. Different one to the ones you normally use. So, please, just let it go.'

I grabbed hold of the banister and forced myself down the last three steps into the main cabin of the boat. Alex was sitting at a table, opposite my dad, who was nursing a drink. I hoped it was something stronger than water. My dad had his hand clasped round the glass and he was busy studying its contents as though he was trying to divine answers from the liquid. He didn't bother looking up when Jack and I entered the room.

It was a dazzling space, as sleek as the outside of the boat. There were black leather sofas, a stocked bar in the corner, polished wood cabinets around two walls and a white carpet so soft underfoot that it made me instinctively want to speak in a

227

whisper. The engine was just a mellow thrum beneath us. There was no real notion we were moving, other than the receding coastline visible through the portholes. I wondered briefly what Carlos would say about where his money was going. He'd probably approve, though he might decorate the place with a few more pictures of the Madonna and a scattering of bikini-clad women. I hoped that Demos still had enough money left over from the purchase of this floating gin palace to lay his traps in Washington.

I crossed to the bank of sofas on the other side of the room, as far away from my dad and Alex as I could get without climbing out of a porthole.

'Hey,' Jack said.

My dad looked up and stared at him. 'So, are you going to tell me what's going on?' he said, waving his arm to indicate the boat, me, Alex, and possibly, well, probably, the fact that both his children had just come out . . . in a manner of speaking.

'Where do you want me to begin?' Jack said.

'Well, for a start – when were you going to tell me?'

'About what?' Jack replied.

'About you. About what you can both do?'

'Well, Dad,' Jack sighed, 'I only just found out myself.'

My dad turned to look at me for the first time since I'd caused the pile-up on the freeway. 'And you, Lila?'

'I . . .'

'How long have you known?'

I took a gulp of air. 'A few years.'

His eyebrows jumped up to meet his hairline. 'A few years? And you didn't tell me? Why on earth not?'

Why not? Good question. Because I thought I was a freak?

'Because I didn't tell anybody,' I mumbled, 'because I didn't want anyone to know. And thank God I didn't tell you.' I could hear the accusation building in my voice, tried to control it, but it was bubbling over. 'Because what would you have done? Cured me? Tried to fix me?' I was yelling now.

'What are you talking about?' my dad asked quietly, looking totally dazed.

'Isn't that what you want to do? Fix us? Like we have a disease?'

I saw the confusion clear. 'No, Lila, it's not like that.' He paused then his voice became softer. 'You should have told me.'

'What, like you told us about Mum?'

He winced. 'What do you mean?'

'I know about Mum being a psy. That she was telepathic.'

She is. Is. Is. Is. Not was.

'What?'

I turned at the sound of Jack's voice. He was staring at me. Oh crap. I'd sort of forgotten to share that little detail with him.

'Lila, what are you talking about?' Jack repeated.

'She was telepathic, Jack. Mum could read minds.'

Jack's reaction was similar to the one I'd had when Demos told me: total disbelief, followed by shock. He blinked a few times, shook his head, then stared at my dad then at me.

'How do you know this?' my dad asked under his breath.

'Demos told me.'

'Demos?' At the mention of his name, my dad's expression shifted then darkened, a muscle pulsing under his eye.

'Yes.'

'Why didn't you tell me?' Jack burst out.

I twisted to him again. 'When? When exactly would I have told you? As you keep pointing out, you were in a coma.' I hoped he wouldn't pull me up on the fact that I had managed to communicate quite a lot of other stuff while he was unconscious.

'What else did Demos tell you?' my dad interrupted. He looked at me for a second before his eyes flashed to Jack.

'He told me about him and Mum.'

'He told you what?' My dad's voice was shaking.

'Just about how they met . . .'

I couldn't continue. I wasn't sure I knew what to say. *Well, I know he loved her and that maybe he still loves her and that he's trying to rescue her and oh, by the way, I forgot to tell you, she's still alive.* Nope. Not that.

'He didn't kill her, Dr Loveday,' Alex broke in. 'Melissa's alive. Your wife is alive,' he said quietly. I let out the breath I was holding.

My dad just stood there, like the air was being vacuumed out of him. He blinked at Alex. 'What? What are you saying?'

'She's alive. The Unit have been holding her this whole time.'

My dad turned to look at Jack and me, seeking confirmation that Alex had gone mad and was spouting crazy conspiracy theories. I didn't know whether to nod or shake my head. So I just stayed absolutely still.

'The Unit aren't who you think they are, Dr Loveday,' Alex continued. 'Jack and I were recruited by the Unit deliberately. We had no idea what they were really doing. Like you, we thought they were trying to stop Demos. That's why we joined up in the first place, as you know.' He gave a little shrug and I longed suddenly to go over to him and take his hand. But I stayed where I was, watching my dad's face turn worryingly pale. Alex kept talking. 'But we've since found out it was all a lie. Everything the Unit told us was a lie. Demos never killed her. They framed him

230

for the murder and took Melissa, and since then they've been trying to contain others like her, people like Lila.'

'Why? Why? I don't understand,' my dad finally managed to croak out.

'Because,' Alex said, 'they're trying to understand the genetic code that makes her and Lila and Jack and all the others the way they are.'

'Yes, of course, they want to fix it,' my dad interrupted Alex, 'but they aren't . . . they can't be containing people . . . why would they be? That's impossible. What you're saying . . .'

'They're containing them so they can carry out research. So that they can create weapons. New weapons.'

My dad actually looked like he was going to laugh. I recognised the signs. The corner of his mouth was twitching into a smile.

Alex's face stayed impassive as though he was explaining an algebra formula. 'Genetic warfare, so to speak.'

The smile vanished. My dad shut his eyes and shook his head. 'I'm sorry . . . I don't . . .'

'All we are,' I interrupted, 'are lab rats for Stirling Enterprises. That's what Mum is.'

My dad switched his attention to me.

'Dad,' I said, 'they're experimenting on us. Trying to figure out ways of making people telepathic or telekinetic and . . . whatever . . . and then once they've figured it out, they'll sell the secrets to the highest bidder.'

He continued to stare at me blankly.

'Imagine it – crazy people able to read your mind.' Suki's face flashed before me. 'Armies of men who can move tanks with a glance.' I took a deep breath. 'Imagine what might happen if the knowledge fell into the wrong hands. Which it's going to.'

The blankness started to fade. Finally my lesson in how a new world order would be created was sinking in. 'And thanks to your research, Dad, they're already well on the road to making that discovery.'

I watched my dad's face crumple. 'What do you mean?'

'They've been stealing your research,' I said. 'All the time you thought you were helping, well, guess what? You were. Only not quite how you thought you were.'

'No. That can't be right,' my dad said, shaking his head.

'She's right,' Alex reassured him.

Something suddenly seemed to penetrate through the fog of his denial. 'Melissa's alive?' my dad whispered. There was a sense of wonder in his voice. I watched as a smile started to break on his lips. But then it vanished into a tight-lipped scowl. He turned to me sharply. 'How long have you known this for?' The anger in his voice took me by surprise, pressing me backwards into my seat.

'Just for a couple of weeks,' Alex answered for me. 'Since Demos caught Lila.'

I saw my dad do the maths, then watched in amazement as his face started to blaze. 'How could you not tell me?' he shouted at me. He looked at Jack. 'We need to turn this boat around right now and go back there. We need to call the police. We need to . . . I need to . . .' He made suddenly for the stairs. 'What are you all waiting for?' he shouted.

'Dad!' Jack called, catching him by the arm as he strode past.

'Dr Loveday . . .' Alex was suddenly in front of them both, blocking the stairs. 'I know this is a shock to you, but you need to hear us out. We can't go back just yet. We've been working on a plan this whole time to get Melissa out of there and to bring the

232

Unit down, but when we found out they were moving Jack, Lila acted sooner. It's thrown the plan off course a little.'

I glared at Alex. So he was blaming me, then.

'But we will go back for her,' Alex continued, his voice soothing. 'Soon. We promise you.'

'No. We need to go back now!' my dad roared and tried to edge past him.

Alex blocked him easily. 'We can't, Dr Loveday.'

My dad threw back his shoulders and stared up at Alex. I could see he was suddenly wrong-footed. The boy he'd known since he was just a kid was now the one giving him orders. My dad, the doctor, was not in charge. Alex was.

'We're waiting for Demos and the others,' I said.

'Demos?' My dad stared at me in bewilderment.

'Yes, Demos,' Alex said, throwing me a look. I could tell he'd wanted to ease my dad a little more gently into that surprise. *Your wife's alive and her ex-boyfriend didn't kill her and . . . oh yes . . . he's actually going to be helping us.*

'Why?' my dad asked. 'He—'

'Because we need him,' I interrupted. 'He's the only way we'll get Mum out of there.'

I realised, as I said it, that it had come out wrong. My dad and Alex turned to look at me, both of them shooting me looks that could kill.

I shrank back in my seat, pressing my lips together. I hadn't meant to imply that Alex wasn't any help at all – that he was irrelevant and we only needed Demos – but from the look on his face that was exactly how he'd taken it. He nodded at me slowly as if he suddenly understood something, shook his head softly and then turned and walked away.

34

The boat pulled into a point with a deck even more impressive than the one at the stern. Two sunbeds were laid out with a stack of white towels piled on the ends of them, as though two bronzed supermodels were about to appear in their bikinis and start posing for a photo shoot. But there was only me, wearing a stupid nurse's outfit that made me look like a stripper. Behind me was a lacquered wooden door leading inside to what looked like a mini gymnasium, but I wanted to be outside, somewhere I could think. This situation with Alex was just getting in the way of the only thing I really cared about – getting my mum back.

Above me was another deck. I skirted the edge of the boat, looking for a way up, and found a little metal ladder. I gripped it tight and scrambled up. Once on the second deck, I flopped onto a cushion and buried my head in my knees, feeling utterly defeated and undone. That's when I heard their voices. It was Jack and Alex. I tiptoed to the edge of the deck and peered over. They were directly below me, partially obscured by the overhang of the deck.

'You don't know that. You're guessing!' Jack was yelling.

'Jack, we can't trust her.'

'Who are you to tell me that I can't trust my own girlfriend?' Jack said something else that I couldn't hear. It sounded like a four-letter word. Not love.

Alex's voice was starting to get louder. 'Until we know whether we can trust her, you can't involve Sara in this.'

'But it's fine for you to bring my sister into it,' Jack snapped back.

'What's that supposed to mean?'

'You shouldn't have brought her back here.'

I leaned further over, straining to hear Alex.

'You think I could have stopped her? You know her as well as I do.'

'Apparently not.' I winced.

'Jack, come on. We had this out already. I'm not explaining myself to you again.'

'She's my sister, Alex. You were supposed to be looking after her. Not taking advantage of her. She loves you . . . she says she loves you.'

'I know.'

I know? That was his answer? What about *I love her too?* What happened to that answer?

'Do you love her?'

Good question, Jack.

My hand gripped the railing to stop myself toppling over. I strained so hard to hear that my ears almost bled, but whatever Alex said in reply was muffled by the engine and the wind. I twisted my head and tried to force the wind to move, to go and batter some other boat. I needed silence over here. The wind dropped, but whether that was just us shifting direction I couldn't tell.

Jack's voice sounded clearly again. 'You should just walk away, then.'

What? I lurched forward then flopped down into a heap on the deck, my legs like worn-out elastic. Why was Jack telling him to walk away? What had Alex said? Had he said no, he didn't love me?

'I promised her I wouldn't leave her,' Alex said tersely.

There was a moment's pause. I tilted my head to catch Jack's answer, feeling myself start to hyperventilate. '. . . if you really want to do the right thing now too, you should leave. We don't need you anymore. It's not your fight. It's *my* mum. It's *my* sister.'

I staggered upright and launched myself towards the ladder. I was going to jump down from the deck and push Jack overboard. Then I'd show him the hundred-year freak wave – see how he could heal from that. But I froze with one foot on the top rung. I didn't move. I didn't jump down and throw Jack overboard. Because Alex didn't love me anymore, so what was the point?

I remained where I was, one leg swung over the side of the boat, immobile, staring out at the ocean, wondering how I was ever going to move again. How I was going to get down in fact. The paralysis was total. Alex didn't love me. Alex wanted to leave me. He was only staying because he'd promised me – out of a sense of duty not out of love.

And then anger surfaced like a piranha – angry, biting and frenzied. I swung my leg back over and started pacing the deck furiously.

The anger was aimed mostly at Jack – but there were spits of it licking like flames towards Alex. I was mad with him too. What had happened to inviting the ass-kicking? To inevitability? To *I love you*? Why had he suddenly stopped loving me? Because I went back for Jack? Because I messed up his plan? It was so infuriating. What was I supposed to have done? Let the Unit take Jack? What was wrong with him that he couldn't understand why I'd done what I had?

I was so busy stamping up and down the deck that I didn't at first notice the wave coming towards us, the wall of water rather – twenty metres high – that had swelled into view. I stopped mid-pace and stared at it, not quite computing what I was seeing. Where had it come from? The rest of the ocean was flat except for the twenty-metre-wide mini tsunami that was headed straight for us.

I had a moment's elation, wild disbelief, that made me gasp out loud. *I did this. I made this happen.* Then I realised we were all going to drown.

I tried pushing it. I squeezed my eyes shut and gripped the rail, begging God and whoever else might be listening to help. The molecules felt fluid and slippery. It was like trying to grip a greased pole with my hands tied behind my back. I couldn't get hold of anything. From underneath the roar of the engine I heard someone yell.

I focused back on the wave, now about forty metres away, my panic rising to meet it. I tried to flatten it down, tried to imagine a flat, calm sea and, when that failed, water pouring down a plug-hole. And suddenly it obeyed, falling under my spell. I drew it downwards, flattening it out like a tablecloth someone had shaken out, and let it float down onto the top of the ocean.

I stood staring at the water, where the wave had been, shaking. How had I done that? I had thought my power was under control and now it seemed I was even more out of control than ever and before had been bad enough. With this kind of power, I could cause natural disasters without even realising it. Maybe I shouldn't look at the water. I squeezed my eyes shut, stuck my arms out in front of me and stumbled blindly towards the door.

'Was that you?'

I jumped about a mile at the sound of Key's voice, almost putting myself into orbit. My eyes flew open. He was standing in the doorway glowering at me.

'It was you,' he said, shaking his head at me. He looked out at the ocean and muttered something under his breath.

I chewed my lip. 'I'm sorry. I don't know how—'

'Can you control it?' he asked, cutting me off.

There was no point in lying.

'Lila, please try,' he sighed. 'I'm not so good at the whole steering a boat thing and Alex is too distracted to show me. So, please, it would help me out if you could concentrate on not throwing obstacles like that one in my way.'

I nodded slowly. 'OK, I'll try.'

'Oh, by the way, Lila, don't get me wrong, the nurse's outfit works and all,' he flushed and stammered, 'if you like that sort of thing, but if you do want to get changed then Alex put some spare clothes in the wardrobe of the master cabin.'

'Oh, thanks,' I said, looking down at my nurse's uniform. It might have worked on Jonas, but it sure as hell hadn't done a damn thing for Alex. I suddenly couldn't wait to get changed into something else.

'By the way,' I said to Key's departing back, 'where are we going?'

'Marina del Rey, near Santa Monica. Not that I've a clue how we're going to dock a boat this size without anyone noticing us. But that's where we're meeting the others.'

He left and I crossed back to the railing and looked out over the now flat expanse of ocean towards the shore. Was Alex going to leave once we got there? How could I stop him? Would he even want to be stopped? Or had he given up on me completely?

238

I needed to get out of this ridiculous outfit then I'd try to talk to him. He couldn't leave. We needed him. I needed him. Resolved, I walked through the door that Key had emerged from. It opened onto a huge cabin in the centre of which was a bed big enough for six people to sleep in. There were mirrors along one side of the room, a large flat-screen television, a desk and two armchairs.

I guessed this was the master cabin and walked to the mirrors, sliding them open to reveal an enormous wardrobe, so large it would probably be big enough to contain even Suki's shoe collection. In one drawer was a neatly folded pile of clothes – underwear, new jeans, a couple of dresses, some sweaters, some tank tops. All in my size, even the underwear. The initial butterfly assault gave way to cramps as I let the silky material slide through my hands.

Then, with one quick move, I pulled off the stupid nurse's dress and slipped on a pair of grey shorts. I was just tugging a black tank top on over my head when Alex walked in. He seemed surprised to see me, but not pleasantly so. He spun on his heel to leave.

'Alex,' I called. 'Wait!'

He turned round slowly, his eyes darting round the room, looking everywhere but at me. 'I'm sorry, I didn't realise you were here. I was looking for Key.'

'You just missed him,' I stammered.

An expression that I couldn't fathom passed across his face. It could have been longing, it could have been disdain. I felt like I was walking a tightrope, that I was balanced on a moment so fine that if I said or did the wrong thing, I would fall and it would all be over. Alex gave me a nod and just like that he turned away again and walked off.

'Alex!' I called after him.

He turned slowly and when he did and I saw the set of his jaw, the hard line of his mouth and the coldness in his eyes, I felt like I'd been slapped.

'Are you leaving?' I blurted out.

A shadow passed across his face. He shook his head. 'No. I promised you I'd never leave you again,' he said, his voice strangely flat.

The relief rushed through me like a hit of something illegal. He wasn't leaving me. I'd got it wrong. But then the rush evaporated. I stared at him for a few seconds. He hadn't moved from his position by the door.

I took a deep breath. 'Are you staying,' I asked, 'because you promised or because you want to?'

He hesitated, his lips pressing together. And in that moment of hesitation it all became clear, like someone had dropped detergent on the oily mess of my brain. He didn't want to stay.

I ground my teeth. I wasn't going to cry. I wasn't going to cause a scene. It was fine. I could handle this. But Jack was right, if he didn't have feelings for me anymore, he should just go. In fact, he could go to hell. I didn't need him.

'You can go. Just go,' I said, my voice catching. 'I release you, or whatever it is, from your promise. You don't need to stay with me. I'm fine by myself. I can look after myself. I don't need you.'

As soon as I said the words, I wanted to slap my hand over my mouth. I wanted to press a rewind button. I waited while the seconds stretched out, desperately wanting him to laugh and pull me into his arms, telling me to stop being stupid. I waited for him to whisper in my ear that he loved me, that I'd misheard, and that Jack was an idiot. But he didn't. He simply nodded in understanding.

'Look, I've got to go help Key,' he said, his face blank, his eyes shuttered. 'We're nearly there and I'm not sure he knows how to dock a boat.'

And he turned, and just like that, he walked away and I crumpled to the floor and started to cry.

35

'Boo! It's only me.'

I sat up from the misery pit I had carved into the bed, and kicked away the barricade of scrunched-up tissues. Suki had burst in on me and was standing like a daddy-long-legs in the doorway, wearing four-inch heels and what looked suspiciously like a designer dress.

'You have missed me. I can tell, Lila.' She skipped towards the bed, but halfway across the room I saw her falter. She tipped her head and started to scowl.

'Why are you crying? Wait!' she demanded, closing her eyes and resting the back of her arm dramatically against her forehead. Her golden eyes flashed open again. 'You did *what*? Why would you say that to him? Are you stupid? Are you totally crazy?'

I started to get off the bed. I didn't want to have this conversation. I wanted to find Demos. We needed to start formulating a plan to get back onto the base.

'What did she do?' Nate said, suddenly popping up behind her. 'What happened?'

'Lila here broke up with Alex. That's why he was so moody when we arrived. Not because he was missing you, Nate.'

'I didn't break up with him,' I interrupted.

'She told him to leave,' Suki informed Nate as they both took up position on the edge of the bed.

'Why would you do that?' Nate yelled, gaping at me like I was mad.

'Because she's stupid. And stop that, Nate. Alex is not going to be interested in you now just because Lila dumped him.' Nate started to protest then shut his mouth.

'I'm not stupid,' I muttered lamely.

'Well, why else would you tell Alex to go anywhere? What will we do for eye candy now? Were you thinking of Nate at all? Were you thinking of me? I think you're incredibly selfish, Lila.' She began to pout and Nate put an arm round my shoulder..

But she was right – I was selfish. I flopped backwards onto the bed. The sheets were damp from where I'd soaked them with tears. 'You weren't here – I didn't have any idea of what was going on in his head. I didn't know what he was thinking. He told Jack . . . well, he didn't tell Jack . . . I don't know. I don't know anything.'

He didn't love me anymore. I couldn't say it out loud. Right now I couldn't deal with processing this fact, not on top of everything else.

'Of course he still loves you,' Suki said, rolling her eyes.

I bolted upright. 'He does? Are you sure? What's he thinking?' The relief was like a toxin hitting my nervous system.

Suki pirouetted round to me. 'He's thinking about what to pack and what the fastest way out of here is.'

'What?' I shrieked.

'He's thinking about what to pack and—'

'I heard you the first time.' I leapt off the bed. 'Why's he packing?'

'I'm sorry, Lila, are you being stupid on purpose? He's packing because you told him to leave. I just told you this. Seriously, did the Unit remove your brain or something? You did tell him you didn't need him. And so did Jack. Why would he stay?'

'But I didn't mean it,' I wailed.

She jutted out one hip and put a hand on it. 'Is Alex a mind-reader?' She waited a beat then answered for me. 'No. And good job he isn't because he might have left you already if he could hear all the mentalness going on in there,' she said, pointing at my head.

'You told him you didn't need him?' Nate suddenly yelled. 'Why'd you tell him that?' He was looking at me aghast. 'We *so* need him. How else are we going to rescue your mum?'

'I know.' Suki pursed her lips. 'We completely need him. Who else comes up with the plans?'

'Demos?' Nate answered, looking confused.

Suki frowned at him. 'Yes, but he isn't hot, Nate. We've talked about this.'

'I didn't mean it,' I said quietly. I couldn't believe Alex had actually taken me seriously. He had to know how much I needed him. 'I need to fix this,' I said, looking at Suki for a solution. She closed her eyes again, biting her top lip. Then her eyes popped open wide.

' . . . Jack! You didn't tell me about Jack . . .' she gasped.

'Jack what?' Nate was bouncing on the bed.

Suki turned to him, beaming. 'Jack is like us too. He can do magic with his body.'

Nate's eyes lit up like candles. 'He can? Wow!' He jumped off the bed. 'Let's go see him.'

'No. No, wait.' I grabbed Suki's arm as she was about to run after Nate. 'What can I do? How do I fix this?' I shook her by the shoulders.

244

Her eyes suddenly went round. 'Hang on. You shoved him!' she shouted. 'I can't believe you shoved him.'

'She shoved him?'

I turned to glare at Nate.

'Yes. And she's always running off on him.' Suki shook her head at me. 'We'd treat him much better if he was ours—'

'Suki!' I yelled. 'Please. Help me!'

She pressed her lips together and shut her eyes. 'I'm not sure what you can say, Lila. But I do know you might want to start with sorry. And you might want to hurry because he's already on the deck. He's just saying bye to Jack. And—'

I didn't wait to hear the rest of the sentence. I was already sprinting down the hallway. I jumped down the steps, pounded down the other hallway and into the main cabin. Demos and Harvey were standing just by the stairs talking with Alicia. They looked up sharply when I ran in.

'Lila,' Demos said in greeting.

'Hi, hi,' I said, rushing past them. I took the stairs two at a time. I had to stop Alex first.

I hit the deck and threw my leg over the side ready to climb down the ladder to the jetty. But then I paused. Alex was nowhere to be seen.

36

'You going somewhere?'

I spun round. Alex was standing behind me on the deck. There was a bag by his foot. I took it in and then looked at his face. It was wary. But that was better than blank. It was better than cold. That's when I noticed Jack skulking in the corner. He avoided my eye, nodded stonily at Alex and disappeared down the stairs. I stared after him then turned back to Alex, my hands shaking.

'Suki said you were leaving.'

'I'm not,' he answered.

I breathed slowly out. 'Then why the bag?' I asked, pointing at it.

He winced a little. 'I was about to leave. But Jack asked me to stay.'

Jack? I looked up at Alex. Jack had asked him to stay? I didn't understand. 'There's no other reason you're staying?' I asked, biting my bottom lip. I could give lessons in subtlety.

'What other reason might that be?'

I looked up and felt momentarily dazed. Alex had taken a step forward and all I could take in was the arctic blue of his eyes, and his lips, half-parted, the ghost of a smile dancing at the edge of them.

'Me?' I half choked the word out.

He took another step forward. 'I didn't think you wanted me

around anymore. I didn't think that you needed me.' His eyes sparked and my breath caught.

I grabbed for his hand, feeling the spark travel into me. 'I didn't mean what I said, Alex. Of course I need you. I can't believe you don't know that. I need you so much that when you're not around me, it hurts. It actually hurts, physically. Here.' I poked myself between the ribs, where I could feel my heart hammering. 'I can only do this because of you. I'm only here because of you.'

He was shaking his head softly. 'So, why did you tell me to leave?'

'Because I heard you talking to Jack.'

The furrow between his eyes appeared. 'You heard that?'

I nodded. 'You didn't argue with him when he told you to leave. And I thought you told him you didn't love me. I thought that's why he told you to go.'

He suddenly shook his head, turned away. After a second he looked back at me. 'Lila, you fool, of course I told him I loved you. That's *why* he told me to leave.'

'Oh.' I couldn't keep the smile off my face. 'You just were so cold with me. And the nurse's outfit didn't seem to make any kind of impression. Whatsoever. So I thought . . .' I looked at the ground. 'I thought you were only staying because you had promised me and then . . . when I asked you, you didn't deny it.'

'You didn't give me a chance to,' he said, shaking his head at me. He took a step nearer. 'And believe me the nurse's outfit made an impression.' He took another step towards me, so he was just a few centimetres away. 'A very big impression.'

I had to tilt my head up now to look him in the eye. He was smiling. My stomach ping-ponged. I was seriously glad I'd kept the nurse's outfit – had stuffed it into one of the drawers – and not tossed it overboard.

'So, you're staying because of me?' I stuttered.

'Of course because of you.' He put his hand under my chin. He was smiling a slow, easy smile now. I felt the shudder run from my knees up to my shoulders and exhaled. The boat rocked and I pushed myself up onto my tiptoes with the next wave and let my lips touch his.

For a few minutes we didn't move. All I was aware of were Alex's hands, one resting in the small of my back, pulling me against him, and the other holding my face gently. And his lips. I was aware of his lips. Like they held the answers to every bit of knowledge in the whole wide world and suddenly I wanted to be the oracle and know it all.

Eventually, we broke apart for air, both of us breathing hard, the air around us almost crackling. I peeled backwards in his arms so I could look up at him. His eyes were back to the way they were before. No more coldness, no more ice. The amber flecks were glowing. The frown line had vanished.

'Alex,' I said, 'it's not just me that needs you.' I thought about Nate and Suki and smiled. 'We can't do this, any of this, without you.'

Alex narrowed his eyes suspiciously at me. 'Have you been talking to a certain Japanese girl by any chance?'

'Maybe,' I said, scuffing the deck with my bare foot.

He shook his head with a grimace. 'That girl . . .'

'No, don't be mad with her.' I took his hand. He was frowning again. 'Alex, hear me out. You can't think we don't need you. Jack's an idiot. And you're an idiot too if you think that. You did all this.' I pointed to the boat. 'You figured out the plan with Carlos and you've rescued me about a hundred times. And I don't think we can rescue my mum without you. Who else is going to figure

248

out how?' I saw the worry and the tension wash across his face and tried to ignore it. 'And I'm sorry I keep running off,' I said, speaking so fast that I was breathless. 'I swear to you that's absolutely the last time.' I took a deep breath, trying to slow down. 'I should have thought about you and how it would make you feel, but I didn't. I was selfish. But I had to go back for Jack. I had to.'

'I understand,' Alex interrupted. 'I was just so scared that I was going to lose you. Do you realise how important you are to me? I had to watch you go – I couldn't stop you – and I didn't know if I'd ever see you again. Do you have any idea what that feels like?'

I pressed my lips together. Yes, I knew what that was like. Once upon a time I'd thought I would have to leave Alex and that I'd never see him again. And it had been one of the worst feelings I'd ever experienced.

I nodded. 'I'm sorry,' I said. Alex opened his mouth to speak and I shook my head to stop him.

'Alex, just listen to me. I need you to understand. When I thought my mum was dead . . . her funeral . . . and the days after, I only got through it because of you, because you were right by my side taking care of me. And when my dad took me to London, the only thing that got me out of bed in the morning, and through every day at that sucky school, was the thought that one day I'd get to see you again. Just knowing that you were out there was enough. So, even before this, even before you actually started rescuing me from bad men with big guns, I needed you. I've been impulsive and crazy and taken chances my whole life because I've always known that you'll be there when it goes wrong. Which it does. A lot. Remember the lake? The sledging incident? The tree in the backyard? And we haven't even got onto almost being captured by the Unit in a Seven-Eleven or getting shot at in Joshua

Tree. And every single one of those times you've rescued me. Every time you're there. You're like my safety net.'

He smiled, a little smile, but the sight of it made my breathing speed up. 'I've always needed you. For my entire life,' I said in a whisper, 'and I'm always going to need you.'

His smile widened, his thumb stroked my jaw.

'Oh, and also Suki and Nate feel the same.'

He raised his eyebrows. 'Are you going to push me out of the way again if I argue with you?'

'I'll try not to.' I grinned at him. 'I'm so sorry. I'm working on the whole control thing.'

He smiled back and it was like a shot of pure adrenaline with maybe some helium thrown into the mix.

'What did Jack say to you?' I suddenly asked. 'Why'd he ask you to come back? He sounded pretty mad earlier.'

'Well, it wasn't as eloquent as your speech.' I pulled a face. 'He said he'd reconsidered. Didn't explain why.'

'What's with that?'

'No idea. But he apologised.'

'Jack apologised? Are you kidding?' I tried to stop the choking laugh from erupting out of me.

Alex nodded, smiling. 'Yeah. He apologised for the things he said. He's still mad with me about not trusting Sara, but he asked me to come back.'

'And us? Did he mention us?'

'Yeah, he said it was OK by him.'

'Are you joking?' I pulled away to check if he was trying to be funny.

'Nope. But he said it through gritted teeth and he warned me if I ever hurt you, he'd kill me.'

250

OK. That was progress.

'I can live with that,' Alex said, looping his arms round my waist and pulling me close against him. 'Besides, I think the only person doing the hurting is you. You're getting strong.'

'Yeah, you wouldn't believe what I can do.' I wanted to tell him all about the water, but Alex cut me off with a kiss, just a gentle, soft touch of his lips against mine.

Someone cleared their throat behind me. 'Oh, excuse me.'

I threw myself backwards out of Alex's arms, dancing across the deck. Alex took a few steps away from me too, clearing some distance, rearranging his T-shirt, running one hand through his hair.

'Dad!' I cried out. 'Er . . .'

'Sorry to . . . um, interrupt . . . I . . . um . . .' My dad's eyes were flitting all over the deck. He turned three hundred and sixty degrees as though looking for something. His glasses perhaps.

'I just . . . I just wanted to talk to you, Lila, if that's OK?' My dad looked over his shoulder at Alex.

Alex took the hint. 'I'll go find the others.' He ducked his head and disappeared down the stairs. I looked after him, feeling the smile lighting up my face. He was staying. He was mine. And my dad had just walked in on us. *Hmmm. Awkward.* I turned to face him, feeling the burn of the blood that had been in other parts of my body retrace a path to my face.

'So, you and Alex, then . . . that's, um . . .'

'Yeah . . .' I interrupted before he could finish the sentence.

'OK, he's a nice boy.' I saw him stumble a little on the word *boy.* Alex clearly wasn't a boy anymore. Was he going to say something about the age difference?

'Has Jack said anything?' my dad asked with a little edge of concern in his voice.

Oh yeah. Plenty. 'He seems OK with it,' I said.

My dad nodded. 'Anyway, that's not what I came to talk to you about.'

I waited. My dad took a deep breath. 'Er, I don't really know where to begin.' He sat down with a heartfelt sigh and indicated the seat next to him. I sat and waited.

'I'm sorry.' I looked up at my dad.

'I'm sorry. I shouldn't have reacted like that when I found out about your ability.' I bit my lip in answer.

'It was a shock. I didn't suspect. I mean, I always thought it was a possibility seeing how it's genetic, but I thought I would know. That you would tell me.'

I caught his eye and looked away.

'Your mother . . .' His voice broke. I looked up. He had his eyes closed. 'I can't believe she's still alive. I just can't . . .'

'I know.' I took his hand. We stayed like that for a good five minutes. The water was slapping the side of the boat and we were rocking gently against the wooden jetty where we'd moored.

'I wish you could have told me,' he said eventually.

'I know. I wanted to, Dad, I really did, but we thought it would be better if we kept it from you. We were always going to tell you eventually. Alex thought it might help if you were on the inside. And Richard Stirling threatened me. If I told you, they would have hurt you and Jack.'

There was a loaded pause while we both considered what we'd escaped. There was no relief because the fact remained that we'd also left my mum behind.

'Have you seen Demos yet? The others?' I asked, my gut twisting painfully. There was still so much to figure out.

'No.' My dad's face darkened.

'He's nice, Dad.'

His expression turned even darker. 'I still don't see why he needs to be involved.'

'Dad, whatever you think of Demos, whatever went on between him and Mum, it was years ago and he's on our side. He's been fighting for her this whole time. Like you have. Like Jack has. We're all trying to achieve the same thing – it makes sense we work together. Besides, you should see what he can do.'

'I know what he can do. I had the pleasure of meeting him once.'

Oh. Demos hadn't told me that part.

'Are you coming? ' I said, standing up.

He sighed and stood up. 'I don't think I have much choice.'

37

Suki and Nate were curled like kittens at Alex's feet. No. More like Sphinxes I realised. Guarding him. Probably making sure I didn't say anything else that might make him leave.

That wasn't going to happen. Suki's eyes narrowed in my direction when she saw me. Nate winked at me and gave me a thumbs up. I shook my head at them. But I couldn't stop smiling. I could breathe again. I could breathe deep without it feeling like a fish-hook was caught in my diaphragm. And then I pulled up short. Amber was sitting in the corner. She looked thinner than before and there was a coldness about her that made me stop from running over and hugging her.

'Amber,' was all I said in surprise. 'What are you doing here?'

'I thought about what Ryder would want me to do,' she said quietly. I didn't know what to say so I said nothing. I just nodded and went and sat next to Alex.

It was only then that I noticed the silence in the room and the tension, so heavy it was almost tangible. I turned. My dad, who had come into the room with me, was now standing in front of Demos and neither man was speaking. Neither man was smiling. They were just staring at each other like two opponents weighing each other up before a prize fight. I had to hand it to my dad – I wouldn't weigh myself up against Demos.

Alicia was standing in the corner of the room. She looked nervous, kneading her hands as she watched them. I dreaded to think what she was reading in their minds, but from the anxious expression on her face I could tell none of it was pleasant.

Harvey was sitting at the table, coffee mug in hand, observing it all with an amused expression on his face. I wondered suddenly whether it was such a good idea bringing my dad and Demos together and was about to stand up and say something – anything to break the tension – when Alex suddenly jumped to his feet.

'Dr Loveday, this is Demos,' he said, stepping over Suki and moving to stand at my dad's side.

'We've met,' my dad said, not taking his eyes off Demos.

'Michael,' Demos said, nodding at my dad in greeting.

'You had to bring my kids into this?' my dad asked. I cringed.

Demos arched a dark eyebrow. 'They're not kids anymore, Michael. And besides, Jack was already a part of it.'

'Maybe we should agree to let the past lie and move forward,' Alex interrupted, stepping between the two men and shutting down the conversation. 'We need to move fast,' he said, 'before the Unit discover what we've done in Washington. We need to time it so they raid Stirling's house and office at the same time we break into the headquarters on the base. It'll create another diversion for us.'

'We need a plan,' Harvey said, licking the edge of a cigarette paper.

I was so sick of hearing those words. Why couldn't there just be a blueprint already in existence? Why weren't we able to just google a solution? Why always this hashing together of crazy ideas – usually stolen haphazardly from my head – until we came up with something suicidally stupid and bound to fail?

But nothing had failed yet, I reminded myself. Though *yet* did seem to be the operative word. We were hanging on a thread of good luck and at some point, with all the weight on it, it was going to snap.

I looked round the room. Alex was chewing his lip. Suki and Nate were bug-eyed, watching us from the floor, Alicia was glaring at Demos and so was my dad.

I wondered all of a sudden how Alicia felt – knowing that her boyfriend was on a mission to save his ex-girlfriend whom he possibly still loved. I cut the thought off before she could read it, but perhaps I wasn't fast enough because she threw a dark look in my direction.

'If you'd let me talk to Sara, we'd have a way onto the base,' said Jack.

'Jack, we can't trust her. There's too much at stake,' Alex shot back.

Jack glowered at him and I noticed Suki edging backwards as if Jack was an unexploded bomb.

'Alex is right,' Demos said, crossing to the table. 'Can we draw this particular line of approach to a close? Unless we're one hundred per cent certain of Sara we don't go near her.'

'Maybe Suki or Alicia could try to read her mind,' Nate offered.

'They can't get on the base,' I countered. 'And if Sara is one of them and if what Richard Stirling said is true, then she can probably block them anyway so there'd be no point.'

'She might not be able to block Amber,' Alicia said.

'What? You want me to walk onto the base and just ask her if she doesn't mind answering a few questions while I check her aura to see if she's lying?' Amber asked caustically.

'Wait up,' Alex interrupted. 'Maybe it doesn't matter whether we trust Sara or not. We can still use her.'

256

We all turned to look at him. 'Think about it,' he carried on, his voice low, making everyone lean towards him. 'What if we made her think that we do trust her?'

I looked at Jack. He opened his mouth as if to say no, but then he seemed to change his mind. 'Keep going,' he said.

'Either way, Sara would let us inside the building. She'd take us down to prisoner holding.'

There was a moment of chilled silence.

'But if she is evil then they'll set a trap. We'd walk straight into it,' said Suki.

'It's not a trap if we have a way out of it,' Alex grinned back at her.

Suki looked puzzled for a moment then her eyes widened as she heard his thoughts. 'Oooh!' She clapped her hands together in glee. 'Double-cross! I like this plan. It's cunning.'

What plan? I hadn't heard any plan, just something that sounded like walking into a prison and bolting the door shut behind us. That wasn't cunning. That was plain stupid.

'Hang on, hang on!' I burst out. 'I don't understand.' Was I the only one who didn't? 'If Sara isn't on our side,' I said, flashing a nervous glance in Jack's direction, 'then they'll be in there waiting for us.'

'Yes,' Alex nodded at me, still smiling, 'but they'll underestimate us. We'll tell Sara that Demos and the others are in Washington and we'll blow the lid there just before we go in so it tallies. The Unit will deploy at least three teams to the East Coast. But Demos and the others will be just behind us.'

'Us?' I asked.

'You, me and Jack.'

'No Lila,' Jack interrupted, shaking his head. 'Lila's not coming anywhere near the base.'

Alex turned to him. 'I don't think we get to tell Lila what she can and can't do.'

I beamed at him. Alex's tone softened. 'But at least this way we're both with her,' he told Jack.

'And me. I'm going too.'

I looked over at my dad. He was clearing his throat.

'Dad . . .' Jack sighed.

'Don't argue with me, Jack,' my dad said, standing up. 'I'm not letting you and your sister go in there while I sit here twiddling my thumbs.' Jack ground his teeth and looked away.

Then I processed. 'The Unit will be inside waiting for us,' I said again.

'Yes. And they'll lock us down in prisoner holding,' Alex nodded, still smiling.

'Yeah? And if they do that, how do we get out? Isn't that the massive great flaw in this plan?'

'They won't lock down. You're already acting like Sara can't be trusted,' Jack cut in.

'We work from the worst-case scenario – that's what we're trained to do, Jack,' Alex replied calmly. 'If she is on our side then great, maybe we'll breeze in and breeze out with your mum, but if she is involved then we need to plan for that.'

'We can disable the lockdown. There might be a way from inside.'

For a moment I didn't know who had spoken because Harvey was usually so quiet. He paused to exhale a smoke ring. We watched it float and hang, just like we were doing, on his words.

'From inside it'll be easy,' he said almost nonchalantly. 'And if you can convince her to disable the alarm system to let you walk inside with Lila and Jack, I might have a way of getting in.'

What? What was he talking about?

'Harvey is a master thief,' Suki whispered, hearing the question in my head.

Harvey gave her a sideways glance. 'Not that masterful, Suki. I got caught, remember.'

My mind flashed back to what I'd read on Jack's computer. Harvey had been in prison for bank robbery. And he'd also escaped. I stared at him. He was a bank robber. A fugitive bank robber. Well, we were all fugitives in a way. But still, *I* was associating with a bank robber! I glanced instinctively at my dad. He was staring at Harvey with barely disguised horror. He didn't find it as exciting as me. But then again he hadn't had the chance to get to know Harvey.

'If you could get inside the building, would you be able to disable the alarm?' Alex asked him.

'Not if it's already going off,' Harvey said wryly. 'Tell me more about the system and I'll tell you what's possible.'

'OK,' Alex said. 'The alarm system triggers if it picks up changes to the electromagnetic field within a five-metre radius of the building. So, if anyone uses a power near it, it sends out a pulse wave that takes out anyone with a power and it locks down the building so no one inside can get out. No one outside can get in either. The system is set up so it can only fire one shot every minute and only in bursts of ten seconds because of the damage it can do to the computer systems. But for the same reason no one is allowed to carry one of those weapons inside the building. They will be carrying guns, though.'

'OK,' said Harvey. 'Get me whatever information you have on the systems the Unit uses. I'll need to do some research.'

'Getting in and getting out is one thing, but how do we destroy the labs?' Alicia asked. 'I'm not leaving there without destroying

259

every last piece of information they have about us. And all their damned research.' She shot a venomous look at my dad.

There were murmurs of agreement from the others.

'What about Lila?'

What about me? I looked at Key.

'What about Lila?' he said again. 'That thing she can do with the water – is it in any way helpful?'

'What thing she can do with water?' Alex asked. Everyone was staring at me now.

'Nothing. I can't do anything with water,' I burst out.

'She can move it.'

Key was making it sound like I was Moses or something.

'I can't – not really!' I spluttered.

Alex had stood up and crossed to me. He stopped and knelt down so we were level.

'Show me,' he said, taking my hand and pulling me up. He led me to the table and set a glass of water down in front of me.

'No pressure or anything,' I muttered, shifting my gaze away from my silent audience to the glass. 'I'm not very good at this.'

I focused on the glass and the water inside shot upwards like a geyser. Only the ceiling stopped its trajectory. Alex hopped back out of its downward path.

'Told you,' I said, shrugging.

Everyone was now staring at the pool of water on the carpet. There was a look of astonishment on most of their faces. I waited for some other reaction, but none was forthcoming.

Demos was the first one to speak. 'What about fire?' he asked, a glint in his eye. 'Can you do the same with fire?'

38

I flopped down on the bed, staring up at the circle of damp on the ceiling. Alex lay down next to me and a wave of energy travelled through my body. If Amber had been in the room, I was sure she would have been seeing rainbows. I instantly rolled against him and felt his arm come round me.

'I don't know if I can do this,' I mumbled into his shoulder.

'You can do it, I know you can,' Alex whispered back. 'You're the most stubborn person I know. You never give up on anything. You just need to practise.'

'No,' I said, pressing myself tighter against him.

'Lila, we're talking about destroying an entire building. I think you need to practise,' he said, trying to pry me away from his chest.

'On what?' There weren't exactly any spare buildings around that I could try blowing up.

'We'll start with candles.'

Why I had to be tasked with destroying a building on a Marine base I had no idea. Surely a rocket launcher would be more reliable, but apparently C-4 explosive and rocket launchers were hard to come by. 'You know, I'm not sure Demos's idea is such a good one. I think we really should go back to the drawing board.'

Alex sat up. 'We don't have time, Lila. We need to move

261

tomorrow. And he's right. We talked all along about bringing down the whole of Stirling Enterprises. We need to destroy all their research and all their data. That way we know they can't come after you.'

'And him?' I asked, meaning Richard Stirling. 'Will he be inside the building?'

'No. We're not going to hurt anyone,' Alex said with a warning tone.

I raised an eyebrow at him.

'Unless we absolutely have to,' he conceded. 'The press will hurt him enough. We're not him, Lila; no matter what he's done or what you want to do to him we let the courts decide what happens to him.'

'The courts will prosecute him for a crime he hasn't even committed. What about what he did to Thomas? What about what he's done to my mum? To all of us? He doesn't deserve to live.'

Alex put his hand on my wrist. 'That's not your call to make. And if the truth of what the Unit and Stirling Enterprises were actually doing ever became public knowledge, what do you think would happen then? You don't think there are other men out there like Richard Stirling – other people who might try to do the same?'

'And if we keep him alive, you don't think that's dangerous too?'

'Lila,' Alex said gently, 'you're not a killer.'

'But you are,' I said, the words flying out of my mouth before I could stop them.

Alex flinched as if I'd slapped him.

'I mean . . . I mean only that you're a trained soldier.'

'Look, Lila,' Alex said and I caught the slight tremor in his voice, 'I have to live with what I did in Joshua Tree for the rest of my life. But I don't regret it. I was protecting you. And I would do the same again if I had to.' He stopped, seeing the stricken look on my face, and lay back down again, pulling me close. 'Hey, it's all going to be OK,' he murmured.

My breathing stopped as his lips found mine. They were warm and perfect and a million miles better than Jonas's had felt. I felt Alex's arms pulling me tighter until I was almost lying on top of him. His breathing was getting faster, his hands running up my spine, tangling in my hair while my fingers were grasping at his T-shirt even as my mind was one step ahead and lifting it up so I could run my hands over the hard planes of his stomach.

There was an urgency in his kiss that I hadn't felt before, something that was drawing us both in deeper, and I was just going with it. Maybe his resolve was faltering. Maybe he'd forgotten about Californian state law. I wasn't about to stop and ask – my lips were otherwise occupied and Alex's hands were on my waist, now stroking across my stomach, caressing upwards—

And then he stopped. Just like that. And I almost deflated and collapsed right there on top of him.

'What? What is it?' I whispered, my eyes flashing open, my face centimetres from his.

In answer he pulled my T-shirt down and rolled me onto the bed by his side. I lay there, staring at the ceiling, feeling my pulse still running at a dangerous rate. He shook his head slightly and smiled. 'The door's open and you're going to make me do something I shouldn't.'

The door clicked shut almost silently and he laughed under his breath. I willed him with every bone in my body to roll me on top of him again and do something he shouldn't. But Alex was Alex.

He took a deep breath and stood, shaking out his shoulders and running a hand over his hair, which I noticed was getting longer. Then he walked to the door and opened it again. Damn his honour. Damn his sensitivity towards my dad and Jack.

He turned back to me, smiling, as though he'd heard my thoughts. 'I don't want to push my luck with Jack.'

I scowled at him. 'I thought Jack was cool with us.'

'I wouldn't say *cool*. He's lukewarm.' He sat back down on the bed, keeping his distance. 'I found out why he changed his mind about me staying, though.'

I sat bolt upright.

'Key.' Alex nodded at the surprise on my face. 'We have Key to thank. He apparently took him aside and told him that sometimes you have to let the people you love make their own choices. That you have to realise you can't always protect them.' Alex grimaced a little at this last part.

'Wow.' I shook my head in amazement. 'You know, when I first met him, I thought he was just a homeless guy harassing me about noodles. I totally ignored him. And he's done so much for me. For all of us. I'm not sure how I'll ever thank him properly.'

Alex stood up. There was a trace of guilt on his face. 'Well, at least you didn't beat the crap out of him.' He headed once more for the door and I exhaled loudly in protest. He ignored me.

'Can you sneak back here tonight?' I asked, trying for innocence and seduction in the same breath.

He narrowed his eyes at me and shook his head. 'No. You're sharing with Suki.'

Oh God. So now I couldn't even think of Alex or dream of Alex because Suki would be along for the ride. I fell backwards onto the bed.

'That's right. You're sharing with me!'

I sprang back up. Suki had appeared with immaculate timing in the doorway. From the glint in her eye and the sly smile on her lips it was clear she'd been waiting for the right moment to burst in. I guessed I should just be thankful it hadn't been five minutes previously.

'And, Lila, feel free to dream,' she said, bouncing across the room and sitting next to me on the bed.

39

'It is so unfair. I never get to have any fun.' Suki stamped her spiked heel.

'Me neither,' Nate mumbled, looking up at her from his face-down position sprawled on the bed.

'Yes, you do. You get to fly around and spy on people,' she snapped back at him.

'You spy on people all the time, Suki. On their thoughts,' I said, sitting up and bringing my knees up to my chest.

She looked at me grudgingly. Then she weighed up what I was saying and decided I was right. Her narrow shoulders huffed up and then down. 'Well, it's still not fair. I want to come inside too. I want to see this headquarters where they do these bad things.'

I winced. The bad things she was talking about were being done to my mum.

'Sorry,' she said quietly, looking at me through her frothy lashes.

'It's OK. I just want to go. I want to go now,' I said, climbing off the bed and going to look out of the porthole. It was getting dark outside, the lights of other boats bobbing up and down the jetty, like candles in the dark. I'd fallen asleep for an hour. Suki and Nate had woken me up.

'Harvey needs to finish his research,' Nate said, looking up at me with his keen brown eyes.

'I know, I know,' I said. It didn't kill my impatience, though.

Harvey was busy online trying to brush up on security systems, figure out what tools he might need to take with him. He claimed he was a bit out of touch having been in prison and not having robbed any banks in the last few years.

Jack, Demos, Alex and my dad were busy refining the exit strategy. Jack was refusing to entertain the idea that an exit strategy would be needed because, according to him, Sara was as trustworthy as a saint, but Alex was insistent on there being a contingency plan.

I sat back down on the bed. 'So, tell me, what happened in Washington?' I hadn't even bothered to ask up until now, there had been so much else going on.

Suki stopped pouting and started bouncing, clapping her hands together. 'It was so much fun. We went shopping. Look – new shoes!' She pointed at the four-inch, crystal-encrusted heels she was wearing. I stared at her, wondering if she was joking

'Oh, sorry, you mean with the drugs and stuff,' she giggled.

Yes, of course I meant that.

'Well, I wanted to keep some.'

'Drugs?'

'No, the money! But Demos wouldn't let us.' She pulled her face into a grimace then lowered her voice, her eyes flashing. 'But I think he stashed some for himself. And I don't think Alex bought this boat on his credit card, if you know what I'm saying?'

I stifled a laugh. It was true. But I didn't care how he'd got the boat, I just hoped one day we'd be sailing it off into the sunset while the others stayed on land beyond the scope of Suki's hearing ability and Nate's flying range.

'But I never get to have any fun, Lila. Why can't I come too?'

267

'Would you please get out of my head?'

'Go where?' Nate asked, confused.

Suki ignored him. 'Oh, oh, but it's fine, isn't it, when you want me to go into Alex's head?' She jutted her chin and rested a hand on her hip.

I ignored her and turned to Nate instead. 'Where did you put the drugs? How did you hide everything?'

'We broke into Richard Stirling's house,' Nate said, rolling onto his back.

'How? How did you get in?' I interrupted. 'Doesn't Richard Stirling live in a fortress? I mean, he's a billionaire.'

'Yeah. Big house. Lots of guards.'

'And dogs. Don't forget the dogs,' Nate added.

'How'd you get in, then?' I asked again.

'Harvey broke in,' Suki said.

'Harvey broke in?'

'Yeah. Easy-peasy for him. I told you, he breaks into banks. Houses are easy. Like a kindergarten game.'

I nodded in fascination.

'We switched the alarm off first,' she said, reading my mind. 'That was all me. I am so clever,' she said, answering my silent *how?* 'I read his dumb guard's mind. I mean really? How silly is that as an approach to security? Telling your guards the code when you know there are mind-readers about? Stupidity like that deserves punishment.'

It did. 'And then what did you do?'

'We hid it – in his safe. Harvey cracked that one too.'

'He's a genius,' Nate piped up.

'Well, in that case, how'd he end up in prison? I mean before, with his power and everything, how did he get caught?' I needed to know. Just in case we could avoid making the same mistake again.

'He got drunk one night, passed out in a bar.' Suki shook her head, giggling.

OK. Easy enough to avoid that one. Just hide all the alcohol.

'How'd he escape?'

'Demos.'

'Demos?'

'Yes, he broke him out of prison. Just walked in and walked out with him.'

'What? Why?' I asked.

'Because he needed someone who could break into the Unit's HQ. This was a few years ago when he was trying to get Thomas out. When he thought Thomas might still be alive. And Demos and Harvey knew each other – they used to work together – so Demos broke him out of prison.'

I closed my eyes and tried to put it all together. Thomas had been caught by the Unit trying to find out what had happened to my mum. Demos had been trying to bring the Unit down ever since so he'd turned to Harvey for help. That made sense. 'Hang on, you said Demos and Harvey used to work together?' I asked, just figuring something out.

Suki looked at me and pulled a face. My jaw fell open. 'Demos? He . . . ?'

'Yes. He robbed banks too,' she said brightly.

'They were . . . ?'

'Yes. Bank-robbing buddies.' She smiled at me, happy I was catching on so quickly.

'No wonder your dad didn't want you associating,' I said to Nate.

'No wonder your dad hates him,' Suki said, looking at me knowingly.

'Yeah and some,' I said. It was true. My dad had plenty of reason to dislike Demos after what had happened between my mum and him.

'Yeah, that's hard for him. What with knowing Jack's his son and everything,' Suki said, her voice thick with sympathy.

I frowned at her. 'Excuse me?'

Her face froze. 'Nothing. Nothing.' She flicked her hair so it fell like a black curtain in front of her.

'Suki . . . what did you just say?'

'Nothing. I said nothing,' she said, climbing off the bed, 'You're hearing things. Crazy voices in your head.'

'No, you said something about knowing Jack's his son. What do you mean?'

'I don't know. Look, it's just something I overheard.' She was flat against the wall, her hands splayed. Her voice became whiney. 'It's not my fault, I can't help it. I can't filter. I just heard it earlier.'

'He's whose son?' I demanded.

'I'm sorry,' Suki cried, 'I shouldn't be the one telling you this.' She dived under my arm and disappeared through the door before I could stop her.

Every step I took seemed to keep time with my heart. Like a ticking bomb. I clutched hold of the banister and crept down the stairs. At the bottom I snuck into the room where they were all massed round the table, heads bent, planning.

There was Jack. He was sitting beside Demos and they were huddled together conferring. Both dark-haired. Both the same height. I heaved in a sticky breath of air then turned my head

270

slowly towards my dad. He was looking from Jack to Demos and I caught the haunted, sad expression in his eyes and it sucked the wind out of me.

My dad looked up and noticed me and I sank down onto the sofa. I couldn't believe I hadn't seen it before. Jack was the spitting image of Demos, apart from his eyes – my mum's eyes – and the fact that Jack was good-looking. But other than that they were almost identical: the widow's peak; the way they both arched their left eyebrow from time to time when something amused them.

It felt suddenly like the world was crumbling or the boat was sinking. I tore my eyes away. I got up and gripped the banister and I climbed the stairs, feeling the sway of the boat almost taking my feet out from under me.

Jack was Demos's son.

Suki and her big mouth. She must have heard it. My dad knew, then. Of course he knew. That's why he didn't want Jack near Demos. Maybe that's what explained the animosity between the two of them. Or at least part of it. So, everyone knew. Everyone, that is, except for Jack.

My room was empty now. Suki and Nate had made themselves scarce. I sat down on the bed and put my head in my hands. Demos had been the man Jack had been hunting for years. Oh God, it was Oedipal or something. Jack couldn't find out.

I looked up and walked to the mirror. *What if?* No. *What if?* No. No. No.

No. There were bits of my dad in my reflection. I had his nose. His chin.

'Are you OK?' It was Alex. He was standing in the doorway. I turned and stared at him, speechless. Then I turned back to the mirror. Alex came up behind me and put his hands on my shoulders and I looked up at his reflection.

'Do I look like my dad?'

'What?'

'Do I look like my dad?'

'No, you look like your mum. You know that. I've told you already.'

I turned round in his arms, tilting my chin. 'And Jack. Who does he look like?'

He smiled at me, shaking his head in confusion. 'Where are you going with this?'

'I think Demos might be Jack's father.'

Alex started to laugh, but when he saw I wasn't, the smile died on his lips. 'What?'

'Suki let it out the bag. But look at them. Go and look at them. They're so alike.'

I saw the sudden realisation dawn. I turned back to the mirror. 'What about me? Is he my father too, do you think?'

'No. No way. I remember when you were born.'

'You do?' I looked at him in surprise. He'd been four, almost five.

'Yeah, of course. Your dad's your dad. You have his nose. And his lashes.'

'That's what I thought.' I glanced in the mirror at Alex. 'So, how is he Jack's dad?'

'You said your mum and dad met while she was dating Demos. Maybe she was already pregnant?'

Oooh, gross. I wrinkled my nose. Is that why they left for Washington? Had Demos known? I looked back at Alex. 'We can't tell Jack.'

272

Alex frowned at me. 'I think your dad needs to tell him. Jack needs to know.'

'Not now. Not on top of Sara and my mum and everything else. It'll take him over the edge.'

Wake up from coma. Find you can heal yourself. Discover girlfriend may be evil. Then discover your father isn't your father but the man you've been trying to kill. No, it wasn't a good idea to tell him. Not before tonight.

Alex nodded agreement. 'OK, after, then. But he has to be told.'

40

I found Suki hiding in the galley. She was sitting behind an opened closet door eating a bowl of dried cereal.

'Sorry,' she said, looking up guiltily.

'It's OK,' I said. 'It's not your fault. I'm glad I know.'

'Did you tell Jack?' she asked.

'No, and you can't either. Or Nate – I know what a big mouth he has. But I think if my dad or Demos wanted Jack to know, he would by now. Anyway,' I said, 'that's not why I'm here. Alex wants you to help me practise.'

'Practise what?' Suki asked brightly. 'Mind-reading? Japanese? Making splashy-splashy with the waves? Kissing? You name it, I am here for you.'

I shook my head. 'No, none of the above. Making fire.'

'Oooh, like cavemen,' she giggled. 'We should invite your brother.'

'Ha ha,' I replied. 'Well, at least we know now where he gets it from.'

Suki linked her arm through mine and we headed back to our cabin.

Asking Suki to help me practise controlling fire was like getting a toddler to oversee a space mission.

'It's only fire, Lila,' said Suki. 'Don't be so scared.'

I was standing in front of a candle barely able to disguise my terror. There was no point faking confidence anyway, not with Suki able to read my mind.

'Just try it,' she urged. 'Look on the bright side: if you cause an inferno, you can always put it out with a tidal wave.'

'Very funny,' I snapped. 'I just don't see why everyone is relying on me. It's so unfair. I've never even done this before. I made a big wave . . . that's entirely different to making fire do what I tell it to. I can't just do it on demand like I'm some kind of performing seal.'

Suki put her hand on her hip and raised her eyebrows. 'Finished?' I huffed. 'Wait here,' she told me and skipped out of the door. She came back a minute later holding a fire extinguisher in one hand.

'Thanks for the vote of confidence,' I muttered.

'Well, I don't want to end up a fireball.'

'Don't tempt me.'

'OK,' she said, lighting the candle, 'now try making it do something.'

I stared at the tiny flickering flame. 'Like what?' I asked.

'I don't know. Make it move.'

I stared harder at the flame, noticing the blue colour in the middle, the dancing black and orange and yellow licking round the wick. The flame seemed to flicker, but I could have imagined it. I concentrated harder. I tried to feel the air around the flame; it felt like pins and needles or like trying to catch fat spattering in a pan. I tried to grasp at one part of the flame that I could sense the edge of. The flame elongated before us, stretching up long and thin until it was at eye level.

I heard Suki breathe in deeply. 'Now make it do something good.'

I felt my grip on the flame go. It dropped back to normal height. I twisted my head to Suki and glared at her. 'You're supposed to be helping.'

'I am,' she said brightly, holding up the extinguisher. Its nozzle was poised in my direction.

I turned round, trying to ignore her, and focused instead on the flame.

'You can do this.'

I smiled to myself and turned slowly. Alex was standing just behind me. 'You can do this,' he said again.

I turned back to the candle, tried to feel for the blue beating heart of it. Then, just like that, I felt it tingle and spark against my mind. I took a firm hold of it and ordered it to jump. The flame leapt upwards, almost to the ceiling, then dropped down again. I pushed it sideways, back down, up, to the other side. Tried a diagonal. It was like a little firework show. I gave an inwards whoop and the candle flipped off the table and landed at my feet. Suki gave a little scream and covered our feet and the carpet in foam.

I looked at Alex. 'I told you you could do it,' he said.

I bit my lip and looked at the charred patch of carpet covered in white froth. I hoped he was right. Or we'd all be toast.

Alex took my hand. 'I have to go now.'

I looked up at him, trying to erase the fear in my eyes. 'Please be careful,' I said. He and Jack were going to meet Sara to set up the break-in. They were taking Amber along for the ride to once and for all settle the issue of whether Sara could be trusted or not.

'It's OK,' Alex said, stroking my cheek. 'Sara will come alone. They'll want to know what we're planning. Why settle for just Jack and me when they could wait a day and get us all?'

41

'Suki?' I whispered in the half-light of the morning. 'Are they back?'

'Hmmmmm?' she murmured, rolling slightly towards me, pushing a purple silk eye mask off her face.

'Are Jack and Alex back?'

She was silent a minute and my heartbeat filled the quiet. 'Mmmm,' she sighed, 'I can hear Jack.' She rubbed her forehead. 'Ow, he's loud. He's angry. I don't want to wake up to this.'

'Why's he angry?' I asked, already knowing with a sinking feeling what that meant.

'Sara,' she muttered and rolled over, pulling a pillow over her head. 'Evil minion.'

'What happened?' I said, sitting up.

'I don't know. I'm sleeping, Lila. Go and find lover boy and ask him.'

I poked my head round the door to the main cabin. The sun was just coming through the portholes, sending slanting shadows across the floor. Amber was standing in the centre of the room while Jack paced in front of her. Alex and Demos were sitting at the table.

'She was lying,' Amber said.

'You're sure?' Demos asked quickly.

Amber shot him a look so venomous that I flinched. Her hair was loose, falling like a blazing halo round her face, which was still pale but more animated than before. She still looked haunted, but there was a tinge of hardness to her grey eyes. I recognised the look well. She was playing the grief game – she had crossed through disbelief and anger, taken a leap over acceptance and had finally landed on revenge where the rest of us had been stuck for some time.

I stepped into the room. Alex smiled wanly when he saw me. He looked utterly exhausted and his eyes didn't rest on me long before darting back to Jack who was still striding back and forth across the room.

'What happened?' I asked warily, my eyes on Jack.

'Amber says Sara was lying,' Jack burst out. 'Because she's the wrong colour.'

'Her *aura* was the wrong colour,' Amber cut in.

'And that's like what?' Jack shouted. 'The equivalent of a lie-detector test?'

'Better,' Amber answered coolly.

'Right, so because you saw some colour in an *aura* you're saying my girlfriend is what? In on all this?'

'I wouldn't call her your girlfriend if I were you. I don't think she feels the same. And yes, I'm saying she's in on it. She was lying about not knowing the Unit had your mum. She was lying about not knowing what the Unit are really doing too. She knows. Believe me, she knows.'

Jack stood still. He shut his eyes for a long second.

'Look, I'm sorry, Jack, I know it's not what you want to hear,' Demos said, walking over to him and placing a placatory hand on his shoulder.

Jack's eyes flew open. He spun round, freezing Demos with one glance. *Like father like son*, I thought to myself, sucking in a breath between my teeth.

'I'll give Sara one thing,' Alex said, shaking his head, 'she's a great actress. She even cried when she saw Jack. Told him she'd do whatever he asked. She had me fooled too.'

Jack didn't say anything. I could see the deep furrows running across his forehead and his jaw was pulsing furiously.

'Amber's always right on these things, Jack,' Demos said. 'I trust her judgement.'

Jack glared at him once more and then he glared at Amber. His face was so readable I felt my heart catch as I watched him trying to gather his feelings and hide them from the rest of us.

'When we go onto the base, when we get inside,' Jack said, his eyes flashing angrily, 'Sara's mine. I deal with her.' He looked at Demos. And then at Alex. 'Understood?'

Alex shot Demos a quick look. Then they both nodded.

Jack strode to the bar and poured himself a double shot of something. He tipped it down his throat in one go. And then he poured a second glass. No one made a move to stop him. I guessed I'd do the same if I'd found out Alex had betrayed me and was torturing my mum.

'So, what exactly did you say to Sara?' I whispered to Alex who was keeping his eyes fixed on Jack.

'We told her that we needed her help to break into the building. We told her it was just you, me and Jack coming with your dad. She's agreed. She'll switch off the alarm system until we're safely inside. I told her I was worried you'd set it off otherwise – said you were struggling to control your ability. It'll allow for Demos and Harvey to follow us inside.'

'So then, it's all set? We're all set for tonight?'

He nodded. 'We just need to alert the press about the drugs bust in Washington.'

'And then I'll call the DEA,' Demos added.

'The drugs people, right?'

'Yep,' Alex answered.

I wanted to listen in to that call. What did you say? Who did you even call? 911?

What's your emergency?

There's a stash of drugs and money in Richard Stirling's house. Here's the address – go check it out. No, this isn't a hoax.

Oh well, Demos was the one man on the planet who could make anyone do anything so I guessed he'd make it work.

'And once we've blown the lid on Washington, we head onto the base. It'll be a huge news story. The DEA raids Stirling Enterprises and their HQ blows up an hour later. It will look like a huge cover-up. The press on both coasts will go wild. Richard Stirling won't be able to just walk away from this.'

No, he won't, I thought, *not if I have anything to do with it. He'll never walk anywhere ever again; he'll be buried in the rubble.*

I glanced at Jack, who was still bent over the bar, staring into the bottom of a glass.

It looked like Sara would be too.

42

I glanced in the rear-view mirror and caught Alex staring at me. A look passed between us and a twinge hit me. If I died today, or got contained, I'd never get to be Mrs Wakeman. Damn Alex and his resolve. If I died a virgin, I'd never forgive him.

Alex turned round in his seat. 'So, let me do the talking, OK?'

I looked out of the back window. Demos and Harvey were following us in a black Toyota rental. Alicia and Amber were with them. No one had explicitly said why they were coming, but it was obvious. Alicia wanted to make sure the headquarters got destroyed and Amber wanted revenge on the people who'd killed Ryder. She was there to make sure she got it.

Key was somewhere in the ether. Maybe he was floating above the car right now. Possibly Nate was too. I wasn't too sure that the command Demos had given him and Suki to stay put on the boat was going to be followed. It was asking for trouble.

Demos was going to drive straight onto the base with the others. It was unlikely he'd have any problems getting through the barricade. He'd just freeze the soldiers from a distance and then drive on by.

'So, we have to buy Demos and Harvey as much time as possible,' Alex was saying. 'Our mission is to get down into prisoner holding, find your mum, rescue her and get out again.

281

Harvey will deactivate the alarm so that Demos can hold the Unit off while we get out. They'll want us all in prisoner holding before they make a move.'

'Are you OK, Dad?' I asked. He hadn't said a word so far.

He gave me a wan smile. He wasn't so used to the subterfuge-filled, fugitive life as we were. I wanted to reach over, pat his hand and tell him not to worry, that you got used to it pretty quickly, but Alex said something and it made us all look up.

'She's waiting,' he said again. I raised my head and scanned the road. We had arrived.

And there was Sara, standing on the sidewalk next to a black SUV, her arms crossed over her chest, her face stricken. I glanced up the street and at the house. Jack stared at it too. It was the first time he'd seen his house in a while.

'Let's go,' Alex said, throwing open his door.

Sara ran to the car and threw her arms round Jack before he could even get out. Wow, she was a good actress. I felt Alex's hand circle my wrist even as the licks of fire started scorching down my veins.

'Lila!' Alex whistled a warning under his breath as if he'd read my mind or felt my anger transmuted as electricity through my skin.

I took a deep breath and tried to smile as I watched Jack's hands travel up Sara's back in comforting strokes. His acting wasn't bad either. He even managed not to throttle her when she started kissing him. She extracted herself after a good half-minute and rushed over to me.

'Lila! You're safe! I'm so glad,' she cried, pulling me into a huge hug. I watched Jack's face over her shoulder. He looked like he was trying to fire laser beams at her back.

'Mmmm,' I said. *No thanks to you.* I patted her half-heartedly on the shoulder, saw Alex's warning glance and squeezed her tighter.

'I wish you could have trusted me,' she whispered in my ear.

Luckily she moved onto my dad and Alex took hold of my curled fists and tugged me back.

'Dr Loveday,' Sara said, taking my dad's hand in both of hers. 'I don't know what to say,' she choked. 'I'm so sorry.'

He stood ashen-faced, looking at her with undisguised loathing, and Jack stepped quickly between them, pulling Sara away from him before she noticed.

'Where are the Unit's teams?' Jack asked quickly.

'Alpha and Beta teams are en route to Washington. We've just caught wind of something,' Sara said with a frown. 'You were right. We think Demos is there.'

I shot Alex a look. So the ball was rolling. The DEA must have raided Stirling Enterprises already.

'OK, let's go,' Jack said, marching towards the SUV.

Sara pulled open the driver's door. We climbed in in silence and it felt like clambering into my own coffin again.

'How are you going to get us in?' Jack asked from up front as Sara pulled away from the kerb. I kept my eyes on Alex's hand holding mine. I could feel his thumb pressing into my palm and I focused on that and not on the fact we were embarking on a suicide mission as though it was just a picnic in the park.

'We'll go in the back entrance,' Sara answered. 'The goods entrance. It's touch-pad entry. I have the code. There should only be a few people around, mainly lab technicians. We can skirt them and take the goods elevator down to the prisoner level.'

Her eyes were suddenly on me in the rear-view mirror. 'I'm so sorry about your mum,' she said. 'I can't believe it's true.'

I looked away, out of the window, and took a deep breath. I didn't want to cause another crash.

'It's true,' Jack answered for me. His hand was balled in a fist at his side and his voice was tight, as though he was being strangled.

We took the turn onto the base a minute later. Sara wound down her window and flashed her laminated ID out of it. The Marines on duty just nodded her through. No stop and search like yesterday morning. They had obviously been primed to expect us and ordered to let us pass.

The barricade lifted. They'd already replaced the one I'd destroyed on the way out the other day. Dusk was falling, the light was bruised and purple and I couldn't help wondering if it was the last sunset I'd ever see. We passed the Unit's headquarters and took the next right, carrying on down a smaller road round the side of the building. The back looked as impenetrable as the front – a solid glass and steel fortress.

'OK, we have to hurry,' Sara said as she parked the SUV by the back door.

We all jumped out, Alex and Jack standing sentry, scanning the surroundings, pushing my dad and me behind them.

Sara crossed to the alarm pad on the wall by two steel doors that reminded me of upright mortuary slabs and tapped in some numbers. I hoped Harvey had done his homework. He had merely dragged long and hard on his cigarette when I'd asked him how confident he was about being able to break in. I wasn't sure what kind of an answer that was, but right now I was going with very confident.

The hallway we walked into was empty and long and lit halogen-white. It looked like a Hollywood filmset for God's waiting room.

284

Our footsteps echoed like righteous thunder. I glanced to the end of it, trying to recall the map Jack had drawn for us. The control room that Harvey and Demos would be heading for was just on the right-hand side before the elevator.

I suddenly had a moment's clarity of vision. We were insane. My dad was completely right. Only mad people would attempt what we were attempting. But, on the other hand, maybe it was so insane the Unit would never suspect it. I had to hope so.

We reached the elevator at the end of the hallway. This was it. I was just minutes away from seeing my mum again and adrenaline flooded my system, pulsing through my body. Sara pressed her ID card against a reader and then pushed the button for level -4. None of us breathed. Alex held my hand tight.

The corridor that we spilled into was empty. The ceilings were low, the fluorescent strip lights so startlingly bright I had to blink. We walked towards a double-thickness glass door at the end. There was another touch pad to its right. Sara tapped in the code. The door swooshed open and we stepped through. It slid shut behind us, sealing us inside what could only be prisoner holding.

The room we found ourselves in was deserted. A bank of computers sat along a central column of desks, their screens blank. Along one side of the room were several white doors, each solid-looking and without handles. The only indication they were doors at all was the thin black outline and the flashing touch pad to the right of each one. Were those the cells? Was my mum inside one? My dad must have been thinking along the same lines because he crossed straight over to them and started banging, calling out her name.

'Where is she? Where's Melissa?' my dad shouted, desperation in his voice.

A slow smile eased across Sara's face.

'Where is she?' Jack demanded.

I saw Sara's face register his tone and her brown eyes narrowed slightly at him. Then, as I watched, she took a stumbling step backwards, her eyes growing round. Her hands flew to her chest, palms outwards. I glanced at Jack again and did a double take. His gun was in his hand and he was pointing it straight at Sara.

'Where is she, Sara?' he asked calmly.

I saw Sara figure it out in that instant – finally understand that we were playing her – that this was a double-cross as Suki had so eloquently put it. Sara's eyes darted to Alex and then to me and finally to my dad, who had stopped calling my mum's name and instead was staring straight at her, with a look of pure hatred.

'What are you doing?' Sara asked, giving innocence one last try.

'Cut the crap, Sara. I know you're lying. Just tell me where she is before I shoot you.'

'You're not going to shoot me, Jack,' she said, looking at him like he was being ridiculous. 'Besides, it's too late for that.' She tilted her head to the camera in the corner of the room. 'Put the gun down,' she ordered in a completely new voice. Her eyes hardened, the softness in her face melting away, leaving only a brittle, hard-angled stranger in her place.

I drew in a breath. Up until then I had been hoping that Amber had got it wrong – that the aura thing was perhaps just a load of New Age nonsense. I glanced at Jack. I could see he was just as shaken as I was. A part of him must have been hoping and praying that Amber was wrong too. But then his expression turned cold and he raised the gun so it was aimed directly at Sara's head.

She didn't react. She just smiled casually. 'You can't get out, Jack. It's too late,' she said.

'Why?' Jack asked.

'Because, Jack,' she sighed, 'your old team are just outside. Well, what's left of them. The ones you didn't shoot. They're watching and waiting for my order.' She nodded at the camera in the corner of the room. 'You're not going anywhere. Neither's your mother. And I should thank you also for delivering your mutant sister to us too.'

Jack weighed her up for a split second before shifting the gun a fraction and firing at the camera in the corner of the room, leaving an intestinal tangle of wires and smoking metal. 'I meant,' he said, training the gun on Sara once more, 'why are you doing this?'

She snorted. 'Well, that's done it. Now they're coming.'

'Answer the question,' Jack demanded.

'Oh, Jack, it's not personal. It was never personal.'

'It's my mum,' Jack growled. 'It doesn't get more personal.'

'It's science, Jack. It's progress. You can't stand in the way of it.'

'Science?' I screeched. 'Science? You think that kidnapping people and torturing them is progress?'

Sara looked at me and laughed. 'Oh, Lila, you do make me laugh. Science is the future. And if one or two people are sacrificed for the greater good – well, so be it. We're learning so much from your mother. We're going to learn even more from you, Lila. And imagine how the world will benefit from that knowledge.'

'Benefit?' I stuttered, taking a step towards her.

Alex stretched his arm out and caught me round the waist before I could reach her. She flinched a little, but tried hard to cover up her fear. I noticed that Alex too had a gun in his hand and that it was pointed at her. Out the corner of my eye I could see my dad, his face frozen, almost expressionless, his eyes unblinking. He seemed too stunned to even move.

'It's OK, Alex, let her go. Let her do her worst!' Sara said quite calmly. 'Go on, Lila,' she taunted. 'Use that power of yours. It'll trigger the alarm. It was reactivated the moment you set foot down here. You'll only hurt yourself.'

I stared at her, loathing seeping from every pore in my body.

'Oh, did you honestly think we didn't know about you? About what you were? Lila, we've known about you for years. Since the scissor episode at your school – remember that?'

I couldn't hide my surprise. That was three years ago. How had they known about that? My lungs collapsed as though my ribs had punctured them.

'We've known about you the whole time, Lila. About what you are. We've just been waiting for the right moment to bring you in. If it had been up to me, I would have contained you as soon as you stepped off the plane from London, but Rachel wanted to see what might happen. She wanted to see whether Demos would go after you, which he did, predictably. We knew where Alex was the whole time you two were off on your romantic little getaway; we could have swooped on you in Palm Springs, but we wanted to wait until we had you and Demos in one place before we made a move.'

I felt Alex's hand tighten its grip on my arm.

'We hoped we'd be able to contain all of you at the same time back at Joshua Tree – make it look like you got shot in the fallout, Lila, and then contain you and no one would have known. You see, we need someone who's telekinetic.' She pursed her lips. 'But you got away. Thank you, Alex,' she said, her voice dripping with sarcasm. 'But then you came back.' She shook her head as though she still couldn't believe my stupidity. 'What were you thinking?'

'If you think you're going to touch her, you've got another think coming,' Alex snarled, taking a step towards her.

'Oh, Alex,' Sara said, laughing. 'You don't really think you're going to stop us, do you?'

The bullet whizzed past my ear. I heard the zip before it smacked into the tiled wall behind Sara's head.

'Enough!' my dad roared. 'Where's my wife?'

My jaw swung open. My dad was holding a gun. I wasn't sure where he'd got a gun from or whether he'd missed Sara's head accidentally or on purpose.

Sara seemed just as astonished. 'Dr Loveday, put the gun down,' she said in an uneven tone.

'She's here.'

I turned my head. Alex was leaning over the bank of monitors in the centre of the room. He'd turned them all on. Every screen displayed a black-and-white portrait of a cell. I scanned across them – all of them were empty and for a moment my heart seemed to tear through my chest. I couldn't breathe or see – black-and-white dots were dancing across my vision – then I realised that was just the jumping static of the screens and there – there was movement. On the far screen. A thin white shape, jerking and juddering in front of the camera, looking upon first glance like a ghost hovering or a smear on the camera lens. I pushed closer, leaning across the desk, clutching at Alex's arm. Even through the jumping static, I could make out the eyes. My eyes. Staring at us. I could see her mouth making shapes. *Michael*. She was saying *Michael*.

'Dad, Dad, it's Mum. It's Mum!' I yelled.

Out of the corner of my eye I caught a flash of movement. Sara had thrown herself sideways, and as I watched, her fist smashed through a square glass box attached to the wall and punched down on the red button inside.

Splinters of glass pierced my brain. I felt my cheekbone smack the tiles and a bolt of pain slice open my head. I heard shouting and the whisk of a bullet past my ear.

Jack was lying by me, his knees bent up to his chest. I tried to reach my hand out towards him, but I couldn't locate my fingers. Vague thoughts, like drips of acid on an open cut, shrieked through my brain. *The alarm. Harvey and Demos hadn't been able to deactivate it.*

Another bullet whistled by my ear. It seemed to ricochet inside my skull. I tried to force myself to stand, to open my eyes at least. To fight. I couldn't give in now. I wouldn't give in now.

A hand started to haul me upright. 'Lila, come on! I need you. Lila!'

I opened one eye, squinting through a film of tears, and saw Alex had his arm round me and was trying to get me to stand. My feet were dragging against the floor, my body hung limp against his side.

'Come on!' he yelled again.

My head tipped back in surprise at his tone, but my feet found the ground and I stood shakily, feeling my head wobble as though it was attached by a fraying thread to the rest of me. The pain was foggy now, less piercing, throbbing in my temples, sending shockwaves coursing down my spine.

'Lila, focus!'

My eyes snapped open. I hadn't realised I had shut them again. The room flipped the right way up. The walls zoomed back in. Sound blasted my ears. The pain was sucked away like a syringe drawing blood. I saw Jack kneeling at my feet, his head bent over, hands splayed on the floor. I bent down towards him, wanting to help him stand, but Alex shook me once more, hauling me round to face the door.

'Lila, I need your help here, please.'

I forced my eyes to focus. But all I could make out was a black mass pounding down the corridor towards us like a huge swarm of bees that slowly pixelated into a solid form. It was them. It was the Unit. They were coming for us – at least half a dozen men stampeding towards us.

'Do something!' Alex yelled.

Then I realised what he was asking me to do and tried to focus. There were splashes of red decorating the walls of the corridor they were running down. Fire extinguishers. I ripped them off the walls, feeling a sharp blast of pain in my head as I did, and mustering the last reserve of energy within me, hurled them like skittles into the mass of men. Two of them doubled over and hit the floor, but the others were already at the door, punching in a code. I scanned the room quickly. Sara was lying sprawled on the floor by Jack's feet and my dad was nowhere in sight, but my brain didn't have time to process that. Alex fired at the control pad, leaving a smoking box dangling from the wall.

The door made a sputtering noise in response. A man on the other side kept punching futilely at the keypad. He gave up and stood aside as another man wedged the butt of his gun into the hinge of the door, trying to force it. A third man fired at the glass.

'The door, hold the door. It's bulletproof,' Alex yelled at me.

Just then the door made a groaning noise. It juddered and wheezed and started to open. I seized hold of it, forcing it shut and holding it there with every bit of strength I possessed. I watched helplessly, gritting my teeth as the Unit's soldiers fired their guns repeatedly at the wall of glass in front of us. The glass bloomed with snowflakes and I felt the tears start to trickle acid-hot down my cheeks. How long before they were through? Even if the glass held, I knew I couldn't hold the door for much longer and certainly not if they fired the alarm again. I had what? Thirty seconds before another one hit me perhaps. What were Demos and Harvey doing? Had they been captured?

'Alex . . . I can't hold it long,' I cried over the noise of the cracking glass.

I was dimly aware of Alex helping Jack to stand. Jack shook him off, steadying himself against the desk, still woozy. It was the first time he'd experienced one of those shots – he wasn't as able as I was to shake it off.

'Let's go.' Alex's hand was suddenly on my shoulder.

I risked a glance sideways. My dad was standing in the doorway of the cell and he was carrying something in his arms.

'Lila, the door!' Alex shouted.

I slammed it closed again, catching an arm and hearing a high-pitched scream. I ignored the sound, struggling to keep my attention on the door when what was behind me was all I cared about.

'Come on, this way!' Alex was pulling and tugging on my arm. I stepped backwards, through the far door, and into yet another corridor, the whole time keeping my focus on the bullet-riddled glass door in front of me.

'Wait here,' Alex said, running past me at a crouch and back into the room. With a fluid movement, he bent and hefted Sara over his shoulder. Then he ran in a crouch back towards me.

Jack waited until he was through then sealed this second door shut before shooting out the control panel. With a gasp, I let go of the first door. The Unit burst through in seconds, sprinted across the room we'd just been in and started hammering and firing at the second door.

Jack took my arm and we started running. I didn't dare glance over my shoulder to see. Every single step I braced myself for the pain and for the fall, my attention on my dad, up ahead of us. Just so long as he got out. Just so long as he got my mum out, it wouldn't matter.

Jack's grip on my arm tightened as he forced me into a sprint. We slammed through the door at the end of the corridor just behind Alex.

'Dad?' Jack yelled, pounding up the stairs ahead of us both.

'Here!' my dad shouted. We flung ourselves up the first flight and found him on the landing, kneeling over a body. I threw myself towards him and he caught me by the shoulder. 'Careful, careful.'

She was dead. My mum was dead. She was lifeless, whiter than white, her lips as colourless as glass. She was lying across my dad's lap, wearing a white hospital gown that blended with the colour of her skin. Jack dropped down next to me and took her hand.

'Mum?' he said, his voice choking.

Her eyes flashed open, startling me. It was as if all the colour within her was concentrated solely in her eyes. They were burning green, filled with life, with memories, with hope, with relief and joy.

'Jack,' she whispered, and a smile flitted across her lips. Her eyes travelled over Jack's face and then to me.

I threw myself forward, feeling Jack at my side, my dad's arms coming round us both.

'Mum, Mum, Mum, I missed you so much,' I sobbed.

Her hand reached up and stroked my hair, my cheek, and gently brushed away the tears that were falling. And then I felt another tug on my shoulder pulling me backwards.

'Lila, come on, we've got to get out of here,' my dad said, leaning down to scoop my mum up once more.

I realised only then we were still in the stairwell. Alex was leaning against the wall, resting Sara's weight. His face was tight; beads of sweat had broken out on his forehead. His focus was on the stairwell below, the gun in his free hand trained on the door.

Jack pushed me up the stairs behind my dad. 'Go, go!' he ordered.

I started running, pausing to make sure the others were following. Jack had dropped back behind Alex and was covering him. I wished he'd just drop Sara on her head so he could go faster.

At ground level, I heard Alex yell at me to wait, but it was too late, I'd already thrown the door back. It hit the wall and my dad who was ahead of me stepped through into the wide-open space of the lobby.

'Ahhh, there you are.'

I staggered back a step. Richard Stirling was standing in front of us. At his side was Robocop. He was aiming a gun straight at my dad's head. My dad stood frozen, holding my mum in his arms as though she was a sacred offering. Her head was thrown back against my dad's shoulder, her eyes were shut and one arm was dangling so low it was almost scraping the floor.

'Going somewhere?' Stirling asked.

The others burst through behind me. I heard Jack swear and then I felt Alex at my side, breathing hard, Sara's body still hanging over his shoulder like a limp sack. I glanced over at him and our eyes caught for a second – his filled with a warning. *Don't do anything crazy,* he was warning me.

Alex turned back to Richard Stirling and the expression on his face shifted, darkened. He raised the gun in his spare hand and levelled it at Stirling's head. As he did so, he took a step in front of me. Jack moved at the same time to stand in front of my dad, shielding both him and my mum. He had his gun pointed straight at Robocop. It was a stand-off.

I took a deep breath. Then pushed past Alex.

'Just let us go,' I said, walking towards Stirling.

'Lila,' I heard Alex growl under his breath.

'Let you go?' Stirling answered with a bemused smile. 'Why on earth would I do that? Right here in front of me I have several hundred million dollars' worth of weaponry in the form of you and your anatomy. A few tweaks here, a little experimentation there and—'

'And you can go to hell maybe?' I finished the sentence for him.

'Oh, Lila, quite the temper, haven't we? It's a struggle for you, isn't it? Keeping control, I mean? We'll need to look into that. I have to say, though, I am impressed. I completely overlooked you, but that's some skill you have.' He turned his attention away from me to Jack. 'And you, Jack,' he said, 'now that's something I never even imagined. When we finally got Dr Roberts talking, we were all quite intrigued and eager to get our hands on you.' He shook his head, his eyes lingering hungrily on Jack's chest.

Jack's reply made me wince.

My dad's response made me wince even more.

I thought about Dr Roberts and what they might have done to him and suddenly felt like I was going to throw up.

Richard Stirling just laughed. It was an eerie sound, rebounding off the high ceiling and marble floor. 'Listen, you played your cards, you lost. I'm just a better poker player. When Demos and his little friends arrive in a couple of hours' time, I'm going to have a full house.'

Hope exploded in my chest almost igniting me. Richard Stirling didn't know that Demos was in the building. He thought he was in Washington. Our bluff had worked! And the alarm hadn't gone off again. I wasn't writhing on the floor in agony. Which could only mean one thing – Demos and Harvey must have deactivated it.

'The building's in lockdown, Lieutenant,' Stirling continued, 'and right behind you coming up those stairs is your old team. So I think maybe you'd be wise to put your guns down now, turn around and walk back the way you came, down to prisoner holding.'

Alex sighed loudly then took a step forward so he was standing by my side. 'I've a suggestion,' he said. 'How about you turn around and walk back the way you came in and we'll follow you out.'

Richard Stirling looked at him, stunned, before smiling tightly. 'Yes, OK, when you've finished being funny, you can do as I say or I can shoot you.'

A sly smile began to form on Alex's lips. 'You could try,' he said.

Richard Stirling's eyes narrowed again, confusion passing over his face. But then it blanked out. His eyes glazed. Beside him, Robocop froze.

I looked up, startled. Demos was standing in the doorway. Harvey strolled out of the shadows behind him.

'You took your time,' I said.

'Made it, didn't we?' Demos answered with a grim smile.

43

Demos circled Richard Stirling and backed towards my dad, letting his attention slip only for a second while he dipped his head to look down at my mum. I didn't miss the way his face softened when he saw her or the way my dad's hands tightened reflexively round my mum. Then, with a grim face, Demos marched straight towards Richard Stirling.

It was only then that I noticed Alicia standing halfway between us and the door, caught mid-step, her hands clutched at her sides. She was staring at Demos, looking like she'd just taken a bullet in her heart.

My attention was diverted by Jack who marched over to Robocop. He dropped the clip from Robocop's gun into his pocket. 'What about the men downstairs?' he asked, crossing to the door that we'd come through, his gun aimed.

It was a good point. They should have broken through the door by now.

'They're trapped down there. I activated the lockdown on that floor,' Harvey said with a little cough.

'But we can't just leave them in there,' I said, 'they won't survive.'

'It's a nuclear bunker – they'll be fine,' Jack replied tersely.

I stared at him. 'What?' he replied, shrugging at me. 'They will be fine. The fire department will find them in a few days' time once it cools.'

'He's right,' Alex spoke up, looking at me reassuringly. 'They will be fine down there. It's built to withstand a whole lot more than a fire.'

'Everyone happy, then?' Demos interrupted. 'Great, then get out of here and off this base before the entire military figures out what's happening in here. I'll hold these guys until we're all set.' He nodded at Richard Stirling and his bodyguard. 'Lila, are you ready?'

'Yes,' I answered, stepping forward.

'I'm staying with her,' I heard Alex say behind me.

'Me too,' Jack said.

Of course they were.

I watched as Alex hefted Sara off his shoulder and it was only then that I noticed the drips of crimson raining down onto the tiles and pooling by his feet. My eyes flew to his face, my heart lurching. His T-shirt was stained dark over his left shoulder and for a moment I thought he'd been shot, but then he handed Sara over to Harvey and I saw that Sara's white top was soaked through with blood.

Harvey stared at her like she was roadkill, his lip curling in distaste. He took a long drag on his cigarette and finally nodded. Alex let go and Harvey held her, letting her hover half a metre off the ground, her fingernails scuttling on the marble floor, her head almost bent double on the slender stalk of her neck. Alex strode to me, his eyes holding mine, checking I was OK, trying to read me.

'Be careful.'

I turned in a daze to look at my dad, his arms locked round my mum. 'Be careful,' he said again. I nodded at him in response and he smiled at me. I watched him leave, following after Harvey.

A few seconds after they disappeared, someone else appeared in the doorway. A flame-haired ghost wearing sleek black jeans, boots and a black sweater. Amber scanned the room quickly and then strode straight towards us, her heels clicking on the floor, her eyes shrouded dark grey. She stopped in front of Richard Stirling.

'What are you doing, Amber?' Demos asked quietly.

'I wanted to see the man behind the Unit,' she answered, not taking her eyes off Richard Stirling. 'What are you going to do with him?'

'We're going to walk him out of here and hand him over to the police.'

Amber wheeled round to face Demos. 'That's *it*? That's your big revenge? After everything he's done. You think that's justice?'

'Amber,' Alex said in a voice as smooth as rain. 'Amber, we talked about this. This will destroy him.'

She looked at him almost pityingly, like he couldn't possibly understand. 'It's not enough, Alex. How can you think that's enough?' She looked at me for back-up and my breath caught in my chest. I couldn't argue. I was on her side. I wanted revenge too. I glanced at the gun in Alex's hand. It would be so easy to flip it up and fire one shot. Just one shot. That's all it would take. Just the lightest pressure in my mind and it would be done. All that pain Richard Stirling had caused, all the badness, wiped out with just a thought, the smallest of intentions.

My eyes met Amber's – the grey swimming like a wet, winter sky. I could do it for her, for Ryder. And for my mum. And for Thomas.

Then I felt the warmth of Alex's gaze on me. I felt his hand rest gently on my arm and my eyes were drawn to his face. He knew exactly what I was thinking. He could see it in my eyes and more than that – he knew me. He knew how my mind worked.

He wasn't trying to stop me, though. There was no judgement in the way he was looking at me, only calm assurance that he was there. That he was leaving it up to me. But his touch did what it always did. It balanced me. It brought me back. Alex was right. I wasn't going to let Richard Stirling turn me into something I wasn't. I knew who I was now – *what* I was. I wasn't going to be hunted anymore. But neither did I want to be haunted by memories.

'Amber,' I said, turning back to face her, drawing in a deep breath. 'It's not worth it. He's not worth it. We've beaten him.'

Her eyes flamed for a moment, as though my betrayal had torn through her and ripped a chunk from her heart. Then, with her bottom lip trembling, she turned back to Richard Stirling's frozen face. For a moment I thought she'd ignored me and was going to shoot him anyway. The gun shook in her hand. I glanced at Demos. Would he stop her? But his gaze was focused on Richard Stirling and his guard, his attention on holding them frozen. I wondered if I could spin the gun out of her hand. But before I could, Amber dropped her arm and let the gun fall to her side.

Jack was the first to move. He put his arm round Amber's shoulder and bent to whisper something in her ear. She half turned, collapsing into him. Jack wrapped both arms round her waist to keep her from falling. He held her until her shoulders stopped heaving, one hand on the back of her head. Alicia then stepped forward and gently pulled Amber out of his arms before leading her out of the room.

When she had gone, Demos spoke to me. 'Lila, are you ready?'

I took a deep breath. 'Yes,' I said, nodding. 'But you should get out of here, Demos.'

'I'll wait until the others are clear,' he answered. I was going to argue, but I felt Alex tugging on my arm.

'Where are we going?' I asked as we started jogging across the lobby.

'Third floor. Where the labs and the server are.'

I nodded. Jack joined us at the elevator.

'I'm not sure it's safe for you two to be with me when I do this,' I said.

'Yeah?' Alex asked as the elevator doors opened. 'Well, I think we'll take that chance.' He bundled me inside and pressed the button for the third floor. I stood there, pressed between Jack and Alex, and closed my eyes, feeling both their arms rubbing against my shoulders. This is where I always wanted to be – where I always felt safest. Between the two of them. It's how it had always been, but I had a sudden sense of foreboding that it was going to be the last time.

The elevator doors opened onto another corridor and I swept the thought away. We had come this far – we were almost in sight of the finish line. We were going to do this. *I* was going to do this. We ran down another long corridor, past a dozen glass-fronted rooms. I caught sight of stainless-steel worktops, banks of computers and futuristic-looking machines – something that looked like an X-ray machine, another that looked like an MRI scanner. The last room on our left made me stumble. It was empty except for a metal gurney. White straps hung down from each corner like zombie bandages. Next to the bed was a shining tray of metal instruments and a machine like the one Jack had been rigged up to in the hospital. This was the place they did their tests. My mum could have been strapped to that very gurney. Alex pulled me forward, past the room.

Ahead of us was a door with a lock on it. Before we were five metres away from it, Jack blew the lock off. I kicked the door back

301

with a quick glance. Inside was a room the size of my bedroom back at Jack's. It was filled with blinking lights and towering stacks of computer servers. This was the heart of Stirling Enterprises, where all the data they had was kept. If we destroyed it, we would destroy all the data they had on us, all their findings. It was a start. Then I'd destroy the labs, starting with the one I'd just passed with the bed and the machines in it.

Jack didn't wait for me to get out a lighter and try to direct the flame. He fired a round of bullets into the server's heart. It smoked and whined in protest.

'That's not going to work,' Alex said. He turned and jogged down the corridor.

'Are you sure you can handle this?' Jack said, looking at me nervously.

I turned my head slowly to stare at him. 'Are you doubting my ability? Because, you know, it totally beats yours.'

Alex was back at our side. He was holding a small glass bottle in his hand. It was full of a clear liquid – alcohol or something from one of the labs. I noticed the skull and crossbones label on its front. 'Get back!' Alex shouted, pushing Jack and me behind him.

'Wait!' I yelled. There were pipes latticing the ceiling inside the server room. Some kind of sprinkler system. I focused all my attention on them and ripped them free, bending and twisting them like pipe cleaners. They screamed in response and we all covered our ears.

Alex smiled at me in pride and then threw the bottle into the room, firing a bullet straight into it as it flew through the air. The bottle shattered loudly, exploding in a giant ball of fire. Instantly licks of blue, green and orange flames began streaking along the corridor and black smoke started to billow around us.

The sprinkler system above us kicked in, drenching us in seconds. *Crap*, I thought, staring up at the pipes. I should have tackled these ones too when I'd had the chance. It was a lot harder to focus with water pouring into my eyes and soaking me.

'Harvey couldn't have disabled the sprinkler system while he was disabling everything else?' I cried over the hiss of the water.

'Can you stop it?' Alex shouted back.

I looked up, squinting through the lashing rain at the pipes above us, my hair plastering over my face. I tried to feel for the edges of the water like I'd done in the shower and when the tidal wave had ripped towards us. I tried to order it to go backwards or upwards or anywhere that wasn't onto us and the smouldering fire. The flames were already sputtering, cowering back into the room. At this rate nothing was going to burn down. *Back the hell off*, I roared in my head, feeling the surge of energy start to build inside me as if thousands of cells in my body were waking up.

The water stopped cascading on us all of a sudden. It was listening to me. It was sucking backwards down the pipes. I pushed it and pushed it as though I was jamming my finger up a hose.

'OK, Lila, the fire! Focus on the fire. We need the fire to destroy this whole floor. We need it to burn fast and hard.'

The flames were darting out of the server room once more, hissing where they were making tracks across the wet surfaces. A single flame sprang along the ground, racing blue and orange towards us. Jack dodged back out of its way and I took hold of it like a snake's head and held it back, away from us, twisting it and forcing it back into the server room. Dense black smoke filled the corridor, throwing itself on top of us like a thick wool blanket that I couldn't breathe or see through.

'Come on, this way!' Jack started pulling me back towards the fire exit.

'Hang on,' I said. 'Hang on.' I could feel the water starting to press again, like my mind was the dam and it was starting to crack. I shoved it backwards hard, letting the flames surge upwards. The pipes started to buckle and whine under the heat, scalding steam evaporating into the smoke. My face felt like melting plastic. I was aware of Jack and Alex calling to me, of someone pulling at my arms, but I dug my heels in and stayed where I was. I needed to make sure it burnt. That everything burnt. I wanted to make sure nothing was left.

I hurled a spear of flame into the glass wall of the lab and heard the splintering crack of glass and the roar as the fire gulped down the air in the room. There was a bursting sound and another huge explosion which knocked me off my feet, throwing me onto my back and sending shooting pains down my arms and legs. Flames arched over my head and a ball of fire raced towards us. In the next instant I felt Alex fall on me, his chest colliding with mine, slamming me flat against the ground, his arms braced round my head. I closed my eyes, curled into him and forced the fire back, back, back. Away from him.

A second later Alex was on his feet, dragging me upright as the flames licked hungrily over his head. Coughing and spluttering, he pushed me the last few steps into the stairwell.

The fire door clanged shut behind us and I felt the cool blast of air hit me. I glanced at Jack and Alex. Alex's T-shirt was clinging to him; the backs of his arms were scorched red with burns, streaked black with smoke. Jack was bent double, coughing, one hand pressed to his chest, the other clutching the banister.

'Come on, let's go,' Alex said, drawing a rasping breath and taking my hand.

304

'No, no!' I said, pulling out of his grip and turning back towards the door. 'I have to stay. We have to make sure it burns.'

'It *is* burning!' he yelled back at me.

Jack's hand was on my back, urging me down the stairs. 'Lila, you did it. It's burning. We need to get out of here.'

I let them both pull me down the stairs, my eyes streaming from the smoke still, my lungs fit to burst, glancing backwards the whole time, wondering if the fire really was burning it all to ashes. We smashed through the door into the lobby, letting it slam behind us. Demos hadn't moved. He was still standing in the centre of the room, his gaze level with Richard Stirling, his shoulders slightly rounded with the concentration it must have been taking to hold him and Robocop frozen for so long.

'Did you do it?' he called out to us.

'Yeah, we gotta get out of here,' Jack replied, running past him. 'Let them go,' he said, waving his gun in the direction of Richard Stirling and Robocop.

'You ready?' Demos asked, pulling a gun from the inside of his jacket.

'Yep, do it,' Jack answered.

Richard Stirling blinked then frowned. He opened his mouth, saw the gun in Demos's hand and shut it again. Robocop fired off an empty round, his gun clicking feebly in his hand. He looked at it in disgust then spat a curse in our direction. He glared at Jack. Jack smiled warmly back at him.

Demos held Stirling's gaze for a few seconds. Then he marched straight over to Stirling and brought his gun up to rest against his temple.

'Demos!' Alex shouted. 'No. We agreed. We're bringing him with us and handing him over to the police.'

305

Demos paused, his eyes drilling into Richard Stirling's. His finger eased down on the trigger.

'Demos!' I shouted. 'Come on! Let's get out before the place burns down.'

Richard Stirling turned to me, a frown creating a furrow between his eyes. Then he looked over his shoulder at the door. Black smoke was starting to slide underneath it, wisping its way towards us. The surface was starting to blister.

Demos still didn't move. Alex waited a beat then he took my hand and pulled me towards the door. 'Come on, Jack!' he shouted over his shoulder.

Jack pushed his gun into Robocop's back and nudged him towards the door. He looked over at Demos. 'Are you coming?' he shouted at him.

Demos still didn't answer. He continued to stand there with the gun against Stirling's temple. The two men stared each other out as smoke started to swirl in clouds around them.

I paused in the doorway. 'We can't just leave him.'

'We're not staying,' Alex shouted back just as a huge explosion blasted open the fire-escape door.

I stopped arguing with him. Plaster and concrete had begun raining down and the flames from the stairwell seemed to gather before leaping in bold streaks across the lobby, towards where Demos was standing, engulfing him in black smoke.

Jack pushed Robocop through the doorway. Alex pushed me through after and I copied him, pulling my T-shirt up to cover my mouth, all the while craning backwards, trying to catch a glimpse of Demos through the flames. What was he doing? Alex was right behind me, though, urging me forward.

The smoke in the corridor was heavy, leaking through the

air-conditioning vents above us and making it feel as if we were running through an underground tunnel. My eyes were burning; the air I was sucking into my lungs was as thick and acrid as tar. I could just make out Jack about ten metres ahead.

I tried to blow the smoke backwards, force it to retreat, and it did a little, starting to thin in places, billowing out to the sides like a cloak. We could at least see where we were going now, the long corridor stretching ahead of us. The back entrance that Sara had led us through at the far end was propped open with something, letting in a sliver of light.

Then we heard a crack, muffled among the roaring of the flames and the rising shriek of sirens from outside. Alex jerked to a stop, his arms flying out to the sides, grasping for me. I grabbed hold of his arm to keep upright. Ahead, I watched Jack stumble, then stagger, his shoulder banging into the wall. In slow motion, with a scream welling inside me, I watched him slide to the ground.

'Jack!' I shouted, my throat burning, shoving my way past Alex to get to him.

The smoke swallowed Jack whole just then and I blew it back with such force that it swept like a hurricane down the narrow corridor, smashing the door wide open and letting in a flood of light. A shadow appeared, striding through the smoke, heading towards us. I barely registered that it was Robocop. I didn't register the gun at all – not until I heard the second crack. Then it was automatic. I hurled Alex out of the way so hard and so fast that the sound he made when he collided with the wall behind me drowned out the sound of the bullet smacking home.

44

It was the force of it that shocked me. It felt like a spear had been hurled into my ribcage. It splintered through the bone, twisting and mauling until I felt its hot, fat body sink into the cushion of my lung.

My knees smashed into the floor, graceless and heavy. Alex's voice roared in my ear before becoming faint and tinny, as though he had been suddenly transported to another dimension. There was another crack; this one sent me tumbling forward, my temple smacking into the floor. Thick, cloying black smoke closed over me, filling my nostrils and my mouth.

An image of my mum floated in front of me. It wasn't the image of her from a few minutes previously, lying like a corpse in my father's arms, but from before, from way back. She was kneeling on the deck by the swimming pool of our old house in Washington, a towel in her outstretched arms. She was smiling, saying something I couldn't hear. She was waiting for me to climb out of the pool so she could wrap me up in it and bundle me dry. I felt my limbs heavy and cold as though I was treading water in a lake of quicksand. I couldn't reach her and a panic took hold of my heart and squeezed with all its might. The image turned foggy and dissolved. And then a thought poked through the darkness, swamping my head. *Jack*. Was he OK? I tried to turn my head to look, but black and red spots jumped and swam in front of my eyes. I tried to call out for Alex, but my mouth felt as if it had been crammed full of rusty coins. I choked on a warm stream of bile that gushed up my throat then rinsed back down.

A sudden jolt. Warmth against my cheek. Wetness underneath me. Hands clutching me. Then footsteps pounding, jarring me with each stride, sending rivers of fire flashing through my veins. And then cool air engulfed me, stinging and vicious against my skin. The softness of arms was replaced by hard, unforgiving ground. Hands were tugging and voices were calling my name, barking orders at me. Then, just as the darkness started to throb and close over me and the pain started to lessen, a stream of molten lava was poured directly into the hole in my chest. A scream tore out of my throat, slicing apart the night air, and seemed to cleave my whole body in two as well. The lava cooled instantly, turning to rock, pressing down so heavily on my chest that I could no longer breathe and the darkness was falling again, heavier this time, a blizzard of black ice which was slowly burying me.

'Come back to me, Lila!'

That was Alex. I had come back to him. What was he talking about? I always came back to him. I always would.

'Stay awake. Come on, wake up, damn it!' He shook my shoulders hard. 'Don't go to sleep. Open your eyes. Lila, listen to me, I'm right here. I'm not going anywhere, but you have to stay too. You can't just give up.' His voice was hoarse, threaded through with panic.

I tried to smile. Why was he panicking? Alex never panicked. I wasn't going anywhere. I just needed to sleep a little bit. If he could just hold me, I could sleep right now. But he'd need to hold me really tight because it was so cold. Freezing in fact. The air con was blasting. Or maybe it was because my clothes were wet from the sprinkler.

Oh. OK. I got it.

And then I was free-falling backwards, tumbling into a velvet-black hole.

'Lila!'

That sounded like Jack. He'd been shot, hadn't he? I'd seen him fall. Was he OK? He had to be OK. He was here and he was talking. That was good. But he could heal. Of course he was fine. I felt myself smile and something warm and wet spilled over my lips and dribbled down my chin.

'Stay with me,' Jack shouted. 'You're not going anywhere, goddamn it, Lila. You never bloody listen!'

I tried to smile again, but something was bubbling in the way. I wanted to spit. But I couldn't lift my head. Jack was asking me to stay. He had finally agreed I wasn't going anywhere. That was so funny.

And I so wanted to tell him how amusing that was. I sighed and let the darkness wash over me.

It was just too bad that I couldn't stay.

This was what people meant when they talked about a bright white light.

This is dying. This is death. It registered in some small recess of my brain where the light was still on. As warm and dark as a womb. I was floating, languid and peaceful, the pain in my chest gone. And suddenly a pinprick of light through the dark, a space, opening and widening, through which the sunlight soared.

And someone was kissing me. No. Not someone. Alex was

kissing me. Kissing me hard, his lips bruising mine, his breath hot in my mouth, tasting of smoke.

'Breathe, goddamn it. Breathe!' he was shouting.

Then his lips were on mine again and he was forcing mine apart, blowing air into my mouth and lungs.

The light swirling round me started to get brighter and hotter. It was sparking, racing in electric ribbons up my legs, flowing down my arms, spinning through the hole in my chest where the bullet had passed. The bone was knitting back together as though it was made of Playdoh.

And then came an enormous judder, an explosion of light and noise and a thump that didn't let up – a pounding drum in my chest. And my head was alive with the sound of it.

My eyes flew open. Alex was hovering a few centimetres above me, his lips reachable. I smiled up at him. He was so damn hot. Even smeared with grime and sweat and blood.

He rocked backwards onto his haunches. He was breathing hard, his T-shirt was soaked with blood, his hands clasped like a stone on top of my chest.

That was fine. They could stay there. I didn't mind.

'Jack, you can stop now. She's back.' His voice was husky, slightly broken.

I turned my head. Jack was kneeling on my other side. His eyes were shut, his head bowed. Then I became aware of his hand, and the heat of his palm where it was resting over my ribcage.

I peered down at it. What was he doing?

He gently lifted his hand away and the heat evaporated immediately. I shivered and my head fell back. Slowly I let my fingers trace their way across my stomach and up my ribcage, feeling for the place where the bullet had smashed its way through. Nothing.

There was no hole, no splintered fragments of bone, no shredded skin. My ribs didn't even feel bruised. But there was blood everywhere. The ground was soaked with it. My T-shirt, which had been pushed up, was drenched in it. Suddenly Alex's hand was on top of mine, flattening over my heart.

'There's no hole.'

My eyes widened.

'Jack fixed you.'

I glanced back at Jack. His eyes were blazing, like he was on fire from the inside. He grinned suddenly. 'Are you going to admit it now? My power totally beats yours,' he said.

I managed to smile. At this point in time I wasn't going to disagree.

There was a charred, bloodstained hole in his T-shirt, over his right shoulder. That's where he'd been shot. He didn't appear to have even noticed, though.

'Come on, we need to get out of here,' he said, jumping to his feet. He was silhouetted suddenly against the inferno of the building behind. Flames were lashing at the sky, black towers of smoke rising into the air.

I had done that. *That's actually pretty cool*, I thought in silent wonder. Then I shook myself. What was I saying? I was an arsonist. There was nothing cool about that.

'Go get the car, Jack,' Alex said, not taking his eyes off me. 'She's lost a lot of blood. I'm not sure she can walk.'

Jack looked ready to say something, but then he got to his feet and jogged off in the direction of the car Sara had brought us in.

Alex put one arm underneath me and lifted me gently onto his lap. My head fell against his shoulder and I tilted my chin up so I could look at him. He was filthy, his blue eyes smouldering through the grime. I traced a finger over his eyebrows. They were singed. God only knew how I must look right now. I didn't feel any pain, though. I was still floating. If this was how Jack felt all the time then I had to concede his power was definitely, infinitely better than mine.

Alex stroked a line down my cheekbone to my lips and I started to float through the stratosphere. 'You have a go at me about leaving you . . .' he said. 'Don't *ever* do that to me again.'

I found my voice. It was raspy. 'Deal.'

He considered me for a moment. 'And while we're on the subject, you also promised me you weren't going to push me around anymore. You shouldn't have done that,' he said, shaking his head softly, his mouth tightening.

'It was about time I rescued you,' I said. 'You know – returned the favour.'

He raised a singed eyebrow, his eyes dancing, the amber firing in them. And then he bent his head and kissed me.

The ribbons of light surged once more up my legs and my heart restarted for a second time.

45

'I can't believe it.'

'Shhh, turn it up.'

Someone hit the volume button. Everyone fell silent. Suki's face appeared beaming on the television screen. The reporter turned to her. 'Miss Nakamura, I understand you saw the entire explosion.'

'Yes, I just happened to be driving past this Marine base with my friend Nate . . .' Nate's head suddenly bounced into shot. He was grinning from ear to ear. Suki elbowed him slightly out of the way so only half of his face remained in the frame. 'And *boom*! The whole place exploded.'

'I can't believe you elbowed me out of the way,' Nate yelled from the corner where he was sitting, watching himself on-screen.

'Nate, they wanted someone pretty in the shot. That's why they interviewed me.'

'Shhhh,' Demos cut them off.

Everyone fell silent again. I lifted my head off Alex's chest. We were curled on the sofa in the main room of the boat. His hand was tracing up my spine, stopping every now and then to stroke under my top where the bullet had gone in. It was making me shudder, distracting me from the news.

The reporter handed over to the studio. A man in a suit and a red tie was staring seriously at the camera, his voice thick with faux gravity. 'That footage was shot earlier this evening at Camp Pendleton Marine Base outside San Diego,' he announced, 'where Stirling Enterprises Headquarters was significantly damaged in a fire. Initial reports are unclear on the causes of the fire, though arson has not yet been ruled out.'

Demos tossed me a grin over his shoulder. I grinned back.

'Arsonist,' Alex whispered into my ear. Again with the shudder.

'What does *significantly damaged* mean? Did we destroy it or not?' Jack asked. He was sitting on the sofa arm by my leg.

'Wait, listen,' I shushed him.

'What about me? Why aren't they showing me?' Suki whined.

'You shouldn't even have been there,' Demos scowled at her.

She stuck her tongue out at him, but he didn't notice. He was listening to the news report.

'The fire coincides with the DEA drugs bust of Stirling Enterprises' offices in Washington DC. Several million dollars' worth of class A drugs and an undisclosed amount of money were found in CEO Richard Stirling's home and office. Four other members of the board have been arrested in joint DEA and FBI raids following an anonymous tip-off to police. The government has reacted by trying to distance itself from Stirling Enterprises, which holds several billion-dollar defence contracts. The White House issued a statement earlier this evening announcing a full inquiry into the highly secretive nature of the defence work being carried out on the base. Certainly the timing of this fire will raise serious questions as to what was really happening on this Marine base.

'One high-level source inside the DEA disclosed that a link had been discovered between Stirling Enterprises and a drugs cartel in

Mexico City.' A photo of Carlos flashed onto the screen. Alex's hand froze on my back.

'Richard Stirling's daughter, Rachel Stirling, an employee of the company, was this evening arrested in Mexico City after yet another tip-off, suggesting the link between the drugs found in Stirling Enterprises' offices and known cartel boss Carlos Mendoza may be more than just simple conjecture.'

I sat up as a picture of Rachel flashed onto the screen. It was grainy film footage of her being handcuffed by four heavily armed Mexican police officers and bundled into a police car. It gave me a moment's mild satisfaction, but not nearly enough.

The voice-over from the studio continued. 'Richard Stirling has not been seen since the raid on his home and offices, but several witnesses have stated that he was on the base at the time of the explosion. He is wanted for questioning by the police.'

Demos hit the mute button. We all stared at him, mute too.

Finally Alex spoke up. 'Where is he? Did you kill him?'

Demos stared at Alex blankly for a second then he shook his head. 'No.'

'Where is he, then?' I asked. My throat still felt hoarse from the smoke and all the blood that I'd choked up.

'I let him go when I heard the gunfire. When Jack got shot.'

'You let him go?' Jack blurted.

'Yes.'

We stared at Demos in grim silence. Even Suki stayed quiet. 'Where did he go?' Jack asked, his voice strained.

'I don't know,' Demos answered quietly.

I sank back against Alex's chest. All that for nothing? He'd got away?

'We destroyed Stirling Enterprises,' Alex said. 'Even if he didn't

316

die in the fire, there's no way he can ever recover from this. He's lost everything. The police will catch up with him eventually. Where's he going to go? His face is all over the news.'

No one said anything. Eventually, Demos turned in a small circle, taking us all in, and then he walked out of the room in silence. I watched him go, my breath catching in my throat. Someone should go after him.

'Where's Alicia?' I asked, looking around.

'She left already,' Amber replied quietly. She was sitting on the floor by Jack's feet.

'Why?' I asked. Amber turned and gave me a look.

Oh. Demos and my mum. It wasn't just what Alicia had seen in the lobby. I wondered what she'd also heard in Demos's head. I couldn't read minds, but even I had seen it. He was still clearly in love with my mum.

'Lila? Jack?'

I looked up. My dad was in the doorway. His face was different. Like life had poured back into his eyes.

'Your mum's awake. Do you want to come and see her?'

I was on my feet already, standing slightly shakily. I was showered and clean, but so nervous and still a little woozy-headed from blood loss.

It had been five years. What would she think? What would we say to each other?

I glanced at Alex then around at the others and suddenly remembered there was so much I had to tell her.

46

Nate's face looked like a tragedy mask. 'We have to go and stay with Grandma.'

'In the Hilton in Acapulco?' I asked hopefully.

'No. In Atlanta.'

I bit my lip and tried not to smile. That was too bad. Way too bad.

'The only good news is I'm going with him.' Suki had appeared by his side. 'Lila, could you help me with my bags?'

I glanced over at the six Louis Vuitton bags stacked in the room. I turned back to her.

'I cannot have this Imelda Marcos woman beating me, whoever she is,' Suki shrugged by way of explanation. Then she smiled. 'Goodbye, Lila. I'll miss you.'

A lump materialised in my throat. Suki pulled me into a tight hug. Nate threw an arm round me too.

'We'll see you in the summer break, OK?'

I pulled back. 'That would be great. I'm not sure where I'm going to be, though,' I said hesitantly, wondering now whether my dad would want to go back to London or whether we'd stay here. Alex had promised me he'd go wherever I was going so really it didn't matter anymore where I was. I was hoping to argue the case for the yacht, though. It seemed like a good enough place to live out the rest of my life. So long as I could share a cabin with Alex and we stayed in international waters.

'I might see you before you see me,' Nate giggled.

'I don't think he'll be flying by to see you, Lila. I think he's more interested in seeing Jack and Alex.'

I took a swipe at him. 'What are the others doing?'

'Well,' Suki answered, 'Harvey's packing. He wants to get back to it.'

'Back to what?'

'Back to work, silly.'

'Harvey has a job?' I couldn't keep the surprise out of my voice.

'I guess you could call it that,' she answered, shrugging one shoulder.

My eyes widened. I held up a hand, not wanting to know any more. 'And Amber?'

Suki smiled slyly. 'I think she's staying.'

'She is?' I brightened instantly. 'Why?'

'Jack offered. She needs some space to grieve.'

'What about Bill?' I asked. 'And Thomas. What about Thomas? Is he OK?'

'They're in Mexico City still. Thomas is better but not quite back to normal. He could really use your brother doing his special magic on him.'

'I could really use your brother doing his special magic on me,' sniggered Nate.

I rolled my eyes at him. It wasn't actually a bad idea, though. Jack doing his thing on Thomas, that is. He'd done it on my mum and it appeared to be working. Hell, if he could bring me back from the dead, he could definitely fix Thomas.

Suki turned back to the bags. 'So, can you help? Or do I have to ask Harvey?'

Demos was standing on the jetty with his back to me. I jumped down and walked to his side.

'How's your mum?' he asked.

I looked into his cool blue eyes, lighter and flatter than Alex's, and saw the splinter of pain buried deep in them.

'She's doing well,' I said, swallowing back the rush of sadness and gratitude that almost choked me. 'Jack did his thing on her. Pretty cool, huh? My dad says she'll be back to normal in no time. She just needs rest now.'

Demos nodded and turned back to look out at the ocean.

'She asked me to tell you thank you,' I said quietly. He didn't respond. 'She asked me to do this too.' I stood on tiptoe and kissed him on the cheek.

His jaw clenched. He took a deep breath and turned in my direction. His eyes were hooded in the dark, as brooding as an overcast sky.

'Keep your brother safe for me, Lila.'

I raised an eyebrow and he laughed. We both knew that keeping Jack safe was no longer necessary.

'Will I see you again?' I asked. My voice actually broke. Somehow, somewhere along the way, love had crept into the equation and it startled me somewhat.

'Yeah,' Demos laughed under his breath, putting an arm round me. 'We're family, aren't we? Or close as.' He twisted me round so I was standing in front of him, holding me there with his hands resting on my shoulders. His expression was serious, his gaze fixed on me. 'Lila, don't tell him, OK? He doesn't need to know.'

320

I sucked in a breath of sea air, let it fill my lungs.

I glanced over at Jack. He and Amber were sitting up on the top deck. He stood up while I was watching and reached behind him for a blanket which he then draped round Amber's shoulders. He noticed me looking and smiled, lifting his hand in farewell to Demos, who acknowledged it with a nod and a smile so fleeting it was gone by the time I could clear my throat and croak, 'OK.'

'How's he doing about Sara?' Demos asked after a while, nodding his head towards Jack.

I shrugged. 'He hasn't really said anything. He asked Harvey if she made it to the hospital, but he didn't seem to care whether she was OK. Not that I care much either. You know – my dad was the one that shot her.' It still surprised me that my dad had actually fired a gun.

'Yeah, I heard.'

'She did kind of deserve it, though.'

'Thought we weren't supposed to be in it for revenge, Lila. Isn't that the big lesson here?'

I grinned up at him.

'See you around, Lila,' he said finally. Then he picked up his bag and walked off down the jetty. I watched him go. A single, dark figure disappearing like a ghost into the night.

Alex found me like that, standing on the jetty, staring into the darkness, which seemed heavier all of a sudden.

'Hey,' he said.

'Hi,' I replied, turning round and sliding my arms round his waist.

'We're all set,' he murmured, stroking my hair behind one ear.

'Where are we going?' I asked, not really caring so long as it wasn't Mexico City and so long as it was going to take months to get there. Months on a boat in the middle of the ocean where no one could find us and where I could get to work on Alex's resolve.

'There's this great beach I know in Mexico.' Alex's voice was so low it actually started my legs quivering.

I looked at his eyes flashing in the moonlight. 'I think I know that beach. It's good for skinny-dipping, right?'

He laughed softly. 'I told you I'd bring you back there one day,' he said, lifting my chin with his finger, his lips so close I could feel their heat.

Finally, inevitably, he closed the distance and kissed me. The synapses in my brain sparked, starting a small electrical fire in my head.

It was OK. At least I knew I could control it.

**AND JUST IN CASE YOU NEED AN EXTRA FIX
OF ALEX, READ ON . . .**

The moment

A short story from Alex's point of view

The last time I saw her was in Washington. Three years ago. Just over.

There's a memory I have from back then that I can't seem to shake. It's of the three of us – Jack, Lila and me – we're playing basketball in my backyard. I think someone took a photo – maybe that's why I remember it so clearly.

None of us were saying very much. We were playing hard and fast, sweating despite the cold. In the car on the way to mine Jack had had a fight with his dad. He was mad – kept slamming the ball against the hoop like he was trying to knock it clean off the wall, not shoot the ball through it. Lila was trying not to cry and I was trying to intercept Jack's passes before someone – or the hoop – got hurt.

The buzzer sounds and I cross the hallway to let Jack in. I know it's him because he always holds his finger on it for as long as it takes me to get there.

'What's up?' he says through the intercom. 'Do you have company?'

'No,' I answer drily. 'I just hang out all day counting down the seconds until I see you again, Jack.'

I buzz him in and while I wait for him to take the elevator up to my apartment I walk the few steps back down the hallway and into the kitchen to turn on the espresso machine. Today is going to be a long day.

Jack is grim-faced and scowling when I open the door to let him in. He kicks past me into the hallway.

'Goddamn my sister,' he says, by way of greeting.

I follow him silently as he heads to the kitchen and watch him as he starts raiding the fridge, tossing aside half a cantaloupe and shaking a jar of salad dressing as though it might contain something more helpful to him in his current mind-set than just olive oil and vinegar.

'Dude, you live like a monk,' he mutters to the empty shelves.

I pour most of the milk carton into one mug and pile in some sugar – Jack takes his coffee milkshake style – top it with a shot of steaming espresso and hand it to him without a word. He takes it, also without a word, and starts drinking, his eyes darting to the window, still narrowed in a scowl.

'My dad's going to freak out,' he says.

I interrupt him before he can get going on what I know will be a lengthy tirade. 'I need to take a shower,' I say, draining my coffee in one bitter swallow. 'I've just got back from a run.' I leave him with his head back in the fridge, muttering angrily at the cantaloupe about how it's got more sense than Lila.

Jack should have warning signs written on him for when he's in a mood like this. Then people would know to give him a very wide berth and time – lots of it – to chill out.

The shower is good. It unknots the muscles in my shoulders and legs and helps clear my mind which, ever since Jack called me, has been trying to process the fact that Lila's coming back.

326

Jack's raging mad but his anger stems from worry – about Lila being here, in California, and the risk that poses. I don't think he's thought about why she's coming. Or processed the fact that something must have happened in London to make her drop everything and book a flight to LA with no warning whatsoever.

As I towel off, I analyse it some more. Jack got the temper and Lila got the impulsiveness in the Loveday family and I've often sent silent thanks to the powers that be for their wisdom in not genetically gifting Jack with both temper and impulsiveness, because he'd be doing time by now if they had. But Lila's never done anything like this before. There must be something behind it. I wonder whether she'll trust me as much as she used to and will tell me what it is that she's running from. And whether I'll still be able to read her. Used to be that Lila was as transparent as a windshield.

I pause, reminding myself not to second-guess her actions. It could be something trivial – maybe she broke up with her boyfriend. But she doesn't have a boyfriend, at least, not that I know of. It could be school – but she's smart. She's doing OK. I shake my head. Who am I kidding? She's not OK. I can tell it from her emails. She doesn't say it in so many words, but it's there, in the gaps between them, in the way she avoids answering the more probing questions I throw at her.

Dropping the towel, I pull on a pair of jeans and a T-shirt, check there's a full chamber in my gun and then push it down the back of my jeans, careful to pull my T-shirt over it. Everyone in this apartment building thinks I work as a personal trainer for wealthy, bored housewives. If my neighbours saw the firepower I carry to go jogging, they'd wonder at my personal-training technique.

327

I stand and stare at myself hard in the mirror, running a hand over my head and the buzz cut I had two days ago. What will Lila see? Will she even recognise me and Jack? We're not the same people she left behind. Three years have passed since we saw each other – two spent in Marine Special Ops training and one spent working for the Unit, hunting down her mother's killers. When I look in the mirror these days, I'm not even sure I recognise myself. It's not the muscle Jack and I have both built up in training, or the scars. Not even the tattoos on our arms mark us out as changed. It's something more than that. Beyond the physical.

We're always on guard, always on the lookout, always wary, careful, suspicious. We've had to master secrets and deceit, while learning at the same time to decipher other people's lies and secrets. We've become adept at closing out the ones we love and even those we might love – at blanking our emotions so there's no chink of vulnerability left visible. We hide our true selves so well that sometimes I worry I'll never find the real me again.

I keep staring unflinchingly at my reflection. This is not a life that Lila needs to know about. When Jack and I are done, when we've caught the man who killed her mother, then we'll tell her. Some of it at least. Not all. Truth doesn't have smooth, soft round edges. It has razor-sharp ones. Holding that truth will only hurt her.

Jack's sprawled on the sofa when I walk into the living room. He's hit play on my iPod deck and I pause in the doorway, trying to hide my smile.

'What is this?' Jack asks, nodding at the speakers. 'I've not heard it before.'

'Just something new,' I say, dropping down onto the easy chair opposite him. It's a playlist Lila put together and sent me a few

328

weeks ago, but I don't think it's such a good idea to bring her name up now he seems to have calmed down.

'It's good,' Jack mumbles, nodding appreciatively along to the music.

'Did you report in to the base?' I ask, changing the subject.

'Yeah, I let Sara know what was happening. Told her we'd be in a little late. You should probably call Rachel, though,' he says, referring to our boss.

'I already have,' I answer. 'We should get going, though. Rachel said they'd picked up some new activity. Possibly a sighting of Demos in LA.'

At this, Jack's head flies up. He swings his legs off the sofa and sits up. 'And you're only telling me this now?' he asks. 'You see – this is why she can't come back. He's nearby. It's too dangerous.' He swears under his breath as he jumps to his feet.

I stand up and grab the keys to my bike. 'She's coming back, Jack, and it's all going to be OK,' I say. 'We'll talk about it later. Right now we need to get to work.'

We pull up outside the West Coast headquarters of Stirling Enterprises – located on Camp Pendleton Marine Base, just north of San Diego. The building sits like a sparkling UFO amongst the smaller, squatter, altogether plainer military installations – barracks, offices and even a hospital – that scatter the base.

We did our training with the First Recon Marines out of Pendleton, so in a lot of ways the base feels like home. Having said that, when I pull up on my bike next to a drill sergeant with purple veins bulging like live snakes under his skin and hear him screaming abuse at a band of new recruits who are sweating valiantly in the midday heat, I can't say I miss those days.

Most of the Unit's employees are trained Marines – at least the soldiers are; the scientists are not. But we're not working under the remit of the US army. Our chain of command is shrouded in layers of mystery, but it's thought that only one or two key people in the very highest, darkest corners of government know what we're really doing.

We're our own secret enclave. And the building on the base which Jack and I are walking into reeks of that secrecy – its reflective glass and steel front means no one outside the Unit has ever caught a glimpse of what's inside. I glance up as we walk inside. There are no guns mounted on the roof, but there are other invisible ways the building has of repelling enemies and I always feel a slight easing up of tension once I'm through the entry system and inside the lobby.

Sixty metres below us right now, as we walk across the marble-floored lobby of this impenetrable building, lies a row of cells, empty except for one. Every time I cross this lobby that's what I think about. What lies beneath.

Empty cells and the fact we've only captured one.

For the last five years Stirling Enterprises has been working for the US government on a project considered too sensitive for the public to ever find out about. Our mission is to contain a group of people called psygens – people with an incurable genetic malfunction that makes them not only different to everyone else – endowed with special abilities like telekinesis and telepathy – but also that renders them incapable of empathy or rational human thought. The Unit psychs claim they're off-the-scale sociopaths.

As if Jack and I needed to be told that – as if we didn't already have proof.

There's no cure. There is only management. Containment, as it's termed. The only problem is that they're fast, they see us coming, they outmanoeuvre us every single time, always staying one step ahead. They have powers we don't, ways of communicating and spying and stopping us in our tracks, which makes containing them a challenge.

We're closing the net on them, though – on the group we're targeting – and once they're contained, maybe then it will be safe for Lila to come back here for good. And maybe then Jack and I might have a shot at living a normal life too. I glance at Jack, who's tapping his foot impatiently, waiting for the elevator doors to close. *Maybe not*, I think. For Jack, revenge is so in his blood, has become so much a part of who he is, I doubt that he'll ever stop hunting them, even after we catch Demos and his crew – not when there are more out there.

Rachel's in full-on debrief mode when we slip into the tactical team meeting. She nods at us, but doesn't miss a beat, continuing to narrate over a rush of images projected onto the wall behind her – maps of downtown LA, some sketchy black-and-white shots drawn from CCTV cameras which she pauses on. They purport to be images of Demos and his right-hand man Harvey – but they're so blizzarded out, it's hard to tell for certain. Rachel wraps up with a reminder for us all to stay focused. *As if we're ever not*, I think grimly to myself, watching her out of the corner of my eye.

Rachel works hard to prove that she's not just in her position because of who she is – despite the fact that her name is Rachel Stirling and her father owns the company. But sometimes she works it too hard. She's good at her job. Everyone knows that. She doesn't need to keep on proving it.

As Jack and I stand, she holds up a hand and beckons us to stay. I sigh. Jack heads over.

'Sorry we were late,' he says.

'Family trouble?' Rachel asks lightly, though her eyes, big and blue and what I imagine to be deceptively innocent, are sharp as needles.

'My sister just told me she's coming to stay,' Jack says. 'Her flight gets in tomorrow around lunchtime.'

'That's unexpected,' Rachel says. She's still smiling, but behind the smile there's a note of irritation. Her eyes narrow slightly.

'I'll deal with it,' Jack says, aware that Rachel's scrutinising him. 'It won't be a problem.'

Rachel studies him for a moment longer, the sheaf of papers she's holding pressed against her chest. 'Let's hope not,' she says with a tight smile. 'We need focus right now, Lieutenant.'

'Absolutely,' Jack says, holding her gaze steadily.

She turns to me. 'We could have used your input, Alex,' she says and I notice that she's opted for first-name terms with me rather than Lieutenant.

I glance up and see Jack winking at me over Rachel's shoulder. I keep my face blank as Jack walks out of the door, smirking. Rachel lets him go. She takes a minuscule step towards me, so she's almost pressing against me, and I'm caught between the table and her. When I glance down, I catch a glimpse of lace bra. I look up quickly.

'Busy tonight?' she asks. I can tell by the way she tilts her head to one side, casually flicking her hair over one shoulder and catching her lip, sticky with gloss, between her teeth, that she's not asking whether I'm busy on call. She knows that I'm not. She signs off all the shifts.

I could take the bait and ask her out. It's not the first time she's put it out there, but every time I've pretended to be oblivious. If Jack knew I'd ignored the hint, he'd never let up. He'd want to know why – but the only reason I could give him is that I'm just not feeling it. Rachel's the kind of girl who's too used to getting her own way, to owning things and having people do her bidding. And besides, I don't want to mix business with pleasure. Last time I did that it ruined my grade-point average.

'I'm going out with Jack tonight,' I say finally. Rachel holds my gaze for a long moment and I blank my expression as I've been trained to do when under interrogation and then edge round her and over to the door. 'I have to catch up with him. He's worried about his sister coming back.'

'Lila?'

I turn, wondering how Rachel knows Lila's name, then remember that it's probably all on record and Rachel will have done her homework. She always does her homework.

'Yeah,' I say. 'Lila.'

Rachel dismisses me with a curt nod of her head and a forced smile and strides out of the door ahead of me, her heels clicking loudly like machine-gun retorts.

Jack nods his head at a girl who's come to stand beside us at the bar. 'Check out the cute girl,' he says.

'I thought you weren't looking anymore,' I laugh. 'I thought you'd turned over a new leaf.'

For the first time in his life Jack's got a girlfriend – as opposed to a girl who he spends the night with, forgets the name of and never calls again. It's been quite a revelation – an entertaining and mildly disturbing revelation. Jack in love makes me believe anything is possible – that monkeys can grow wings and fly, that world peace can be achieved and that one day our work with the Unit will be done. The upside of Jack's metamorphosis into a love butterfly is that I've been able to witness it and laugh my ass off.

'I have turned over a new leaf,' Jack says. 'I'm looking for you. It's about time you hooked up with someone. It's been way too long.'

'You know the rules,' I answer.

If anyone knows the rules, it's Jack. He always learns them, mainly so he can go right ahead and find a way to break them.

'Who's saying you have to date anyone?' Jack grins.

I grimace. 'Not my style, Jack.'

He says something then about Rachel and I decide I need to redirect his attention elsewhere. 'What did the email say?' I ask, pointing at his iPhone, which he's clutching in his hand. Jack hands it to me.

Surprise! the email from Lila reads. I'm coming to LA. My flight gets in at around midday. Lila x

'Something's up,' I say, handing the phone back.

'Not necessarily,' Jack says. 'You think this is the first time Lila's been hot-headed? Seriously, dude, you do remember my sister, right? Short, blonde, impulsive as shock therapy? Stubborn as a mule who won't take no for an answer?'

Does Jack ever listen to himself? Does he appreciate the irony of this statement? I shake my head at him in wonder.

'Hey, I'm not short or blond,' Jack protests as he catches the look on my face.

'It could be about a boy,' I venture.

Jack stares at me blankly. 'A what?' he asks.

I choke back the laugh. 'A boy. You know? A Y-chromosome

334

holder? You don't seem to notice them as much as you do the X-carriers.'

'What are you talking about?' Jack asks, 'A boy? She's just a kid.'

I hesitate, wondering how Jack is only just doing the maths on this one now. 'She's seventeen. She's not a kid anymore.'

Jack looks like he's about to go all Incredible Hulk and burst out of his clothes before rampaging through the bar. He jumps off the stool. 'If any boy ever lays a finger on my sister, I'm going to kill him,' he says.

Again I stare at him in silence, thinking of all the girls Jack has laid fingers and much more of his anatomy on besides. Poor Lila. If she ever wants to have a shot at a normal life, as in one that doesn't require a vow of celibacy, she needs to stay in London.

Jack sits back down. 'You think that might be it?' he asks, looking pained.

'I'm just speculating,' I say, not wanting to fan his rage. I think back to the time Lila had a crush on me when she was about seven. She put a Valentine's card in my school bag. Seeing how the bag was sitting in the hallway of their house at the time, the suspects were narrowed down to just two: her or Jack. Hand-drawn pink hearts and ponies weren't really Jack's thing, so natural deduction left Lila. I never said anything to her about it, not wanting to embarrass her, but if I was honest, it was also because even then I knew how Jack would react.

'When did you last speak to her?' I ask.

'A couple of weeks ago,' Jack answers. 'She seemed OK.'

'She seemed a little down to me.'

'When did you talk to her?' Jack asks, sitting up straighter.

I curse myself mentally for mentioning it. 'She emailed a couple of days ago,' I say carefully. Then add quickly, 'Go gently, OK? She's been through a lot.'

Jack glowers at me. 'She shouldn't be coming. She needs to go back to London. I'm sending her straight back.'

'You can't, Jack. Let her stay a few days – a week. Find out what's up. You owe her that. We owe her that.'

I think about the last time she was here – that image of us playing basketball rears up once more in my mind's eye. Lila looked lost, afraid. And we ignored her. We were so set on joining the Unit we didn't stop to think about her or how she might feel. I think further back, to the time before that – to the funeral. She'd just lost her mother and the only thing she needed right then was Jack. But Jack had flipped out and taken off. I stayed with her instead, partly because there had been no one else to take care of her – her dad was inconsolable, weighed down by his own grief – but mainly because I wanted to. But since then I haven't taken care of her well enough. And neither has Jack. We've been so focused on revenge and on the bigger picture that everything else has fallen by the wayside.

'It's not safe for her here,' Jack says, interrupting my thoughts.

'We'll keep an eye on her. She'll be fine,' I murmur, almost to myself. I'll keep an eye on her and I won't let anything happen to her, not just because she's as much a sister to me as she is to Jack, but because frankly I'm scared of what Jack would do if anything happened to her. When his mum died, he lost it completely. Losing Lila would send him over the edge. Would probably, I think, send us both there.

The girl leaning against the bar behind Jack suddenly speaks up. 'What does one have to do to get service around here?' she purrs. 'Strip naked and dance on the bar?'

Jack has turned at the very first syllable to check her out. She's wearing a dress so clinging and tight that it invites much scrutiny. I'm sure that's the point and I glance away. But Jack, of course, is straight in there like a shot. Even though he's obsessed with Sara and would never do anything behind her back, it's as if he's genetically programmed to flirt with all women. And all women seem unable to resist his charms.

'You could try that,' he says. 'We wouldn't stop you.'

'Jack,' I say in a warning tone. We need to focus on what we're doing with Lila not on chatting up random girls who look like they've stepped out of a manga cartoon. I signal to the barman and the girl turns to me and asks if I'd like anything. I wonder how old she is. She's wearing a lot of make-up and four-inch spiked heels, but even so she's tiny and there's no way she's old enough to drink.

'No thank you,' I say politely, my thoughts back on Lila.

I can hear Jack striking up a conversation, but I don't engage. Until I hear the girl say something that makes my head fly up.

Jack and I stare at her, confused. I swear she just told us she was a mind-reader.

'Ha ha, just kidding!' she's now saying, laughing loudly. 'I just know that this is where all the Marines hang out,' she adds.

A Marine groupie. Great. I turn in my seat and stare at the TV over the bar, feigning interest in the game. Jack makes some comment rich in innuendo and I hear my name involved in the sentence. Yes, I decide with a sigh, I'm going to kill him later. In his sleep.

The girl is quizzing him now about bad guys. If only she knew, I think to myself. We're about to catch a very bad guy indeed. Very soon. And when we do, we'll finally make him pay for everything he's done.

337

'Soon?' the girl asks, her voice practically a shriek. 'How soon? As in tomorrow? What did he do, this very bad guy?'

I turn to stare, a shot of adrenaline already flooding my system as I move fluidly off the stool. 'I didn't say that out loud,' I say.

The thought has taken just a second to process. She's one of them. She's a psy. How else did she read my mind? My hand closes instantly round my gun, tugging it free from its holster at my waist.

Jack reacts too, reaching an arm out to grab hold of her, but she's gone, darting through the crowd faster than a jackal, weaving under arms and spinning through the door out into the front lot.

We're on her heels, barging through the mass of people in the bar, the others from our Unit aware of our shouts and already following our lead, stampeding after us, yelling at each other, and we all tumble out into the front lot just as she throws herself into a car that's speeding away, its door still hanging open. And there's a shadow in the front seat. A face that I'd know anywhere, that haunts every moment of my life and Jack's. It's Demos.

Then everything goes blank.

Twenty-four hours later and still no leads. But we have her name. Suki Nakamura. All day we've been plugging it into the systems and pulling up intel on her. She's a new one. Recruited by Demos and sent to infiltrate us, we believe. Though if that was an attempt at infiltration, I wonder at Demos's recruitment and training criteria.

'This girl can spend,' Jack says. He's standing at the kitchen table poring over the paperwork I've brought over: all the bank statements, credit card bills, airline tickets, hotel room service receipts, school records, immigration information and identity photos I spent the day accumulating while Jack was out picking Lila up from the airport.

'She certainly can. The amount of shoes she's bought in the last three months alone could sink a battleship.'

I keep my eyes on the door, my hearing tuned for any movement from upstairs where Lila is still sleeping. I haven't seen her yet and I'm aware that my focus isn't fully on the paperwork Jack's rifling through. I'm distracted and have to still my fingers which are drumming the tabletop. It's like there's an electric hum in the background, created by her, and the sound of it, the vibration of it, is jarring me, not allowing me to focus fully on what Jack is saying.

'So, what else did you find out?' Jack repeats.

I zone out the hum and try to concentrate on the paperwork. I start outlining what I've discovered about Suki Nakamura, the latest of Demos's recruits. 'Twenty years old. Grew up in Tokyo. Her father's a businessman. He's funding her "studies" here in the US. I doubt he's aware that his daughter's a psy or that she's currently running him into debt while simultaneously rescuing the US economy from financial Armageddon.'

Jack shoots me a wry, impatient look.

'But we haven't had a trace of her since yesterday,' I finish. 'She's gone to ground.'

Jack frowns and I'm with him. Suki's our first lead in months and we let her slip right through our fingers.

'She'll show up again,' I reassure Jack, who's studying the photographs of Suki now – each of them passport shots that show a girl with straight-cut bangs, shining eyes and a grin like a Cheshire cat.

'You think she'd be that stupid?' he asks.

'She gave herself away pretty quickly in the bar, didn't she?' I answer. 'I don't think we're dealing with a superior mind here.'

Jack sighs. 'He was there. He was right there.' He's talking about Demos. 'Goddamn it, Alex, we could have caught him. He's playing with us. It's just a game to him.'

'One slip-up, Jack,' I say quietly, 'that's all it will take. Next time we'll be ready. We're going to catch a break, I feel it. They're tracking Suki – as soon as she uses any form of ID, spends a cent on her credit card, registers her name at a motel, signs into Facebook, we're on it.'

Jack scowls some more at the photograph of Suki, before tossing it onto the pile. 'I'm on call tonight,' he says.

'You want me to come over if you get a call-out?' I ask. Then add quickly, 'Just in case Lila wakes up and you're not here?'

'That would be great. Thanks.'

And just then we hear movement overhead. Lila's finally awake. Jack immediately starts gathering up the papers on the table and stuffing them inside the folder, which he then takes and slides into a drawer beneath a cutlery tray. He crosses to the stove and switches on the hob before turning back to me. 'Remember,' he says, 'we say nothing of this to Lila, OK?'

I nod.

After a few more minutes we hear a creak on the landing and then a pause as she hesitates. Jack and I both cross to the door and walk out into the hallway.

I reach the bottom of the stairs before Jack and look up. And there she is. Lila. Taking the stairs two at a time, head bowed, hair flying, looking as though she's being chased. She glances up just then and I catch sight of her face, and am instantly struck by how different she looks – not at all the Lila I remember – but before I

340

can process the change, what it is exactly that's different about her, she trips on the next step and comes flying towards me. I catch hold of her by the tops of her arms and steady her.

She stays like that, her head against my chest, not moving. Her hair is tickling my jaw, her hands pressing against my stomach. For a handful of seconds neither of us moves. And then she pulls away abruptly and my arms fall to my sides and I realise with a shock that takes a few seconds to register that I hadn't wanted to let her go. I dismiss the thought almost as soon as it arrives. It's only that I've missed her and here she is. Right here in front of me. But at the same time, seeing her again feels just like it does when summer finally comes around after an endless winter. You're shocked by just how much you've missed the warmth and the smell and the ease of it.

'Lila,' I say, 'it's good to see you.' I open my arms up wide. 'Do I get a proper hug?'

She steps forward into my arms, this time pressing her hands lightly and slightly tentatively round my waist, and I pull her tight and feel the tension in her body ebb as she takes a deep breath and presses herself closer. This time I pull away first.

I study her. The girl that left three years ago is not the same girl standing in front of me now. That skinny, slightly awkward kid with bangs and braces, who seemed to always be wearing an over-sized T-shirt, has been replaced by a girl on the cusp of something I'm not sure whether to call beautiful or stunning. A voice in my head pipes up loudly, reminding me that she's neither. She's JACK'S SISTER. I shouldn't even be looking at her in that way. It's Lila. Forget about her being Jack's sister, she's practically MY sister. And yet . . . I'm not sure how else to look at her. You'd have to be blind not to think she was attractive, beautiful even. I might

341

be her brother's best friend, I might have known her since she was born, but I'm still a guy. And I'm definitely not blind.

I follow her into the kitchen, all too aware that I can't stop staring and that I need to redirect my eyes northwards and my thinking elsewhere. I will. I just need time to absorb. To absorb and process and then I'll be able to see her once more as JACK'S SISTER.

'Been a long time,' I say when we're facing each other again in the kitchen. 'You're looking well.'

Lila gives me a small smile, her eyes – are they contacts? Because I'm sure they weren't that green last time I saw her – keep skirting the floor, her hands moving self-consciously to tuck her hair behind one ear and then to pull up the strap of her tank top which has slipped down over one shoulder. No more oversized T-shirts either, I note. She's still flushed from sleep, but pale beneath that, the freckles across the bridge of her nose faded. Her hair's darker than it used to be too, and longer, but it suits her.

I pull out a chair for her and she sits and I lean against the counter, keen to observe her, interested to see if I can read what's going on from her body language. She's guarded. Definitely hiding something. She won't hold my gaze for long and her hands keep flitting to her thighs and I have to force my own gaze to stop following them. But she's not as transparent as she used to be, I realise. It's more like she's opaque – the windshield has shattered. It's clear there's something beneath the surface, I just can't make out what it is. Yet.

'So, what's the deal, then?' I ask. 'Why the escape to southern California? London not rocking enough for a teenage girl, so you've got to check out the entertainment factor of a military town?'

342

Even as I say it, I see the way she winces and her eyes dart to Jack, who's busy frying steaks but clearly listening to every word. He's held his cool – hasn't yet asked her why she's here. And to his credit, after much persuasion, he didn't hand her a return ticket as soon as she got off the plane.

'Kind of, something like that,' Lila mumbles in response. And then she looks up at me and holds my gaze and she smiles a smile so full of undisguised happiness that her whole face lights up with it and it makes me catch my breath.

And that's when I know for sure that I'm in trouble.

Acknowledgements

Thanks to:

John and Alula for the best adventure of my life.

Nic, Vic and Sara for all their love and support along the way. I miss you guys more than anything – more even than red wine and chocolate brownies from K&C.

Tara, once again I owe you hugely for making Lila sound American, and for role-playing Mrs Johnson – you were great, you should have been an actress.

Lauren – spectacular friend and co-conspirator, thanks for the American language edit and for the fun times at BL literary nights.

Olivia and Julia for being my teen test readers. You guys are brilliant and funny and I wish I could write as well as you do, Olivia.

Lindsay and Josh for the nutso psycho whackjob advice.

My mum for letting me practise my story-telling at a young age by allowing me to forge my own sick notes and fake her signature on them.

My dad for his technical advice on how to blow things up and the physics of sprinkler systems. (Is it physics? I still don't know.)

The fantastic bloggers out there whose passion for reading and writing is something I am hugely grateful for. Especially those of you who make Alex your book boyfriend of the week.

MyAnna, Jess and Jess for the belief in these books and for all you are doing to widen the audience.

Till Kruss for my wonderful website and for being my personal German-flavoured Larry David.

My agent Amanda who never stops encouraging and supporting my writing despite the number of random ideas and crazy jottings I throw at her.

Venetia, my editor, and Lydia, Catherine, Mel, Caroline, Rumana and Nick at Simon & Schuster for all their hard work and support.

Jenny Cooper at Waterstones who has been so supportive of all my writing. I really appreciate it.

Jane Tait for your brilliant copy-editing skills on which I rely far too heavily. I'm glad that you know the correct use of the subjunctive tense because I clearly do not.